STACKS

Library of Truth

Kathy J. Forti

RINNOVO PRESS
Stackslibraryoftruth.com
Stackslibraryoftruth@gmail.com
Facebook.com/stackslibraryoftruth

ISBN: 978-0-578-29915-0
Printed in the United States of America

Foreword by the Author

STACKS is a work of fiction. Names, characters, businesses, events and incidents are the product of the author's imagination. Any semblance to actual persons, living or dead, or actual events is purely coincidental.

Prologue
The Harbingers of Fate

He stood bathed in a pool of luminous light. Like an actor fretting his hour upon life's stage, in a spotlight of uncertainty, there were no scripted lines to fall back on. Not now. The light provided some modicum of comfort in the darkness that surrounded him, but deep in his soul he knew it would come to this. A man alone, awaiting his fate. He could almost hear the seconds ticking down towards the inevitable.

It was a somber moment. His 60 plus years comprised a lifetime of dedicated service. Few, if any, would ever know of his guardianship of some of the country's most deeply hidden secrets. There would be no family or children of his bloodline to remember his work. He would become a forgotten blip on the nation's historical register.

Every bone in his body felt weary, yet his mind was keenly sharp and aware. He felt a slight droop in his shoulders and schooled himself to straighten his posture. Even now, in this desperate hour, his impeccably dressed signature three-piece suit and pin-striped bow tie were in order. He would forever pride himself on maintaining dignity and decorum, no matter what the cost.

These were uncertain times for everyone. He could only trust himself to do the right thing when the time came. But in his heart Roone Sawyer hoped for a last-minute reprieve.

A beautiful and seemingly ageless woman appeared before him now. She towered over him, as always, despite his almost six-foot stature. By some standards she might be described as an Amazon—a force of nature to be reckoned with. He had known this woman for several years now and she had never let him down, despite the fact he knew very little about her. She was an enigma and preferred it that way. Her age, where she had originally come from, or how she came to be who she was, would remain a mystery. Perhaps he would never know. There was so little time left. So many unanswered questions.

But this woman knew everything about him. In fact, she seemed to know everything about everyone down to the finest detail. Period. When they first met, he thought she was some kind of intellectual goddess. But now he knew better. Were they both just chosen players in some greater simulated reality, he wondered?

She quietly allowed him to finish his last thought. A slight smile touched her lips as she waited for him to be the first to speak. Patience was something she had an abundance of or she would have never lasted in her job.

His lips were bone dry. He was more nervous than he thought. "I've seen the records..." he began. He knew she had seen them, too. Perhaps she had even written them.

"I had hoped for more time to prepare," he finished, wetting his lips.

She seemed to take his words in stride. "Thousands of others who came before you were also unsuccessful."

That surprised him. How many others, he wondered? He knew it should give him some peace of mind that he wasn't the only one to fail, but it didn't.

"Yes, but perhaps with more time I could change that..."

She gently cut him off. "I am sorry, but I cannot help you. It is already written in time and is out of my hands."

Roone hung his head. He was not the type to plead an unwinnable case. In some ways he regretted having looked at his personal file. He knew it had been a mistake the very moment he did. A glimpse into one's own future is never a good idea. His curiosity and thirst for information had finally done him in.

What he had learned from his file made decisions even

harder. There was no certainty he still had time to get key information into the right hands. It would be his last duty of service—his final mission.

Roone slowly nodded. He understood the terms. There was no avoiding one's fate. A devoutly religious man, he murmured a silent prayer for the Lord to show him the way. He still had work to do this very night.

The woman only smiled. She had played out this scene so many times before. There was always a bargaining stage before acceptance finally took hold, and this man was no different.

"Without wisdom, knowledge is oftentimes a double-edged sword." Then, with just a hint of sadness, which surprised even him, as she seemed at times to be without emotion, she added, "I will miss you, my friend."

~~*~~

Like every day at this hour, the cold inky waters of the Potomac River swelled with a stream of private excursion yachts motoring their way upstream, back to their home docks after a day of sport fishing on the open waters off the Chesapeake Bay. Overhead, gulls hovered, tracking the smell of discarded fish bait, hoping to catch a tiny morsel from fishermen gutting their hauls of Atlantic sturgeon, striped bass and trout from the decks of their charter boats.

The early evening sun quickly faded as dusk stole in to replace it. Hints of a spectacular sunset of blood orange streaked across the sherbet sky. For some it was known as "the magic hour"—a photographer's dream. From the shore, a lone fishing boat could be spotted trailing behind the crowd of returning boats. Onboard, four men, red-faced and clearly inebriated from a day of too much sun and beer, packed up their over-priced fishing rods and expensive Bamboo brand gear. They, like everyone else, were ready to call it a day.

Like hundreds of other political lobbyists in the Nation's Capitol, they too would write off this day's fishing jaunt using generous expense accounts that had little to no accountability. It was standard practice in Washington, D.C. Everyone did it.

The captain of the boat, a seasoned sailor who despised drunkenness but tolerated it nonetheless, looked forward to depositing his obnoxious passengers on dry land and seeing the end of them. He had taken their verbal abuse only because they had paid him so generously for the day.

However, the constant complaints about not catching any "fuckingly large" fish had finally gotten to him. Expensive gear, totaling in the thousands for one fishing rod alone, did not substitute for seasoned skill and patience at sea. He sighed deeply. Another 15 minutes and the marina would be in sight and these parasites would be out of his hair forever only to be replaced the next day by more just like them.

He sped up the boat, passing an illuminated Jefferson Memorial as nightfall quickly descended. Without warning the boat suddenly jerked and fishtailed starboard. His passengers staggered and fell against the railing spilling beer all over his highly polished wooden deck. The engine came to a dead halt.

"Hey, you little shit!" one of the guys yelled up at him, "Can't you drive a fucking straight line?!" The others laughed uproariously at the guy who always used the "F" bomb. The engines continued to whir.

The captain held his tongue and threw the boat into reverse. Whatever the obstruction was, he hoped it hadn't damaged his prop. The raucous laughter died out at the same time a large black plastic bag, bound in a crisscross of rope, popped to the surface.

One of the men rushed for a grappling hook off the back wall, yanked it off and leaned over the boat's edge. He hooked the half-submerged bag on his first attempt and let out a whoop of excitement. It was clear he was hoping to haul in what might be the biggest catch of the day.

"You think its money or drugs?" he asked the others, pulling it towards the stern.

The captain jumped down from the bridge and quickly took charge. "Move aside!" he ordered.

He grabbed the hook out of the man's hands and yanked it in. A dark dread came over him. The bundle was large. His prop must have sliced through some of the ropes holding it underwater. The men helped him hoist the unwieldy bundle over the side where it dropped onto the deck with a heavy thud.

"Maybe its Osama Bin Laden," one of the men joked with a raucous laugh. "They never did retrieve that son-of-a-bitch's body."

"Don't touch it!" the captain warned, cursing under his breath. He had a strong premonition that this new development meant they would not be docking any time soon. He hoisted himself unto the bridge and radioed the Coast Guard for help. A quick glance back at the deck made him swear aloud.

"Get the hell away from it!" he shouted angrily.

But it was too late. The big burly guy with the foul mouth had sliced the black bag wide open with a pocketknife. A pale white arm, severed at the shoulder, fell out onto the deck. The men stared back at it in speechless shock. Inside the bag, eyes wide open, the bloated face of a dead young male stared back at them. The roped noose wrapped tightly around his neck told them all they needed to know.

Groans were heard all around. One man, his hand to his mouth, rushed to the side of the boat and promptly vomited. The captain groaned for an entirely different reason. It meant it would be hours of questions and reports before going home. They should have left well enough alone and tossed the bag back into the dark inky waters for someone else to find. Everyone knew the Potomac was a dumping ground for all kinds of trash, especially the human kind.

Table of Contents

Chapter 1

On any given day, the serenity of Capitol Hill and its spacious manicured lawns hosted visitors and tourists from near and abroad seeking a glimpse of the workings of one of the most powerful centers in the world – the United States Government.

While all appears calm on the surface, there is a heightened police presence monitoring every street and entrance on The Hill 24 hours a day for security threats. Checkpoints and concrete barriers cordon off vehicle access to all but those with high clearances. Underneath this bastion of government power lays a hidden labyrinth of color-coded underground tunnels and walkways that encompass the entire Capitol complex.

A daily stream of ID laden legislators and aides make their way through these tunnels that connect the Library of Congress buildings, the Rayburn, Longworth and Cannon House Office Buildings, the Russell, Dirksen and Hart Senate Office Buildings, the Halls of the Supreme Court, and the power hub centerpiece of it all – the United States Capitol building.

This morning the sun has not yet risen on the copper covered dome of the Rotunda of the Thomas Jefferson Library of

Congress building. It is 6:03 AM, several hours before the Library opens for the day.

A sizable squadron of police cars, their overhead red lights flashing in the pre-dawn light, flank the length of the 1st Street SE main entrance. A lone ambulance pulls up, blocking the middle of the street. Two paramedics wheel out a gurney but seem in no particular rush.

A sudden and unexpected death has occurred in the Capitol complex. The victim is a well-known and highly respected personage on The Hill. A man who controls and oversees the daily workings of a vast body of knowledge encompassing the Thomas Jefferson, John Adams and the James Madison Library structures. The man is Roone Sawyer--*The* Librarian of Congress. The mode of demise---"death by hanging".

~~*~~

The first floor of the Jefferson Library was already swarming with officers from the Emergency Response Team of the United States Capitol Police (USCP), by the time Lieutenant William Hanlon flashed his badge at Security and made his way across the marbled floor of the Great Hall. He had been in the building hundreds of times since childhood, and yet the grandeur of its Italian Renaissance architecture, stained-glass skylights and marbled statues never failed to elicit feelings of unequivocal beauty and awe.

Lt. Hanlon was a 33-year veteran of the USCP force and damn proud of it. His height always made him stand out, towering above most of his men with a natural take charge presence. People automatically stepped aside when he entered a room. The man radiated the confidence of someone who knew what needed to be done and the best way to do it. His reputation for getting to the down and dirty facts and quickly was well known. While he

2

demanded the same no-nonsense approach from his men, he wasn't averse to rubbing people in high places the wrong way—if it got the job done. Experience had taught him toughness and lack of fear were the only way to survive in Washington. That, or be eaten alive by the jackals.

When he received the early morning homicide call, he knew the exact location of the Office of the Librarian of Congress and needed no direction. It was right across from the treasured Gutenberg Bible display. He hadn't known Roone Sawyer personally, but Hanlon knew enough to know this was only a ceremonial office and hadn't been officially used since 1980. The official Office of the Librarian of Congress was in the Madison Building, so Sawyer hanging himself in this office he found rather odd. It could be the guy was trying to make some kind of statement by his death room of choice.

Within scant seconds after surveying the scene, Hanlon felt the back of his scalp itch, an inherent tell-tale sign that what his eyes were seeing did not totally add up. He had witnessed a number of dead bodies during his work on the USCP force--mainly legislators keeling over from heart attacks at their office desks. He knew the type and could usually spot them right off. They either were power obsessed or had something to prove. They rarely took a break. Some were Senators and Congressman who preferred to sleep in their offices rather than go home. Others simply could not afford to rent a place in this expensive city. Making one's congressional office into personal living quarters wasn't permitted, but in this town lots of things were overlooked.

Lt. Hanlon had pretty much seen it all, but this was a first. There had never been a suicide hanging inside the illustrious halls of the Library of Congress since its establishment in 1800.

From experience, Hanlon was not one to jump to conclusions. Homicide or suicide, they couldn't rule out anything. The place was being dusted for prints and the items on the highly polished oak desk, a small personal laptop and several reference books were being catalogued into evidence.

For all practical and immediate purposes, he knew Forensics would call it an apparent suicide. Questions remained as to how Sawyer managed to hang himself from a low brass railing that ran along an alcove atop one side of glass paned bookshelves. He noticed there was a somewhat hidden balcony up there. Did Sawyer fling himself over the low railing? If so, it would explain no evidence of an over-turned chair on the floor beneath him.

Hanlon's scalp continued to itch. It seemed like a lot of work to kill oneself. Gunshot to the head, pills, wrist slashing would be a hell of a lot easier and more common. Yet, the guy opted for a thickly corded noose around his neck, like a staged lynching.

The night janitor, a 30-year-old Latino, had stumbled upon the dead Librarian during his early morning cleaning routine. The young employee, Juan Ramirez, was still visibly shaken at his grisly discovery. He claimed he knew Sawyer. Everyone did. Apparently, it wasn't unusual to see him walking the Library's Halls at night. After all, as Master Librarian the guy must have felt like he owned the place.

Ramirez pried his eyes away from the forensic photographer snapping pictures of the gruesome scene. Sawyer's lifeless face stared back at him, like a rag doll. Ramirez' eyes watered with emotion he quickly tried to hide. Instead, he shook his head muttering, "Mother of God" under his breath. As the photographer finished his work, Hanlon's men moved in to cut down the body. A gurney stood by waiting to claim the newly deceased.

Ramirez now teetered on the verge of hyperventilating as he tried to avoid looking. "Mr. Sawyer was a good man. This is terrible thing. Terrible," he said continuing to shake his head.

"When's the last time you saw him?" Hanlon asked.

Ramirez shrugged. "Maybe around... Oh I don't know. It was

shortly after I got here at 11:00 PM. I figured he was getting ready to go home or back to his Madison Office. He looked very tired."

Hanlon motioned to one of his detectives. "Brodie, get library security over to the Madison Building to open Sawyer's office. See what you find. And send a detail over to where he lives as well."

He could always rely on Detective Alfonso Brodie for the detail work. The guy looked like he just stepped out of the centerfold pages of a fashion magazine. He was the penultimate snappy dresser, groomed mustache, gelled hair and a forever smile that made all the ladies' heads turn. But the guy wasn't of that particular persuasion. As if Hanlon cared. Brodie was his smartest and most thorough detective on the force. He usually left no stone unturned. He was confident that Brodie would find something to make sense of this death.

"And find out who's in charge of this place under Sawyer," he added.

Ramirez spoke up. "That would be Althea Linfred, sir."

Brodie was already heading out when Hanlon shouted back, "And get that Linfred woman over here ASAP."

The media would hear of Sawyer's death in no time. Capitol Police federal radio bands were more secure than the regular metropolitan police bands. But news traveled fast in this town. USCP media center would have to put out a press release pronto. Within hours this town would be a gossip mill of theories on why Roone Sawyer had killed himself. The scene might look like a suicide, but Hanlon was calling it an apparent suicide for now until they learned more from Forensics.

There was a laptop and books on the room's highly polished mahogany desk in a room no one was supposed to use. The visitor's railing just inside the doorway allowed people to view in, but not trespass. The whole scene felt staged. *Why*, was something he was determined to find out.

Chapter 2

Zach Eldridge had not slept well. Not that this was unusual. His brain was still on overload and would often take an hour of serious nightly Qigong to quiet his mind enough to settle into sleep--only to then have an active night of dreaming. His dreams were often otherworldly and at times possessed a high degree of strangeness. Yet, at times those same dreams provided unexpected answers as well.

His brain was wired differently than maybe 98% of the population. He was normal by every other standard for a 28-year-old white male with above average intelligence who had come from a family of chronic over-achievers. But Zach had what the psychological experts termed, "Acquired Savant Syndrome" for lack of a better term to call it. He wasn't autistic, or developmentally delayed or even physically impaired. He just saw the world around him in numbers, a form of mental and visual synesthesia that stimulates several senses simultaneously. It caused Zach to possess some unique abilities. Everything in his world had a mathematical signature. Numbers were his friends and because of it he could process any equation at lightning speed, which was why he was often ranked a genius on intelligence scales.

His brain felt like it was hooked into a giant super-computer that kept on spitting out calculations and looking to solve problems both night and day. If he put himself through a series of meditation in motion exercises several times a day, which the ancient Chinese practice of Qigong provided him, his brain often found some semblance of stillness. Sometimes just visually practicing the exercises in his head, while practicing deep breathing techniques, could provide a calming effect as well.

His savant syndrome was both a blessing and a curse. Even now, as he reached for a cup of coffee, his brain had already silently calculated distance, weight, temperature, and how long it would take him to move the mug from the kitchen counter to his lips. It might be useless information to most people, but his brain craved a continual data input like others hungered for food.

He hadn't been born this way. At the age of seven, Zach had suffered a concussion after being hit in the head by a baseball. It knocked him out cold and ended forever his Little League days back in Greenwich, Connecticut. He woke to find he was seeing things he hadn't seen before. At first it was only seeing colors as numbers or fractal images, but then odder things began to happen over the years. Brain imaging showed the right side of his brain was slightly compromised from the head injury and as a result his left-brain, particularly his parietal lobe, had become over activated to compensate for the damage.

He was grateful that he didn't also hear voices. He was not schizophrenic, paranoid, delusional, or any other diagnostic code. He was just different. There were others like him in the world, but not many. His specific anomaly was visual memory acuteness for all things mathematical. Zach had extensively researched the phenomenon and found the experts believed we all had genetic memory that lies dormant, and sometimes due to head injury, stroke, seizures, or other sudden accidents this intelligence becomes unlocked and easily accessible.

Zach had already been born with an above average IQ according to testing standards--mostly due to heredity. His physicist father was exceptionally gifted with an IQ of 160 and his mother about 130, so he had been blessed with good intelligence genes from day one. But due to his sudden injury, it elevated him into the profoundly gifted range of 180.

Head injuries were usually the main cause of such phenomenon. He had read about a woman who had hit her head in a car accident and immediately started seeing dead people. Another had become telekinetic and could make objects move. It only confirmed the fact that science knew and understood very little about the true workings of the human brain. To avoid being labeled different, or weird, Zach had learned early on to keep the knowledge of his exceptional brain workings to himself.

With his acquired talents, and his ability to retain unlimited amounts of information, Zach could have easily become a neuroscientist, an engineer, a physics genius—maybe even another Nikola Tesla. Instead, he became a library information analyst--a solutions expert. Maybe even the best, but few would ever know it.

Zach knew that he could look at any information system and restructure and re-organize its databases for better efficiency with very little effort. He could see it all laid out in his head, like a math problem, and he could put it through exercises without having to put it to paper. It was his own unique and special talent.

At an early age he had discovered that this talent could be used to attain higher knowledge, commit books to memory and conveniently remember everyone's phone numbers. Peace of mind came to him within the world of books, so it was only natural for him to seek out his life's work within a library structure.

While life had thrown him a curve ball, it had also given him a unique gift—the capacity to easily assimilate complex details and find solutions. Because it came so easily to him, he had quickly taught himself over 20 different computer programming languages. Fortran was a language he had whizzed through in no time, having a natural ability to construct and implement algorithms, which fascinated him.

Had he desired a lifetime of government service he could have easily been recruited into any of the intelligence agencies. But none of that interested Zach. He preferred to fly low under the radar. He liked his loner life, and while many found him both sociable and likable, he counted few close friends. By design he had learned early on to keep his unusual abilities hidden as much as possible. He didn't talk about himself—didn't even like to, so others often found him a complete mystery. He preferred that even his family just think of him as quirky and assume he was not living up to his true familial potential. He did not want to turn into anyone's test subject guinea pig and he knew that could easily happen.

Zach had spent his early 20's at the New York City Public Library working collections consolidation, cataloging, circulation, rare manuscripts, even the media center. Over the years he had been assigned to several branch libraries in Manhattan, Brooklyn and Queens. For those who worked with him, he was a real "Zach of all trades" in the library system world.

It wasn't as if he needed the money or recognition. Zach had been born an Eldridge Family Trust Fund baby. As an only child, he would eventually inherit it all. Born to Camille and Martin Eldridge--his mother was currently a two-term Senator from the State of Connecticut and his father an aerospace engineer and astrophysicist who traveled the world involved in projects he rarely, if ever, talked about. Zach barely saw either of them growing up in his family's Connecticut estate. He saw his nannies and the household staff as being his true parents.

His great grandfather, Zachariah Eldridge (whom he had been named after) had made his money on the New York Stock Exchange during World War I in war reparations and would later go on to be a one-term Governor of Connecticut before dying in a plane crash.

Compared to the rest of his family, Zach was the odd-ball under-achiever. It usually didn't bother him, except when his mother made excuses to her friends in front of him. He preferred to keep his distance for this very reason.

Back again in Washington D.C., he opted to stay in his family's unoccupied flat in DuPont Circle, a last-minute decision on his part. He had a key. And no one really knew he was here or what brought him. He preferred it that way. If things panned out for him today, he would start looking for a place of his own.

A month ago, he had set in motion plans to rent his SoHo condo on New York City's Lower East Side and take off for Britain's Oxford University. It had long been a dream of Zach's to search out rare Pythagorean manuscripts at one of the oldest research havens in the world--the Bodleian Library. That plan would have to wait.

Less than 24 hours ago, Zach had received an unexpected and mysterious message from a former friend and colleague. "I need you to come to Washington, D.C.," it instructed. "You must leave immediately."

The note had been sent via private messenger service and warned that discretion was of paramount importance. His friend stated that there was a 'special black hole assignment' waiting for him in Washington and no matter what happened, 'It would be advised to look for problems that need attention in the closed Stacks. It will require your unique expertise and insight.'

The message was certainly cryptic. If his friend, who he trusted completely, needed him, then it must be serious. He booked a flight that evening. At 9:00 AM this morning they planned to meet and Zach would finally learn the finer details.

Zach was definitely intrigued. Despite his lack of sleep, he felt hyped at this unknown new prospect. His flight from New York's JFK had arrived in Reagan National Airport after midnight and it was now 7:00 AM. Rest would have to wait until later.

Without much thought, he instantly calculated exactly how long it would take him to shower and change and maneuver through the city. His memory automatically retrieved up a D.C. Metro System map from the depths of his brain. One cursory glance told him he needed to catch the Red Line from DuPont Circle, transfer at Metro Center, and take the Blue Line to the Capitol South station. It would be a two-block walk from there. His visual memory was quite acute and more accurate than Google Maps. He never got lost.

Wherever he travelled, Zach preferred to be early and avoid any unnecessary anxiety of being late. He derived great comfort from scoping out his surroundings in advance. Getting the feel again for the D.C. area was not something he openly relished. It had been several years since he found a need to be in the same city where his mother worked. They were not on the best of terms and hadn't been for a long time. He made a mental note to avoid the Hart Building where her offices were located.

Zach turned on the bedroom television, hoping to catch the local weather report. A commercial about some new restaurant in Georgetown was airing, reminding him he needed sustenance. He hadn't eaten since lunch the day before. It would have to wait. He couldn't fit that into the time he had allotted himself to make his meeting.

He hopped into the claw foot tub to take his standard three-minute shower. He was never one to dawdle. He lathered up experiencing the strange sensation that he was on the verge of a new chapter in his life. He didn't want to be late. The excitement at seeing an old friend again was something he normally didn't feel. But this was different. It had been several years since they had last conversed. Life had taken the two of them in different directions.

Over the sound of the running shower, the television was loud enough for him to overhear the morning's breaking news:

"Metropolitan D.C. Police report the body of a third unidentified young male victim was discovered last night by a group of boaters on the Potomac River. The public demands to know…Is Washington in the grips of a serial killer? Stay tuned for more details as they develop…"

Chapter 3

Detective Brodie powered down the personal laptop belonging to the Librarian, Roone Sawyer. What he had seen had made his stomach sick. He motioned for the other detective to box up the computer and have it safeguarded in a secure evidence locker.

Sawyer hadn't tried to hide anything, which is what the USCP discovered upon entering his home. The laptop was still powered on, sitting out on a living room coffee table like a bright beacon of light to anyone entering the premises. It was the first thing Brodie noticed when he and his men had gotten access to the deceased's 12th floor penthouse in Foggy Bottom's Watergate South Complex.

His men had already completed a thorough search. The place was clean. In fact, it was immaculately clean--no dust anywhere on any of the surfaces. House cleaning might have been in that day, but he doubted it. Brodie made himself a reminder in his notepad to check on it anyway.

No dishes in the sink either. The refrigerator was full of fresh food and a cut of sirloin steak that looked like it was meant for dinner that night. Not something suicides tended to do---go out grocery shopping before they hung themselves. The wine cabinet was filled with fine cabernets. The guy certainly had good taste.

While the rest of the apartment provided nothing of real significance, the laptop was the real bombshell. Brodie had only seen enough to know what they were dealing with. Who knew what else the computer might reveal once digital forensics combed through it.

Brodie rang up Hanlon, knowing he was waiting for his report.

"Whatta you got?" Hanlon asked, not wasting time.

"We found the same suicide note on his personal laptop which we found on the one at the Library near the body..." Brodie began.

"Great," Hanlon said matter-of-factly, moving right along. "That makes all our lives a lot easier."

Brodie hated to be the bearer of bad news. "It gets more complicated."

"What the hell is so complicated?" Hanlon shot back.

On the other end Hanlon could hear Brodie's sigh. He never liked the sound of Brodie's deep sighs.

"Sawyer left a confession note to other crimes as well."

Hanlon swore. "Fuck, don't tell me..."

"There's pictures," Brodie finished. "Lots of pictures. And it cites the one detail of the recent deaths we withheld from the public. That all the deaths were by strangulation from a noose around the neck."

This time Hanlon was the one to sigh. "Shit!"

~~*~~

Within Zach's short 15-minute train commute to the Capitol South Metro station, the bright warm rays of summer had been

16

quickly replaced by the ominous appearance of storm clouds moving in. He knew he had enough time before the rain came through.

It was 8:49 AM and the Library of Congress had already been open for exactly 19 minutes. Zach took in all these facts along with computing that it was 449 feet distance from the Metro to the First Street S.E. main entrance of the Library of Congress. It was an easy walk on most days, and usually uneventful, as he remembered.

While his brain silently noted the eight pairs of Corinthian granite columns that graced the Library's façade, the three sculpted bronze entry doors leading to the first floor, the 33 heads adorning the window keystones of this grand architectural structure, his attention was also drawn to the presence of two police cars and a WWGO-TV news truck parked outside. A young and attractive female reporter, along with her station's cameraman, were positioned on the steps blocking curious pedestrians as they readied for a live stream feed.

Zach glanced at his watch. He had only a few minutes to spare. He made a wide berth around them. The female reporter noticed him but didn't miss a beat as the camera rolled.

"This is Cali Cavaleri for WWGO-TV News outside the Library of Congress with a breaking story…"

This town is breaking news central today, Zach mused.

"Early this morning Washington awakened to the shocking and sad news that a well-respected figure in the community, *The Librarian to the Library of Congress*, Roone Sawyer, died last night inside this very Library which he oversaw for the last five years…"

Zach stopped dead in his tracks, feeling an inner earthquake of shock begin to hit. His feet refused to move past the 12th step of the first set of stairs. Twelve is a perfect number--the number of completion. Double twelves were an even more significant portent for him.

Roone was dead. His friend *was* dead! How? Why? His brain was suddenly stuck in fourth gear, speeding along with non-stop questions.

Zach gasped for breath at the reporter's next words.

"Until the investigation is complete, Capitol police are calling it an apparent suicide…"

~~*~~

It took several minutes for Zach to collect his thoughts and move past the shock that threatened to paralyze him. In the 42 steps that took him to move from sidewalk to the Library entry, his life had shifted and taken a major turn. Something had gone terribly wrong. He might never learn why Sawyer had summoned him to D.C. on such short notice, but whatever it was Zach was determined to get to the bottom of it.

He knew Sawyer was a religious man. Unlike Zach, he had studied biblical scripture in depth--probably every version of holy texts in existence. It was one of his primary interests and had been for years. Like Zach, Roone had also been a loner with unusual quirks.

But, based on his friend's strong beliefs, Zach was pretty sure suicide was out of the question. The notion was preposterous—even absurd. Roone thought killing was the worst travesty a man could ever carry out. Somehow, Zach knew he would prove this.

A solemn determination suddenly coursed through him. His tall lean body moved forward with new purpose. He buttoned his dark blue blazer and straightened his tie. Roone had specifically said that 'there was a critical job waiting for him and no matter what happened, he was to take it without hesitation'.

Zach braced himself for whatever was to come. Even with

18

Roone gone, the Library was still open for business. Very little would ever shut it down, outside of a possible pandemic. He moved through the Library's double entry doors into the main vestibule where he emptied his pockets, nodded to the two security guards on duty and dropped his backpack onto a security scanner belt. He passed through the metal detector easily which then opened onto the Library's Great Hall--an ornate masterpiece of Masonic statues and symbols flanked on both sides by marble staircases. Like everyone else, he paused a moment to take in the enormity of this great institution, the breathtakingly stunning artistry and the magnitude of knowledge it contained.

It was clear to Zach that employees, and even visitors, were now hearing the news about the death of his friend for the first time. Whispers could be heard throughout the Great Hall, followed by audible gasps. An older woman, who was in all likelihood a long time Library employee, passed him with tears in her eyes.

Towards the back of the Great Hall, two uniformed Capitol policemen stood guard in front of a yellow taped off area that included the Gutenberg Bible display. The public restrooms had escaped the sealed area, which meant the alleged suicide happened in the office off to the left. It was the first Librarian of Congress's office dating back to when this room was initially opened in 1897 but was now for only ceremonial use. This was where Roone had instructed Zach to meet him at exactly 9:00 AM—the very scene of the crime. And Zach was pretty sure it *was* a crime scene. Someone had wanted Roone dead and had acted upon it.

Zach took it all in. He calculated his best approach. He opted to pretend as if he had heard nothing and see how far it got him. He approached the sealed area and was immediately stopped by one of the uniformed officers.

"Sir, this area of the Library is closed to visitors today," the officer instructed.

"I have an important meeting with the Librarian Roone Sawyer," Zach told him. "I was instructed to meet him here this morning."

A frown flitted across the face of the older officer. He was debating whether the meeting might have any significance to the case. He hurriedly murmured under his breath to the other officer on duty, before turning back to Zach.

"What's your name, son?"

"Tell him Zach Eldridge is here. He knows me."

The officer pointed towards an alcove niche by the Great Hall's marble staircase, which displayed the bust of Thomas Jefferson. "Wait over there."

Zach observed the officer walk off to contact someone who might be in charge. He was resigned to waiting, no matter how long it took. Would it be a homicide detective or a Library executive who would come calling to ask him questions? Perhaps both.

Zach moved over towards his assigned waiting area in the Great Hall, which was fast filling with visitors starting their free Library tour. His attention was drawn towards an attractive redheaded female docent, whose reddened eyes showed recent signs of tears.

He immediately noticed that her entire countenance was filled with numbers of eight--an unusual amount in his experience. There were eights on her lips, her hair, her torso, and they seemed to be moving and spinning in and around her, beckoning to him. He found himself unconsciously moving towards her small tour group, catching her words as if flotsam floating on strands of air.

"... the eight statues around the Great Hall represent the Goddess Minerva in all her many forms," she said stifling a small sniffle. "The Minerva of War carries the torch of learning in one hand and a sword in the other representing..."

Zach watched mesmerized as she paused to wipe her reddened eyes with the back of her hand.

She seemed terribly embarrassed and apologetic at her display of emotion. "I'm so sorry, ladies and gentlemen. Please bear with me. The Library has just gotten some very sad news about the death of one of our staff members whom we all loved…"

Her eyes welled up again, threatening to open the flood gates. It was so endearing. Zach reached in his backpack for a package of tissue and extended it towards her. She flashed him a brilliant smile which only intensified all the eights spinning around her. She was all lit up like a Christmas display. He was totally transfixed. She mouthed a silent 'thank you' to him and quickly dabbed at her eyes. Without missing a beat, she resumed.

"All right, everyone. If you'll follow me to the center of the floor, you'll see a large brass inlay shaped like the sun, pointing to all four cardinal directions—north, east, south and west. It was very important to the Founding Fathers that government buildings be built on directional ley lines and lined up with the stars to insure guiding wisdom in all governing matters of their new Capitol. Notice the 12 medallions of the zodiac that border the Great Hall, representing the heavenly constellations …"

Zach heard her words, but his mind had been hijacked by her abundance of swirling luminescent numbers. He had never seen that many eights before on anyone. Eight was his favorite number. Good things happened to him when he saw eights. He was born on the 8th of November. Today was June 8th. It was an auspicious sign. In that very moment, Zach realized that whoever she was, they were destined to meet again.

His thoughts were abruptly brought back to reality by someone stepping into his line of vision. They blocked his view of the red-haired woman with the sad eyes. He saw the gold badge on the cop's belt, before he saw the guy's face. They had sent a plainclothes detective to see what Zach knew. He would tell them nothing.

Thirty minutes later, after convincing the police that he was there for a hiring interview and nothing else, he was ushered over to the executive offices of the Library located in the Madison Building. Zach was seated across the desk from a stout woman in her late 50's with short-cropped hair who looked like a military drill sergeant.

The nameplate on her desk identified her as Alfia Linfred, Deputy Librarian of Congress, which meant that she was now Acting Librarian of Congress due to Roone Sawyer's untimely demise.

Deep frown lines were visible between her eyes marking a lifetime of chronic squinting. Her face wore little to no makeup, except for eyebrows, which had been drawn on with great precision. She stared at her computer, reviewing a file Roone had entered into the system—a file most likely on one Zach Eldridge.

Linfred sat back in her chair, raised one painted eyebrow at him as if looking through him. She wasted no time getting to the point.

"Let me be perfectly frank with you, Mr. Eldridge," she began, enunciating his last name. "I wasn't aware you were scheduled to start work here today. These are matters for Human Resources and..."

Zach headed her off before she could pass him off to HR. "Roone---I mean, Mr. Sawyer, contacted me about a critical position that would require my expertise. I moved from New York yesterday in anticipation of starting today."

He paused, deciding how much to say. "I was so shocked and saddened to hear of his death. It just doesn't make any sense."

Linfred looked away. "Well, these things never do."

"He told me he was looking forward to working together again," Zach added.

Her head snapped to attention. "You knew him personally?"

"He was one of my undergraduate professors at Yale. I was his teaching assistant. I also worked under his direction when he ran the New York City Library before he came here."

Linfred peered back at her computer, taking a new interest in Zach's file.

"I see from his file notes that you have a Masters in Library and Information Services with a specialty in mathematics and system security analysis."

Zach nodded, adding with a small smile, "I clean up messes in complex information systems. I'm the Harvey Keitel of libraries."

Linfred stared blankly back at him, not getting his meaning.

He shrugged. "You know—the fixer character in the movie *Pulp Fiction.*"

She visibly bristled. "Mr. Eldridge, I find your attempts at levity inappropriate to say the least. Perhaps you would feel more comfortable coming back and doing this another day with Human Resources."

Okay, so she had no sense of humor. He tried again.

"Mrs. Linfred. I meant no disrespect. I left my life in New York behind to come work here. There's no point in my leaving and coming back another day. Roone implied that there was a special assignment here which he wanted me to start on immediately."

Linfred sat up straighter. She leaned slightly forward in her chair. She was definitely curious. She glanced back at her computer, rescanning it.

"I don't see any reference to a 'special assignment' anywhere in Mr. Sawyer's notes. Can you be more specific?"

Zach recalled Roone's cryptic message. He had called it a 'special black hole assignment' with reference to the closed Stacks. It meant something of importance was either missing or misplaced and no one had a clue to its whereabouts. It happened a lot in large libraries, even with visitor security bag checks and scanners detecting theft on the way out the doors.

Sometimes, as much of 10% of an entire library collection could go missing at any one time. It was known as the 'black hole'. Correcting this problem didn't require Zach's system analysis skills, but some serious tracking ingenuity instead.

He was puzzled why Roone wanted to get him here so quickly only to locate a black hole? There had to be countless others already employed at this Library he could have been put to the task. So there had to be something else of greater importance Roone had in mind.

Linfred tapped her pen on the desktop, impatiently waiting for his answer.

Zach flashed her his most confident smile. "Yes, I can. He specifically said I would be assigned to collection management in the closed Stacks." It was a lie, but close enough to the truth from what Roone had implied. Roone's message had clearly warned that discretion was of the utmost importance. He would bet a million dollars his friend had not trusted Linfred. She seemed all too eager to jump into Roone's vacant seat.

Linfred pursed her lips. "Hmm. Well, I guess we'll just have to see about that."

She quickly rose from her chair, signaling the meeting was over and walked him towards the door. "I'll check with Human Resources and get back to you. Federal security checks are required for employment here and…"

Before she could finish her sentence, she spied two police officers carrying out a laptop from Roone Sawyer's office next to hers. She hustled over and stood in their path.

"What are you doing?" she demanded. "That's Library property!"

Detective Brodie stepped in to intercede. "We have a search warrant, Ma'am."

For the briefest of seconds, she seemed too shocked to speak. "Let me see it!" she insisted. "I'm in charge here."

She scowled as Brodie produced the papers to show her. It served to immediately deflate her authority. She stood back, biting her lips while several boxes of files paraded past her watchful eyes.

Amidst the commotion, Linfred had clearly forgotten about Zach's presence. She seemed lost in thought, almost worried, as the officers moved towards the elevator.

"What are they looking for?" Zach asked softly.

Linfred shrugged. "Foul play, I presume," she answered without thinking.

"They think Roone was killed?"

Linfred quickly regained her composure and sense of dignity. "I said nothing of the sort, young man. But who knows. He was secretive and had problems…"

This surprised Zach. Roone was the sanest, most well-adjusted person he had ever met. "What makes you say that?"

She shrugged again. "He did odd things. A few times I caught him in the closed Stacks talking to himself."

Zach wasn't about to point out that studies considered talking to oneself a sign of intelligence. "I often talk to *myself*," he admitted.

She gave him a pointed look. "Then I'm sure you'll do quite nicely in the Stacks."

~~*~~

On the basement level of the Capitol Police station, inside a cluttered dark room illuminated only by the light emanating from a multitude of computers labeled with coded evidence numbers, two digital forensics technicians slowly sifted through the files stored on Roone Sawyer's personal hard drive. Lieutenant Hanlon stood by patiently, looking over the shoulder of one of the on–duty technicians. He found himself frowning with undisguised disgust as the operator scrolled through image after image of graphic hard-core pedophilia. The technician then proceeded to open another folder containing even more lurid images.

"There's hundreds more pictures," the technician reported. "We examined all of his computer hard drives and the one found in his Watergate apartment was the only one containing pictures along with the names and dates of all his victims."

Hanlon grimaced, peering closer. "Are those the male bodies from the Potomac killings?"

The other technician nodded. "He made notations on crime scene pictures like trophy cataloging. Besides knowing a noose was used in the Potomac killings, they also contain other homicide details never released to the public. Some of it is pretty graphic."

Hanlon shook his head. "I can see that. The sick bastard. No wonder he hung himself along with the rest of his victims."

Detective Brodie entered, silently closing the door behind him without anyone noticing. He snuck up on the group intently viewing pictures of naked young men in compromising sexual positions.

"Hey, didn't you guys get the memo? No viewing porn during work hours."

"Can it, Brodie," one shot back at him. "You want to sift through this junk, then be my guest."

Hanlon signaled for the technician to shut it down. He turned to Brodie, "Looks like we found our serial killer."

"The Librarian?"

"Yes. Sawyer," he said, moving towards the door. "Notify Metro Police what we've got so we can wrap this case up."

Chapter 4

Zach didn't wait long to hear acceptance news from Human Resources. Being the son of a U.S. Senator, something he had intentionally failed to mention to Linfred, meant swift federal clearance. He knew he would be fast-tracked through the system. The Feds had a file on every politician's kid. He knew that from hacking into their databases in the past. He had conveniently learned from the hack that there wasn't much to take note regarding one Zachary Eldridge except his lineage connections and employment records. As far as the Feds were concerned, at least on paper, Zach led a relatively boring life. There wasn't even a parking or traffic violation on his record.

In the interim before starting as a new employee of the Library of Congress (known on Capitol Hill as the LOC), Zach found himself grieving his old friend. His memories, as always, were vivid and detailed. Roone had been a mentor to him and almost a surrogate father figure when his own father was off doing whatever he did in the astrophysics world.

There were times Zach wondered if his father really worked undercover for one of the many foreign or domestic intelligence agencies. He was forever jetting off to places in the world where governments either collapsed or suddenly became war zones upon his return. His father could be very vague about what he did for a living and his mother certainly never discussed it. Both his parents were enigmas.

Roone Sawyer, on the other hand, was the only one Zach had ever trusted with the full extent of his savantness. It was Roone who had advised him on how best to use his abilities and expand his knowledge in areas other than math computation. Yet even Roone had warned him to be careful. The world didn't always take kindly to freaks and geeks. The less they knew the better. Since secrecy seemed to prevail in his family, before long he found himself also taking on that aspect of the Eldridge family persona.

Zach knew he was different. He knew his brain did not function in the same way normal people's brains worked, but he also knew his heart was in the right place and he would eventually find those that accepted him for who and what he was—like Roone did, or rather had done. There were few people he could relate to, even now, for which he desired to engage in a true friendship. Libraries were his home, his sanctuary, and books had become his non-judgmental friends.

Right now, he focused on research. It was his brain food. Within a 24-hour period he quickly absorbed a stack of history books and detailed maps about the LOC, committing to memory every room, gallery, and important artifact that it currently contained. He wouldn't readily remember every little detail, but his brain functioned as a giant search engine. Facts were stored somewhere in his memory vaults for easy retrieval whether significant or non-significant in nature.

The LOC contained more than 168 million items and approximately 12,000 new items were entered each day. It was a staggering amount of material for any Library to keep track of.

Massive data, comprised of books, commissioned art, rare manuscripts, both bound and unbound, as well as large photo and digital collections had to be managed. Even with an annual budget close to $700 million it was a gargantuan task for its three thousand plus employees. Zach could understand why they might have a 'black hole' problem.

The LOC had grown exponentially since 1815 when its founder, Thomas Jefferson, had first donated 6,000 books from his personal collection to start the new Library of Congress after British soldiers burned down the original one in 1814. Congress eventually approved the payment of the grand sum of $24,940 for Jefferson's collection, which had works in it from all different languages. That once small library had eventually grown into the largest library on Earth.

On any given day, thousands of visitors passed through this great institution, greeted by over 300 volunteers, researchers and tour docents—like the redheaded woman. His thoughts briefly returned to her beautiful green eyes—a rare genetic anomaly. The chances of having red hair and green eyes were—he quickly calculated--less than 2% of the world population. It wouldn't be hard to find out who she was. He would wait until he had internal LOC access to the volunteer registry to look her up.

His thoughts drifted back to his main purpose for being here—Roone Sawyer's cryptic message and subsequent death. Zach never considered himself psychic, but he knew without a shadow of a doubt that his friend had not committed suicide. Therefore, he had to have been murdered. By whom, and why, remained something still to be discovered.

~~*~~

On his first day on the job, Zach breezed through "New Employee Orientation" and was immediately handed over to

Library Services (LS) Collection & Preservation division where a sweet African-American woman named Lydia showed him around.

Lydia was subbing that day for her Supervisor, who was out sick with the flu. She was an apologetic one and didn't have a clue what to do with Zach or who to deliver him to. She kept referring to an assignment sheet she had in-hand which referenced his job description details and station location.

"It doesn't exactly say," she tried to apologize again. "But I believe I am to escort you to the Supervisor of the Main Reading Room, which is Estelle Friedman."

Lydia ushered him through a back maze of corridors on the first floor that led into the secure private domain of the Main Reading Room. Oddly enough there was no direct route into the Main Reading Room from the visitor's entrance, which seemed a rather strange architectural flaw. Any member of the public, age 16 and over, had to first possess a special photo "Reader Identification Card" to get in before going through a security scanner. This was the key access point to the world's best research portal in the world and it was tightly controlled. Security strictly banned all liquids, food, backpacks, large purses and most importantly, cell phones, inside this domain. The list of other non-allowable items was quite long.

Zach gained immediate access upon flashing his employee ID that hung from a lanyard around his neck. Employees were required to wear their photo ID at all times. This allowed them to speed past the visitor metal detectors and required bag search line leading into the Reference Librarian Room—the antechamber to the Main Reading Room.

As he moved down the center aisle of the Reference Librarian Room, Lydia motioned for him to go directly into the Main Reading Room.

"Go take a look," she instructed. "Give me a few minutes to

locate Mrs. Friedman and we'll get you settled in."

Zach was grateful for the opportunity to go it alone. He had never been inside the Main Reading Room, despite having seen pictures of it in multiple books. His parents had never taken him inside this Library as a child--probably fearful he would never want to leave.

Like any place Zach saw for the very first time, initial impressions were important to him. It told him a lot about the energy of the place and its structure in the mathematical universe. Everywhere he could see numbers dancing around—on people, through people, hidden away in little alcoves. What he was sure would be experienced as a chaotic intrusion, maybe even a nightmare for many, was something he was used to. At times it was even quite comforting. It told him his brain was in order and functioning in a state he had come to experience as normal. He immediately felt at peace in this new setting. All around he could see that the creators of this magnificent space had strived for harmony and balance.

He walked around the reference desk in the center of the room, pacing out its length and the parameters of the three-story octagonal shaped area. His eyes were drawn heavenward to the semi-circular stained-glass windows beneath the domed ceiling. He smiled appreciatively at what appeared to be an all-knowing giant eye in the center of the dome. Around the eye-like mural were the U.S. State and Territorial seals, all 48 of them with the inscribed date each was admitted to the Union.

Sixteen bronze statues were placed along the balustrade of the galleries. Eight recessed alcoves occupied the outer edges of the room where library computer terminals were made available for research and where the open Stacks were available to Library members. Most of the LOC collections were online, but not everything. In this enclave of knowledge, in-depth research of more obscure materials always had to be done in person. One had to physically experience this place to truly feel the depth and magnitude of knowledge it offered. Zach wondered how many authors had started writing their books in this very room.

Zach walked over to the Central Desk where two reference experts were processing green slip requests. He scanned the titles of books being called up. It always interested him to learn what people wanted to read. Today it was state legislative records, foreign law reviews, history books—the usual Washingtonian reading material.

Across the reading room, in Alcove 7, another employee was placing each researcher's cache of reference books on their designated shelves for easy retrieval. Copiers and printers sat in one corner, scanners at both sides of the room and city telephone directories near Alcove 4. The place ran efficiently. He took note of every last detail. If they turned off the lights, he was confident he could find his way through every nook of the place blindfolded. It was now all in his head. Forever committed to memory.

Zach made a 360-degree turn. He observed only a handful of people occupying the 236 desks in the great room. He glanced up to see people viewing him from the glass-walled visitor's mezzanine on the second floor above. There was always someone watching. Must be some hidden stairways, along with cameras up there as well, he thought. His attention was drawn to the inscription on a sidewall: "Science Is Organized Knowledge". There were hundreds of such sayings throughout the Library. In time, he would come to know them all.

His eyes zeroed in on the gilded bronze clock on an upper wall. It had been beautifully placed against a gold mosaic of zodiac signs and a life-size bronze figure of Father Time clutching a scythe. He immediately noted that the clock was not keeping accurate time. Either someone was forgetting to wind it or its internal mechanism was damaged. His fingers itched to examine it, find out the cause of its failure and to correct the time to set things right again. The thought occurred to him the time error might have some intentional meaning, or certainly by now someone would have set it right. Zach had come to find that in life everything had meaning, and in time it would reveal itself. He smiled at his last thought and made a mental note to learn more about that clock.

He recognized Lydia walking into the room alongside a woman who must be his supervisor. Estelle Friedman was not at all what he had expected--short, round, friendly and a sprite of a woman, who barely came up to his chest. But what she lacked in stature for her 55 years, she made up in confidence. The first words out of her mouth after introducing herself were, "Mr. Eldridge. I see you are a young strapping lad with an intelligent face. I have a job for you, and I think you are going to like working here."

Unlike Linfred, who was serious and demanding, Estelle wore a big bright smile and could make heads turn with her unusual laugh--which, in the confines of a quiet library, could be a real liability. However, she didn't seem to care or take offense if others shot her a look of disapproval. Zach liked her immediately. She was genuine and had a rosy-pink aura around her, which meant she was a nurturer. He was not at all surprised that she took him quickly in hand like a mother hen taking care of her newest chick.

Within no time, Zach found himself in the controlled environment of the closed Stacks. The temperature never rose above 67 degrees and the humidity stayed under 47%. The very rare manuscripts and books required constant monitoring at all times for preservation purposes. Thankfully, that was not part of Zach's job.

The closed Stacks provided a good degree of privacy and autonomy for those who labored 'down under' in the windowless and sometimes darkened confines of this tomb-like denizen. Zach felt at home in such places. The interruptions would be minimal here while he tried locating 'special requests'—meaning materials that had gone missing for long periods of time. It was only a small part of the 'back hole' problem.

Zach's station in a back nook of the Stacks contained a computer, a small desk lamp and very little else. The overhead fluorescent lighting running down the center aisle could be harsh on his eyes at times, but since many of the rows lay in perpetual darkness, waiting for some interested party to trip a light sensor motion detector to their contents, it would be okay. He was used to it.

There were open Stacks in all the Library's reading rooms, but the general public never got to see the closed Stacks of the Main Reading Room. It was hidden behind locked doors that spanned the perimeter of the octagonal-shaped room. Very few people had access to it. The staff could request items via the Library's online computer system or a green call slip, but they were always delivered in person and retrieved when finished.

The closed Stacks were not artistically beautiful like the rest of the Library, just mainly uniform and functional in an austere way. Here one would find long corridors housing row upon rows of floor-to-ceiling metal shelving holding not only reference books, but also aisles containing over 22,000 small wooden drawers housing more than 22 million card catalog entries. Some went back over a hundred years and were still legibly handwritten in black ink.

Zach keyed in his computer access code and brought up a list of special requests under his department. It was fairly long with requests dating back at least three months. Another folder cataloged actual file requests that had never been found going back several years. This could be a folder or file which contained original maps, notes, diaries, photos—or any number of loose materials pertaining to an item, which either could not be bound or perhaps was of a subject that might be confidential in nature.

Zach scanned the pages of entries and immediately zeroed in on one particular request, a file marked ZE, which wasn't a listed LOC classification. Class Z books were generally bibliography materials under Library Science. The final classification for General Information Resources was always ZA. A ZE code had to be a misclassification or a typo on someone's part.

He wondered if the LOC was using extended Z classifications, which were unique to other Library systems. Zach did a quick systems search looking for any classifications that might come after ZA. Nothing. He went back further in the request lists and found a few other ZE entries, which were even older. A few of the ZE entries had a Congressional office address code after the request. Quite a few were marked SH-211. He brought up the Congressional Directory to see who was assigned that code.

Interesting. Someone from the Senate Intelligence Committee *really* wanted this file. It was evident that they had failed to locate it, but nevertheless kept trying, repeatedly. Why? Now he was *really* curious. There was no explanation on record of what the file contained.

Behind him, Zach heard the sound of wheels rolling down the marble aisle. It invaded his thoughts and the silence of the Stacks. He turned to see who had entered his domain and saw a gangly mail clerk pushing a metal cart towards him. His badge showed he was a summer intern.

"You Zach Eldridge?" the kid asked.

"Yeah?"

The kid held up a small package. "You got mail," he said handing over a lightweight package.

"It's been sitting around the mailroom for a few days. No one knew where to deliver it," he explained scratching his head.

"Thanks," Zach said.

"No problem. Sorry it took so long," the kid said, turning his cart back around. "My name's Richie. Stay warm, man. It's like a meat locker down here."

Zach nodded, barely hearing him as he moved off. The small package in his hand weighed very little. Who would be sending him mail already? It was sent inter-office courier, with no sender name or department listing. He ripped it open and carefully dumped its contents onto his desk.

Three items stared back at him. An old brass key with the initials JF emblazoned on it. A small hand-held electronic device, that looked like a phone, but clearly wasn't, and a picture of a large statue of a woman holding a spear up towards the sky, who looked somewhat familiar to him. Underneath the woman was a hurriedly scribbled message: "Nothing missing. Nothing broken."

"What the...?" Zach stopped in mid thought. It was a familiar sounding saying. Where had he heard it before?

His memory immediately shifted back to an earlier time, many years ago, when he had first started working at the New York Public Library, Manhattan Branch. In his mind's eye he recalled the vivid memory of Roone Sawyer, sitting alone in an empty reading room with a dimly lit table lamp casting shadows down on a large open book set before him.

It had been a wintery New York City night, with outside temperatures hovering near zero and the wind howling up a storm. The general public had long ago gone home due to extreme weather warnings. Only a few employees still remained straggling towards exit doors, donning warm winter coats before bracing themselves for the frigid cold outside.

Zach remembered he had been one of the very last employees to leave the building. As he passed through the reading room, slinging his backpack over a shoulder, he saw Roone Sawyer was still there--his white hair neatly combed back, with his tweed suit and signature bow tie making him easily recognizable from across the room. Zach had surmised awhile back, when he was his teaching assistant at Yale, that the man was a consummate bachelor. He had no one to go home to. The Library was and always would be his home.

Zach had called out to him in passing. "Kind of late for you, Professor. I thought I was the only one still here."

Roone looked up and smiled in recognition. "This is my favorite time of day and my favorite place," he admitted momentarily sitting back in his chair. "Home can wait."

He looked around him like a man in command of his domain. "Zach, there is no comparison to the quiet stillness of an empty library, surrounded by knowledge that has survived for centuries. These books..." He looked down at the book in front of him, its pages worn with age. "They help to clear away the cobwebs in one's mind after a long day."

Zach moved towards him and could see the book he was referring to was an Old Testament version of the Bible written in Hebrew.

"I never took you for the religious sort," Zach remarked, nodding toward the Bible.

Roone removed his wire-rimmed spectacles and laid them down beside the ancient text.

"Religion and spirituality are two separate things, my friend," he explained. "These scriptures speak to the very essence of man's soul—to one's relationship with the Divine. It is beyond religion. It is ancient wisdom and when one has attained wisdom, one has it all."

He looked directly at Zach continuing. "There is an old saying... Nothing missing. Nothing broken. Remember it..."

"What does it mean, Professor?"

Sawyer repeated the phrase like a mantra. "Nothing missing. Nothing broken. It means being at Peace with God. The Hebrews call it 'Shalom'. Completion. Oneness. Fulfillment. It is what every man strives for in his human journey."

Sawyer returned his glasses to the bridge of his nose and went back to his scriptures. "I mark the passages that remind me of this sense of human purpose. It serves as my password to what lies beyond..."

Zach had sat down with his friend, being drawn towards his philosophical words. And between the two of them he found himself debating with his old Professor the esoteric and scientific meaning of the word 'nothing'.

"If 'nothing' means lack of physical existence," he pointed out, "then does it reside in a cosmic vacuum or outside of space and time? Therefore 'Nothing missing. Nothing broken' could mean something else entirely..."

They had spent hours talking about the nature of the Universe and the concept that perhaps there were other parallel universes out there affecting all of us. Such ideas resonated with him, pushing him to explore deeper thoughts about the nature of man and reality with his friend. He could have spent all night talking such ideas, expanding his mind and laying open the possibilities that man was not finite at all, but infinite. He would never forget the conversation. 'Nothing missing. Nothing broken,' indeed.

Zach recalled his old Professor's words like they had been spoken to him only yesterday. There was no doubt in his mind that Roone had sent him this package. Perhaps it had been his last act before dying. The absence of such a great mind and mentor made the loss seem even more profound.

For some unknown reason, these items had been important to Roone. They meant something. They had been handed down to Zach for him to discover their deeper significance. In fact, in Zach's world, where everything meant something, his professor would have known this. Was this why he had urgently contacted him at such short notice?

He picked up the brass key stamped 'JF'. He had no idea whose initials they might be. The key didn't feel like a standard door key. It might open a cabinet or a small door. The key looked fairly old and, from the grooved uneven design along the sides, like it had been roughly hand cast.

Most of the Library's office and private rooms had security keypads outside each door, so that ruled out it being an LOC door key. The energy of the key felt like a "1" which, to Zach, meant it was the starting place. This key unlocked something Roone wanted him to find. His initial contact warnings about secrecy and discernment meant that he trusted Zach to discover the items' meaning without him having to divulge it in a communication that could be intercepted.

His attention was drawn to the odd phone-shaped device. It was black and had no brand name or identifying marks. Nor was there any visible power switch. It fit nicely in the palm of his hand, was quite cool to the touch, but its true purpose eluded him. He had never seen anything like it and Zach was a real gadget freak.

The device was comprised of some sort of lightweight polished metal, which didn't include aluminum or steel alloys. He tried etching a small mark on it, but it was scratch proof. He purposely dropped it, but it showed no sign of cracks. It was as hard as titanium. Was it some new experimental magnesium-based alloy? He would have to test it for heat resistance when he got home. Lighting a match in a Library was bound to get him fired.

He put the black device in his shirt pocket for safekeeping, tucked away with the other items in his backpack, and returned to work. Seconds later, his cell phone was beeping like mad with a string of message alerts--so much for the uninterrupted peace and quiet of the Stacks.

Zach scrolled through his phone to see they were all news

reports coming in concerning Roone Sawyer. He had set his phone to alert him to any new developments regarding his friend. What he now saw made him swear vehemently. He felt ready to explode.

Chapter 5

The news was dead wrong. They were painting Roone as a pedophile serial killer, which was not only preposterous, but outright defaming to who the man truly was. He was a scholar, a moral and compassionate man. A man with such clear boundaries that not for a second did Zach believe any confession to such crimes they might have found could be legitimate. Someone was clearly framing him and that someone might also be his killer. With no family, there was no one to defend Roone Sawyer's legacy, except Zach.

He had tried to calm himself down after hearing the news by attempting a few tried and true Qigong exercises right there in the Stacks before his brain blew a gasket. Anger could do that to him, which is why he avoided it at all costs. When it did happen, his mind went into overdrive and his visual cortex started spitting out swirling fractal images in vivid colors with three-dimensional numbers superimposed over whatever was in his line of vision at the time. It was like a fireworks display carried out in fast forward motion. No drug could stop it. It was what he was feeling right now.

Zach immediately stood up and shifted into his Qigong Tiger sequences. It was the only way to control the energy coursing through him by becoming one with the energy and re-directing and releasing it. He dipped into the movement, 'Tiger Seizing Prey', and started to feel himself regain control of his emotions.

He managed to steady his breathing and focus the energy in his body through a deeper method of meditation he had incorporated into this particular form of Qigong. He felt the bands loosen on his vision, but his senses were still acute. From experience he knew he also needed to get some food or drink into him. He had skipped lunch and his glucose level was probably low, which didn't help when such things happened.

Zach headed for the underground tunnels leading towards the Madison Building Cafeteria. Normally new employees needed a map to navigate the labyrinth maze running under the Capitol Hill buildings, but Zach knew the route from committing the tunnel system to memory even before he started.

He found himself coming to a complete stop outside the vending machine room under the LOC instead of going towards the food shops and café inside the Madison Building. All he really needed was some quick protein. That would have to tide him over until later.

It was 3:23 PM and only a few people were milling about inside. Zach fished out his credit card, inserted it and pulled out a tuna sandwich from a refrigerated slot. He quickly unwrapped it and practically chucked it down. His taste buds recorded it as above average for vending food. Someone had added sweet relish to it, which he liked. He made a healthy drink selection, opting for water, even though his secret poison would always be Dr. Pepper.

Zach swore softly under his breath when the water bottle he'd just purchased failed to drop down into the well. He gave the machine a little shake with an added bang for good measure. It dropped down into the bottom dispenser with a thud. He leaned down to retrieve it, just as a vision of the red-haired woman came into focus. He found himself straightening up to his full 6-foot height, attempting not to stare, yet amazed that with the sight of her his head and vision immediately cleared.

She was standing in front of a vending machine only 10 feet away trying to make what looked like an important decision. He watched her chew her bottom lip for the briefest second before pushing a selection button. She must have felt his eyes on her, admiring her, taking in everything about her he could see and surmise, because she suddenly turned her head and glanced his way. He smiled. A second later she smiled back. He felt his pulse quicken and decided to introduce himself.

That's when synchronicity and his luck went sour and his supervisor, Estelle Friedman, came into the vending room. She spotted him and made a direct beeline for him. The red-haired girl turned away.

"How's it going, Zach?" she asked, juggling a coffee in one hand, and selecting a chocolate brownie to add to her afternoon snack with the other.

"It's going okay, Mrs. Friedman," he answered, still observing the red-headed woman retrieve a bright red apple from the fresh fruit machine and put it towards her mouth. Zach groaned inwardly watching her take a bite. He had really wanted to talk to her.

Mrs. Friedman followed his line of sight. She cleared her throat, interrupting his thoughts.

"Best pick up your jaw and put your tongue back in your mouth, young man," she said with a knowing smile. "Don't go getting any ideas about that one."

Zach suddenly had her full and undivided attention. "Why? Is she married?"

"No."

"Boyfriend?"

Mrs. Friedman shrugged. "I've heard she doesn't date."

Zach frowned. "Is there something wrong with her?"

Mrs. Friedman let out her funny, but loud little laugh. A few heads turned. "Heaven's no. Meghan is one of the Library's sweetest and most sought after docents. Everyone likes her."

Meghan. Her name was Meghan--meaning "pearl". It suited her.

Zach stifled a smile. It was apparent his boss had a little bit of a gossipy side about her. He decided to use it to his advantage. "So, what's her story?"

Mrs. Friedman finished her coffee and tossed the cup in the trash. He watched her stash the brownie in her purse, probably for a late afternoon snack. He trotted alongside her, back through the tunnel, hoping to learn more about this Meghan woman. His supervisor was only too happy to share her knowledge.

"Meghan's a widow. Her husband was an Air Force pilot who died in Afghanistan about six years ago. They were married only six months when his plane crashed. She was pregnant at the time."

Zach had to ask. "She has a child?"

Mrs. Friedman nodded. "Yes. A daughter."

"You think she's still grieving?" he asked.

They were fast approaching the cellar level elevators to the Library. "Well, many have asked her out, but she always turns them down. So don't go breaking your heart trying," she added with a hint of motherly advice.

Together they silently waited by the elevator doors, each lost in their own respective thoughts. Zach's were clearly on Meghan. Mrs. Friedman's were clearly on work and quite possibly her chocolate brownie.

"Now if you have any work-related questions, just call me," she added as the doors to an empty elevator slid open.

"Yes, I do," Zach said following her in. "Do you know what a ZE classification is?"

There was a rather long moment of silence before she spoke. "The Library doesn't use any such classification."

"Then why do I have 12 special requests for materials starting with that classification?" he wanted to know. "Some have gone missing for quite some time."

The elevator doors slid open to the first floor. She walked out with Zach on her heels.

"Is there something I need to know or should I spend a lot of time actually looking for something that doesn't exist?'

She hesitated, pulling him over to the side of the corridor while others passed. Whatever she was about to reveal made her somewhat uncomfortable. She spoke in hushed words. "The Library *did* have an unlisted ZE classification at one time, which pertained only to classified government information that was kept in a private vault connected to the Library's Congressional Reading Room."

While Zach had heard of the place, he had never seen it. The Congressional Reading Room was off limits to the general public and most LOC staff. Only Members of both chambers of Congress could access this exclusive room styled after London's old world men's clubs. He wasn't sure if his Senatorial mother would even be allowed inside.

One had to be assigned a special key code, unique to their person, to get past the door's guarded security system. Visitor records were meticulously kept, especially if one brought in a special guest. Located at the very end of a quiet corridor, on the southwest corner of the first floor, few people knew of its hallowed existence. One would not find its location marked on any LOC map and for good reason. Those that came here usually came to escape the scrutiny of Capitol Hill, knowing their privacy would be unquestionably respected.

"Where is this ZE vault information kept now?" Zach asked.

Mrs. Friedman shrugged. "I believe all such classified

information was moved over to the National Security Agency."

Mrs. Friedman had given Zach much to think about back in the closed Stacks. Could it be that the NSA had not retrieved all the Library's ZE classification materials when they had cleared out the 'vault' and someone knew this? Had that person been Roone Sawyer? Or other unknown parties as well? There was a chance these missing ZE materials had not been returned to the Congressional Reading Room vault and had somehow landed up back in the closed Stacks.

If possible, Zach would have to find out when this NSA acquisition took place? He had a pretty good idea by checking back to when the earliest ZE request on his list had been made. His answer was approximately 11 months ago.

Zach spent the next two days searching through hundreds of special file folder boxes that appeared to have never been opened in years. Shelf maintenance and cleaning couldn't get to all these areas, especially in a library this large. Dust particles could be a real hazard, which Zach had grown accustomed to over the years. He always donned gloves and a special mask he had devised for himself to limit exposure time whenever he found himself in the more inaccessible areas of the Stacks. Over the years he had read too many studies about librarians getting asthma, lung cancer, skin allergies and other respiratory problems for him to not exercise a healthy modicum of caution.

In his search, he found several misplaced items on his list and experienced the brief thrill of a treasure hunter finding what others had not. There was an old saying in the Library world that 'Books shelved incorrectly are as good as lost'. It was the number one cause for 'Black Hole' problems. Yet, despite his progress, Zach still found no evidence of any mysterious ZE materials. The irony certainly hadn't escaped him that ZE were his own initials.

On his second day on the job Zach personally delivered some of the requested items to the "reserved call shelves' in the Main

Reading Room. Researchers often had their own reserved shelf assigned to them for a 7-day period where books could be placed on hold just for their use. Zach could have sent these reference materials up in the book elevator that ran under the Central Desk, or with one of the other Stacks workers, but it was a good excuse for him to search through the open stack alcoves as well. He wanted to get a good feel for where everything was located.

Over at the Desk he caught sight of a young well-dressed woman asking questions of Harold, an older gentleman and one of the many rotating reference librarians assigned to the Main Reading Room. She was scribbling notes on what looked like a reporter's small spiral notepad. She looked vaguely familiar and then it hit him where he had seen her before. She was the TV reporter he had seen on the entrance steps of the Library reporting on the breaking news of Roone's death on his first day. A day he would never forget. The words she had spoken had torn right through him to his very core. Roone Sawyer was dead.

He hadn't caught her name at the time, but he would never forget that voice. She worked for the local station WWGO-TV. This time she had no camera crew with her. There was a determined and hungry look to her face, like a dog going after a bone. He knew exactly why she was there. A good reporter never missed the chance for a follow-up scoop. She was probably there to do more character assassination on Roone. Who else had she interviewed trying to get information? What had she learned?

He debated whether to go forward and get involved or not, when Mrs. Linfred seemed to appear out of nowhere. She marched right over to the woman and promptly read her the riot act.

"Ms. Cavaleri, please get your skinny reporter ass out of *my* Library and stop harassing *my* employees!"

Zach observed the reporter practically blanch at the confrontation. Linfred wasn't one to mince words. You knew where she stood. She either liked you or she didn't. He probably came into the latter category. And as for this Cavaleri woman, well she was someone Linfred had obviously encountered before, and the decision was in. She had been declared an enemy of both Linfred and the Library.

Then to make matters worse, Cavaleri's cell phone went off with a series of loud text beeps, which made Mrs. Linfred's temper border on DEFCON status.

"No cell phones in the library!" she practically screamed at her. "You know the rules! And next time go through the Communications Officer!"

Cavaleri glanced down at her texts, mumbled a half-hearted, "Sorry. Gotta run!" And with that she made her escape.

The exchange was witnessed by most everyone in the reading room. Linfred looked around in annoyance, daring anyone to say something. She zeroed in on Zach, who immediately looked down hiding a small smile. All around people's heads returned to their books and laptops. Linfred harrumphed loudly and marched back out of the room having made her point.

Chapter 6

Cali Cavaleri oftentimes felt like she had a monkey on her back. All her life she had wanted to be a journalist and while she had come far, she had fallen even farther. And, as her therapist had undeniably pointed out time and time again, she had no one to blame but herself. She had made some very poor choices in her nine years in the broadcast news business after coming to Washington. It had literally driven her to drink. She had what those in denial would call a 'little drinking problem", but to those in recovery Cali was an addict. She drank too much and she knew it.

Back in college she had been quite the star student in her New York University Journalism Department. Her professors had loved her, and she had loved a few of them back in return—oftentimes passionately. People told her that with her looks and brains she could make it anywhere. Unfortunately, she had bought that hype hook, line and sinker. It didn't take long to discover that the news business was a dirty cutthroat field—a swamp. You had to be willing to compromise and lower yourself if you wanted to get ahead. Only the very resilient survived and she was a survivor.

Like so many others who had stars in their eyes, Cali thought it would be different for her. That was her first mistake. Magical thinking had caused her to believe that she could become a star reporter or an on-air personality without having to start from the bottom and work her way up.

After graduating at the top of her class from NYU with a degree in broadcast journalism, Cali had put together what she thought was a killer audition tape. It contained all the stories she had covered at the University's busy little TV station. She wrote her own news copy, produced her own stories, edited them, and even had a short gig as an On-Air host. She had diligently shopped her audition video all over the country, sending out about 100 USB sticks and resumes. The only station she heard back from was a small station in Skull Valley, Arizona—not exactly a thriving metropolis. The population at best was around 800 and the median age was around 53 years old. There would be no dating life whatsoever for her there unless she sauntered over to nearby Whiskey Row in Prescott.

Arizona seemed to be calling her. Skull Valley needed an intern and a weekend weather girl and they needed someone right now. It was the hardest thing she had ever done, but she swallowed her pride and took it. She desperately needed a "starter" job.

Skull Valley's weather, like most of Arizona was sunny, hot and sunny, and fire season was really hot and dry with the occasional summer monsoon thrown in to break up the monotony. She never could get used to rains that brought an annual invasion of tiny frogs that seemed to find their way into places frogs should not dare to venture. She hated bugs and insects and screamed whenever she saw a scorpion skittle across the floor.

Cali was really a city girl through and through. She had expected to start her career in a small station in New York City, not Skull Valley, Arizona. Even the name of the place should have been taken as a sign. But Cali endured because the people at the station were nice and she had a gift for gab—even with the farmers and the locals, and all those NRA card-carrying, concealed weapons folk. While she would never admit it to any of her liberal city friends, she took up firearms training and found it was something she was surprisingly good at. One can never have too many skills, she thought. And one never knew when her Annie Oakley abilities would come in handy. However, this was one talent she did not include on her resume.

She found interesting Yavapai Indian stories, interviewed Hopi Elders on tribal prophesy, reported on a few stray UFOs, which the area seemed to have more than the usual amount of, and was beyond ecstatic when one of her stories on Arizona drug rehab center corruption made a network news feed. That got her a job offer at a Phoenix station, where she was assigned to cover the metropolitan crime beat. She had a good nose for sniffing out political corruption and after four years in Phoenix she made the big jump to WWGO-TV in Washington, DC—where her taste for fine Chardonnay wines escalated and she soon found herself knocking off a bottle or more every night to unwind.

As a WWGO reporter she had her on-air segments as well as her own Twitter feed to report stories. She was still young-looking for 30 and hip enough in her reporting style to have amassed a sizable following. Then it all went to hell. Her astrologer told her it was due to a 'delayed' 28-year Saturn return cycle in her natal chart, compounded by other difficult transits, which were a bitch to navigate. Damn those planets! At least it gave her something to blame, even though she didn't understand it at all.

What really happened was that she had fallen into bad intel, the fake news trap, and wasn't thoroughly checking out the veracity of her sources. She had gotten lax. One of those sources happened to be an undercover operative, a USAP, as they were called, meaning he was from an "Unacknowledged Special Access Program" who also just happened to be on the FBI's counterintelligence task force. She also happened to be having a torrid affair with him. He was drop dead gorgeous and inventive in bed, so her trust factor was clearly compromised. In the end he had been feeding her false information. Great sex could be a deadly compromiser of good judgment. It was a hard lesson to learn.

When a news story blows up on you in Washington, you get quickly labeled. Then with a few too many glasses of wine sloshing through her after a long shift, she had tweeted out some rather inappropriate barbs at some of her political critics. She was mortified when she discovered the next morning what she had actually tweeted. There was a big gap in her memory from the night before and she suspected she had probably blacked out. She had to do a mea culpa to all her followers, including the Speaker of the House whom she had drunkenly targeted.

The next morning she encountered the firing squad in a pseudo intervention, which included the station's owner, Elizabeth Vandam, her executive producer David Freeman and some Brunhilde witch from Human Resources. She was severely chastised for her behavior and warned that unless she dragged her "skinny little reporter ass" into treatment (as that Linfred bitch had referred to her), she would be looking for a new job sooner rather than later.

Cali Cavaleri obediently did what she was told. She checked into a 30-day rehab program and was ordered to attend weekly therapy thereafter. Lucky for her, the station's health insurance plan paid for it all.

Upon release she hit every 12-step program the city had to offer trying to find the right fit. She quickly learned who the political addicts were in this town---all of them from lobbyists to senators. Some tried to attend an out of area group to avoid recognition, but Cali made the rounds and learned who went where. The one perk she hadn't expected from getting sober is that addicts often form silent alliances with other addicts—like an unofficial brotherhood or sisterhood trying to help each other out and support them. Because of it, Cali could get scoops on stories faster from a fellow addict than from someone who wasn't.

The 6:00 o'clock news hour was quickly nearing and traffic in the newsroom always became more chaotic with last minute copy going to the editor before making its final destination to a studio teleprompter feed. Overhead TV monitors lined a sidewall flashing stories their affiliate station in New York was airing along with the usual local network feeds. A young acne faced delivery guy had just dropped off what smelled like a pepperoni pizza. The cheesy smell wafted across the newsroom over to Cali's cubicle.

She had just finished a Wendy's cheeseburger and was wiping ketchup from her lips. There were several half-finished and now cold coffee cups strewn across her desk along with leftover fries. She knew she was substituting an alcohol addiction for a caffeine one, but hell nobody was perfect. At least she wasn't a chain-smoking nicotine addict as well.

Above her desktop monitor was proudly displayed all her many-colored sobriety tokens--red, gold, green and a dark blue one for six-months. That's how long she had now been sober. She had carefully glued them on her cork board to both remind and inspire her that she was getting her life back together.

A framed photo of a lone goldfish sat on her book shelf, a yellow sticky taped to it proclaiming: 'My Family'. She hadn't been on speaking terms with her own family for years. Both her parents were alcoholics, her father now dead from liver cancer and her mother still barely alive in Queens probably still living with her druggie boyfriend. A part of her still blamed them both for passing down their god-awful genes to her. It was something she was still working on in therapy—overcoming the blame game.

In her therapist's office was a cross-stitched pillow, which boldly read: "If it's not one thing, It's your mother. Get over it!" She was really trying hard not to be a mommy basher. All she really wanted was a hard-earned break.

Cali had her headset on, blocking out the din from the busy newsroom around her. She felt extremely focused today and had awakened feeling a small ray of hope. She had no idea where it came from, but she would take it. It was a good sign. Something was changing. She could feel it.

She glanced at the large wall clock across the newsroom knowing she was on a tight deadline. She had been on hold for almost ten minutes now waiting for someone with the Capitol Police Communications Dept. to verify one of the victim's names. When you have been accused in the past of having gotten the facts wrong, a bit of paranoia sets in making you want to check and double check everything. It was something she would probably live with for the rest of her life. Finally, someone came back on the line. She sat forward in her chair, her fingers flying over the keyboard.

"Give me the spelling of that name again," she asked, repeating it. "J-a-n-g-s-u-p-a-k. Got it, thanks!"

She hung up and transmitted the copy to her news editor. The station's Evening News Producer, Frank Carlisle, poked his head into her cubicle.

"Anything new on the killer librarian story?"

She reached for one of her unfinished cups of coffee. She grimaced at its cold bitter taste, then swigged it down anyway. Caffeine would always be her best friend now that she had severed her close relationship with wine.

"Well, I finally got the name of the last victim those boaters found—a 16-year-old Korean kid. Capitol Police claim all the victims were underage. The cops think these kids might have been smuggled into the country since there are no records of any of them in immigration files."

Frank nodded. "Might be part of a human trafficking network."

"That's what I was thinking," she said. "I'm looking into it…"

"And they're sure the Librarian did it?" Frank was always second-guessing the cops.

"The police found hundreds of compromising photos of the victims on Sawyer's personal laptop. They also found password-protected files with some pretty gruesome stuff."

Frank shook his head in disgust. "The guy's better off dead."

Cali shrugged. "My source tells me they're not sure if Sawyer killed himself out of guilt and remorse or he was being blackmailed and afraid the truth would come out. However, I'm not entirely buying it," she added. "If he was being blackmailed to avoid detection, why leave a suicide note confessing to it all?'

Frank shrugged, glancing at the monitor. "Listen, I've got a new assignment for you."

Cali swiveled around in her chair to face him. "Can it wait a day or two? I've got this gut feeling there's more to this Librarian story than we're getting."

"Cali, the public wants something new to fixate on. The Potomac Killer story is already old news."

"Maybe," she reluctantly agreed. "But the Library employees I spoke to all paint a different picture of Sawyer."

"Like what?"

"They all said he was a devout Catholic, biblical scholar, and had a heart of gold. It seems he never missed the 7:30 morning mass at St. Patrick's," she reported. "Others say he never left the Library. It was his whole life, so something doesn't add up."

Frank was a dyed-in-the-wool skeptic. "The pious ones usually fall the hardest." One of the producers handed Frank that night's news script and kept walking. Frank glanced down at it, scanning the lineup.

"Anyway, my hands are tied," he said without looking up.

"How come, Frank?"

Frank was antsy to go. He started walking in the direction of the news studio. "Elizabeth Vandam—you know, the woman who signs your paychecks, says she's tired of seeing child killer stories on her station. It makes everyone uncomfortable—especially her. Time to move on…"

Cali rose from her chair and followed him down the newsroom aisle. "C'mon, Frank. Just give me a little more time. I'm sure I'll find something."

Frank stopped abruptly and looked her straight in the eye. His voice had an underlying warning tone. "Cali, listen to me. Don't push your luck. You're still on disciplinary probation until the end of this year. One more mess up and Vandam will have you writing your own obituary. Do I make myself clear?" He left her standing there, but her thoughts were already reviewing other options.

Chapter 7

The black phone-like device was a real enigma. Zach had been up all night reviewing the most recent metallurgy reports trying to pinpoint what type of alloy the little gizmo thing was comprised of. It didn't react to heat or fire, even with prolonged exposure. He had run some tests and so far, it didn't scratch, dent, melt, bend, or reveal any secrets of its true purpose. Where had Roone gotten it? And more importantly, what was Zach supposed to do with it? If only Roone had left behind instructions, even cryptic directions if nothing else, instead of leaving him guessing.

The device, which Zach now called "Gizmo", was either a top-secret experimental alloy our government was producing that hadn't been publicly unveiled or it didn't come from this world. It also occurred to Zach that the answer might be both.

Gizmo failed to set off any of the security scanners in the Library, which on one hand was a relief. It also did not show up on any x-ray machine monitor either. It was like it didn't exist in the material world and only Zach could see it. He didn't believe it was invisible, but he was seriously wondering whether Gizmo had some sort of automatic cloaking ability that kicked in under either unwanted and/or technological scrutiny. That meant it fell into the artificial intelligence realm.

Until Zach could figure out just what Gizmo was capable of, he kept it on his person at all times. This morning, he had a sudden thought that if it was AI then it might respond to direct orders. As he walked through the Library's security scanner he instructed Gizmo to allow his presence to be known. As soon as he thought the instruction, the scanner started beeping. The guard asked him if he had forgotten to empty his pockets of all metals.

Zach sheepishly shook his head and feigned confusion. He retraced his steps, instructed Gizmo to default to shield mode, then walked back through the scanner. This time the scanner remained silent. The Guard shrugged and waved him through.

Zach could hardly contain his excitement. Gizmo was not only AI, but consciousness-assisted technology, meaning it could organically respond to the conscious thought and intent of its operator. In the few days he had kept it on his person, Gizmo had harmonically tuned itself to Zach's consciousness and found him compatible within the parameters of its internal programming.

What he realized with a great degree of awe and reverence was that he had in his hands something scientists had only talked about in theory, yet never as a reality. As far as he believed, consciousness assisted technology was something relegated to the future. How had such a device come into Roone's possession? And why had Roone felt it important enough to pass on to Zach? And for what purpose?

Zach made a quick beeline for his secluded little nook located at the very end of a long aisle of rows within the Main Reading Room's closed Stacks. He purposely avoided conversation with some of the other Stacks workers who occasionally made their way past his special request desk wanting to engage in gossip or small talk. In his mind, Zach knew he had a job to do here, and time was of the essence.

He held Gizmo in his hand and verbally instructed it to 'turn on'. Nothing happened, which is what he feared would occur. He tried a few other computer commands, before finally just thinking "Engage Program". A mild tingling sensation was felt in the palm of his hand, followed by warming heat, but nothing else. The thought "Disengage" turned it immediately cool to his touch. Okay, so far he had accomplished silently turning it on and off, which was nothing earth shattering in nature, but definitely a start. Zach quickly concluded that Gizmo responded more efficiently to simple thought commands. Its programming had to be primarily in code.

But all programming arises out of language and Zach understood this. The language of the universe was mathematics—an area Zach was quite proficient at. For starters he ran through Fibonacci number sequences in his head, then Lucas sequences, then variations of the most well-known sacred geometry that encompassed all of nature. Nothing. He then went on to simple and complex physics equations. Still nothing. From there he tried commands in ASCII codes, then in several different types of Binary Codes, all consisting of a two-symbol number system of zeros and ones in eight-digit segments. Again--nothing. Gizmo blankly stared back at him.

After several hours of unsuccessful attempts at formulating programming scripts in every computer language he knew, Zach had a sudden epiphany. The two other items that Roone had included in the package sent to him might provide a clue. There was that old brass hand-cast key--perhaps it was simply symbolic in nature—like opening a door to understanding. Then the picture of the statue with the message: 'Nothing missing. Nothing broken.' Remembering his debate with Roone about the nature of 'nothing', he would have transcribed the message to mean 'missing and broken'. He wasn't sure what was broken, but he sure as hell knew the reason he was here was because there were a lot of special request files missing.

Zach ran up the list of missing items on his computer screen and began mentally repeating each file's given Library Code along with the instruction to "Find". Still no reaction from Gizmo. He switched gears and started transposing the assigned Library Index Codes into Binary Code. Nothing happened until Zach got to the government classified ZE category. Gizmo suddenly went hot all over.

"You liked that, little buddy?"

So, this was going to be a hunting game like Hot & Cold. Gizmo was leading him towards the prize. A game Zach was beginning to thoroughly enjoy. He suspected the AI in Gizmo knew this. Okay, he thought. I am going to make a compressed binary script file for all 12 missing ZE file numbers and let's see what you've got.

Zach's brain could run through number sequences faster than the speed of light in a lightning storm. It did so now in rapid succession like a mathematical mind mantra on speed. Energy coursed up his spine and flooded every cell of his body with tentacles of pulsing light. He knew immediately he had cracked the code.

Gizmo turned red hot in his hand. All around him the bookshelves and walls began rippling in a watery mass. They took on speed, becoming waves of coiling and swirling energy around him like a giant silvery slinky. The room seemed to shift on its axis.

He held on for dear life as his whole body vibrated as if it was being wrenched apart by a hurricane force. There came a loud sonic boom, which ripped through the very fabric of time and space, creating a dimensional portal into the unknown—a wide gaping black hole opened before him. The pull of some magnetic force took command and Zach was instantly sucked into the swirling vortex, clutching Gizmo to his chest as his body traveled at warp speed through a long dark pulsating tunnel.

He had the brief thought that he might be dying, and this was the tunnel transport often referred to in near-death experiences. He immediately abandoned that thought when he shot out of the tunnel backwards and landed on solid ground, only to find himself sitting in a pile of file folders that clearly displayed the Library's ZE government classification markings.

Stunned, Zach looked back at the black hole he had just emerged from in time to see it close back up, leaving a solid metal wall in its place. No doorways, no handles, not a trace of what had just been there.

"Holy shit!" He looked down at Gizmo still in his hand, only to see his little buddy had turned completely white and was as cold as dry ice. He must be pretty pale himself after what happened. What the hell *had* just happened?

Zach whipped his head around to gauge where he landed, besides smack dab on top of those missing ZE files. His mouth dropped open in stunned disbelief. For as far as his eyes could see, massive walls of highly polished silver drawers reached high into the sky with no visible ceiling. He could NOT see where this massive bank vault-like place began or ended.

Zach slowly rose to his feet and stepped over the ZE files, reminding himself he would get back to them later. He was fairly certain he was no longer in the LOC, nor on Capitol Hill. Wherever he was it had been one hell of a roller coaster ride getting here.

A quick sweep of his body confirmed he was still in one piece. Thank God. The vibratory force that had coursed through him in the tunnel had ceased immediately upon being spit out into this place, replaced by a deep and immediate sense of calm. He liked that.

His brain also felt different here—more balanced. The usual mathematical chatter in his head, which he dealt with on a daily basis since his head injury, had quieted. Inside, he felt centered and serene. For the first time in years, Zach experienced a sense of normalcy.

He stepped out into the vast spaciousness noticing that every row was bathed in a white silvery glow. Oddly enough it gave him a sense of strange familiarity. He knew he had never been here before, but perhaps he had seen such a place in his dreams. He pushed that thought aside for later analysis.

The place was brightly illuminated by some light source that went beyond electricity, beyond light bulbs or even batteries. This lighting was capable of curving evenly around walls, filling every crevice. Not a hint of darkness anywhere and no shadows. Weird. No light fixture he knew of was capable of accomplishing this. Could he have travelled to the future where such technology might be possible?

He scrutinized this new environment he now occupied. The air was fresh and sweet with a hint of some fragrant flower—not exactly roses but close to it. The temperature was perfect, with little to no humidity. There was an even flow of air all around him—again from some unknown source. He hadn't spotted a vent anywhere in sight.

It was easier to breathe deeply in this place. His lungs expanded and contracted easily. Ancient Yogis had been teaching such practices for centuries as a pathway to higher states of consciousness. Was he in a state of expanded awareness now?

His brain felt like it had been swept clean with an infusion of O3 ozone, a more powerful compound than oxygen on the Periodic Table. It was now razor sharp and acutely focused. Word and memory retrieval were noticeably heightened. He felt euphoric, even high. Damn, even his body felt lighter and taller.

The stiffness he often felt in his neck and shoulders, from long days pouring over computer screens and hauling around books and catalogs, was gone. No sign of ache or fatigue anywhere in his body. Would a medical review right now show him breaking the age barrier and becoming biologically younger?

Had he stumbled upon the Fountain of Youth?

So far, not a soul in sight to answer his questions.

Where to look first? Zach moved closer to the silver drawers and found his first impressions had been wrong. It was an illusion. They weren't actual drawers that opened up. There weren't any visible drawer seams or handle pulls, only a series of engraved symbols and markings that ran up and down the wall. Zach sensed there was a vault of valuable information behind the silver facade, but how one accessed it was the million-dollar question.

He recognized the engravings to be Ancient Sanskrit in origin, but he could be wrong on that. Unfortunately, Sanskrit wasn't one of the five spoken languages Zach had mastered. Not too many people around these days to converse with in the old language. But if he had to, he could learn it rather quickly. He made a mental note to himself to start if, and when, he got back.

Instinctively he ran his fingers over the markings, feeling the raised characters and grooves under his touch. The metal felt cool to his fingertips. Once again, he felt a tremendous reserve of energy just under the surface waiting to be awakened.

His curiosity hitched into over-drive, followed by desire. What lay behind the engravings? Would they reveal themselves to him? Speak to me, he mentally commanded.

A jolt of white heat shot forth from Gizmo causing Zach to step back in surprise. A ripple of energy streamed through the engravings and slowly morphed into a full spectrum holographic moving image in brilliant Technicolor. Incredible! There were just no other words for it. Nothing rivaled this even at Disney World!

Zach stepped back further to see more as the image grew in size and scope. In the upper right corner, over-laid into the hologram was code as well as date, place and time---which went back---holy shit! It was hundreds of thousands of years ago during a time when giants walked the Earth. Geographical coordinates were displayed within the hologram, which would have placed it right where Antarctica is today. However, this land mass was fertile, no ice or snow. Was there a pre-Antarctica civilization no one knew about?

The moving image played like a travelogue video showing beings that were over 10 feet tall in stature. They inhabited a modern world and possessed technology and space vehicles that roamed the skies. Zach was reminded of the epic Sanskrit stories written about in Ancient India's Ramayana and Mahabharata. It appeared these stories might not be myth after all.

What had happened to this race of tall beings? How had all trace of them been historically lost? Zach saw a continuous blast of laser light weaponry that turned the silica in the desert sands to hardened green glass and humans to dust and ashes. The Earth shook and pulsed with the onslaught. There was his answer. They had destroyed themselves by some ancient form of atomic or nuclear energy, leaving man to start over. And with that the hologram vanished into thin air, back into its silver time capsule.

Unbeknown to Zach, he was being closely observed--his progress monitored as he ran his hands along the long wall of markings wanting to discover more.

In a nearby Control Room which monitored this realm, The Record Keeper watched Zach's myriad attempts to access other holograms of information. His lack of success showed frustration coupled with determination. It brought a smile to The Record Keeper's face. This one had tenacity.

The first hologram reveal had been a gift merely to see how he handled information. His curiosity and desire for learning pleased The Record Keeper. The kid's thoughts were easy to read. His analyzing skills were a cut above the others. His IQ was in the high triple digits, but he also had a good degree of common sense, which would take him far. Where others had failed, this one might very well be the one.

The Voice had already alerted The Record Keeper to the newcomer's presence upon arrival. "Portal 3 entry. Identity: Zachary Edward Eldridge, Age 28, Library Technician, Library of Congress, Washington D.C., United States of America…"

There was a pause, as always, before The Voice asked the final question: "What action do you wish to take?"

The Record Keeper had been expecting this newcomer called "Zach". In this realm, nothing came as a surprise. All was already known and so The Voice was dismissed.

"I'll take care of this one."

~~*~~

Zach felt a rush of energy and sensed the presence of a being seconds before it materialized before him in a holographic image. It was of a woman. A tall, blonde and androgynous looking woman whose age was undeterminable. While she looked to be in her early 30's, her eyes looked much older, as if she had seen a lot in life. He watched in amazement as she morphed in and out of the hologram. Was she real or just his imagination? She stared at him, and he stared back, not expecting her to converse and was taken aback when she finally did speak.

"Hello. Zach,"

She knew his name. That blew him away. "Who are you?"

"I am Satya. The Record Keeper."

It might be a stupid question, but he had to rule out the obvious. "Did I die?"

He didn't feel dead. In this place he felt very much alive. But then he had no point of reference for such things. While stories of near-death experiencers recounting traveling through a tunnel of light to other heavenly realms was nothing new, he didn't believe this was the case with respect to him. At least, he hoped not.

"No," she said. "You arrived through Portal 3 and are in the

L-O-T."

That didn't tell him much. "What's an L-O-T?"

"The L-O-T is the information depository of the Library of Truth."

Satya pointed down to his feet. Beneath where he stood, on an inlaid white marble floor, was a gold geometric design, which he had failed to see. Its mathematical shape was formed by two disks of the same radius intersecting. The center of each disk lay on the perimeter of the other. He recognized the sacred geometry of the Vesica Piscis. However, the Sanskrit meaning inscribed eluded him.

"It says… Truth alone triumphs, not falsehood," She pointed out. "The truth which makes men free is often the truth which men prefer not to hear."

And with that, she stepped out of the holographic vehicle and stood before him in the flesh. She was slightly taller than his six-foot stature, which he rarely encountered in a female. Her body was tightly sheathed in a white long dress that hugged her seamlessly like a second skin. She moved past him, motioning him to follow.

There was a quiet gracefulness in the way she seemed to glide down the aisle. One was struck by the innate strength and confidence she exuded in the way she carried herself. Here was a woman who naturally took command and expected others to follow. Zach found himself falling into step behind her and trying to keep up.

She tilted her head slightly towards him with an assessing eye. "I see you have a real hunger for knowledge. That will serve you well in your life's mission. In fact, it is a necessary factor."

There was something in the tone of her last words, which made Zach stop short. What would she know about his life's mission?

She sensed his confusion and immediately changed the

subject. "Did you like what you learned from your first viewing of your planet's history? That was my little gift to you." She smiled at him for the first time.

He knew, of course, she meant the holographic information about the giants that walked the Earth thousands of years ago. Well, hell yeah. That was like giving drugs to an addict. Zach was an information junkie and there was no self-help group for those of his kind. That little newsreel had caused his curiosity about the Library of Truth to instantly skyrocket from zero to 100 in a nanosecond. He craved to learn more and he suspected she damn well knew it.

"The LOT is the depository for all universal knowledge," Satya explained. "In your world, those that came before you refer to it as the 'Akashic Records' or the 'Universal Mind of God'."

Never in his wildest imagination would he have believed such a place even existed. Who had created it? How far back did it go? Was the LOT in another dimension? There were so many questions in his head. For the first time in his life, he didn't know where to begin. He, who preferred to take a methodical and systematic approach to all new endeavors of discovery, was now functioning on a whole different set of cylinders.

She continued down another row, making a sharp turn around a corner, which opened onto an even larger section with pure gold walls. Zach was struck speechless. This gold was so brilliant it might be beyond 24-karat. His hand instinctively darted out to touch it. It was much harder than gold bullion and other precious metals he had knowledge of. Was it actual gold or some new other-worldly alloy, like Gizmo? If so, its worth had to be beyond calculation.

Zach was acutely aware that they had not run into another soul in this entire place, which was curious. He also noticed that while many areas of the walls contained Sanskrit engravings, some areas did not. There were blank highly polished surfaces while others had only a singular symbol. He was about to ask Satya the meaning of this, but again she headed him off.

"You are only here for a limited time today," she explained. "So, listen carefully... Only the true historical facts are stored in the LOT. There have been no alterations or spin, as some humans call it, to any of the events recorded here—and they are ALL here. Nothing is missing and nothing has ever been broken nor erased."

Zach immediately flashed back to the message Roone had left him—'nothing missing, nothing broken'. Was this the place he was *really* referring to?

"How far back do the records go?" he asked.

"The LOT has existed since the beginning of linear time, as you know it. Since the very beginning of creation."

Which meant, billions of years of records. The LOT had to be the size of at least a thousand Libraries of Congresses. And it went back to Creation? Would he find here the true story of how man began and for what purpose? Excitement coursed through him. This place was total brain candy. He wanted to take up residence--like now.

"Be careful what you ask for..." she warned.

Holy shit! Did she just read his mind? He reigned back in his thoughts and returned to basics. "And this place is connected to the Library of Congress?"

"Well, yes. Under certain circumstances."

"What does that mean?"

Satya carefully weighed her words. It was always tricky how much to divulge to a newcomer. "The LOT is not in your dimension but several dimensions and sub-dimensions beyond Earth. You have gained access to it for a good reason--to learn the truth. That is all I can say right now."

They came to an abrupt halt at the edge of a vast whiteness blocking off any visibility or hint of what might lay beyond. Satya touched a section of gold wall that displayed a singular infinity symbol. "This place you see before you is the sole domain of The Record Keeper. Where this symbol is found, means it is inaccessible to all without my acknowledgement and consent. I have stored an event in here that is only for your eyes. Please pay careful attention."

Zach watched her make a quick thumb to index finger gesture with an added flick of her wrist. No sooner had she done this than streams of colored light began spilling forth from the Record Keeper's vault.

Her gesture was very similar to a Gyan Mudra hand position used in meditation to open knowledge and consciousness. Satya stilled in a focused trance-like state, as if she herself was solely dependent on summoning up what she wanted him to see.

Strands of rainbow-colored light spiraled around them with a mesmerizing and hypnotic energy force. They danced on the air, weaving and entwining, before taking recognizable shape and form. This time the holographic moving images filled the entire room and Zach was able to step inside alongside Satya.

A mild electrical current rippled through him from head to toe. I'm inside a hologram he thought to himself in amazement. It was real and it was alive. Inside, it became difficult to distinguish what was present and what was past. One might think they were actually living in non-linear simultaneous time.

Zach's eyes went from soft focus to extreme clarity in seconds. His awareness was so sharp he immediately recognized where he was despite the fact he had never physically been there before today. He was looking down from the second-floor open balcony onto the Main Reading Room of the Library of Congress. The Visitor's viewing gallery was right above him and he knew that the area he was now walking through with Satya was off limits to most everyone.

It was after hours because a quick glance over the railing confirmed that no one was below in the Main Reading Room. The gilded bronze clock on the wall, which was never on time, despite the life-size figure of Father Time standing watch over it, now displayed the time as four minutes to eleven o'clock. Satya led Zach towards a partially opened door located directly behind the large bronze clock.

Zach stopped dead in his tracks when he saw his friend, Roone Sawyer, inside the small space, opening a smaller door on the back of the famous clock. The excitement at seeing his friend again overwhelmed him. He moved forward to embrace him but was blocked by an incredible wall of energy.

"Only observe," Satya instructed, holding her hand up.

That was harder for him to do than he would have thought. He watched Roone pretend to wind the clock, while he deftly slipped a small leather-bound book from the inside pocket of his jacket and tucked it down inside the clock's housing. Roone looked around quickly to assure he was still alone before locking the clock's door. He then appeared to look directly at Zach and hold up the key in offering, as if he knew Zach was right there watching him. It was both unnerving and puzzling.

Without thinking, or realizing he had the power within the hologram to do so, Zach found himself able to use his own eyesight to zoom into any area of the event for closer scrutiny. He did so now only to discover the old brass key Roone had used to open the clock was the very exact key he had sent Zach in the package containing the picture and Gizmo. An even closer zoom in showed it also displayed the initials 'JF'.

Zach had an immediate "ahha" moment. He recalled reading that the artist who designed the clock was John Flanagan--hence the 'JF' initials. This realization was rapidly followed by understanding Roone's words: "Nothing missing, nothing broken". Translation: 'Missing' files. 'Broken' clock. Perhaps he would have figured that clue out in time, but now he didn't have to. If Roone knew about the LOT, would he have also known that

70

Zach might see the viewing of this event someday and make it easier for him to decipher its meaning? Had he staged the clock event for that very purpose? Whoa. That would open a lot of other possibilities.

"Did Roone know about the LOT?" he tentatively asked.

"Of course," Satya replied matter-of-factly. "Would you like to know how he died?"

She threw out the invite like she was emotionally neutered and asking him to tea. Zach took a moment to think. He wasn't sure he wanted to see a man he knew and loved hang himself. But he had to know for certain if it really was by Roone's own hand as the authorities claimed. He checked his emotions and nodded.

Satya flicked her fingers in the same motion she had done before. A veil of white light quickly descended around them and time seemed to go in fast forward mode. When it dissipated, Zach and Satya were standing in the far corner of the Ceremonial Librarian's Room on the first floor of the Library of Congress. Roone was already inside the room--the room where he would die.

Zach watched Roone set down a small laptop computer and a few books on the highly polished surface of the round table that occupied the middle of the room. Slowly he moved over to the sidewall where a glass-enclosed wood cabinet displayed pictures, commemorative plates and some of the original Librarian's books. Roone opened the cabinet and proceeded to re-arrange a few items that were not placed to his particular liking. He stood back reviewing his work with a wistful smile. One could tell he loved this room and his Library. Zach recalled how his friend had always been a stickler for things being put back in their proper place. The guy had been a neat freak at times, even up until the very end.

Roone carefully closed the cabinet's glass door and slowly turned back around. His eyes swept the room, noticing that there

71

were two burnt out light bulbs on one of the several bronze wall sconces lighting the room. Zach could see him make a mental note to have that taken care of right away. It would be a sloppy reflection on the high standards Roone had set for the Library's upkeep.

Roone's eyes strayed to the American flag displayed on a ceremonial stand next to the very first Librarian's desk. He went over to the flag and let the soft fabric rustle through his fingers. Roone was a man who deeply loved his country. He would always be the first to drop whatever he was doing and personally escort military servicemen or veterans on a tour through the halls of any library he worked in.

Zach recalled these memories now, yet he still wondered what Roone was doing. He continued watching his friend pull out the black leather chair behind the desk, sink down into its tufted cushion, then swivel around to face the window behind him. He seemed lost in his own private world—a solemn yet sad look in his eyes. His lips moved as if in silent prayer and Zach realized that Roone knew he was nearing his life's end. His actions were of a man who was saying goodbye to his beloved Library. But why?

There was a sudden sound at the door and Roone swiveled back around to see a maintenance worker enter the room carrying a ladder and several light bulbs.

"Sorry to disturb you, sir," the man said moving towards the light fixture near the door. "I just need to replace a bulb in here. I'll be out of your way right quickly."

Roone nodded to him. Someone had most likely already reported the broken bulb. Now he wouldn't have to.

Zach's attention was drawn to the maintenance worker. His head was clean-shaven, he had a hefty build like a nightclub bouncer, and the knuckles of his right hand were tattooed with strange exotic symbols. Zach could see sets of fours swirling around his body, signifying darkness and death. The guy radiated the energy of a bad storm front.

Zach took an unconscious step backward. He could sense evil in the air. Whoever this guy was he certainly didn't look or feel like an after-hours maintenance worker, despite the ladder and replacement bulbs he carried.

The two men exchanged a few pleasantries, then the man went about changing the broken light bulbs. Zach watched, but his chest and body tightened on high alert. When Roone got up from the desk and retrieved his laptop and books from the table, the man was folding up his ladder. Roone wished him a good night and stepped past him towards the door. That was when the man lunged from behind.

Zach leaped forward to save his friend, but once again met an energetic wall of resistance that pushed him back. He was powerless to provide any assistance. He helplessly watched as the man applied pressure to Roone's carotid artery, causing him to immediately pass out. The killer wasted no time roping a thick noose around Roone's throat and yanking hard enough to snap his neck and finish him off.

Zach felt sick to his stomach. He cried out in pain, his breath coming in quick gasps. He couldn't bear to watch the killer string up his friend and stage the whole phony suicide. He turned his head away, feeling his eyes well up with tears.

"I've seen enough," he whispered.

Chapter 8

Zach *had* seen enough. He was still pretty shaken up. What was still missing was WHY Roone had been assassinated? Based on what he had observed, and knowing Roone had been such a likable man, the pieces just didn't add up. And his mind, which hated missing data, really needed to make sense of it all.

However, no sooner had he expressed a desire to get out of the holographic record to escape the agony of watching such a brutal killing, than he found himself back where he initially landed in the LOT, next to the pile of missing ZE files with even more questions than answers.

His confusion mounted. He had no recollection of how he had gotten from point "A" to "B" in the blink of an eye. Total brain wipe. Which was disconcerting to say the least. Satya towered over him with a slight look of impatience, waiting for him to reclaim his senses.

Her next words were a direct order, all business again. "You need to go."

"I want to know *why* he was killed?" he demanded. Zach could be just as bossy when he needed to be, which was now. He wanted answers. He had come this far and he felt no inclination to leave until he learned the truth behind the killing.

Satya shook her head. "I warned him to be careful. A little knowledge can be a dangerous thing."

"What did he know?"

She sighed. "He knew enough about the illusions of your world to get him killed. I told him the truth can kill you, but he chose not to heed my warning."

"Who was the guy who killed him?"

She shook her head again. "For now, I am only able to show you what happened in the official record. Yes, this man killed him. And yes, this man framed him for murders he did not commit." She stopped, weighing her words carefully. "There are limits and boundaries that I must adhere to. I can say no more."

Satya thrust one of the missing ZE files towards him. "Here, take this one. That should suffice for now. The rest of the files shall remain here."

Without another word, not even a goodbye, or it was nice meeting you, the portal yawned its jaws wide and swallowed him whole. He went hurtling back through the tunnel at an even faster rate of velocity. His body went numb with shock. Seconds later he shot out of a blue ceiling panel, inscribed with the words "the Light of Truth," into the Members of Congress Room. Somehow, he miraculously managed to land both feet on the plush Oriental burgundy carpeting.

His eyes quickly swept the interior of the oak paneled room with its ornate wood carvings, grand arches over tall doors, and matching Italian marble fireplaces at both ends of the long rectangular room. Thank God the room was empty, sparing him having to explain to anyone how he had managed to drop out of the gold beamed ceiling without damaging its seven magnificent paintings representing the Spectrum of Light.

Zach wondered if the mode of re-entry into his world from the

Library of Truth would always be, ironically enough, through the sixth ceiling panel known as the "Light of Truth". Time would tell. He glanced down at his wristwatch. Only a few minutes had passed from entry in and out of the LOT. It felt more like several hours had passed. Yet, in both worlds time appeared to be functioning on an entirely different spectrum.

He checked his pocket, relieved to find Gizmo still there, no longer white but back to his normal black persona. The double doors inside the Members of Congress Room were closed to the public. Oftentimes the room was used for private meetings, but today there was no guest speaker podium or the usual assortment of round tables and chairs set up for such an event. Luckily, he was alone—for now.

Zach paced the room trying to sort out his experience. His body was buzzing with energy from head to toe. As always, he needed to engage in movement to quell his non-stop thoughts. What a strange and other-worldly experience. Yet the LOT was real and not a dream. A Library within a Library, but in another dimension and everything recorded was the God's honest truth. The concept stretched his imagination. He felt a moment of giddiness, almost elation, to have found such a place.

Did the LOT's records only go backward in time, or did they also show future events? That would make information hidden there extremely valuable—to a lot of people. Which made him question who else might know about the LOT. Roone had obviously found his way there, so there must be others. And, what *had* his friend discovered to get himself killed in such a grisly manner? Satya wouldn't tell him everything he wanted to know. Why? Who was she protecting? The killer? His mind formulated questions faster than a speeding bullet. Still, there were no answers.

Satya had thrust a ZE file into his hands before ejecting him from the LOT. Would it provide any clues? He examined it now.

It was a thin folder with no visible 'Top Secret' markings on its exterior. Inside he found a few sheets of parchment paper with hastily scribbled notes. The script had been made with an old quill and ink pen, which showed advanced signs of fading from the passage of time. How old the papers were he could not determine. There were no dates on the notes. But they clearly had been written before the invention of the ballpoint pen.

Zach carefully lifted the handwritten papers and found underneath an equally old and weatherworn map of a large landmass—what might be a continent. He turned the map over and found the marking "P1" on its back. Nothing else.

He took out his cell phone, which oddly enough had to be re-booted. It had completely shut down somewhere between the two worlds and it had erased a few apps in the process. He didn't have time to figure out which ones only that his social media apps were suspiciously missing—whatever that meant.

He accessed the camera and snapped pictures of everything, just in case the file folder happened to conveniently disappear again. It was clear someone on the Senate Intelligence Committee was obsessed with finding this missing file and they hadn't given up after all this time. Its contents were indeed curious but didn't appear especially revealing in nature. They meant something to somebody. Zach was willing to bet the person who had requested it would shit in their pants with excitement learning it had finally been found. But he intended to thoroughly examine it before he gave it up.

He tucked the mysterious file under his arm and headed for the closed conference room doors. No sooner had he exited the room than he encountered his supervisor Mrs. Friedman hurrying down the hallway. From the intentness etched all over her usually cheery face, she appeared to be on a timely mission. A stack of files were clutched to her ample bosom. The second she spotted him her face flooded with relief.

"There you are. I was looking everywhere for you."

He held up the file in his defense, hoping to avoid further explanation. "Look. I found one of the older missing ones."

He held tight to it, but she grabbed it, if only to examine and verify its file number for herself. One eyebrow shot up in surprise the moment she recognized the ZE designation. "Oh my. I guess there are still a few of these still around. Where was it?"

"Well," he hedged. "It was kind of laying around in a different records room."

"Hmm." Her brows knit together. She pursed her lips—about to ask which records room then decided against it. She didn't have time for long stories. She placed Zach's find on top of the stack she now carried.

"Did you find any of the others?"

"I'm still working on it."

A door suddenly opened at the end of the corridor. Zach glanced over to see a plainclothes security agent step forward to accompany three men exiting the private confines of the Congressional Reading Room. There were two older men, followed by a young male in his early 20's whose lanyard identified him as junior Senate staffer. Every senator and representative's office had a staff of these Congressional aides who usually arranged special tours on Capitol Hill for either constituents or high-profile contacts. They were assigned to do legislative research, handle administrative details and run errands all over town for their bosses. Which meant one of the other men was most likely a Senator.

The older men looked vaguely familiar, especially the tall robust gentlemen wearing a U.S. Senate lapel pin. Talbot. Yeah, that was his name. Senator James Talbot from Maryland. The senior member and Chairman on the U.S. Senate Select Committee on Intelligence.

While Zach preferred to stay out of the political realm, having been subjected enough to its machinations during the years his mother ran her numerous political campaigns, he knew enough to know Talbot was a good ole boy with powerful horse-trading skills.

Talbot was as tall, gym-fit and attractive as the other guy was short, stocky and lacking in any discernable physical appeal. His sagging facial wrinkles, paired with deep grooves under dark appraising eyes, gave him the appearance of a Shar Pei pup. It was an odd pairing at first glance, yet the shorter guy radiated more power and influence than the Senator.

Zach couldn't place the face. Someone who remained behind the scenes, most likely. However, the two acted like old friends. Both were pushing mid to late 60's and were cut from the same cloth with a taste for fine custom-made suits and designer silk ties.

The Shar Pei guy glanced into the Members of Congress Room, the room Zach had just exited. "Beautiful ceiling," he commented. The Congressional Aide was quick to agree.

"Yes, indeed it is, Mr. Stavros. Not only beautiful, but quite unique in its artistry..."

Constantine Stavros. Zach recognized the name. This was a guy who kept his face out of the news because his wealth afforded him that privilege. He was a billionaire many times over in the global banking world. And a man who destabilized and toppled governments just because he could—probably for the sheer fun of it. His reputation preceded him, but he rarely made public appearances and was known to be a bit of a recluse. Zach wondered what brought him to Capitol Hill and the Library of Congress on this day.

The Aide continued his informational narrative. "Those murals represent the Seven Spectrums of Light: The Light of Science, Creation, Excellence, Research, Poetry, State, and that blue one over there is Senator Talbot's favorite...The Light of

Truth." The Aide ushered Stavros inside the door to allow for closer viewing.

Zach eyed The Light of Truth ceiling painting he had just emerged from. Did Talbot know about the panel's hidden portal?

Mrs. Friedman took that opportunity to approach the Senator, handing over the files she had brought with her. "Senator Talbot, your items are all here as requested. And good news..." she nodded towards Zach. "One of my staff was finally able to locate that missing file your office has been wanting for some time..."

Zach watched her hand over the coveted file. A part of him wanted to snatch it back, hoping to have more time reviewing its contents, but perhaps the snapshots he had taken would be enough. Talbot eyed the ZE labeling, fingering its edges, yet refrained from opening it. Zach watched him carefully. Under hooded eyes, Talbot was doing his best to hide his excitement. He wanted what was in it but didn't want to show it.

"Ah yes, the old map file," he smiled matter-of-factly. "I had thought we would never see this one."

Apparently, he did know what it contained. Zach was itching to ask him about its contents. However, he had a keen sense of preservation and sensed it was probably better to not display any interest, for now. The pictures on his phone he could analyze later.

"Thank you, Estelle."

Talbot looked genuinely appreciative. "I was just telling my friend, Mr. Stavros, that the Congressional Library staff, are the most dedicated research professionals in the world."

He waited a beat before adding, "And I must say, as well, that I was very sorry to hear the terrible news about poor Mr. Sawyer."

Estelle stiffened. "Yes. We all were."

Zach stood there mutely, feeling invisible beside Mrs. Friedman. If they only knew what he knew.

Talbot's face turned solemn. "Quite shocking to say the least.

However, Sawyer will certainly be remembered for his contributions to this great institution."

Stavros and the Congressional Aide emerged from the Member's Room. Stavros' ears picked up upon hearing the dead Librarian's name. He didn't pretend to hide his true thoughts on the subject.

"Appalling and disgusting news," he sneered in distaste as if a bad odor had invaded his personal space.

There was no stopping him. "How did a man of his kind, with such a deviant appetite for youth and blood ever get selected to head up the Library of Congress in the first place? That's what I would like to know."

Zach could not contain his reaction to Stavros' disdain.

"Mr. Sawyer was no killer," he stated with certainty. "The truth will come out."

Everyone's eyes swung over to stare at his boldness.

Stavros shrugged, dismissing him. "The truth is always ugly to admit."

Talbot looked at Zach quizzically. "Young man, have we met?"

Mrs. Friedman piped in, ready to smooth over any ruffled feathers. "Senator, this is Zach Eldridge. He's new to Washington, but extremely thorough and capable in his job. Zach was able to locate your 'map file' when no one else could. This Library is lucky to have him."

Zach nodded towards the Senator. "I'm happy to be of service, sir. If you have any future special requests..."

Talbot was now eyeing him curiously, his brow knitted together in thought. He cut Zach off before he could finish offering further help. "You look familiar. Eldridge? Hmm. Any relationship to the Connecticut Eldridge's?"

"Yes, sir." Zach admitted without saying more.

A light bulb blinked on in Talbot's head. Of course. A smile spread across his lips followed by a hearty laugh.

"You're Camille's kid, aren't you?"

Zach didn't like to talk about his family connections. "Yes, sir," he said quietly.

"Well, I'll be dammed! Did you hear that Constantine? We've got Senator Camille Eldridge's son waiting on us today…"

Zach pushed down the feeling of embarrassment that always came with someone suddenly seeing him in a different light once they connected the family name and fortune. Mrs. Friedman was now looking at him curiously. Stavros seemed the only one not impressed.

Talbot slapped Zach on the back. "Good to have you, son. Welcome to Washington!"

~~*~~

Almost 10,000 miles away, in an area of the world where few men dare to venture, where cold winds average around 15 mph and temperatures can reach a frigid minus 95 degrees Fahrenheit, a yawning deep crater, several football field lengths in diameter, spans a jagged frozen tundra. Four U.S. Military vehicles, marked 'Extreme Snow Transport', patrol the perimeter of a large gaping chasm. Their headlights bob along in the never-ending inky darkness which blankets the area both day and night.

Antarctica. The mid-winter sun disappears for months in this desolate continent. The routine rarely varies for the defense contractors who work this isolated station in such a remote corner of the world. While their duties demand long, oftentimes monotonous hours, outdoor shifts rotate every 30 minutes. It takes time to acclimate to the extremely dry cold of this icy wasteland. Extreme exposure is the silent but deadly enemy for everyone who works here.

The men who patrol this obscure base possess high-level

security clearances within a black-budget division of the Defense Intelligence Agency. They are paid well to do their job and, more importantly, keep their mouths shut.

Dressed in heavy thermal snow suits and masks that protect against all forms of radiation, the men on duty slowly move vehicles and equipment onto a hidden freight elevator, the size of an open gymnasium, which transports all supplies deep down into the frozen earth.

Overhead a stealth darkness suddenly blocks out the starry night sky. The men briefly pause to glance up to catch its uncloaking process. Bright running lights visibly appear on a large chevron-shaped craft, as it silently hovers over the crater hole. The men move into their positions. Experience has taught them to immediately curtail whatever they are doing and brace themselves against the rotating winds such craft stir up. Seconds later, they watch the ship descend and disappear down into the interior of the Earth. The sight is a common occurrence for them. They silently return to their work duties.

Miles underground, in a darkened yet comfortable theatre-style room, 12 floor-to-ceiling screens continuously monitor 12 secure tunnel locations. Each screen is marked with an identifying number and its exact coordinates, which pinpoint its geographic Earth location. Access to this room and the information displayed on each screen remains in the hands of only a select committee consisting of the 12 people who call themselves MINERVA.

Each member has a responsibility to uphold the MINERVA agenda, and each will have their own team of people that have been hand-picked to support such efforts. Members are not elected but chosen. It is a time-honored tradition that has never changed. What happens in this room, and the decisions they make, affect the lives of every man, woman and child on the planet.

At this very moment the screen marked "P3" remains conspicuously dark. Two men, cloaked in silhouette, one tall, the other shorter, stare at the blank monitor.

"It went offline this morning," the shorter man explains in a hushed tone. "There appears to be an unidentified problem in the D.C. portal that we haven't been able to get any intel on."

The other man, with a noticeable degree of authority, frowns before letting loose a torrent of anger. "And I'm just hearing about it now? God damn it! Can't anything be done right in this god forsaken place?

"I'm sorry, sir. We're doing our best." The shorter man assured.

"Best is not good enough," the other man pointed out. "Replace the tech guys immediately with those who don't make such critical mistakes."

The shorter man silently nodded. Such was the nature of his job.

The man with authority's voice became steely. "The last time this happened it was sufficiently dealt with so the problem would never repeat itself. And now you're telling me it's happened again? Do you want to be replaced as well?"

"No, sir. But I must inform you that we don't think it's a technical problem. We have reviewed all the logs. Everything is running perfectly, but for some unknown reason P3 just suddenly went completely dead. Even with a potential breach, that's not possible with how the system has been set up."

The man with authority had run out of patience. "Fuck it, man! I don't want to hear excuses. Just fix the god damn thing!"

A booming voice is heard over the room's private intercom system, bringing the men's conversation to an abrupt end.

"Sir, the Committee members have just landed," the voice informs.

The man with authority extracts a cigar from a humidor box

on a conference table and lights it. He puffs on it before replying. "Give them an hour to acclimate and then we begin. There is much to discuss."

Chapter 9

After 28 years, Meghan March was still sleeping in the childhood room she had grown up in on her parents' estate in Bethesda, Maryland. The room's decor was still filled with all the yellow flounces and lace frills her mother had selected for her back when she herself was a child. But after her mother died six years ago, shortly after Meghan's own husband Brett had also died, she had returned to her family home and didn't have the heart to change anything—or leave. She talked herself into believing her father still needed her. There had been enough trauma and change in a short period of time for everyone in their family. Familiarity was something she needed and craved--and so she hadn't altered a thing.

Meghan didn't like to dwell on the fact that she wasn't as independent as she would have liked to be at this stage in her life, but she had Izzie's welfare to think about, not just her own. She looked down at her daughter, who lay curled up against her sleeping soundly, her blond hair wildly framing what could only be called an angelic face. Her child's warmth seeped through to her, making her feel languid and cozy. Meghan smiled. She loved these quiet mother-daughter moments. Making Izzie had been the best thing she had ever done in life—so far.

A fierce storm had rolled in late last night with booming thunder and lightning followed by a torrent of much needed rain. Around 1:00 AM Izzie had crawled into her bed seeking comfort from the thunder. Her six-year-old daughter was rather sensitive to loud sounds and, at times, was plagued with vivid dreams and nightmares.

It was already 6:30 AM and Meghan had things to do for her father's party that night. Normally she would have gotten up even earlier to make it into the Library where she volunteered as a docent several days a week. But this week had been especially emotionally trying with the news surrounding Mr. Sawyer's death. He had always been so helpful and nice to her when he learned she was writing a book about the Library's many hidden treasures. There were others who worked at the Library, both staff and volunteers alike who were also finding the salacious details hard to believe.

Perhaps no one ever really knows anyone, even when they think they do, Meghan thought to herself. Her own mother had committed suicide from what was officially called an 'accidental' overdose of sleeping pills. Meghan hadn't even known her mother used pills or that she was seeking professional help for anxiety and depression. It was sad that her father never wanted to talk about it. So, poor Mr. Sawyer might have been secretly tormented as well by his own internal demons.

Meghan tried to slide out of the bed without disturbing Izzie. But Izzie stirred, her blue eyes fluttering open, then getting big when she realized she was no longer in her own room. She must have forgotten. Izzie sat up rubbing the sleep from her eyes.

"Mommy is it still raining outside?" she asked sleepily. Izzie hated to be confined indoors. Once she got moving, she never stopped. She was an explorer and got into everything.

Meghan opened the blinds, letting in streams of sunshine.

"Yeah!" Izzie said happily jumping out of bed. She went to kiss her mother good morning, then headed back to her own room next door. She stopped at the door and looked back at Meghan who was heading for her bathroom.

"I forgot to tell you something very important, Mommy."

"What's that honey?"

"I saw an angel in my dreams last night."

"You did?" Meghan said matter-of-factly.

Izzie had such an active dream life that this revelation was not out of the norm for her. Since she was two years old, Izzie claimed she saw things even when she was awake. The professional experts said she would grow out of it and not make a big deal about it, so Meghan hadn't. But by age six, she had yet to 'grow out of it'.

"Oh yes," Izzie gushed. "He was a tall angel with a very nice smile and face. He took me to a special place in another world that was so beautiful that I didn't want to come back."

Meghan frowned. She didn't like the sound of such things. "What about me, honey? Mommy would miss you if you didn't come back."

Izzie giggled. "Oh Mommy. Don't be silly. Maybe you could come too." And with that, Izzie danced out of the room.

Her daughter was so happy at times. Meghan did not ever want to discourage such feelings of joy. The world had enough darkness in it that one needed all the little rays of sunshine a child could shed on it. Meghan knew that perhaps she was too protective a mother at times, but Izzie was truly different than other children. She was precocious, engaging and yet too damn clever at times for her own good. Her daughter could point out a lie faster than a polygraph tester. She claimed she could see the lie.

Around adults Izzie had learned to keep such thoughts to

herself. But around other children she felt they were fair game and made her detection skills known. It became a social liability. The other kids skirted around her, not knowing what to make of her strangeness. If she weren't so cute, she would have been treated like an outcast.

Meghan had opted to home-school Izzie, instead of sending her to a private school. Tutors were employed who had experience with gifted children with over-inquisitive minds. Meghan was not sure whom Izzie had inherited her special gifts from. Izzie's father was smart and had graduated from the Air Force Academy at the top of his class with honors. But he was a straightforward "by the book" kind of guy. Everything had to be in order, logical and explainable by science and experts or it didn't exist in his world. He would scoff at anything even remotely esoteric, paranormal, or "woo woo", which Izzie seemed to personify.

In fact, Lieutenant Brett March was so much like her own father, ambitious and controlling that she failed to clearly see these tendencies until after their marriage where he too wanted to dominate her life. The more she pushed back, the more controlling he became. The old adage that women often marry their father certainly applied in her case. She had followed in the footsteps of her mother's relationship with Meghan's father and look where that led--to heartache and suicide. She had been too young and naive to see the similarities, but she was no longer anyone's fool.

She had met Brett through friends at a social gathering at some glitzy home in Georgetown. He was several years older, wearing his Air Force uniform and had literally taken her breath away when she first laid eyes on him. He winked at her and flashed her one of his famous smiles. Her heart pounded wildly in her chest when he came up to her and introduced himself. She now knew that shyness drew him to her like a magnet, signaling that she was a woman he could easily mold into whatever he expected her to be in his life.

Coming from privilege, she had led a fairly sheltered life. She had never lacked for anything except perhaps a good education in common sense. From early on she had been schooled in finding the right husband, having children, and being a "good wife". It was Meghan's first serious relationship and she loved it that he was a man with experience and a promising career in the military. He fit the bill regarding everything she was told would give her a happy life.

Back then she thought it was love at first sight, but it was more like lust. She was still a virgin, although she would not admit that fact to anyone for fear they would think something was wrong with her. But she had her urges and was more than willing to give up her virginity under Brett's insistence. He literally swept her off her feet with his charm and charisma. He had that seductive effect on women and had he lived she suspected he would have eventually cheated on her. But fate had intervened and spared her that heartache.

The marriage had been a mistake since day one, but the only good thing that came out of it was that it was short-lived and, of course, she had Izzie to show from it. That alone made it worthwhile.

So far Izzie had shown no signs of her father's controlling temperament. She remembered all too clearly how everything in his closets and desk drawers had to be arranged in alphabetical order and spaced accordingly. His towels had to be folded just right. His underwear ironed. He would use soap only once and then insist it be discarded. Meals had to be on time and cooked to perfection. And if something wasn't done right, according to his strict standards, she would hear about it. On a diagnostic spectrum he probably had obsessive-compulsive disorder, but even the hint or suggestion of seeing a therapist would send him into a rage.

Meghan found herself forever tip-toeing around him to avoid conflict. She became hyper-sensitive to his moods, and this was occurring while she was pregnant with Izzie. No wonder Izzie could be overly sensitive at times. Meghan had unknowingly handed down this trait to her child.

There was a part of her that felt great relief when several months after their marriage the military plane he was piloting crashed at Andrews Air Force Base due to mechanical failure. She would not admit to anyone the freedom she had felt upon hearing the terrible news, just like she had never admitted to her long-held-onto virginity. There was secret shame that she could harbor such thoughts and emotions about her daughter's father, but his death had finally given Meghan her life back.

Upon his untimely death, she suddenly found herself thrust into the role of a young widow with a child on the way. Life can do that to you. In the blink of an eye your whole life changes and propels you down a totally unexpected path. Her strength and resilience re-emerged and saw her through the double death of both Brett and her mother. She would never want to relive that year ever again. Now she just wanted to look forward and create her own future for her and her child, despite the fact she still lived in her parents' home. Yet it did provide her some protection.

Deep down she didn't know if she could trust her judgment regarding men or relationships ever again. She never wanted to give her power away to anyone like she had with Brett. The more she capitulated to his needs and desires, the more he wanted and took. She had become a Brett pleaser in that relationship, fearing he would stop loving her and reject her if she didn't. She hated herself for being so weak.

Now she found herself skittish about dating. But she was acutely concerned that if she ever took another husband, they had to totally accept Izzie, because Izzie meant everything to her. Besides, most men were not looking for a relationship that came with a young precocious child. And that was a deal breaker she had come to accept.

Meghan knew she was still young and attractive. She also knew she still turned heads on occasion and put it down to her flaming red hair, which was a recessive gene handed down to her by her maternal grandfather. Yes, she was lonely at times, even with Izzie, but she pushed those thoughts out of her mind. She was of the belief that if she was meant to be in another relationship, all the signs would be there, and it would just naturally happen organically. Like divine intervention. That thought comforted her and kept her going when her spirits were down. Until then, she would focus on her child, her work and, of course, seeing to the hostess obligations and catering details of her father's party that evening.

~~*~~

Zach realized with a start that his life had just gotten more complicated—a complication he didn't want, or need, but one thrust upon him whether he liked it or not. How could he NOT do anything with the knowledge he now possessed.

The LOT had totally messed with his brain. While it felt like its usual 'normal' on his return to the Library, he already knew how incredible it felt in the LOT and he wanted that sharpness and acuity again. Damn!

What to do? Things appeared to be royally fucked up. Satya had shown him Roone's murder expecting him to do something about it or she would never have lured him into her holographic universe in the first place. Hell, yes, he would find his way back there. Whatever it took. The LOT was a thousand times more interesting than the LOC. Had it been up to him, he might not have come back.

His phone buzzed persistently in his pants pocket. He checked the screen where it identified the caller as "Mommy Dearest". That was the second call from his mother since this morning. He ignored it, just like the first one, and let it go to voice mail. Instead, he headed for foreign language services where he pulled all the books available on Ancient Sanskrit. Zach had work do to and he was eager to get started.

He paused in the Main Reading Room to look up at the wall clock. Still not the right time, he noted. Missing time, broken clock. From what he had learned in the LOT everything now took on new meaning. There was a secret hidden inside the mechanism of the clock, which Roone had left behind. Zach suspected the small leather-bound notebook might have been intentionally left for him. He had the key to unlock the clock's door, but how he would gain access to the clock without alerting others was not going to be easy. He would have to come up with a viable plan.

But first he got on the LOC inter-agency communications system and hacked his way into building maintenance to search all repair requests. There he found no records at all for a light bulb replacement in the Ceremonial Librarian's Room on the night Roone had been killed.

He went back a whole week prior to the killing just to make sure, yet still found nothing. Surely someone would have noticed it long before that night if it indeed had gone out. Someone, or the killer if he was working alone, must have unscrewed the two bulbs in question prior to the killing. But how would they know Roone would be in that room at the time in question? Alright, so he didn't have an answer yet for that either.

He then searched the personnel files of all maintenance workers and found no pictures of any staff member that even remotely resembled the killer. Somehow the guy had found his way into the Library after hours. Would security footage have picked it up?

Hacking into the LOC security system was a little trickier

without leaving any traces behind, but Zach managed to do it by finding password credentials for the Inspector General of the LOC, who then unknowingly requested it be sent to his personal computer terminal which Zach then re-routed through several worldwide hubs to an anonymous IP address he could access from anywhere.

From there it would be easy bringing up security cam footage from all the entrances throughout the day. The guy could have also made his way into the LOC during public hours, then hunkered down somewhere to wait. Zach was pretty confident security footage was archived and stored for more than a week. This would have to be a home project. He couldn't take the chance of being caught red-handed looking at LOC video cam frames in the Stacks.

His cell phone buzzed again. His mother just would not give up. This time the alert was marked "Urgent". He reluctantly answered.

"Yes, Mother. What is it?"

On the other end he could hear her giving a staffer an order to secure her car.

"You haven't answered your phone," she admonished. Well, that was obvious.

"I had to hear it from the FBI that my son has secured clearance to work at the Library of Congress. Then just a little while ago Jim Talbot told me you have already started!"

He could hear the unmistakable annoyance in her voice. His mother did not like to be the last one to know what was happening in this town, let alone the business of a member of her own family.

"You spoke with Senator Talbot?"

"Why, yes dear. We *do* work together."

Now he was curious. "What are you working on together?"

"Don't be obtuse," she scoffed before changing the subject. "If you had listened to my message, you would know I flew back to Washington last night."

It was hard to keep track where she was these days…Washington, Connecticut, on some Senate junket… who knew? As always, she would be staying at her place on Capitol Hill on a tree-lined street within walking distance of the Supreme Court and her Senate Hart offices. His mother loathed inconvenience. Instead of taking quick public transportation, which she would never do in a million years, she also refused to navigate Beltway traffic and opted instead for a personal driver who was always on call. If his mother could have secured lush living quarters right inside the Senate she would have had it all wrapped up in no time. Instead, she was only a heartbeat away and never had to worry about any long commute.

Every day she would slip her unbearably high heels into her leather bag and exchange them for designer brand sneakers to accomplish her daily brisk walk to work—come rain or shine. His mother was a consummate calories counter. He was certain she knew exactly how many steps she managed to squeeze in before the end of each day and God forbid if it was under 12,000 she would make up the difference on a treadmill before going to bed each night. His mother feared gaining weight as much as she feared growing old and fading from power. Her weekly spa bills reflected this.

Zach had known she would eventually find out they were working within blocks of each other—practically a stone's throw away. She would expect to see him more, so it came as no surprise when she informed him of the reason for her call.

"There's a special event I'm attending tonight. You're invited as well," she began. He silently groaned. Here it comes. The Kennedy Center for the Arts? A concert at the National Cathedral? Dinner at the White House? His mother was a social and political butterfly.

"Jim Talbot is hosting a little event at his home in

Bethesda…"

That got his attention. He waited for the guilt ploy tactic to be thrown at him.

"I would like to see my son. You never…"

"I can't," he cut her off. He had security cam footage to review at home and start learning Sanskrit. Two infinitely more interesting options than a night out with his mother.

"You can and you will," she stated firmly. "It will be good for you to meet influential people in this town, and I will not take 'no' for an answer." She paused a beat. "I assume you're staying at the DuPont Circle flat. I'll be sending a car around for you at 7:00 PM. Don't you dare disappoint me."

"Is Dad with you?"

"No." She didn't seem inclined to say more.

"Where is he?"

She let out an impatient little sigh. "Your father is in Antarctica right now…"

His father's work as an astrophysicist took him to some far out and remote places, but Antarctica? What were the odds of hearing about Antarctica twice in the same day? He didn't even have to calculate the odds. It was rare.

"What the hell is he doing there?"

He could visualize his mother's frown of disapproval. At least he hadn't said WTF. He was pissing her off with his questions. Unfortunately, he seemed to be good at that.

He could feel there was a poisonous zinger coming his way like a curare-tipped arrow going straight to its target. Here it comes, he thought, bracing himself for the impact.

"Perhaps if you were a better son and spoke with your father more often you would know such things."

Zach said nothing. Okay, point taken, but his father could call him as well.

"I have to go. Oh, and Zach—tonight's black tie. I trust you won't show up in a Henley and Vans."

Chapter 10

Senator Talbot's large sweeping estate on the Potomac, which could have easily accommodated an arboretum and petting zoo from the looks of it, was only a 15-minute car ride from Zach's flat.

His mother's designated driver pulled up a long gravel driveway behind several other vehicles sporting government plates. Like a solemn procession they inched their way towards a busy valet stand that fronted the main entrance where drinks were already being served.

Zach noted the grassy manicured lawns and old stone mansion were lit with a cascade of brilliant lights. Sunset was fast approaching and from the look of things, this was no small social gathering as his mother had led him to believe. It was a full-blown Washington circuit party. The kind he hated. The good news was that it would be easier to blend in with the crowd and make an escape after an hour--if he could survive that long. His social duty to his mother would then be fulfilled. No one would be any the wiser if he left early and headed home.

Zach sighed. Okay, let's get this over with, he thought. He

quickly stepped out of the back seat of the Suburban and unconsciously finger combed his hair before straightening his tie. His black Canali tux was elegant by most standards to satisfy his mother's dress code demands. However, even now, he was itching to ditch the tie and be free of this gathering at the first chance he got.

Zach waived the driver away to deal with valet parking and followed the music down candlelit steps leading towards a large flagstone veranda. Senator Talbot had an impressive home, even by Washington standards. Against the panoramic and sweeping backdrop of the Potomac River, the grounds had several lush rose gardens, a sizable swimming pool with a spa and off in the distance, almost hidden and not wanting to be seen, was a child's swing set and treehouse. Zach found that curious. It looked like it didn't belong in such a place. So, a child either lived or visited here.

He scanned the milling cocktail crowd, which were well over 100 guests and growing. No little shindig, here. Zach had kept his driver waiting at least 30 minutes, because he couldn't pull himself away from the LOC surveillance footage. He knew his mother hated when people came late, which he was intentionally doing. It would irritate her need for order and certainly push her buttons when she saw him saunter in late. But he really didn't care. He was here, wasn't he?

Events with throngs of people played havoc on his senses. He would avoid them like the plague and his mother knew this. Everywhere he looked numbers were spilling out of everywhere. In his mother's misplaced guidance, she thought she was providing him some type of positive aversion therapy that he would eventually begin to enjoy. Wrong.

The place was filling up with people and his head was reeling with color, numbers and snatches of women's high-pitched laughter wafted across the veranda. He recognized a few faces from the news and celebrity tabloids, which was always the case in D.C. Zach didn't bother to look around for his mother. Instead, he headed straight for the bar. He ordered himself a Corona beer from one of the bartenders who was pouring wine with one hand, champagne with the other, and alternating with a few shots of hard alcohol for the diehards.

Nearby a three-piece ensemble of musicians on violin, cello and piano broke into an Amy Whitehouse version of 'Love Is a Losing Game'. Not in this town, he thought, where people had affairs with whoever would bring them one rung closer up the power ladder. He eased back against a shady elm near the bar, watching the lights flicker across the Potomac. He slowly sipped his cold Corona.

He had forgotten to eat that day with all that had happened, and he knew he had a low tolerance to alcohol, especially on an empty stomach. He snagged a shrimp canapé with cream cheese from a passing waiter's tray. The filling oozed onto his fingers, so he downed it in one bite. At home he would have just licked his fingers clean. Here, he reached for a napkin from another waiter's tray and managed to clean his hands.

Zach turned back around only to find a little sprite of a girl in a pink tulle dress, with blonde curls and wide blue eyes staring him down with an open mouth. Probably the swing set child. Her eyes brightened as she continued to silently move her mouth in little "O" shapes.

"Hi there," he said at last.

It took her a few seconds to finally find her words. "Are you an angel?"

He couldn't help but smile. "Hardly."

"Angels aren't supposed to lie," she said, placing her hands at her hips, challenging him to disagree.

The kid was adorable. He found himself squatting down to her level. "Yes, I know." He gave her a sly appraising look. "Are you an angel?"

She broke into a fit of giggles. "You're funny."

That's when he looked up to see his mother standing over him with a champagne flute in her perfectly manicured hand. He immediately rose to his feet.

"Excuse me, dear," she said, waving the child aside and leading Zach away by the arm. He glanced over his shoulder and gave the little cherub a goodbye wink.

"Hello, Mother. So good to see you again."

She plastered a fake smile on as they passed other guests. "Oh, stop acting like I'm a stranger," she warned under her breath. "You never were a good liar." Her smile faded for a brief second. "You aren't still mad at me, are you?"

Sometimes Zach just didn't have the energy to argue with her. His mother could be so tiresome and nagging at times. They feared her in the Senate for those very reasons. She could make others squirm. "This is neither the time nor place for that discussion. I came. You saw me, and now I'll be leaving."

Not to be deterred, she ignored his words and deftly steered him towards the other side of the terrace where a group of men had gathered. She gripped his arms as if daring him to let go. "Nonsense you fool. Swallow your pride. You owe me at least an hour of your time."

"What makes you think I owe you that much?"

She sighed in exasperation. "Someday you will thank me for doing this. Not everything in life can be learned from one of your books…"

He was about to say something when the group he was being maneuvered towards parted and Senator Talbot came into view holding the hand of that bright eyed little blonde girl in the pink dress.

"Camille," he said, nodding towards Zach. "I see your son has decided to join you. How wonderful." He looked proudly down at the child. "Have you two met my granddaughter, Isadora?"

The child looked up at him. "It's Izzie, Grandpa. You always forget. My name is—just Izzie."

Talbot chuckled. "Okay. 'Just Izzie'."

Zach's mother found the child's words amusing. "How utterly priceless. The Chairman of The Senate Select Committee on Intelligence being told he has faulty memory."

Talbot ruffled little Izzie's hair. "Well, I've certainly been accused of much worse."

Talbot turned his attention to Zach. "So, tell me, son. Are you finding your new job at the Library of Congress fulfilling?"

He saw Izzie's eyes widen and that little 'O' appeared on her mouth once again.

"Senator, it's been surprisingly more than I expected."

His mother rolled her eyes. "My son the Librarian. He adamantly refuses to consider politics or even the family business. Jim, maybe you can talk some sense into him. God knows, I've tried."

Izzie was the one to break the tension. She pulled on Zach's sleeve. "I love the Library. My mommy works at the Library, too." Izzie craned her neck scanning the guests. Her eyes lit up when she spotted her mother coming towards them.

"There she is!" she cried.

Zach turned his head and was totally dumbstruck. The most beautiful sight he might ever see was heading his way. Meghan March wearing a strapless blue sheath dress, with her flaming red hair pulled back in a tight chignon at her neck, was smiling at him with some semblance of recognition. This was Izzie's mother? Damn.

She simply took his breath away. A better word was gob smacked. There was an explosion of 8's coming from her head like a holiday fireworks display going off. He immediately forgot about wanting to leave. Perhaps he *would* have something to thank his mother for after all. Imagine that. Meghan March being Talbot's daughter!

There was another excited tug at his sleeve. "What's your name?" Izzie wanted to know.

He leaned down and whispered. "Just Zach."

He witnessed Izzie's million-dollar smile. She grabbed his arm and hauled him over to her mother, bridging the distance. "This is the angel I was telling you about, Mommy. I finally found him. His name is Just Zach--and he's a rainbow person."

~~*~~

Meghan had already noticed the man talking to her daughter. He looked vaguely familiar in a way she had yet to identify. The mother in her wanted to swoop in and immediately intercede. Izzie knew better than to talk to strangers without a family member present. But Izzie could be a chatterbox at times if something intrigued her. And this tall young man obviously did. She had the fleeting thought that her daughter might grow up to be a flirt. It terrified her to no end that she might not be able to protect her from the world's predators. She pushed that thought out of her head. Worrying about it now would be futile.

Izzie's bedtime had already come and gone. She promised her daughter an extra hour after watching her beg for more time to show off her new pink dress and "look for angels," which was her newest obsession since this morning. Tomorrow she was sure it would be something else.

Watching her daughter, she was both surprised and curious to see the level of excitement in her eyes. Izzie was not only staring at the man but looked completely enthralled with him. This was highly unusual, so Meghan stepped away from her father's guests to observe the interchange. She scrutinized the man more carefully wanting to see what her daughter was seeing.

He was an attractive man in a serious sort of way. She noted that he looked at ease in his formal evening attire and could tell that it was custom made and not off the rack. He came from money. She was drawn to his eyes, which signaled that he felt uncomfortable at such events. Maybe he was just shy. Why did he look so familiar?

And why come to a party and avoid the other guests, but readily strike up a conversation with a child? She found this curious. She didn't know if she should find it endearing or see it as a red flag concerning her daughter's safety. Most of the other guests were too busy making connections to give a minor the time of day. But yet Izzie had marched right up to him and Izzie had pretty good radar for what she called "rainbow" people. She claimed she could see rainbows around nice people and black and red if they were bad. Without question she usually avoided the black and red type, so Meghan could only assume the man was indeed a good "rainbow" person.

He had opted for a familiar beer rather than the expensive wines and liquors that were offered, which suggested he was genuine. His jaw was clean-shaven and well defined. His thick dark brown hair was stylishly slicked back and his eyes were gentle and kind when he talked to Izzie. Something Izzie said he found extremely amusing. She watched a smile spread across his face. Her child could be quite precocious at times. Who was he?

Camille Eldridge certainly knew him, because she walked right up to him, totally ignoring her Izzie, and brought him around like a mother hen. Realization hit her and she immediately saw the family resemblance. He was probably Camille Eldridge's son. How very interesting. Then it hit her. Her father had mentioned that he had met a young man at the Library today who was related to Senator Eldridge and that…

She suddenly remembered why he looked so familiar. The memory of him handing her a Kleenex, then seeing him again in the vending room came flooding back. She didn't know where he worked, but he was definitely a Library of Congress employee. She liked most everyone she knew from the Library. Too bad his mother was a power-hungry bitch. She would try not to hold it against him.

Meghan did not like Senator Eldridge one bit. In fact, she found her extremely distasteful. While she tried not to be judgmental, but she suspected, no she actually knew, that Camille Eldridge was having an affair with her father and probably had been for some time. Did her son know this? What would he think about his mother cheating on his father with another man? Perhaps nothing, since it was done all the time in Washington.

As a widower, her father was free to see whomever he wanted. She wanted him to be happy, but she couldn't see that happening with Camille Eldridge. The woman was fake, phony and plastic, just like a lot of Washington socialites who had designs on men of power and influence like her father. But she supposed it wasn't any of her business.

Meghan sighed and brought herself back to the present. The man's name was Zach Eldridge—Izzie's "angel" find. He didn't look like an angel. He was watching her closely, actually somewhat curiously. Had her thoughts given her away? She smiled back at him, not wanting to appear rude. She sincerely hoped he was nothing like his designing mother.

~~*~~

Zach watched the play of emotions flit across Meghan's beautiful face and wondered what had caused her moment of consternation. There were energetic chards of glass coming out of her head. Her thoughts read like an open book. Something had seriously put her off. Hopefully, not him. Did he look too eager to meet her?

106

He extended his hand. "Zach Eldridge," he said introducing himself. She shook it and he noted how soft and smooth her skin was. "I didn't know you were Senator Talbot's daughter. It's a pleasure to meet you. It seems our parents know each other."

He glanced over towards his mother who had already forgotten him and moved on. To *his* consternation he saw Talbot press a hand against his mother's back, then let it drop lower in an intimate fashion. It was so subtle the guy probably thought no one saw it. Holy fuck! He hadn't seen that one coming. This could definitely make things awkward. He hoped Meghan hadn't seen what he had.

His mother's affairs were legendary, like Norman conquests. No wonder his father stayed far from home and didn't come back for months on end. The last thing he wanted to think about was his mother having wild sex with another man. He wished his parents would just get a divorce and put each other out of their misery. He suspected the reason they didn't was neither wanted to deal with the financial fallout it was sure to entail.

Izzie quickly butted in. "Mommy, Zach works in the Library, just like you. Did you know that?" She didn't wait for a response from either of them. "I didn't know angels could work in libraries. That is so cool."

Meghan smiled apologetically. "She's on an angel kick today. It seems you've been chosen."

He liked the sound of that, 'being chosen'. "I've seen you at the Library. You're a docent..."

She nodded. "And you're the guy with the Kleenex. Yes, I do remember. Thank you. I was pretty upset that day."

Izzie's head followed their conversation like a ping-pong ball being lobbed back and forth.

He moved closer to avoid others overhearing. "Well, it was pretty understandable. I knew Roone Sawyer for many years. I was his teaching assistant in college and he was my mentor. We worked together in New York City and he recruited me to work at the LOC."

"Really? I'm so sorry. It must have come as quite a shock."

"It did." He was silent for a moment debating whether to say more about Roone's death.

Izzie let out a little audible yawn. She was rapidly winding down having already lost interest in adult conversation. Meghan drew her closer.

"I really liked him and so did Izzie. And believe me, Izzie has a pretty good sixth sense about people. He sometimes allowed her to come into the Main Reading Room despite the age restriction. I've been having trouble believing any of those things they've said about him..."

Zach nodded in agreement. If only she knew. He let her continue, loving to watch her as she talked and emitted 8's. He was hopelessly smitten but didn't really care. He felt alive around her.

"I miss him. Mr. Sawyer was helping me with research on a book I'm preparing on the Library's unique collection of statues. No one knew that Library like he did."

Meghan saw his spark of interest at what she had said. She watched him reach in his jacket pocket, pull out his cell phone and bring up a picture. "Can you tell me something about this statue?" He handed over the phone. Izzie hung on her mother's arm and craned her neck wanting to see.

Meghan recognized it immediately. "Oh, it's the Minerva of War. There's a pair in the Great Hall atop each marble pillar, at the base of both staircases. The other is the Minerva of Peace. These particular statues were done by the artist Herbert Adams. He also did the Library's two bronze entry doors, marked 'Truth' and 'Research'."

She looked over at him curiously. "You probably walked right by both these statues many times."

She pointed out the details in the photo. "The Minerva of War holds a short sword ready to strike and in the other hand a torch of knowledge and learning. There's a predominant Minerva theme in other areas of the Library as well, like the Mosaic at the top of the stairs by the Visitor's Gallery. I also hear there is a rare Minerva in the Congressional Reading Room's private balcony, or perhaps there was one there at one time, but I've never seen it."

"Have you been inside that room?" he asked.

"No, unfortunately. I've asked my father several times to get me in, but he seems to think it's a man's domain and I have no business there. He can be so Neanderthal at times."

Zach made a mental note to get them both inside. Key code pads were not a problem but running into someone inside who knew you shouldn't be there could be.

Izzie's eyes were droopy and at half-mast. She was fading quickly. She snuggled against her mother like a human pillow. "Mommy," she whispered sleepily. "Can I go to bed now?"

"Yes, honey," she said running her hand through Izzie's curls. "We'll go right now."

Meghan took Izzie's hand. "I'm sorry. She's had a very busy day. Will you excuse us?"

Zach would have liked to keep talking with Meghan. That would be worth sticking around for. "Will you be back?" he asked hoping to make it happen.

She nodded a "yes" before taking her daughter in hand.

He watched her leave and knew he must be grinning like a silly idiot but didn't care. There was something about her that made her irresistible, along with little Izzie. The feeling was new to him and frankly it scared him. He didn't scare easily.

Zach quickly rejected the idea of having another beer while waiting for Meghan's return. He wanted to have a clear head. Blending into the background was something he could do well, so he kept to the shadows with a clear view of the sliding glass panel of living room doors, where Meghan was sure to return from.

He watched the other guests enjoy themselves under the small white lights that illuminated the grounds and terraces. He was sure politics was the subject of the evening, or some bill in the House that was up for a vote. After a few drinks, a few couples ventured out onto the portable dance floor and were swaying to the medley of tunes the musicians had struck up.

On one end of the terrace, the caterers were bringing out tapas trays of stuffed mushroom croquettes, chicken empanadas, Spanish crab cakes, fried calamari, spicy meatballs, smoked salmon on cucumbers and goat cheese crostini. It all looked good, but Zach had no appetite for any of it. He wondered how long it would take to put a six-year-old to bed. In his head he was trying to calculate bath time, brushing teeth, perhaps a short story and then lights out. He would wait however long it took.

Zach noticed Constantine Stavros over near the bar talking to a few other men who were unknown to Zach. His eyes moved on until another familiar face crossed his line of sight. A bald-headed man. His eyes swung back and zeroed in on the man. His heart practically leapt out of his chest. His pulse raced. Holy shit! It was the same guy who killed Roone! What was he doing here?! Zach watched him move quietly through the milling guests, past Talbot and his mother, then past Zach who barely breathed, not moving a muscle. The man never noticed him. He was sure of it, as he moved with purpose spotting his target straight ahead.

Zach saw him stealthily move towards Constantine Stavros, who apparently recognized him, and whisper something in his ear. Stavros nodded and inclined his head, dismissing him. Zach quietly took out his cell phone, pretending to make a call, and snapped a quick picture. The killer retraced his movement across the veranda without stopping to converse with anyone else. He made his way towards the steps leading to the front of the house. Was he leaving the party?

Zach immediately sprang into action. He followed him, pretending to be talking to someone on his phone to avoid attention as he bounded up the stone steps after him. As he came around the corner to the driveway entry, he slowed down. The guy was up ahead having a smoke, waiting for the valet to bring around his car.

What was this guy's connection to Stavros? Bodyguard? Hired thug? To his relief Zach spotted his driver at the end of the long drive. He texted him to come get him ASAP. He needed to leave right now.

Barely seconds later Zach could hear his driver's ignition turn over and the sound of wheels on gravel as he pulled out of line heading toward him. Both cars arrived at the same time. The killer took one last drag on his cigarette and tossed the butt onto the stone drive. He got into a new black model Mercedes and took off.

Zach snapped a picture of the guy's license plate and jumped into the back of his own waiting car. He knew he was tossing aside a second chance with Meghan, not being there when she returned from putting Izzie to bed, but he had to find out who and what this guy was all about—and what his connection to Stavros was. The universe was dropping an opportunity right into his lap and he couldn't let it slip by.

"Don't let that car out of your sight! There's an extra $100 in it for you," he told his driver, buckling his seatbelt, as his driver took off at a fast clip down the driveway and through the open iron security gates in hot pursuit.

The killer drove like a NASCAR driver. His sporty black Mercedes wove in and out of the traffic on the Parkway, providing a challenge for Zach's driver to avoid being spotted tailing him. After about 30 minutes, the Mercedes pulled over to an off ramp. Zach's driver slowed down, following from a close distance as they came up to a streetlight. Without warning a silver

SUV cut in front of them while the traffic light was still yellow. The Mercedes sped through the yellow light, but the SUV stopped as it turned red.

Zach swore under his breath seeing his prey get away. "Can't you go through the red light?" he asked the driver.

"No sir. I cannot." He replied before adding, "Not for $100."

"Whatever then. C'mon man--move!"

It didn't matter. By the time they safely proceeded through the intersection there was no sign of the black Mercedes. Gone. But not out of reach. Zach brought up the picture of the guy's license plate on his phone. He would soon find out who he was and where he lived.

The driver looked at him through the rear-view mirror apologetically. "Sorry, sir. What would you like me to do now?"

Zach drummed his fingers impatiently against the seat. He really wanted to go back to Meghan, but he had work to do. "Take me home."

He knew he would be up late tracking down leads and hacking into secure systems looking for answers. Things were becoming more complicated by the minute. In his head he was making a mental list that kept growing. Somehow, he would make sense of it all.

Chapter 11

Cali Cavaleri hated exercise with a passion, but since she enjoyed eating she had come to the conclusion it was a necessary evil she would endure to keep her TV job, just like sobriety. Drinking had served a dual purpose. Besides helping her escape her dull lonely life, it had also suppressed her appetite. She skipped meals and drank them instead. It kept her forever thin, preventing a need for diet pills to keep off the dreaded fat, which had alleviated any anxiety about packing on excess camera weight. Of course, when she stopped being a wino that all changed. Her appetite came raging back with a vengeance.

Station management would pretend, on the record of course, that a little "healthy" weight didn't matter. But they lied. It mattered a lot. They would get around workplace discrimination laws by making jabs about her caloric intake rather than come out and tell her to lose weight or look for another job. "Helpful" books on the latest diet trends were anonymously left on her desk when she was out on field assignment. She suspected her female competition at the station was intentionally mind fucking her. They were all pencil thin. It didn't take a rocket scientist to get the message. If she wanted to eat more than 1200 calories a day, she had to jog her little butt off in the morning and sometimes in the evening with a four-to-five-mile run. And now, she too, was part of the pencil thin club.

She sprinted up the steps of her condo, wiping the sweat from her brow with her sleeve. It was going to be another hot day and she had about 30 minutes to shower and change before the camera crew swung by to pick her up to cover a story on Save the Chesapeake Bay's newest environmental agenda. It was an easy assignment.

On her way towards the shower, she hit the switch on her expensive, but oh so worthwhile new espresso maker, now displayed like a shrine on her kitchen countertop. She craved that much needed caffeine jolt to jumpstart her day. It was her new god. She realized that she had successfully overcome a wine addiction, only to replace it with a coffee fixation. They couldn't fault her for that. Hey, no one was perfect.

While she waited for her first shot of the day, she logged into her laptop on the kitchen table checking for any last-minute instructions from her assignment editor. As soon as she opened her laptop, the screen was overtaken with an image of a man, his head clean-shaven, with the bold caption: "Roone Sawyer's Real Killer. Now Go Get Him!" She jumped back in startled surprise. What the hell?! She hit the keypad. It immediately brought up a typewritten note from whoever had the audacity to hack into her computer. It read:

"The man's name is Lee J. Vargas. His vehicle is registered to BGC Solutions, a private security intelligence contractor located in Arlington, Virginia. He lives at 2517 Nordica Way in Tyson's Corner. I have proof he strangled and killed Roone Sawyer and framed him for human crimes he did not commit. Look into Vargas' connections to Constantine Stavros. You will be receiving time-stamped footage of Vargas' entry into the

Library of Congress on the date in question. Trust no one."

Cali frowned and stepped back. She felt a moment of fear, swiftly replaced by anger. Had the sender of the note also snooped around into her private files on her computer as well? She had an erotic novel she was working on (which was her surrogate for sex these days), also numerous Washington sources for inside leaks, and most damming of all—her sobriety diary. Her whole freaking life was on her laptop, and someone had gained access to it. Fuck! Fuck! Fuck!

For a long moment she was more consumed with her own privacy being violated than who Roone Sawyer's possible killer might be, but then the journalist in her kicked in. Who had sent this to her? And why? Were they just another anonymous source trying to turn in their crazy neighbor?

Cali could paper her bathroom walls with the confessions she'd gotten this past week alone--all persons claiming to have inside information on the Potomac Killer aka Roone Sawyer. Yesterday a dwarf, who sent along a picture of himself without a shirt and laying back against some fluffy flowered cushions, had confessed to not only being the real pedophile killer but also the secret lover of that Librarian guy Sawyer. Seriously, one could not make this shit up. There were a lot of sick puppies in this town, and some of them she had even dated.

She took a screen capture of the note and pic and texted it to her phone, just in case it should mysteriously disappear from her laptop. When she went to check to make sure her other files had not been wiped or corrupted, movie footage popped up on the screen and played in a continuous loop. What next? Would her computer also self-destruct?

Cali peered closer. Sure enough, it was time-stamped Library of Congress, the entry access door, date and time—and there was the bald-headed guy. He was wearing dark glasses and a baseball cap, but it was definitely him. He had quite a distinct nose, very patrician. He must have had an access code because the time displayed showed entry during Library after hours.

She was confused. Had the police been so sure it was an open and shut suicide case that they had never requested security footage from all entry points for the day? That would be hard to believe. She knew Lieutenant Bill Hanlon of Capitol Police and he bordered on being anal in his investigations. He wouldn't have missed this detail, would he?

She saved the footage and texted herself this file as well. She grabbed her espresso and tossed it back like a tequila shot. There, just what she needed. She was feeling better already. Someone had some explaining to do. But right now, she had a job to see to.

~~*~~

Zach knew the second Cali Cavaleri had accessed the information he had sent her computer. He also knew it would probably freak her out, but definitely get her attention. People's computer IP addresses were not terribly hard to anonymously interface with and place undetectable key codes into their registry. The intelligence agencies had been doing it for decades. Zach had simply created his own personal back door into Cali's computer, bypassing NSA email surveillance. He knew everything he was doing was illegal, but he was pretty sure he had left no trace back to him. Certainly, no one at the Virginia Department of Motor Vehicles would ever notice the breach of their driver's license and plate database.

It had been a long night going through the footage of all Library entry points for the entire day of Roone's murder. He could have written an algorithm script to make the search easier, but for this he wanted to be sure with his own eyes.

He quickly ruled out that Vargas might have hidden in the Library earlier in the day. It was clear from the footage he had gained easy access, which meant someone had given him a maintenance entry. So, he knew Vargas was not working alone. How many others might be involved in the murder was something he wanted to access in the LOT records.

He discovered someone had inserted code on the footage causing it to skip over a few frames. They just happened to be the same frames of Vargas' entry access. If Zach had not been carefully watching each frame's time stamp, he might have missed the skip over. But he had. Someone had gone to a lot of trouble to make sure the security footage was doctored, yet undetectable. Had surveillance footage for the day gone missing entirely, it would have raised too many red flags. This told him he was dealing with professionals.

Gizmo sat on the desk in his flat throughout the entire security footage review. Zach tried to activate him using the same mental algorithms he had used before, but nothing moved the little guy. Verbal commands failed as well. The device had no battery, so Zach was at a loss to explain Gizmo's sudden lack of response or its source of power. Could it be Gizmo only responded while in the Library itself? He would put that theory to the test soon enough.

Zach had easily functioned on less than two hours of sleep before. And that was a direct result of the neuro-circuitry in his brain being different. Once his mind latched onto something it was hard to let it go. It energetically fed itself and was self-sustaining. Some might call it wired, but it allowed him to get a lot of work done while others were sleeping.

On an ordinary night he might read through one or two books and commit them to memory. This is how he had mastered computer languages so quickly. Tonight, he found some time in the early dawn hours to start learning Sanskrit, the "mother of all languages". Sanskrit was said to be the purest language, a sacred language handed down from the gods.

Zach really wanted to know what was written on all those silver and gold walls in the LOT. If it meant the key to opening knowledge, he would learn it faster. He opted to start with the older Vedic version versus Classical Sanskrit. Many of the ancient sacred texts used this version, so it seemed like a logical place to start. He quickly realized learning it also required logic, which he was quite good at. It suddenly became a whole lot easier and almost fun to learn. He knew he would master it in no time. For now, he would have a good idea, maybe not totally accurate just yet, of what the LOT inscriptions meant. Wouldn't Satya be surprised!

Instead of going directly to his little office niche in the Stacks the next day, Zach scoped out the second-floor balcony area overlooking the Main Reading Room where Roone had hidden something inside the great clock's interior. There were private offices along that hallway and, although lightly trafficked, it would still be pretty risky for anyone seen trying to open the locked maintenance door behind the clock's housing.

Zach leaned up against the wall, quickly looking both ways to make sure the coast was clear. He had no idea whose offices were along this hallway. Right now, no one was in sight. He quickly tried the key in the outer door, watching the corridor. It didn't fit. No surprise. That would have been too easy. The old key in his hand only opened the clock, not the exterior door leading to it. This would require locating a much newer type of key from maintenance, or the deft ability to pick a lock. Under the circumstances, he concluded the latter might be a much easier feat to accomplish. He would return.

There was a flood of new research requests from the Main Reading Room awaiting Zach when he returned to the Stacks and, since they were short-handed that morning, he pulled reference books from all over the Library. Most of the researchers were writers of some sort or another--novelists, government policy wonks, genealogists, historians, etc. Oftentimes they came for access to the more obscure materials not digitized or able to be found on the Library's online computer system.

They had access to the periodical volumes, congressional quarterlies, bound almanacs, State voting records, directories of all kinds. Many reserved study shelves both in the Stacks and in the Main Reading room to hold their reference requests. Zach would make a delivery run several times a day to accommodate their needs in addition to working on his own projects.

He had just finished dropping off several reference volumes on "Immigration Procedures and the Law" when he spotted Mrs. Friedman heading his way.

She handed him a thick binder. "Here, add these Senate Committee Reports to Shelf Number 12. They just came in."

Zach put the binder on the cart. "What's the name on the shelf?

"Cali Cavaleri."

He wrote down the name on a green call slip, despite knowing all too well who she was.

"That's the WWGO-TV reporter, correct?"

Estelle nodded. "That's the one. She'll be in around 2:00 PM."

He hoped it had something to do with the Vargas lead. "What's she researching?"

Estelle shrugged. "Not sure. She specifically requested this week's Foreign Relations Committee Yearly Report on Human Trafficking. It's a hefty volume."

That gave him a moment of pause. Oddly, he hadn't considered that angle. Human trafficking? He stared right through Mrs. Friedman, lost in a myriad of thoughts. His mind was racing with possibilities. He had to get back into the LOT right away. And if he could, this time he would come prepared.

He made some hasty excuse about a pile of work awaiting

him, which he needed to return to immediately. That being said he promptly turned his book cart around, tossing Cali Cavaleri's report materials on Shelf 12, and hightailed it back to the Stacks. Mrs. Friedman watched him race off, not knowing what to make of his sudden and odd departure.

~~*~~

Cali Cavaleri nervously drummed her pen atop her desk, still holding on a line Capitol Police had patched through to Detective Bill Hanlon. She hadn't even shared with her producer or any of her bosses what had appeared on her computer screen this morning. She kept hearing the words of the note in her mind: "Trust no one."

Well, she couldn't do her job if she didn't trust someone. But past history reminded her to go slowly and go cautiously. She could be walking into another 'fake news' trap. The last one had practically destroyed her professional credibility. She wanted to feel a few things out with Hanlon first. She hoped he wouldn't blow off her call. Cops generally hated reporters. Thought they were all scum of the earth, wanting to sensationalize everything. Well, not all of us are story whores, she thought.

She breathed a sigh of relief when she heard his voice finally come on the line.

"I'm eating a Philly Cheese Steak sandwich right now and it's getting cold. You've got 60 seconds, Calvaleri. What do you want?"

She gulped. He was pissed that she had called on his lunch break. Not a good place to start. "Hey, Hanlon. Good hearing from you, too," she began. "I'm tying up some loose ends on a story on Roone Sawyer, and I wondered if your guys checked the security footage for the Library that evening."

"Fuck. You think we're total morons?"

She waited. "Well, did you?"

Hanlon sounded like he was ready to hang up on her. "Of course we did."

Did she have to pull answers out of him? "And you found nothing?"

He sounded impatient. "That's right."

She knew she was going out on a limb. "My sources tell me differently. I'm texting over a footage clip. When you've had a chance to review it, let's talk."

There. She hung up knowing she had just opened a big can of worms. She texted the footage to his cell phone, which she hadn't wanted to initially use, and waited by the phone counting the minutes. It didn't take long. Her phone was buzzing angrily back in no time.

"Where the hell did you get this?" he demanded, without even saying hello.

She had certainly gotten his attention. "I can't say."

"Can't say or won't say?" he insisted on knowing.

"A little bit of both." She hurried on. "So, would I be right in assuming you haven't seen these particular frames before? Or that you haven't yet identified the man in the frames who is clearly entering after hours?"

His answer was noncommittal and steely. "I'm not saying anything."

She couldn't help but bait him—just a little. "I know the man's name, address, and who he works for. And it's not the Library. So, Bill, if you want to share something with me, I might be persuaded to share a little with you."

"Fuck you." He hung up.

Cali smiled. She was onto something big, and he knew it. She was certain she would hear back from Hanlon before the day was over. She had something he wanted.

~~*~~

Zach skipped lunch, grabbed an Uber and made a quick run over to the International Spy Museum Store on L'Enfant Plaza. Twenty minutes later and over $500 lighter, he walked out carrying a high-end black designer watch and hip reading glasses. Both were equipped with high- definition stealth mode video recorder capability. At the last minute, he also threw in the ultimate espionage lock pick tool, which might come in handy. One never knew. He was a firm believer in being prepared.

Gizmo had never left his sight since he first laid eyes on it. He kept it in a pocket along with his cell phone waiting to see if it turned on under any other circumstances. So far nothing. Since it had cloaking capability, Zach never had to worry about it being detected by security or anyone else, but nonetheless he kept it on his person and hidden from sight.

Back in the Stacks he took Gizmo out of his pocket. He had already retrieved the Antarctica file from the LOT, or rather Satya had pressed it into his hands. There were others, most likely also in the LOT to avoid detection. Zach knew where they were and so did Gizmo. Too much had happened since yesterday to closely examine the Antarctica notes and map the had snapped pictures of before handing it over to Meghan's father. His to-do list was growing by the minute.

Once again, he rapidly went through the binary code script sequence in his head, which was now on a continual loop akin to Mach speed. It encompassed all the still missing ZE file codes. At the same time, he instructed Gizmo to "Find" the files. And just like that the little guy turned on hotter than a furnace in winter and the walls started rippling again. Within seconds, Zach was ripped backwards through the same hole in the portal and back into the LOT.

This time, instead of initial disorientation, he picked himself right up off the floor (he would have to work on a better landing for next time) and headed down the aisles of knowledge. He was determined to learn how this library system worked without Satya's assistance. Only then would he be able to get the answers he really sought. He started with the Sanskrit inscriptions, hoping his crash course in this new language would point the way.

Satya watched Zach from afar through visual pathways in her mind's eye. Nothing was unknown to her. She saw everything as if she was right there with the person. Yet, this one she found to be unlike any of the others. First off, he had a higher degree of intellect, an immense hunger for knowledge, and quick deductive skills that made him so much more interesting. The poor thing didn't even know the extent of what he was destined to accomplish--yet. And she would not be the one to tell him either. That would wait. Everything was about timing. His path would eventually unfold before him and allow him to see the bigger picture. She knew she would be there for that, too. She was the witness to all things profound and mysterious.

Zach's baseball head injury at age seven had been no freak accident. That, too, was predesigned to fit with his life journey. The contents of Zach's personal life file were known to her long before he ever found his way into the LOT. She knew its finer details intimately and, for that reason, she made sure no one would ever be able to access it under any circumstances—not even Zach. That was the first mistake Sawyer had made. Curiosity had led to his learning of the date of his own death. All past, present and future memory were stored in the LOT and that made it a dangerous place—for some.

Normally she would immediately greet and assist each entity which gained entry into the LOT. There were those she liked and there were those she didn't. She was not there to judge their motives, only to follow protocol that had been established for hundreds of millions of years. If one found their way here, she was required to assist them. How they used the information gleaned in the LOT vaults was entirely up to them. Man had free will and she was essentially barred from interfering. However, there *were* occasions which necessitated her bending the rules just a little bit to protect the innocent. Her only constant was to assist and advise each visitor to use the information wisely and not for service to self. Of course, there would always be those who didn't heed her warning, which was their choice, but their actions eventually would be addressed in time by a higher authority beyond her level.

Satya smiled to herself. Zach had put on his "special" reading glasses to decipher the inscriptions and was already randomly opening holographic records. There was an easier way to summon what he specifically needed, but she was confident he would figure it out in time. Let him experiment. He was like a child with a new toy, and she felt an odd level of maternal protection. She could feel his level of excitement with each discovery.

She knew perfectly well what his intent had been coming into the LOT with his "surveillance" tools. Technically that would be prohibited, but she chose to look the other way with him. His intent was pure and that held weight with her.

Zach eventually found his way to the gold section and her "special" cache of files. One of these protected records had allowed him to see and experience the events leading up to his friend's death. These were the records she had warned him from trying to access without her consent. It was obvious he really wanted to get back in. She could hear his thoughts as well as see he was having a moral dilemma about what to do. Should he or shouldn't he?

He stepped back having made his decision. He would not touch them without her go ahead. His integrity had won out. She liked that. And because he had a sense of honor, she allowed the file he wanted to open to him once again. It beckoned him to dimensionally step back in and re-experience it. This took him by complete surprise. He hesitated only for a second and entered the hologram. As he did, she inserted a thought, in her own words, inside his head.

"Go ahead and record the details with your silly little spy tools—then go use it wisely."   She already knew he would.

Chapter 12

Cali checked for time. She was running later than she had anticipated. Due to a backlog of breaking news stories, she was stuck waiting her turn in the editing room. Her story on environmental efforts to Save the Chesapeake Bay, a general interest piece at best, was not a newsworthy enough priority to cut ahead of the others. She resented having to wait in line. She wanted to get back to some hard news stories and silently cursed her news director for palming off what she considered to be a fluff piece to fill air-time.

Now that she had finished the environmental piece, she noted there was still a small window of opportunity to run over to the Library and get the newly released Annual Foreign Relations Committee Report and get back to the station in time for her segment slot on the Nightly News.

Buried in the back of the Report, typically sandwiched between other more interesting Committee findings, the Report often addressed the current human trafficking problem. Data and statistics stuff. There might be something in there worth mining for her proposed follow-up story on the Potomac victims. She knew only too well that this was a subject very few wanted to talk about let alone hear the details on the nightly news.

But Cali's instincts told her to keep looking. After all it wasn't like every reporter in town was chomping at the bit to get a copy of the Report. She would have bet a year's salary she was the only journalist in town who requested a copy be put on reserve for her.

Her NYU journalism professors had taught her well. Ferreting out background information was the hallmark of a good reporter. But it meant putting in the extra time and effort, which was fast becoming a dying art with some of her professional colleagues.

The Annual Committee Report ranked the most egregious top tier three trafficking countries in the world for the year and restricted non-humanitarian aid going to them. That meant loss of big bucks for certain governments and companies if they ranked high on the list.

Cali was fairly certain the Potomac Killer victims were all illegals smuggled in by sex traffickers. None of them was in the immigration system database or registered as a citizen of the United States. She knew this because she had checked and double-checked with her sources. If Roone Sawyer was framed and didn't commit the crimes, as her anonymous source alleged, then there was an even bigger story out there waiting to be told.

Cali fumbled around in her pocket for her Reader's Photo ID card and passed it to the guard on duty outside the Main Reading Room. One practically had to strip down to the bare essentials to enter this hallowed research space. Today she carried in only a notepad, pen and laptop, which was pretty much all they allowed. Her tote bag and purse were currently being held hostage with a diligent cloakroom attendant on the ground floor.

A staffer source on the Foreign Relations Committee had told her there was something she should look into on the committee's latest annual report. Senators on the committee had been pressured to whitewash it by persons at the U.S. State Department as well as United Nations diplomats. Unfortunately, this Report was not yet available for access on the Library's online computer system. She would have to make copies of it—something she couldn't assign a station intern to do. And besides, she didn't want to alert others at the station to what she might be working on—at least not until she could put some meat on the bones of the story.

The Report was waiting for her on her reserve shelf inside the Main Reading Room. She took it over to the Alcove 4 station, which was what she called her "Middle East" office desk. Here she was surrounded by reference books on Islam, Iraq and Arabic countries. It was a quieter spot than the other alcoves, which was how she liked it. Few would recognize her here, or worse, ask for her autograph. Then there was also the added convenience that Alcove 4 had a Desk 46 Library computer already cued up to their online database. She never had to go far if she needed additional searches. She wanted to compare last year's Annual Report with this newest version and see if it indeed appeared to be "whitewashed".

No sooner did she open her own computer when, once again just like this morning, her screen was taken over by her anonymous source. A video was cued up and this time the caption read:

"Here's your proof. Use earbuds or they will throw you out of the Library. You're welcome."

Startled, and now somewhat paranoid, she immediately did a complete scan of the Main Reading Room, her eyes darting everywhere. She could feel that she was being observed. Had they watched her reaction to reading the note on the screen? Whomever they were she would show them that Cali Cavaleri was not in the least bit affected by this new turn of events. She smiled to the room at large. There!

Yet, the nagging suspicion remained. Could it be a Library employee or someone else who was hacking her computer and trying to scare her? There were about 20 people scattered throughout the reading room, but no one was paying her any noticeable attention. She thought she heard footsteps on the balcony above her containing the Alcove 4 Stacks, but the sound moved on and was quiet. She waited a few seconds before putting in her earbuds, as instructed, and started viewing the film. Within seconds she knew she had good reason to be scared.

Never had she thought she would ever witness a real murder in such gruesome detail. It was alarmingly chilling. She desperately wanted to shut it off, but she became mesmerized by witnessing the final moments of another human being's demise. The footage didn't look fake or staged, but all too real. She watched it to the very end, then replayed it. That might cause her shrink to diagnose her as sick and twisted, but her reporter persona tried to stay detached and impersonal and get the facts straight. Which were: Roone Sawyer did not kill himself, and the bald-headed guy had clearly offed him, then proceeded to put damming evidence on Sawyer's computer to frame him as a pedophile and killer. But why? That was the million-dollar question.

Who had filmed this and how could they record such an event unless they, too, were part of this murder scene? Not in a gazillion years could this film ever be aired on the station's nightly news. Since the murder had taken place in a Federal Library Building, the station would be raided for withholding evidence not only from the Capitol Police but also from the FBI.

Cali had only one viable option under the circumstances. She forgot all about the Committee Report. It would have to wait. She collected all her belongings, placed a quick phone call, and hurried down the steps of the Library and into a waiting TV station van.

Zach felt newfound energy coursing through him. He was on his way to vindicating his friend and that gave him new confidence. He could only hope that Cali would do the right thing and not bury the story under pressure from unknown persons. He would know soon enough. Perhaps within less than 24 hours. If so, she would scoop everyone else in the news field.

Zach had purposely picked Cali to be his leak. He had done his research well. Cali had messed up and hadn't made the best of choices, which had stalled her career. But he knew she would work this story simply because she had something to prove to herself and others. He understood that. And, Zach had always been a champion for the underdog.

Cali Cavaleri might never know who he was, which he preferred, but he didn't mind being her "deep throat" source. There was good reason for getting a reporter involved, versus going directly to the police. He wasn't sure he could trust any cop in this town, especially those at the top. Too many of them had their allegiances, just like members on The Hill.

This was an inside job, but under whose influence and direction he hadn't yet figured out. By using Cali, he could remain anonymous and insure that enough parties would know what had happened to get the true story out there. He preferred not to think about the potential danger he might be putting her in. In the end it would be her choice what she did or did not do with the information.

He had formulated grand plans of his own on how best to use the information in the LOT. If the choice was his, he would have spent every waking moment in this new sanctuary of knowledge getting answers to everything. But that choice was not his to make. When he tried to go back a second time that day, Gizmo failed to respond to the entry algorithm. He could only surmise that there might very well be a daily time allotment for each visitor. He would test that theory tomorrow.

For him, it had been a real revelation to learn that he could spend hours inside the LOT, like he had yesterday, and yet return to his dimensional world a minute or two later from when he had left it. This meant he could come and go as he pleased. His absences would not attract unnecessary attention.

The LOT was a strange, yet wonderful place to him. He was just starting to get the hang of how to open and retrieve records. Contrary to what he initially thought, the Sanskrit inscriptions were not the key to opening the stored holographic events, but they did provide helpful time and dating factors. The key to unlocking what one desired to know was based on intent. He hadn't stumbled on this strategy until the end of his first visit that day. Which was another odd thing. He always knew when it was time to leave, whether he was consciously ready to leave or not. He would experience a build-up of energy in his head. This caused the complete sense of normalcy and peace that he usually felt while there to quickly fade. Instead, it would be replaced by a persistent itchy feeling that it was time to go. He wondered if it was time sensitive to how long he was actually there or did it signal someone else's entry into the LOT?

Satya had not made her physical presence known throughout today's visit, but he felt her presence in his head, which was even more unnerving at first until he got used to it. He had a strong suspicion she was quite adept at reading other people's thoughts. And to his surprise, he could hear her words directed to him. He never thought of himself as being clairaudient, but in the LOT it seemed quite normal to have this extra sensory ability.

Zach's thoughts returned to discovering that intent was a powerful force inside the LOT. Whenever he had a strong desire to know something, Gizmo would react like an alter ego. The device's surface temperature would go from cool to hot in seconds. He had the thought that he needed to get back to the Library to get Cali his damming footage, when suddenly he was propelled back through the portal in a whirlwind.

Some of the most interesting moments in Zach's life had happened when he least expected anything to happen. He likened it to being in a meditative "neutral-idling state," as he called it. Others would term it "staying in the now". It was difficult staying in such a zone, when his mind was pulsing with a never-ending cascade of ideas.

Even now, the thought occurred to him that if he could instruct Gizmo to cloak himself whenever coming through a security checkpoint, so that the device failed to register on any surveillance monitoring device, then what might Gizmo be capable of accomplishing of the same nature for Zach? He knew Gizmo was not really invisible to the naked eye, but cloaking allowed it to bypass human awareness of its presence. This could prove to be invaluable.

Zach decided to give it a try. He took off his employee ID lanyard from around his neck, gave Gizmo the instruction to cloak them both and walked right past security and into the private domains of the Congressional Reading Room, where the Senator from California was just exiting. No one even glanced at him.

Zach made a quick tour of the room with its gilded gold ceilings and arched windows which flooded light into every corner, showcasing its decor of finely crafted tables and desks. There were burgundy and gold striped couches against the wall, a television tuned to a local news station, and a carved stone fireplace capable of providing a warm fire during cold winter months. The place was a political sanctuary that oozed coziness and warmth.

Zach found the rumored hidden staircase he'd heard about. It led to a private balcony overlooking Capitol Hill where he saw a vaulted safe tucked away in a niche containing who knows what, as well as a rare gold statue of Minerva—the one Meghan had referenced hearing about. It was smaller than the ones in the Great Hall, but this one was securely displayed in the corner of the room, on a solid pedestal, which appeared to be made of gold. Not gold leafing or gilding, but pure solid gold. It was not behind glass or under security protection and yet it had to be worth a fortune. Upon running his hands over it, he was surprised to find that it emanated a unique energy signature. How very odd. He snapped a quick picture of it for Meghan.

Downstairs he heard people enter the room and decided not to push his luck. He exited the balcony staircase and moved towards the exit. Amazingly, no one stopped him. Not even the guard on duty. With this new ability, Zach suddenly felt invincible.

He was not the type to waste time with a new-found ability. He directed his attention to the 2nd floor balcony overlooking the Main Reading Room. If his luck held, he would try unlocking the great bronze clock's housing and find out what Roone had hidden there. Whatever it was, Zach knew it had to have been left for him to discover.

The corridor was empty, with one office door slightly ajar. He passed the open doorway glancing inside to see a male figure sitting at his desk tapping away on a computer. He quietly padded by and paused outside the exterior door to the clock's mechanisms.

Exercising caution, he reinforced the thought command to Gizmo to continue to engage shielding mode. Again, he glanced both ways before taking out the lock pick tool. It was a straight pin and tumbler lock, nothing fancy. He inserted a small tension wrench into the bottom of the lock while inserting a pick into the top. The instructions advised applying a slight torque to the wrench while raking the pick back and forth. It was easier than he thought. It took only two tries before the key and driver pins lined up with the shear line and the lock sprung open. Good Lord, did people know that locks were this easy to break into? So much for the illusion of safety.

He was just about to open the door handle when two people emerged from the office door across the hall. Zach froze in place, not moving a muscle. One of them was Alfia Linfred. Crap!

He became as still as a deer caught in the headlights. "Nothing to see here," he kept repeating in his mind, looking straight at her. She glanced his way, looking straight at him, but said nothing and passed him by still in conversation with a Library division head.

Oh. My. God. His erratic breathing took a few seconds to re-normalize. Before someone else came through, he softly opened the door and closed it with a click behind him. Using the flashlight on his cell phone he scanned the dimly lit area in front of him. The clock's bronze housing was enormous—and dusty. He stifled a loud sneeze. Working in dusty Library's for most of his adult life had not helped his allergies one bit. Looks like maintenance hadn't been back here for some time.

He spotted the small door to the clock, just like he had seen in Roone's holographic memory of the event. In his pocket was the key. He inserted it into the lock where it turned easily. Zach flashed his light inside the interior and there it was—stuffed all the way in the back and wedged to the side to avoid easy detection--the leather-bound book Roone had hidden. Zach pulled it out, realizing immediately that it was not a book, but a journal. Inside were page upon page of handwritten numbers starting at the beginning with the small, almost indecipherable letters 'ZE'. Zach knew coding when he saw it. His friend had taken extra precautions to mask the information inside in code in the event someone else found the journal first.

Zach couldn't help but smile at the irony of it all. Even in death, his friend was still trying to feed him cryptic instructions he knew Zach would make sense of. He carefully tucked the journal inside his shirt and turned to leave. He hesitated then turned back around. Someone needed to take up the task at hand with Roone now being gone. Zach might have the only remaining key to the clock's housing—certainly the original key.

He searched for the clock's winding key, which was on a hook inside the housing, and proceeded to wind the clock fully before replacing the key back on its hook. The ticking was loud and strong like it should be.

There was still one more thing to do. The clock's inaccuracy had been bothering Zach since he first started working there, so he took a few seconds to properly adjust the clock arms to reflect the correct time. He stepped back. There. He felt better already. He was now, unofficially of course, the Library's new timekeeper.

~~*~~

Back at the TV station, Cali was doing mental cartwheels. She was going to break this story on tonight's news that new evidence pointed to Sawyer being murdered. She was able to get two experts from her station's tech department to verify that the video footage of Sawyer's death had not been digitally tampered with by using overlays or any other special computer graphic interface effects. God bless her source. It *was* the real thing.

Out of professional courtesy, and not to get her ass thrown in jail for hiding criminal evidence, she once again texted a copy of the murder footage over to Hanlon. They were fast becoming good buds because he called her back immediately. By now he must have programmed her number on his speed dial.

The first words out of his mouth were again: "Where the hell did you get this?" Followed by a more demanding, "And who else has seen it?"

She didn't want to antagonize him by being too snarky, much as she would have liked to. Never burn your bridges was something she had learned early on in life, especially in the news business. You never knew when you might need that person again to come through for you. But, in all truth, she was doing his investigative work for him and he could at least be a little nicer.

"No comment to the first question and to the second…my executive producer and two video experts who verified its authenticity," she stated calmly. "We're running with the story tonight on the late evening news."

She could practically hear his head explode on the other end. "You can't do that," he said with finality. "You're interfering in an open investigation."

"Relax, we're not airing the murder footage, but it's pretty clear Roone Sawyer did not kill himself. That's big news the public will want to know about. And maybe he didn't do that other stuff as well, which means you have a bigger problem at large. Like a serial killer." So there. She had made her point.

She knew he knew he had a problem. He capitulated, just a little, which had to be very hard for him. Hanlon was old school. "We did find hidden code in the original security footage, which we're looking into how it got there," he admitted before adding. "From facial recognition, we now have a lead on the murder suspect."

"Just a lead?" she prompted. "His name is Lee Vargas. He lives at 2517 Nordica Way in Tyson's Corner and works for BGC Solutions in Arlington. When were you planning to arrest the guy?"

She could hear him swear under his breath. "Now, I gave you something, Bill. All I ask is that you tell me the minute you nab this guy so I can have my exclusive. In exchange, I will share whatever else comes my way on this case. Pinky promise."

She hated to have to kiss up to Hanlon or any cop for that matter, but there weren't a whole lot of other options. The Capitol Police were exempt from Freedom of Information Act (FOIA) requests unlike Metro. They could withhold names, identities and any evidence from the public they chose until the cows came home. That is unless Congress allowed the release. Which was highly unlikely in her case, especially since the Madame Speaker of the House still hated her big mouth guts.

But she understood Hanlon. He had a job to do, and no cop wanted to be in league with a reporter. To them it was like working with the devil himself. But, at least, the Lieutenant was a reasonable man.

"I'll get back to you." And, once again, the dick hung up on her.

Cali grabbed a camera guy and re-shot a new breaking news segment, inserting stock footage of the Library and Sawyer, but this time with the killer's identity and face. She would have it cued up and ready to go. It gave her a sense of hope that her career was finally back on the fast track, however timing was everything. Her nervous system was on overdrive waiting for the go-ahead on Lee Vargas. Five minutes before air-time she got her confirmation call confirming his arrest.

Her confidence came surging back knowing that Lt. Bill Hanlon would now owe her. Those whack-a-doodle bitches at the station could all eat shit. Finally, she had caught a break.

Chapter 13

Last night's news was the first thing Zach saw upon awakening. All the media outlets in D.C. were now running with the lurid news of Roone's gruesome murder and the national stations were following suit. Lee Vargas' face was plastered everywhere along with his surprise evening arrest at his Tyson's Corner residence. News was now coming in that Vargas had lawyered up with one of the biggest criminal defense attorneys in D.C.

Zach experienced a moment of deep satisfaction, knowing his part in revealing the truth, but it was becoming clearer he had only scratched the surface and more would need to be uncovered in order to prove Roone's innocence. Someone with deep pockets was probably protecting Vargas.

It was too bad he had missed Cali's breaking TV news segment. He would find it on the web later and see what kind of job she had done. Lack of sleep from the following night and the intense pace of yesterday had caused him to crash shortly after he returned to his flat. He wasn't sure what time he had passed out still hunched over his laptop.

All Zach remembered was figuring out the algorithm and key decoder, which was easy enough because Roone had used Zach's initials as the cipher and ran it in a diagonal pattern. Once he started deciphering the patterns in Roone's journal—sleep overtook him so fast and furious he was out for the entire evening.

His mouth was drier than dust and he could feel a tightness crawl up his neck that was stiff from last night's work. He guzzled down some water and rubbed a hand over the dark stubble that covered his jaw. One glance in the mirror told him he looked like hell. His rumpled clothes from yesterday hung on him. That hadn't happened in a long time. Nothing a shower and shave, along with some focused Qigong, couldn't quickly fix.

It was now apparent to Zach that his work priorities had taken a drastic and sudden detour. Work at the Library would now become secondary to his true work inside the LOT. He hadn't even scratched the surface of how this information might be used. A new plan was formulating, and he was beginning to see exactly what he needed to do.

Getting back into the LOT was becoming easier each time. Getting back to the Library from the LOT was another matter. There were glitches. Zach couldn't always predict where he would be ejected back out into his D.C. Library world. The first time it had been through the ceiling panel of Truth in the Members of Congress Room, yesterday he had come out near a video display in the Bob Hope Gallery on the ground floor. He had scared an old lady taking pictures of the "Hope for America" political memorabilia from decades ago. Zach had yet to figure out why he never came back out where he initially started. Like everything else, there had to be a reason.

Back in the LOT he decided to take a different approach to

accessing information. A place this dimensionally advanced shouldn't need call number identification, card catalogs, online bases or the archaic systems still used in the Library of Congress or other libraries around the world. Which is why Zach started experimenting with the power of INTENT. His decision was immediately rewarded. He discovered that Gizmo, being consciousness-assisted technology, was able to easily interface with the LOT's system of classification and storage and merge it with Zach's mind. He remembered an ancient Sanskrit saying: "The mind of man is a library unto itself." Had they been referring to the LOT?

He directed Gizmo to find information showing him why Roone was murdered and who was responsible. A whirlwind of dark colors began shooting out from the silver wall vaults, furiously merging into a swirling hologram that Zach saw completely in his mind's eye even before it opened to him to become one with its visual memory.

He felt the extreme temperature difference of this environment immediately. It was so real his brow felt hot and sweaty and breathing became more labored. Little beads of perspiration ran down his back making him noticeably uncomfortable. He had entirely too many clothes on for such a place. Steam came up through vents in the floor and it appeared he was now in a well-insulated sauna room. He recognized the half-naked man with a towel draped over his lap to be Constantine Stavros. The same man Senator Talbot had been squiring around in the Library the other day. Stavros' eyes were half closed, but there was no mistaking who he was.

He observed Stavros reach for a ladle in a wooden bucket alongside his bench and slowly pour cool water over his head, sighing as it streamed rivulets down his sweaty body. The steam room door suddenly opened and Lee Vargas, wearing nothing, silently entered. Some nasty looking tats were inked across his chest along with a patchwork of battle scars. His face was expressionless. He stood at attention, waiting for Stavros to acknowledge him, who finally nodded for him to sit down on the same wooden bench a few feet away. The two men were alone in the steamy cell.

Vargas was the first to speak. "The pipeline just delivered another shipment. Very young. Mostly male. They're being seasoned and branded for tonight's event."

Stavros grunted.

Vargas continued. "I can assure you that you and the others will be extremely pleased, not to mention highly entertained. They're all prime specimens—some virgins as well."

"Excellent," Stavros inhaled the steam deeply into his lungs. He was silent for a moment, lost in thought, before finally adding. "Make sure you get some good close-up recordings of the Ambassador. No males, only very young girls for him. He won't be able to resist a threesome. It's our insurance policy should he get cold feet on our trade deal. You know the drill."

Vargas nodded. "Anything else?"

"Yes." Stavros frowned. "Regarding that meddlesome Librarian, Sawyer... I trust you destroyed anything which might link back to M."

"M? Whoa. Wait a minute... Who is M?" As Zach asked the question aloud, the visual memory did an immediate freeze frame in response to his request. Without realizing he had the option to direct the event's rate of play, Zach waved it to continue. It did.

Vargas was quick to assure his boss. "I didn't find anything in Sawyer's apartment, nor in the Library which might compromise the organization. As always, I was very thorough. He was an easy kill."

"What about the press?"

"They've been alerted to suppress any follow-up reporting."

Stavros was quite pleased. "Excellent."

Both men lapsed into silence. The discussion appeared to come to an end. Vargas grabbed a wet towel and placed it around his neck. He rose and moved to leave.

Stavros cleared his throat. "Oh. And one more thing..." Vargas stopped, turned around, hesitating at the door. Stavros removed his lap towel and stood displaying his full nakedness. "Don't you ever use the river again to dump dead "kiddie litter". Find another way to get rid of the bodies. I'm on some goddamn advisory committee to Clean Up the Potomac. Seeing such human pollution in our waterways I find quite upsetting."

Zach had seen enough. Stavros had ordered the kill on his friend. Was Roone murdered because he knew that Stavros was behind an international sex trafficking ring that was blackmailing people in high places? Had Roone learned about it in the LOT or somewhere else? Perhaps the answers were hidden in the journal Roone had left him, which he had yet to completely decipher.

His thoughts kept coming back around to his "M" question? Who or what is "M"? He instructed Gizmo to find the "M" file. From the amount and density of dark streams of light coming from all over the LOT at once, it was like a non-stop attack of information coming straight at him. Zach hadn't seen anything like this before. The information had to span decades of time and, if so, how would he know where to begin? He immediately halted the onslaught. In his gut he sensed he was opening one gigantic bucket of worms and needed to move more slowly.

Best to work backwards. He instructed Gizmo to open something more recent on "M" and a hologram instantly formed to show him a table of 12 people, sitting in a dimly lit room, surrounded by large visual monitors displaying live-stream images. He recognized Stavros as one of the 12 sitting at a large conference table. There was one other familiar face in silhouette, but before he could identify the person, Satya moved in like a force of nature. She stood in front of him, becoming a human shield as the information behind her faded and dissolved, blocking off further review. With vacuum force, the streams of information got sucked back into a vault faster than the blink of an eye and all returned to an empty silence between them.

Zach sensed Satya was not pleased with him, but the minute she finally spoke he knew her words came more out of concern than anger--quite possibly even protection. This intrigued him. Did she think he would meet the same fate as Roone?

"You learn quickly," she began. "I have left you free to experiment and discover, but it is now time to go."

Go? Was she kidding? He was just getting started. "Tell me who or what is 'M'?"

"I guarantee you will not like what you hear," she replied.

From her overall reaction, he had already come to that same conclusion. "Then, just tell me what I need to know."

It was a fair request. Satya knew he would eventually learn everything anyway. It was already destined. While there was some knowledge not yet ready for human dissemination, she could not protect him forever or she would not be properly doing her job. She nodded and told him the only thing important to know—for now. She was sure there would be repercussions to pay. She softly spoke the words that might seal her own fate.

"M is Minerva--the source of evil for all humankind."

And with that she vanished, sending Zach hurtling back through the portal and emerging out of a bookcase in the Young Reader's Center of the Library where story time was currently in progress. He was met with a sea of young faces who, in unison, sat forward in their chairs staring at him in silent amazement. One of them was young Izzie March whose eyes were as round as saucers.

Zach put his finger to his lips beckoning the children to silence. He slowly lowered himself to the floor sitting cross-legged with his back up against a bookcase filled with children's books. He was prepared to wait it out and not draw any further attention to his unorthodox entrance. He settled down to join them. He loved a good story.

The Library had volunteer teens who often acted as "ambassadors" to help out during the daily children's events offered at the Center. Today's story reader looked to be about 14 and the selection was, "*The Door to the Secret City*" about a boy named Freddie who visited another world. Zach had to smile at the irony of that choice considering the more than 600,000 children's books available in the Library to select from.

Izzie had not stopped staring at him. He removed his recording glasses and put them in his shirt pocket before giving her a little wave of recognition. Slowly she turned back to the story reader and resumed listening. Oh brother. Now for sure she would think he was an angel having dropped out of the sky. Every few seconds, Izzie would glance back at him sitting on the floor to make sure he was still there.

He was quite certain she would give him the third degree the first chance she got, which of course she did. The minute story-hour wrapped up and the reader closed her book, Izzie marched over to Zach demanding to know where he had come from.

"Are you an angel from heaven? Who sent you here? Have you seen my Daddy? Are you trying to earn your wings like Clarence?" she said before stopping to take a breath. "And how do angels come through bookcases?"

"Whoa." He held up a hand. "Someday I'll tell you but right now I have to keep it a secret. It's confidential stuff. It might jeopardize my mission." If only she knew how true that was.

"Oh," she said, clearly disappointed. She thought about it for a few seconds. "Okay. I guess you might not get your wings if you tell me." She paused a second before another thought popped in her head. "Can you tell me if you're here to help my Mommy and me?"

That was a tougher question, as he really didn't know. He believed in being as honest as possible with kids. They were great lie detectors regardless of what adults thought.

"I hope so," he said softly and meaning it. "And speaking of your Mommy, where is she?" He rose to his full height from his perch on the floor.

"You're a very tall angel," she said craning her head back and studying him. "I saw you in my dreams, you know. I knew you were coming."

He hid a smile. "You did?"

"Yes, I did. I know my Mommy doesn't always believe what I tell her, so I sometimes keep secrets so she doesn't get that look on her face."

Zach tilted his head in her direction. "And what look is that?"

Izzie knitted her brows together, her eyes squinting then going wide in an exaggerated manner. "That look. It means she's worried—and she also gets very quiet. I think she thinks too much. And maybe she still misses Daddy. I just don't like to see her unhappy."

"Ahh. I see what you mean. I think she might get that look if you told her I was an angel."

Izzie nodded solemnly. "Yeah, I know." Then she laughed. "She would think I was really crazy, huh?"

He wanted to change this whole angel topic. "Izzie, where's your Mommy now?"

She grabbed Zach's hand and pulled him towards the door. "C'mon. I'll show you."

Izzie dragged him down the hall, past the Coolidge Auditorium where a ladies meeting was just letting out. She darted and bobbed through the throng, never letting go of his hand as she raced across the Library, coming to a dead stop in front of the Information Tours Desk where the person behind the desk appeared to know her well.

"Hey, Gladys. Where's my Mommy?" She asked.

Gladys pointed towards the orientation gallery where a group of about 25 people were watching the Library's historical film presentation. "She's getting ready to start a tour. Better hurry."

Zach spotted Meghan before Izzie did. She was standing off to the side of the benches in the small presentation area. As always, she looked radiant. She was dressed quite officially in a blue suit and low-heeled shoes. Izzie skipped towards her, all excited.

She looked back for a brief second at Zach and beckoned him to follow. "C'mon. I need to ask my Mommy something really important." She gave her mother a quick hug and immediately launched into her plan.

"Can Zach come to my birthday party tomorrow?"

Whoa. He hadn't seen that one coming. He smiled sheepishly at Meghan. She looked back apologetically at him. "Honey, your birthday is tomorrow, but your party is on Sunday. I'm sure Zach has more important things to do."

No, he didn't have anything more important to do, if it didn't involve being around Meghan. He had an even better idea. "I'd love to come to your birthday party on Sunday, but how about I take both you and your Mom out to a special dinner tomorrow night to celebrate your big day?"

Izzie's eyes lit up with excitement. "Can we do pepperoni pizza and root beer floats?"

Zach looked to Meghan knowing he was totally putting her on the spot. "If your mother says 'yes' then most definitely."

Izzie hung on her mother's arm, jumping up and down with hopeful glee. "Mommy--please say, yes. Please! Please!"

Meghan gave him a questioning look, which said: 'Are you really sure you want to do this?'

Hell, yes. He nodded, flashing her a brilliant smile. Izzie liked him. It was a start. Of course, she thought she was dealing with an angel on a mission, but if it got him closer to her mother, he would take it and shamelessly run with it.

Chapter 14

Cali was starting to get used to having a 'deep throat' source. Whoever they were knew her nightly news schedule deadline. Not too late and not too early. Enough time for her to make it in the nightly news line-up or knock another breaking story of lesser interest lower down in the cue. Whenever her computer was taken over, as it had been twice before this week, her pulse raced with new possibilities versus fears of being hacked.

Yesterday, everyone was looking at her like the new emerging queen of investigative journalism. Today was like hitting the motherlode. At exactly 3:33 pm alerts came in on both her phone and her computer of an URGENT incoming message:

"Ask yourself why C.S. would want Sawyer killed? Follow the money."

Oh. My. God. Cali could hardly believe her eyes. The murder video was bad enough, but this little gem showed Constantine Stavros admitting to his complicity in the murder! And naked as well! How in God's name was she going to air something like this? If she sold it to a rag magazine, or even Stavros himself, she could make millions and just retire now. But then she, too, might land up dead like Sawyer.

She glanced up to see Frank Carlisle, her producer, heading down the newsroom aisle straight for her little cubicle. He didn't stop to make small talk about sports scores with any of the male writers, which he often did. The look on his face told her something serious had just gone down.

"Grab a crew and get over to the Central Detention Facility. I just got word that Lee Vargas committed suicide."

She was stunned. Vargas had been silenced just like Sawyer. "How did he do it?"

"Hung himself. Ironic, huh?"

More like karmic justice, she thought. But now she knew there were bigger fish to fry. "I just got this in from my source, Frank. I think you should look at it. It's pretty damning stuff." She played him the Stavros video, watching for his reaction.

Frank looked stricken. "Fuck… Elizabeth and Stavros are very good friends."

Elizabeth Vandam was the owner of WWGO-TV along with a number of other multi-media family-run conglomerates. Would she try to kill the story to protect her friend? Did Stavros have Vargas killed to silence him from pointing the finger at him? She realized that this was one of those stories that would have to go through the legal department as well. They could get slapped with a false accusation or libel and slander case and Vandam might deep-six it for that reason alone, even with the naked part blurred out.

"Send me a copy of that video, now," Frank instructed. "I'll need to take this upstairs first."

Red storm warning flags went off in her head when she heard that. She knew she had to preserve this footage in the event it mysteriously got erased off her computer.

"Sure thing," she acquiesced. "I'll do that now and then get over to the jail."

As soon as Frank disappeared, Cali not only sent a copy to him, but to her private cloud storage server as well. Begrudgingly, she texted a copy of the video to Lieutenant Hanlon. After all, she *had* promised him. He had better be her insurance policy. She definitely didn't want to land up spending her remaining days in some witness protection program trying to avoid sex trafficking murderers. Everyone knew Stavros was a very powerful man with global tentacles. Who would have thought he was also a pervert and pedophile?

~~*~~

Bad news often spreads like wildfire. Less than 30 minutes later, Stavros heard about the video's existence from Senator Talbot who got it directly from Elizabeth Vandam—both known messengers of doom. His executive assistant had to pull him out of a very important meeting with the Board of Governors of the Federal Reserve System to inform him the Senator was on the phone and it was URGENT that he drop everything. That only served to piss him off. No one told him what to do--ever.

Stavros left the conference room and walked the few steps to his private office to take the call away from prying eyes. "What's so goddamn important I need to be pulled away from business? It had better be good, Jim."

He listened, his eyes bulging in anger. He sat down in his chair, trying to steady his breathing so he wouldn't have a heart attack. Fear flooded through his veins. Vargas had been eliminated, so how had this new information leaked out?

"So, you're telling me some smart-ass reporter has the goods on me? A video? That's impossible. Is this a joke or are you just fuckin' crazy?"

Stavros brought up his personal email on his large screen desktop.

"Yeah, I see your link…"

He clicked on the link and his screen brought up the footage of his flabby round and sweaty body in the sauna of his home—spilling his guts out to that flunky, Vargas. Fuck!

"Kill this video! Do you hear me? Take care of any copies immediately." He had never been so angry or scared. But he was Constantine Stavros. No one screwed with him or any of his enterprises. He would get even. He hung up the phone still swearing. "Fuck those fuckers!"

~~*~~

Zach was diligently at work deciphering the code Roone had used in his journal. He had reserved this task for the privacy of his own place, on his own security-protected equipment and not in the public confines of the Library. Truthfully, he wasn't sure what was safe in the Library anymore. Minerva might be anywhere and everywhere. He reread the first passage, which Roone had written rather cryptically:

"If you have gotten this far, it means I am no longer there to guide a friend and you have found your own way into ZE3. I'm sure you have already surmised, on some level, what you may be dealing with. My records, if you can access them through 'S' should tell my full story. The layers are multi-faceted and run deep. The players are everywhere. The task at hand was something beyond my ability and scope. I trust that you, my friend, will be more successful…"

Zach made some notes. S=Satya, ZE3=LOT. He hesitated, then scratched out the last entry. Why the designation '3'? Were there other LOTs? He put a question mark next to it. Most definitely he needed to access Roone's life files, but would Satya let him? Hadn't she already quarantined Roone's death record away from prying eyes? Who else might want to see it? As for the "players", he assumed this referred to Minerva. He continued reading:

"Be careful what you look into, as there is no turning back. This was a painful lesson for me. As you can see, I am no longer. There is a record of everything. Past, present and future are all simultaneous events in ZE3. There is no linear time as you know it…"

Zach laid down his pen and leaned back in his chair. The enormity of what he had just read really hit him. No linear time. It meant anyone could predict future events and probable outcomes with LOT knowledge which were all happening simultaneously. So far, he had only been accessing the past and there were enough questions there to fill several lifetimes of investigation.

This put a whole new spin on things. Was Minerva using the LOT for their own worldwide gain? That would mean anyone interfering with their plans or horning in on their knowledge base would get them immediately killed—like Roone. They would come after him. No matter how clever he was, he knew they would find him. It was only a matter of time—and perhaps one unfortunate slip up on his part.

Zach's phone alert brought him back to reality. The alert notified him that WWGO-TV had just run a breaking story by Cali Cavaleri. She was reporting from the steps of a detention facility that Lee Vargas, murderer of Librarian of Congress' Roone Sawyer, had just committed suicide inside his jail cell.

The County Coroner's van was nicely fitted into the background frame as two EMTs whisked out a gurney carrying a white draped body towards their emergency vehicle. Apparently, Vargas had hung himself without a soul ever noticing or stopping him. Security cameras on his cell block had all conveniently malfunctioned. Fat chance of that ever happening, Zach thought. More likely he, too, was murdered.

Zach waited for the final bombshell part of the news story to be unveiled. The big Stavros' confession tape revealing the billionaire was also behind the Potomac killings, had arranged multiple deaths to cover up his crimes, was corrupt and dirty--but it never came. Someone had gotten to Cali. This was the story of a lifetime, and she was sitting on the most explosive part?

His anger and frustration caused fireworks to go off in his head. Colors and numbers started crashing into each other like bumper cars at a carnival. He immediately went into a series of Qigong postures to quiet the energy and regain control. It was often within these meditative states he had his best insights and ideas. When the numbers started turning into geometric shapes of form and order, he felt a flooding sense of calm and wellbeing move in. After around 30 minutes of mind and body therapy, he knew he would have to take matters into his own hands. He could no longer count on Cali to do the work for him.

Zach knew his way around the Dark Web, the forum chat rooms, and how to remain anonymous with the other freaks and geeks, and hackers out there while leaving no trace. Yes, the NSA tracked everything, but using some of their own algorithm software for intelligence gathering, one could still manage to insulate themselves from detection and remain anonymous if they were smart and clever enough.

Before the night was over, Zach had uploaded an unmarked, untagged version of the Stavros Steam Room Confession to every media source, newsfeed and hacker's forum of any note. By dawn tomorrow everyone in the world would know about Constantine Stavros' dirty little secret.

~~*~~

Cali awakened in the darkness of night to the pressure of a hand shoved up against her mouth stifling her scream. Someone or something was on her bed, looming over her. All she saw was a dark male hulk. She kicked out struggling--trying to reach for her Glock 42 handgun she kept in a nightstand drawer by the bed. She couldn't reach it. Her knee made contact with the man's balls and she went for it. He grunted, feeling the pain. Good, take that you bastard!

She was half out of her mind with fright. And now she could sense he was mad. He captured both of her hands in a tightened grip, straddling her so she was unable to move. She watched in fear as he leaned down close to her ear.

"Be a good girl, Cali," he whispered. "Stop struggling. All I need is your source, so talk and I'll give you whatever you need."

Oh. My. God. She would know that voice anywhere. It sent instant tingles through her body down to parts that had lain dormant for a while. Fuck the bastard! He still had the power to make her seek out his hardness, his blatant sexuality, like a wanton craving a much needed fix.

They were polar opposites in so many ways, but magnetically they would be forever drawn to each other. Fiery, passionate, and even now, as in the past, her body continued to betray her even though she knew better. Damn him to hell for doing this to her!

FBI Agent R. J. Bond felt her go limp beneath him. He knew she would cave. She was a creature of desire. He removed his hand from her mouth and let it linger, slowly caressing down her neck.

"Fuck you!" she spat out, taking a breath while glaring at him.

She had always been a little spitfire, and this time was no disappointment. He loved that about her. But he had his own life to lead and it didn't entail a long lasting relationship with her outside of the occasional sex marathon they might engage in every blue moon.

She had accused him on numerous occasions of being commitment phobic. He shrugged off the assessment. Even if true, he would never admit she was right or that he loved his job more than he could love her or any woman for that matter. They were entirely two separate compartments in his brain—Women & Work. He kept a lockdown on the first one—especially with Cali. She was like kryptonite to be around. Distance was born out of necessity.

In his line of work, those around you could get easily hurt—especially loved ones. He dealt with all kinds of shady characters. Some legit, some not so legit. He had enough shit on his conscience to torment him. He didn't need worrying about her safety weighing him down as well. Yet, there was something about Cali that made him keep coming back, like some karmic plague. She had something the Agency and other interested parties wanted from her. And they had sent him in to get the job done because he knew how to handle her. He agreed only because if they had sent anyone else there was the possibility she might really get hurt.

He ran his hand under the silky sheets, touching warm bare skin. As always, she was buck-naked. The little minx never did like wearing pajamas. He felt his blood run instantly hot. She never failed to turn him on, just through close proximity. Hell, yeah, he would be dammed to hell for doing this!

"Now Cali, that's no way to treat an old love," he scolded in a low yet seductive tone. His fingers slid down her throat and caressed her soft skin. She knew he could be deadly enough to squeeze the life out of her in seconds, but he moved lower. Her breath hitched in her throat as he began circling and teasing her now hardened nipples. It sent bolts of lightning straight down to her pussy, which was already wet and waiting for him. A soft moan escaped her lips. Damn him!

He continued to tease her private parts with his fingers. Her hand reached out to cup his hardened dick, but he gently pushed it aside. He was already compromised enough. He had information to obtain before his dick would be allowed to find any relief.

There was too much blood flow moving to his lower half right now, not enough to his brain. He remembered the purpose of his mission and plunged two long fingers deep inside her, eliciting a louder moan. She was dripping wet with desire. His fingers sought out that sensitive spot on her upper vaginal wall, where he could keep her on the edge indefinitely, while rubbing her clitoris. He knew what she liked and he prided himself on it. Her breathing quickened as he rubbed harder. Her eyes were shut--pure bliss written across her face. He could feel her inner lips tightening and contracting…

"I know you want this, baby," he whispered. "Come for me--hard and fast and I'll fuck you all night the way you like. Just tell me whom you're working with first. Who is your video source?"

Cali's brain kicked into overdrive sending her body to a screeching halt. What the fuck?! Did he take her for a total idiot? An easy mark? He just wanted her deep throat source. The bastard always wanted it his way. Two could play this fucked up game.

She rolled hard to the side, catching him off guard and forcing him to roll with her until she was on top and straddling him. Now who was the dominant one? She quickly made fast work of unzipping his pants, freeing his hardened manhood and impaling herself on it. If he had any psychological fears of "vagina dentata," then he better start worrying. She clenched her vaginal lips tightly around him, milking him. A loud groan escaped his lips and she watched his eyes roll back in his head. Oh, yeah. She could easily devour him now if she wanted to.

She began riding him, letting her own orgasm rip through her then immediately pulling out before he was done, leaving him hanging. A total cock tease. Yep, guilty as charged. Her feminine warrior energy did a little dance of triumph. Don't ever fuck with me again, it said!

"Now tell me who sent *YOU!*" she demanded, slapping him across the face. "And after tonight don't you ever even think of coming back here again you traitorous piece of shit!"

Chapter 15

Constantine Stavros had spent a lifetime giving orders, running financial empires, and setting international banking policy. His minions spanned the globe, knowing he could make or break their fortunes with just a well-placed word in the right person's ear. When he spoke, others always listened. It had been that way for decades since he had made his first million illegally at the age of 22 transporting oil and gas parts, then second-hand military equipment to third-world nations and banana republics who were on U.S. government sanctions lists. Some of the arms equipment he managed to procure was nothing more than junk saved from the scrap heap. On occasion it was known to blow up in some revolutionary's face, but that was never his problem. Lives were expendable in both war and business. His business policy was 'take it or leave it'. Only a fool promised a "money back guarantee".

What he was and would always be was a global specialist in "Plan B" services. He saw options others never saw. Truthfully, he didn't care who or what anyone's personal politics were. Over the years, he found that the most cut-throat revolutionaries were easier to deal with. These animals were grateful for anything they could get their hands on to accomplish their ends. Maybe they were more like him than he wanted to admit. He had killed and he knew they would kill him in a heartbeat if they could. Many of these mercenaries were funded behind the scenes by elites to sow discord and chaos in order to reap the profits of the country once its government fell. It was an age-old tactic that had been going on since the beginning of time. Truth be known--humans were quite stupid. But the dumbest always paid him well.

Stavros' worldwide team of legal experts could find loopholes within any situation and conveniently sidestep the law. Some openly referred to him as a "King Cobra". He could slither out of most anything. His business practices were toxic like a snake's venom. The royalty and elites were often the first ones who came running to him for help and guidance. Ethics be damned.

Stavros prided himself as being an equal opportunity opportunist. His life, at least the white-washed version of it, read like a Horatio Alger rags to riches story. A poor immigrant from Greece, he had made opportunities in his life, not always legal, but which nevertheless made him a very wealthy man. As a result, he had bought up struggling banks and provided financial secrecy havens for governments and the rich and powerful. The banking world gave him legitimacy--an open door, but human trafficking was the icing on his cake. Selling sex was a commodity that never ran out of buyers--the younger the better. Thousands of kids, both kidnapped and sold, were smuggled each month into other countries to feed the insatiable desires of the most twisted of minds. His own network was mammoth and far-reaching. No one would ever suspect Constantine Stavros of running the world's largest sex slave trade.

Up until now, Stavros had always considered himself

"untouchable", quintessentially exempt from the rule of law unlike the rest of society. He was and had always been protected by the most powerful of men that made up the brethren of Minerva. For decades he had sat on the board of Minerva, one of the elite 12 individuals whose decisions ran the world. Their source of information was infinite and all-knowing. Their individual identities had all been sworn to secrecy. At no time, would they ever divulge their true purpose within the ranks of Minerva.

Minerva knew exactly what he did best, and they used him to sexually entrap others to play their games of conquest and capitulation. Minerva had made each and every one of the 12 members rich and powerful beyond their wildest dreams. It had made them godlike to decide others' fates.

Now, for the first time in his life, Stavros found himself on the other side of the fence having to explain that damn fucking video. No sooner had he hung up the phone on Jim Talbot giving him the bad news than Minerva's agents had swooped in and whisked Stavros away to the other side of the world for an "unscheduled meeting".

He took his usual seat with the other men sitting around the large round conference table, noticing that many avoided direct eye contact with him. It was a quiet, somber assemblage. He watched the Supreme Governor of Minerva, who no one ever addressed by name, look around the table, nodding to each man, before picking up his pipe and taking a few thoughtful puffs. The meeting had begun.

"Connie, we have a serious situation..." he began. Minerva's long term "Governor" had never addressed him by his nickname in all the years he had served on the board. This did not bode well. Stavros wasted no time getting to the point.

"Gentlemen, I can assure you that there are no breaches in MY network," he began pointedly looking to each man. "It is virtually impossible to obtain a video conversation inside my own personal sauna. This I can guarantee."

"Yet someone did," the Governor calmly pointed out.

This questioning of him was preposterous. "The entire building is swept for bugs twice, sometimes three times a day. There are no cameras inside the steam room and the walls are lined with impenetrable steel!" Stavros was trying to keep the frustration out of his voice, but the calmer they got the more agitated he felt. The balance of power was slipping, and he sensed the meeting was not going in his favor.

The man to the left of the Governor, recognized respectfully as the "Counselor", spoke up. His words were chilling. "Your problem has now become our problem. It threatens us all. How do you intend to correct it?"

"Correct it?" He had barely time to catch his breath before they brought him here without any notice. That was a bad sign. He could only remember that happening once before during his time with Minerva.

Stavros sat forward in his chair. He would find who was behind this video leak if it was the last thing he ever did. But right now, he would have to request something he had never done before.

"I demand primary portal access into the LOT for answers."

His request was met with dead silence. Access into the LOT was reserved only for the Governor and the Counselor, which he had always thought was a handicap to the rest of the group. Up until now he had kept that opinion to himself, but it was the only way to get at the truth.

"Well?" he said impatiently, drumming his fingers on the table.

A few of the members immediately glanced towards Minerva's Governor and Counselor for their reaction. Both men remained silent, their thoughts unreadable, but tension could be felt all around the table. No one challenged those in charge of Minerva, ever. It was unthinkable and dangerous. Stavros had just broken a key rule.

The silence in the room stretched on for what seemed an indefinite period of time until the Governor finally rose from his chair. All eyes were upon him as he took a long drag on his pipe and motioned Stavros to leave, dismissing him with a slight wave of his hand.

"Please wait outside while we discuss this matter."

Stavros remained unmovable in his chair.

"Leave now," the Governor repeated.

Stavros lost his tongue, fury coursing through him. "I am a long-time member of this group and I respectfully demand to stay. I will not be dismissed. I can fix this!" The second it came out of his mouth he knew he had made an even bigger mistake—perhaps the last one of his life.

The Governor calmly extracted a black device from his inner jacket pocket and extended it towards Stavros. A second later, Constantine Stavros slumped to the ground unconscious. Security came in and immediately removed him from the room.

The Governor sat back down in his chair, the black device securely tucked back in his pocket. "The man has become a liability to Minerva. We have others to take over his network and fill our needs." He paused, taking a dramatic puff on his pipe, before calmly suggesting a solution. "I propose immediate re-harvesting."

Again, no one said a word. Everyone there knew what that meant. They had each taken a solemn oath to Minerva to serve unquestioningly in order to reap the vast rewards. Each year in a ritual ceremony they would re-take that same vow of obedience for the power it reaped. It was understood by everyone that should any of them be compromised, death would be the only answer.

The Counselor looked to each person. "Are we all in

agreement?"

The question was really a non-question. The rules would be adhered to no matter what. A universal nod of agreement was seen around the table. Constantine Stavros would be no more, but business would go on as usual.

~~*~~

There was clearly a problem in the LOT. Minerva had never lost a live-stream video feed to the Library of Congress portal, but here it was several days later from when it first happened and they had still been unable to remedy the situation or pinpoint its cause. This was very disturbing on many levels. All surveillance in and out of the LOC had been completely severed. And while Minerva suspected a breach, there was no way to be certain. Satya was being noncommittal in their efforts to find answers.

Both the Governor and the Counselor had gone into the LOT demanding to get to the bottom of things. That Stavros thought *he* would find answers in the LOT was downright laughable when even they were at a loss. The issue of a possible portal breach was something they had decided not to openly discuss within the member group. They had purposely met in another conference room to avoid anyone viewing portal monitoring screens and asking probing questions.

The Counselor confirmed what the Governor had also experienced.

"Yes, Satya is being difficult. She is nowhere to be seen for any help. Record events are sometimes missing, or I find other events substituted in their place. It's never been this disorganized in there before. Something is not right."

The Governor was also concerned. "She's hiding the truth from us. She may be working with another group—possibly even against us."

"Can she do that... Hide the truth from us?"

It was a good question. One the Governor didn't have an answer for. He had never accessed Satya's personal files in the LOT to shed light on her responsibilities and duties, if such a thing was even allowed. The woman, or whatever she was, had always been there, from what he knew, and would probably still be there long after all the rest of them were dead and gone. As always, she continued to remain an enigma.

"She may need to be replaced," he thought aloud. But what if she was immortal?

"Yes. Perhaps she could be re-harvested as well," the Counselor suggested.

They both fell silent contemplating that option. Who in the world would they replace her with? Yet, something needed to be done right now. There was an information road block to who or what had caused the Portal 3 live-stream to go dead, as well as who had used the LOT to access that damning video on both Vargas and Stavros, who were now thankfully eliminated.

Loose ends were always immediately taken care of by the council. Nothing could ever point back to Minerva. They had existed this long, and they would continue to exist for centuries to come. The Governor reminded himself to look back in Minerva archives and see if something like this had ever happened before.

They had put out feelers in the intelligence community to look at who was feeding that TV reporter Cavaleri information and who was behind leaking it to the global internet. They were now watching very closely. All their sources were on high alert. While Minerva could easily eliminate that troublesome TV reporter at any given moment, they might not catch their true leak if they acted too hastily. M-12 could wait it out a little longer. Eventually they would find their mark.

More importantly, they feared what other information this person or persons might have obtained on Minerva and how they would use it? Satya knew something and she wasn't talking, which was very disturbing.

The LOT had been their sole information playground for centuries. How could someone even dare threaten their power and control of global knowledge? It filled both men with dread and rage. They, too, could be eliminated unless they did something about it now.

Chapter 16

Cali was madder than hell. Who had leaked her Stavros tape on the internet? She sure as hell didn't believe it was anyone at the station. Only Frank, Vandam and Legal had seen it. Was it someone on Lt. Hanlon's team?

She had called Hanlon first thing this morning, after dumping Bond out of her apartment and hopefully out of her life. Thank you very much for that spectacular orgasm! Bond had told her nothing and she had told him nothing in return, only because she didn't have a clue who her deep throat source was. And with the viral spread of the video all over the global internet, possibly a gazillion hits by now, it thankfully served to draw the heat away from her. She certainly hadn't found a way to anonymously give every corner of the planet a birds-eye view of Stavros' shrunken little dick. A disgusting thought, which even now was hard to erase from her mind--unless, of course, she replaced it with Bond's. No. No. No. Cancel, clear, delete. She was not going down that road again.

Unfortunately, her mind was not yet ready to let go of that vivid image. Imagine him thinking he could wheedle info out of her just by dangling his big dick in front of her! The thought made her swear like a truck driver--perhaps a bit too loudly. Heads bobbed up across the newsroom cubicles to stare at her. Okay Cali, get it together. Enough already. Shut the fuck up!

Now Hanlon was telling her that not only did his team not leak the video, but now Stavros had gone missing as well. No one had seen or heard from him. Just vanished into thin air. His private planes were still in their pristine hangars, his fleet of expensive cars were all accounted for, and his cell phone records had been wiped clean. How very convenient!

But where did that leave her? She was back to square one, unless her source could send her a proof of life video of Stavros alive and well cavorting on some private island somewhere. Perhaps he might have even decided to fake his own death to escape justice? The rich and powerful were certainly capable of pulling off such a thing. Would that be the next shoe to drop?

Cali was damn frustrated with this turn of events. This was all Elizabeth Vandam's fault—and Frank's, too! Had they allowed her to do her job and report this breaking scandal, instead of giving Stavros the heads up to hightail it out of the country, and out of extradition range, then right now she would be basking in her scoop of the decade. Now that everyone who possessed an internet connection had probably already seen the damning tape, it was totally worthless to her.

Don't think for a moment she hadn't made her feelings known to Frank. Spineless little weasel. Were they in the business of reporting the news or protecting rich and powerful people who thought the law didn't apply to them? She continued to fume. At times like this she wished she could still drink. A bottle of Malbec would do just fine right now to numb her seething anger.

She made a note to attend an AA Meeting in Georgetown tonight to exorcise such demon thoughts. Backsliding was not an option—now or ever. Silently she remembered to recite the AA

Serenity Prayer instead of calling her sponsor:

"God grant me the Serenity to accept the things I cannot change, the Courage to change the things I can and the Wisdom to know the difference."

Oh yeah. She was already thinking more clearly. Next time she would have the wisdom to bypass corporate altogether and post it on her Twitter account instead.

~~*~~

Zach awoke that morning knowing that today would mark a turning point for him. He felt excitement deep within him, despite not being able to point to anything in particular which he could attribute it to. He assumed it might have something to do with meeting Meghan and Izzie after work to celebrate Izzie's 7th birthday. He had made reservations at Il Rinnovo in Georgetown, knowing Izzie would get the best Meat Lover's Napolitano pizza he knew of. It had always been a favorite Italian restaurant of his since it opened in 2010 and his family knew the owner.

Special arrangements had been made at Il Rinnovo just for Izzie. He had tried to think of everything to make it perfect. Down in the condo's parking garage he pulled the cover off a slate grey Lexus LC-500 that his family used for guests. It started up on the first attempt and had an almost full tank of gas. He would drive it to work today so he wouldn't have to rely on an Uber later.

Zach wasn't sure if tonight could technically be classified as a "date" date. He might secretly hope so, but he knew women could be squirrelly about labeling such things. It was best not to let his thoughts and desires get ahead of him. Better to let things develop and just give them both a fun evening. He hadn't had much fun in a long time, outside of last night's flooding the world-wide web with the Stavros video. The internet had gone wild. It was one of the most viewed viral videos of all time. The media platforms kept trying to censor it and pull it down, but it kept popping up again everywhere. Zach bet Cali Cavaleri had wished she had acted sooner and not killed the story. She was probably, right now, cursing him for pre-empting her scoop. Next time she would think faster on her feet—if there was a next time.

Which brought Zach back to his plan. The morning news was filled with reports of Stavros' timely disappearance. The Feds had gone to arrest him and he had slid right through their fingers without a trace. Zach intended to rectify that. The man needed to pay for his crimes. The firing squad would be too good for him with all the deaths he had been responsible for.

Zach had every intention of going into the LOT today and finding out where the man was hiding. Nothing would stop him from tracking him down. Now that everyone knew Stavros' face and what he had done, no place would be safe for him.

But Mrs. Friedman kept giving him new assignments on top of his existing work: writing new algorithm scripts for processing foreign data entry, doing an update of the missing items from the rare manuscripts vault, and just when he thought he might sneak away to the LOT, she brought by some new interns to show how to pull information from different Stacks all over the Library.

Since time essentially stood still in this Library when one was in the LOT, you would think it wouldn't make much difference if he snuck away or not for a few minutes, but he had literally not been able to get a moment's free time to himself and he couldn't take the chance of activating entry into the LOT from the men's room and someone seeing him disappear. Finally at the end of the day, about 30 minutes from when he planned to meet up with Meghan and Izzie at the Library's main entrance, he was able to steal himself away to the Coolidge Auditorium, on the Ground Floor, which he knew would be empty at this time.

Zach slipped past the posted red and white lettered sign informing the public "The "Auditorium Is Closed". He peeked through the porthole windows of the double entry doors, confirming no one was inside, then entered. Only a faint dim light from onstage lit the auditorium interior. He didn't need illumination for his purpose. He sat down on the first step leading down to the stage, retrieved Gizmo from his pocket and quickly started the algorithm sequence in his head.

He heard a slight sound near the door, but it was already too late. The walls were rippling and re-entry had begun when he felt a small hand grasp his shoulder from behind. Too late, he realized Izzie March was now holding onto him for dear life, a terrified look on her pale face as they were both sucked through the portal at warp speed. He had the presence of mind to grab her tight against him and wondered how in hell he would ever explain this to her or her mother.

They landed just where he thought they would land inside the LOT, but this time he was careful to break her fall. Pretty in pink, she landed atop him like a ball of fluffy cotton candy. Still bug-eyed and disoriented, he quickly righted her to her feet where she wasted no time in stepping forward—her eyes going in all directions to view the vast expanse of silver vaults.

Her mouth was wide open in that funny little "O" expression he had seen before. "What is this place?" she asked in a whisper.

A small hiccup escaped her, followed closely by another. She slid her hand to her mouth in embarrassment before adding, "Oh. My. Is this where angels go?"

He would have to do damage control quickly. "It's a library inside a library," he began, scrambling to his feet. "It's where stories and memories are kept."

"I've never seen this part of the Library before. Does my Mommy know about this?"

"No, I'm pretty sure she doesn't. It's a secret place. Only a few people know about it and how to get here."

He was averse to ever asking any child to keep a secret from their parent, so he treaded carefully with his next words.

"I think if you told her about this place, she would get that worried look on her face that you told me about."

She frowned deeply, scrunching her brows together with another hiccup. "That look?"

He nodded, picturing Meghan doing much more than that look if she found out he had just propelled her daughter into another dimension.

Izzie seemed to take that under some consideration. Her brain reviewed her options and a decision must have been made. She suddenly smiled and skipped forward, happily taking his hand in hers. "Okay. Show me what you do here."

He scrapped his plans for finding Stavros' hideaway. Not with Izzie here, especially considering she might remember Stavros' face from their party. Her grandfather knew the man. He wasn't sure how familiar Izzie might be with him as well. He would come back later to deal with Stavros.

Another hiccup escaped her lips as she ran her hands over the shiny smooth silver walls. "This one is warm," she said putting both hands up to feel it. She then put her ear up against the wall to listen. "I can't hear anything inside. What kind of stories and memories are kept here?"

"All kinds," he replied. "Would you like to pick a memory you want to see?"

She tilted her head to the side not sure. "Like what?"

"Maybe something that you've always wondered about. Something special…"

Her face lit up at once with an idea. "Can I see a memory of my Daddy?"

Zach wasn't sure if this was such a good idea since he knew nothing about Brett March. Where was Satya? She would know the right thing to show Izzie. But Satya was nowhere to be seen. Probably because Satya did not want to be seen by an almost seven-year-old little girl who might start talking about her. He was on his own on this one.

"Okay. I think we can find a memory that entails both you and your Daddy."

"But he died before I was born. I've only seen him in pictures," she said sadly. She looked at Zach, nervously twisting the fabric of her pink dress between her fingers, trying to hide her disappointment before whispering, "We have no memories together."

"Well, let's see about that." He suddenly had an idea. "I think we can make this an extra special birthday present. What do you say, Izzie? Are you game?"

She nodded and hiccupped. "Oh yes. What do I have to do?"

"Think about how much you want to see your Daddy and I'll do the rest."

He watched her close her eyes and screw up her face in an earnest attempt to make her wish come true. He amplified her intent with his own. The streams of rainbow-colored lights started shooting out from everywhere. The kid was going to love this.

Zach nudged her. "Open your eyes, Izzie."

He watched her eyes light up like a Broadway marquee as the display of colors swirled from all around into formation. Her little hands came together, clapping in sheer delight while her feet began a happy dance.

"Oh, my. Oh, my," she kept repeating, her hiccups miraculously gone. Izzie held her breath in awe at the vision coming to life before her. A hologram picture emerged of both her mother and father dining at a restaurant. He prompted Izzie to follow him into the memory, where she immediately went to her parents and started talking to them.

"Mommy and Daddy—it's me Izzie." When they paid no attention to her and continued to speak to each other, Izzie spoke louder. "Can't you see me?"

To Zach's dismay, he recognized the eatery as Il Rinnovo, the very restaurant he had planned to take both Izzie and Meghan to this evening. What were the chances of that happening? About one in a thousand or, to be more exact, one in 2235, the number of restaurants in the D.C. area, not counting current closures or openings. A useless fact, but his brain couldn't help doing the calculations.

He tried to listen in on their conversation, but Izzie kept pulling on his hand impatiently.

"Why can't they see me, Zach?"

"This is in the past, Izzie. Listen closely. Your Mommy is telling your Daddy that they are going to have a baby. That's you they're talking about."

Izzie got really quiet. She went over to her father, wanting to touch him, but came up against a hard energetic wall, just like Zach had in earlier holograms. She looked perplexed, then like she wanted to cry, but she held back her tears. Zach sat down at the table where her parents were dining and let her sit on his lap instead as they watched the memory play out together.

While Izzie was enthralled with watching her father's face and hearing the sound of his deep voice, Zach was paying closer attention to the subtext going on between the couple. He felt like a voyeur watching one of Meghan's most personal moments. There was a part of him which tried not to think about how intrusive this was—like reading someone's diary.

"My Daddy is very handsome." Izzie remarked watching him eat his pizza.

"Yes, he is," Zach quietly replied.

"He was a test pilot for the Air Force. Mommy told me he was top of his class."

Zach smiled. She was really enjoying seeing her father. More interesting to him was the revelation that Brett did not seem completely enthralled at the news he would soon become a father.

He hoped Izzie had not picked up on that fact. He heard Brett ask Meghan if she had forgotten to take her pills and how had this happened. Had she not been careful? Meghan barely picked at her cannelloni pasta. She moved her fork around the plate listlessly. A fake smile was plastered across her face. There was no light in her eyes. Even he could see she was terribly disappointed with her husband's reaction. Something was definitely wrong between these two. The love seemed to have gone out and he felt it best to get Izzie out of there before she realized it.

Meghan dropped her fork on her plate, her face quickly turning a pale shade of green. She pushed her chair away from the dining table, covered her mouth and made a hasty beeline for the ladies' room. She was ill. He wasn't sure if it was from Brett's lack of interest or morning sickness. Izzie jumped off his lap and went chasing after her mother.

Brett wolfed down his pizza and continued to look put out. He fiddled on his phone, sent a few text messages and didn't seem even remotely concerned that his pregnant wife had just run off sick and had yet to return.

Zach then witnessed another perturbing event that he was also glad Izzie had not seen. A pretty young waitress came over to the table asking Brett if he needed anything else—dessert maybe? She smiled at Brett and he flashed her an interested smile right back. Zach then watched the two blatantly flirt with each other. Brett curtailed his shameless displays when he saw Meghan returning to the table, Izzie trailing right behind her.

Izzie stood next to Zach, making a disgusting face. "Ugh, she threw up! I guess she didn't like that cannelloni." She looked down at her feet, suddenly becoming quiet and thoughtful.

Zach immediately rose to his feet. He had seen enough. The memory immediately stopped because he wanted it to stop. Every last remnant of Meghan's pregnancy announcement dissipated back into their silver drawers and they were back in the silent

LOT once more.

Izzie looked up at him beseechingly. "Can't we see just one more?" She turned all doe-eyed on him. "Pretty please? For my birthday?" He was such a sucker.

"Alright. Just one more. What do you want to see?"

"Can I see my Daddy flying his plane?"

That seemed like a harmless request, just as long as it wasn't the record of her father's actual plane crash. Neither of them wanted to see that. Zach set his intent for her and the process of accumulating all the bytes of data of the record came streaming into focus. This time Izzie kept her eyes open to watch the entire hologram form in front of her. As soon as it came to a complete stop, she ran right into it, no hesitation at all, already knowing what to do. Zach was only a few steps behind her.

The two of them found themselves on a busy runway at Andrews Air Force Base in Maryland where a squadron of F-35 stealth fighter planes, conducting touch and go training exercises, were taking off one right after the other. Ground crew control, wearing headphones, hand-signaled to pilots positioning themselves next in line for take-off. These grey sleek planes hit the skies under the control of experienced military aviators who knew how to handle fighter jets.

It was an incredible sight watching a plane do a vertical takeoff straight into the air then going to supersonic speed in less than 60 seconds. Zach knew that in the years that followed this same fleet of planes would be temporarily grounded due to manufacturing defects. He wasn't sure if this contributed to Brett March's plane crash and ultimate death, but he remembered Congress having investigated the defect problem.

The noise all around was deafening and Zach and Izzie put their hands over their ears to protect them. That's when Zach realized he had the ability to watch the event without sound or lowered volume. He gave the intent for the latter and they were both able to remain on the runway, sight unseen, as fighter jets flew over them—some so close he could practically read the tread on their tires. He felt just as excited as Izzie to observe this air show.

"Where's my Daddy?" Izzie wanted to know.

And with that thought, her father's plane was highlighted in the skies as it came in for a landing. His plane came to a complete stop right in front of where they stood on the runway. Brett March, looking like a real combat pilot, extracted himself from the cockpit and jumped to the ground wearing a green Air Force flight suit with an array of test pilot patches and the insignia designating his fighter squadron belonged to a special operations wing of the U.S. military.

Brett removed his helmet and aviator glasses and gave the maintenance crew worker heading his way the thumbs up sign. His short blonde hair rippled in the wind as he signed off flight papers and walked off to talk to another pilot doing a pre-flight check.

"Pretty cool, huh?' Zach said to Izzie.

She nodded in agreement, totally spellbound. He could see she had a bad case of hero worship. There were stars in her eyes as she followed her father's every move--memorializing it for all time. He felt a twinge of paternal protection that she was growing up without a father. While his own father was very much alive, it also felt like he no longer existed in Zach's world. They almost never spoke anymore. Izzie must be feeling that loss as he sometimes felt the loss of his own father.

"I have blonde hair, too," she stated matter-of-factly. He put his hand on her shoulder and led her quietly out of the hologram without protest. Reliving other people's memories could be emotionally draining, even as an observer.

"We need to get back," he told her. "We still have to meet your mom for your birthday dinner."

She thought about that, pursing her lips. "I wish I could stay longer and watch movies all day long."

"Your Mommy would miss you a lot if you stayed."

"Can you bring her here, too?" she asked hopefully.

He shook his head. "I'm sorry. That's not a good idea. I probably shouldn't have brought you here in the first place."

"But you didn't!" she pointed out. "I did it on my own! I was leaving the Young Reader's Room when I saw you go into the Auditorium. I was curious to see what was going on in there, so I followed you. Going through the tunnel was scary, but exciting. I'm glad I did, or I never would have seen where angels go---right?"

Well, he wasn't going to correct or argue with her logic. More concerning was what she might say once they got back to their own Library world—which was where they better get going right now.

He squatted down next to her. "Izzie, listen closely. I need you to hold on to me very tightly going back so we get back safely. Do you understand?"

She nodded her head and clasped both hands around his neck. "Okay, Zach." He rose to his feet picking her up against his chest to a standing position.

Having a second person along during the exiting process threw another unknown variable into the algorithm equation. Zach had no idea if it would make a difference. It hadn't seemed to upon getting there, but it crossed his mind he needed to proceed with caution.

He reached for Gizmo in his pocket and began the algorithm return sequence. Before he could stop her, because he had his hands full just holding her, Izzie reached out for it and put her hand over Gizmo to touch it. It turned red-hot in a split second, the portal opened, and they were both sucked through it.

Immediately, Zach felt a noticeable difference. Perhaps it was because he was returning with Izzie this time, who was practically doing a chokehold on him, but he knew something was very strange. The portal's energy had dramatically changed. It slowed down, then sped up in an alternating grid like pattern, then shot them both out of a stone slab into dark murky WATER. Water that was up to his waist. Holy shit!

Izzie practically crawled up his body frantically trying to escape the water drenching her pink stockings and lapping at the edge of her dress. He could feel the cold water penetrate his clothing.

"Where are we?!" she cried, scared out of her wits.

Zach didn't have a clue where they were or what had gone wrong. They were enveloped in total darkness all around them. He felt blinded by his inability to see even a few inches in front of him. There was no visible sign of light from anywhere.

Yet, Zach had the strange sense that something or someone was watching them. The feeling persisted and became stronger. He noted the water and air around them felt electrically charged. Was there something down here putting out an electromagnetic signal, or worse yet, was the area radioactive?

"I don't know." His sense of trepidation about possible contamination caused him to hoist her onto his tall shoulders to avoid any further water contact. She clutched him tighter.

"Hold on, Izzie. I'll get us out of here." He hoped he sounded more confident than he felt. With one hand he grasped both her legs to his chest and with the other fumbled around for his phone flashlight inside his shirt pocket. Izzie held on tightly to his head, her small hands covering his ears, but he could still hear her little whimpers. She didn't like being in the darkness. He would have hell to pay for this for sure when and if they made it back.

His flashlight came on illuminating the area, showing they were in some type of sizable underground chamber with water tunnels. He shone the light all around, thankful for having bought a waterproof cellphone. He quickly checked to find his battery charge at only 50 percent. It had lost some power in the re-entry sequence, but it hadn't stopped all together like last time.

The portal had unceremoniously ejected them out with a burst of energy onto a submerged stone slab. How they had managed to pass through thick stone, he wasn't sure. This was certainly turning into one hell of a day for surprises.

Shining the light down into the water, he could see that the rectangle-shaped slab had strange hieroglyphic markings that were worn and undecipherable. Something floated by them causing Izzie to scream. If water rats were down here, he might start screaming as well. But he was pretty sure they were not in sewerage water. It smelled too clean, despite the silt. But he had to stay calm for her sake. He flashed the light on it.

"What is it?" Izzie asked, looking down and to see if it was alive.

It surprised him when he recognized they were floating strips of wet papyrus paper tangled around slats of brown rotted wood. He frankly didn't know what to make of the yellowed parchment debris. Who used such things anymore? Papyrus paper was sturdy and waterproof and could stand the test of time, so dating it might prove futile. His analytic mind was in high alert in this strange environment. It was calculating distance, depth, air temperature, chamber wall material. In fact, there looked to be mica in the tunnel walls and the water itself had slight traces of salinity. Were they near the sea?

He flashed the light into a far corner and spotted the remains of a decayed wooden platform that was tilted to the side and sinking into the silty water. Much of the wood debris in the water must be from this collapsing structure, which might have once functioned as a small boat dock.

There was an entrance to a water tunnel in the opposite end of the chamber, which could lead anywhere--maybe to even more dark watery tunnels. He realized he was running out of options and had to make a decision quickly. He was grateful Izzie was not wailing up a storm. She seemed to be taking it all in, as curious as he was.

He waded towards the tunnel, feeling the weight of Izzie bearing down on him and the chill in the water, when his light picked up the reflection of a shiny object. He swung the light in that direction to discover a hand-wrought iron ladder hidden away in a recessed section of the wall.

"Look. A ladder!!" Izzie shouted, barely containing her relief. He headed that way instead. The odds were better that it might be a more direct route out of this watery hole than the tunnels. He could only hope and pray.

When he reached the ladder, he found there was a step up to a narrow ledge. And yet, several of the iron rungs were rusty and submerged under water. He suspected that this place, wherever they were, was susceptible to flooding. A hidden spring, or an outlet from the sea at high tide perhaps?

Zach tested the ladder's strength and it appeared to hold, but he couldn't be certain about the rest of it. Better to let Izzie, the lighter of the two, go first.

"I'm going to be right behind you, so you don't fall," he instructed, lifting her off his shoulders and onto a dry lower rung. She clung to the ladder in the dim light.

"Just go very slowly. Think of it as an adventure, Izzie. Okay?"

She murmured a soft "Okay" and bravely reached for the next rung.

"Wait a minute," he added before she could move up the ladder.

Izzie paused, looking back at him uncertainly. He spun around and quickly clicked several flash pictures of the space and the hieroglyphic stone slab they had emerged from. It had to have weighed several tons, so he hadn't even attempted to lift it open. While he inherently knew they needed to go back the way they had come, he had a burning desire to know where they were. He would figure the rest out soon enough—he hoped.

"Okay. Let's go," he said hovering close behind her back as they slowly climbed each rung together.

The ladder was old, but still strong. The two of them steadily climbed about 50 feet until the ladder brought them to another dirt level, which was completely dry, airless and dusty. Here they found another expansive chamber with seven large cavities carved out in the stone-wall to house some type of large object. Zach scanned the space with his light until it came to rest on two niches in the wall, which contained mammoth size black granite sarcophagi with slightly ajar heavy stone lids.

Izzie ran over to one trying to jump up to getter a better view of its contents. He went over and held her up so they could both peek inside.

"It's empty," Izzie said, clearly disappointed, before adding. "This is a very strange place." Once out of the watery hole, she was quickly regaining her confidence and curiosity.

He couldn't agree more and suspected when he saw the papyrus that they were no longer in Washington, D.C. Where were they and were they in current time? If they were back in real time, then right now Meghan would be looking for her daughter and terrified that she might have been abducted. What to do?

Izzie looked up at him, suddenly worried. "Zach, do you think there are snakes down here?"

"Nah." He sincerely hoped not. They needed to get out of here. There was another ladder on a far wall, leading closer to the surface. Just keep climbing he told himself. Once again, he snapped a few pics and motioned for her to follow him.

This time they climbed the ladder 25.8 feet, which didn't bring them to the surface, but into another spacious but empty chamber where the temperature felt noticeably warmer. Izzie looked almost disappointed to see there was no new discovery on this level to explore.

Again, they spotted a larger shaft over to the side with double side-by-side iron ladders, one looking much more rustic than the other. They opted for the newer ladder and slowly worked their way up what was to be an even longer ascent. He admired Izzie's stamina. She was a real trooper. No complaints and he suspected she was secretly thrilled to be along on this unexpected adventure. By Zach's calculations they had traversed approximately 147.3 feet from the water tunnels down below to the surface and the kid wasn't even dragging.

He felt the cool clean shafts of air hit his face as they reached surface level. He could see the nighttime sky lit by a bright full moon through the padlocked metal gate that would lead them back out to the real world. But first the padlock.

He examined the large keyhole lock. The old lock tumblers were easier to trip and less sophisticated than the newer ones. His new-found skill at lock-picking made this an easy task. From his now wet wallet, he extracted a small pick and within seconds sprung it open. He could see from Izzie's astonished look that he had just impressed the hell out of her.

They stepped through the gate into cool desert sand. All was quiet, not a soul around. The rays of the full moon illuminated directly ahead of them an old excavation site with limestone and granite block pillars resembling an ancient temple. Zach turned around already knowing where he was and what was behind him. He turned Izzie around to face what he was sure was her first ever look at the Great Pyramid on the Giza Plateau in Cairo, Egypt. As always, it was magnificent under a full moon.

"Wow!" was the only word to escape her lips.

Zach had been here before, but he hadn't known about the existence of the deep shafts leading down to the water tunnels and the dimensional portal now submerged under the stone slab, which led directly to the LOT. Had the ancients known about it? Had it been part of the Pharaoh's death ritual where he would float on a boat through the underworld to the next world where he would find enlightenment? The imagery was symbolically displayed on temple walls and ceilings. This would put the ancient stories, believed to be myth, into a whole different categorical understanding. This might be why they were obsessed with the ascension process into the next world. Did it all come back to the LOT? 'Wow' was right. This gave him a lot to think about. Might there be other portals scattered around the world as well leading back to his Library of Truth?

Zach put those deeper thoughts on hold for now, knowing he would get back to them. Right now, he had to find a way to get Izzie and him back to the Library pronto.

Zach could see lights in the distance from the crazy traffic of Cairo. Well. that certainly answered one question. At least they were back in the same century as the invention of electricity. But were they back in real time? Cairo was six hours ahead of Washington time or around 11:30 PM. He was supposed to be meeting Meghan and Izzie at the Library entrance right now for their dinner date.

But Izzie was reluctant to move. She stared up at the Great Pyramid, rubbing her eyes, not quite believing it was real and perhaps she was just dreaming it. Heaven only knew what was going on inside her little brain at that moment. He didn't have long to find out.

"How big is it? What's inside of it? Can we go there?" she rattled off before taking a breath and stating. "This place is soooo cool!"

Despite her visible enthrallment with the novelty of it all, her physical appearance was markedly bedraggled and dirty. Her porcelain complexion was now smudged. Her blonde curls were matted from sweat of being in a warm airless place. That once perky pink dress was closer to the color of dusty sand. Never in a million years could he explain her appearance away to her mother. He could only imagine, having waded through silty water what he himself might look like. But curiosity was the keystone to knowledge, so he took the time to answer her questions…

"When the original marble casing was still visible it would have been 480.69 feet tall, but now it's only 449.5 feet high. That's still very tall. At one time, it was once considered the tallest structure in the world, but not anymore. If you measure each side, it's approximately 755.75 feet wide with a total perimeter around of about 3023.22 feet." He tried to keep it simple for her age but had to add the most important factor: "The Great Pyramid is very special. It's based on the Phi ratio in sacred geometry..."

She rolled her eyes. "A pie? That's so silly."

"No. Not that kind of 'pie'. This is spelled P-H-I."

She seemed to be through with the concept of Phi. "I bet there's a gazillion stones."

"Not quite. It has 2.3 million blocks of limestone and granite with some weighing as much 80 tons each."

"WOW! Is there a mummy inside?"

"No mummy," he said. "They've never found a mummy inside any of the pyramids, but many have been found beneath the ground where we stand."

"Oh." She looked down at the sand. "They don't come out at night, do they?"

He hid an amused smile. "Nope. They've all gone to the afterlife."

"Oh. Is that like heaven?"

"Yeah, like heaven."

"Can we go inside the pyramid and look around?"

"Not this time." He fudged on that answer. Hopefully, he

would never find himself in this predicament with her a second time to even consider such an option.

He knew he was already screwed being here, so he figured he might as well show her the Sphinx. "Follow me," he said before whispering. "There are night guards on the Giza Plateau. So, let's try to not get caught. Stay close."

Izzie's eyes darted about in every direction. "What will they do if they catch us?" she whispered back.

"Throw us in an Egyptian jail."

From the cascade of number twos he could see streaming out of her little head, it was evident she was worrying about the likelihood of such a horror actually occurring. He had to remember not to say such things, even in jest. She was just a kid. Besides, they had Gizmo's cloaking ability--a backup plan he decided not to share.

"Don't worry. I won't let that happen to you." She looked only slightly assured. The stream of twos slowed down, but she furtively hugged the shadows close to him. They avoided using his flashlight, fearing they would be detected, so there was only moonlight to guide each step. Sand moguls and loose stones were still strewn all over this ancient archeological site. One could easily trip and fall, and he didn't want to take the chance of having either of them hurt. Slowly and steadily, he led her down from the public's elevated viewing platform to ground level where few were allowed entry. All was quiet in the darkness of the night.

Zach had still not figured out a way to return them to the Library of Congress or the LOT. His mind searched for a solution--any answer. They couldn't stay here in Egypt. And they couldn't fly back without causing a hell storm among multiple parties—especially Meghan. They didn't even have passports. He took a moment to reflect, leaning up against the stone dream stele located between the great paws of the Sphinx, behind the prophet's pulpit. Think, Zach, think, he told himself.

That's when he had an unexpected revelation. It flooded over him like a wave of serenity, followed by a cosmic opening, an expansion of consciousness where all options were suddenly made known to him. It was the most profound moment of clarity he could ever remember having. Not even in his deepest meditation had this occurred. Perhaps it was what the Masters strived to attain, because it was beyond words. It WAS.

In this state his mind he felt Oneness with the LOT and to all information it possessed. In that moment a direct link was established, patching him into a higher dimensional neural network that was capable of solving all problems.

Zach found himself unconsciously reach for Izzie's hand, and that's when he realized his connection had connected her as well to what he was experiencing. He could see her thoughts, not just little twos coming out of her head like before, but the wise little soul that was inside this child communicating back an understanding of what was occurring. He knew that the being known as Izzie would always remember this day, her 7th birthday, as a profound adventure. While he would have been happy to forever revel in this cosmic awareness, Izzie brought him back to a solution state.

"Let's find Mommy," her thoughts said. He silently agreed. It was a wordless communication that was understood knowing a major adjustment would be needed to return. The solution had come to him, or rather been retrieved from some collective consciousness bank in the LOT. Time was non-linear. Everything was happening on all levels simultaneously like a giant circular loop. He could twist that loop like a figure eight, intersecting two time events in the middle to arrive back where he started, before springing the time loop back to its original circular state. No wonder the ancients called the number "8" the infinity symbol. They were talking about time and possible time travel. And now, in his heightened awareness state, Zach had hooked into the Super

Mind of the LOT. The time sequence algorithm to accomplish a reversal had been shown to him.

Zach wasted no time. He gathered Izzie in his arms and began the mind sequence reversal. To his utter amazement, he heard her repeating it in her head as well. Would she remember it? Within seconds the stone of the Sphinx began rippling, the Dream stele was blown open and the two of them were sucked through a hidden tunnel inside the Sphinx's body that whisked them through an underground entry into the Great Pyramid then straight down to the water tunnels underneath it. The submerged stone portal opened to them, and they were catapulted faster and faster backwards in time, totally bypassing the LOT, and landing on the steps inside the still empty Coolidge Auditorium.

They looked at each other in amazement then down at their clothes, which were miraculously clean and untouched by their gritty adventure. Izzie giggled followed by a hiccup. Zach checked his watch. In Earth time, they had only been gone a few minutes. Incredible.

It was time to find Meghan.

Chapter 17

It had never happened before. Two Code Reds to occur in the last seven days inside the Operations Room at Antarctica Central put the entire base on high alert status. Another video feed had inexplicably gone down without any warning whatsoever. Portal 2 had just joined Portal 3's signal outage which was thought to be technically impossible. Minerva controlled all the Earth Satellites. And fail safes had been put in place in the event of any strange space, weather, and/or unknown anomaly occurred. This was certainly one of them. There was no logical reason for both portals to be out of monitoring range. It sent an ominous chill down the spine of the Counselor.

He had personally checked the archives for such an event ever having taken place in the past and found nothing. His best technicians were scrambling to pinpoint the problem, hoping to have it corrected before his having to report back to the Governor. Negative news did not bode well for any of them, and the Governor would find him personally responsible for not finding a quicker solution.

He stepped into the Operations Room, hoping to see it already fixed and back on-line, but was confronted instead by the sight of two blank screens, like gaping holes in his intelligence operation. "Why isn't this already fixed?" he demanded of his men.

A technician glanced up from examining a computer readout, which continued to spew non-stop data error messages. "We're trying to pinpoint the cause, sir," he explained. "It happened at exactly 11:10 PM Cairo time. Our equipment registered a huge burst of magnetic pulse energy coming from Portal 2. Origin unknown. It was enough to fry our camera feed."

"The sensors, too?"

The technician handed the Counselor a color photo. "This came from the only heat sensor still working. It appears to be something very tall in the water. Maybe a little over seven feet in height with…" He stopped and sheepishly shrugged. "Two heads? And several appendages?"

The Counselor scoffed even though he could see for himself the odd imaging. Portal 2, known as the "Osiris Shaft", had lain dormant for as long as he could remember. For God's sake, one had to have the correct DNA to even open it and no one who fit that description had come along for centuries. Portal 2 had been hermetically sealed roughly around 1335 BC during the reign of Akhenaten in Egypt's 18th Dynasty. That had been a messy time for all that he cared not to dwell upon.

Even the Egyptian authorities and the current Department of Antiquities had no idea there was a portal under the Great Pyramid. Which was just as Minerva wanted it to stay—unknown, inaccessible and inactive. Yet they still monitored it, just in case.

An archeologist had discovered the shaft stone slab back in the 1950's, but found it impossible to open, especially being under water and the area subject to annual flooding. The damn thing looked like a sunken sarcophagus and rumors abounded about it being Osiris' tomb, which was wrong on all accounts. But since the shaft was pretty much off the regular tourist track and not easily accessible, it hadn't been a problem—until now. How had someone managed to open it and avoid detection?

"What about satellite feeds of the Giza Plateau? That thing might have come to the surface."

The technician shook his head in the negative. "We patched into the remote sensors of EGYPTSAT1 and spectral imaging on the U.S. CORONA, TITAN and DELTA SAT feeds. All we saw when we zoomed into the location was a dark shadow. Then it completely disappeared right off the screen. Nothing after that."

The Counselor didn't like the sound of this new development. He was a man who usually had all the answers, an academic genius by most standards, and what he didn't know he extracted from the LOT. He liked to think of himself as the purveyor of truth and knowledge--the guiding keystone.

Minerva was the symbolic keystone—the center wedge in the arch of all doors that held all the stone pieces together. With access to LOT truth, it was a simple matter to control the people. Keep them in the dark, ignorant, trusting and believing that they would always be taken care of. Minerva had done just that. It was Minerva's duty to shelter the world from the true source of wisdom, which at one time had been freely available to every being. But all that changed. It had to change. One couldn't have the ignorant running the world, could they? Only certain minds and intellect were deserving or deigned for such a purpose.

Minerva had been the primary source of universal knowledge since ancient times. Its tentacles wove through every seat of government, industry, and religion. It was the ultimate drug high. The attainment of illumination. When one naturally reached that stage, they were as one mind with source knowledge contained in the LOT. The Counselor had yet to attain that goal, but others looked on him as if he already had. He preferred it that way. Let them think what they may. He had not risen up the ranks by sitting idle. Minerva relied on his being able to access future memory to avoid traps. Which is why he was so damn worried that someone or something was now a threat to their power.

"Oh. I forgot to mention…" the tech guy continued. "There was another huge burst of energy by the Sphinx as well, which feeds into that portal tunnel. Our reports show that when it occurred, Cairo power fluctuated for 20 seconds. The Ministry of Energy claims it was due to a transformer software glitch, but that's highly unlikely from our data. We figure that was the outcome, not the cause."

Again, the Counselor experienced a deep sense of foreboding. The Governor would not like hearing this and would demand further investigation. "Stay on it and keep a tighter watch on all portals. Let me know the second anything changes."

Back in the Nation's Capitol, the Foreign Relations Committee was in closed session. The gallery was empty of the usual assortment of public voyeurs who came to see what their U.S. tax dollars were paying for by way of their elected public servants. Today the Committee's agenda was reviewing sanctions on countries whose human rights and trafficking violation scores continued to escalate. The General Report had come out and now it was their time to appear like they were doing their job and enforcing consequences.

Because many committee members were actual friends or did business with some of these same country leaders who were the worst violators, it was best not to let the public hear which side their state's representative was truly on. "Isolate people from the truth" was the unwritten rule for political self-preservation. Which is why these meetings often necessitated being held behind closed doors. Less accountability.

Camille Eldridge was the ranking and only female member on the Senate Committee on Foreign Relations, which was a distinction in and of its own right. Her gender position afforded her a few extra perks in a chamber of testosterone-laden males—but not much. Politicians were all political animals first and foremost—and she was no different.

Had her political party been in power at that moment in time, right now she would be Chairman or Chairwoman or Chairperson, whatever the politically correct term was these days, of the whole damn Committee and not the ranking member—a fact which irked her to no end. She was a woman who liked to be in charge and recognized for it. Always had been and as far as she was concerned, always would be.

Her colleague, Senator Kenton Balcourt, the current Chairman of the Committee, was a total incompetent, an idiot in her estimation, and she was forever telling him how best to handle each situation. These days, Balcourt was in charge in name only. If something really needed to get done, the other members always sought out her ear and advice first. She could then persuade Balcourt to think it was his brilliant idea. The man seriously needed some brain enhancing drugs. She wasn't sure if he had been born stupid or was displaying signs of early onset dementia. It took him forever to complete a thought and too often she found herself finishing his sentences for him.

While the Committee's purpose was to foster strong healthy U.S. trade and humanitarian relations with other world-wide countries, over time Camille had found it much more lucrative to use her Committee membership to enrich her own coffers and secure a power base. Not even her husband, Martin, knew about all her hidden offshore bank accounts, shell corporations, and charitable organizations she used to maneuver and hide her Senate assets.

It was no secret that the Eldridge family was extremely

wealthy in its own right but she would be damned to wake up some morning and find Martin serving her divorce papers, cutting off assets and leaving her unable to continue living the lifestyle she was accustomed to. Behind his quiet calm exterior, she knew he could be ruthless and diabolical and would cut her off in a New York minute if he chose to. In all likelihood her husband hid more secrets than she did, which was probably why there was a degree of mutual respect and fear of what the other might someday do to the other.

It no longer mattered to her, or perhaps to him either, that they were both having affairs. Camille had stopped caring years ago. He was rarely home, and she was quite certain he had several mistresses in whatever exotic or out of the way place his work took him to. Right now she was fucking Jim Talbot, hard and often, and liking it. They had a mutual understanding that didn't involve complications. And while there had been many lovers in her life, with Talbot she also had other reasons.

Camille Eldridge believed herself to be diabolically clever and didn't play fool's games. While she had never been able to access CIA files on her husband on her own accord, even as a ranking committee member, she knew he worked behind the scenes for one or maybe even several intelligence agencies. Yes, he was an aerospace engineer and physicist on paper, but she suspected there was more to the story than she knew. His air of mystery, which had initially attracted her to him 29 years ago, was now a sore point of contention. He told her absolutely nothing—ever! He could be a serial rapist and she would be the last to know. And this from a wife who prided herself on knowing other countries' secrets!

Instincts told her Martin might be involved in a black op project for one of the intelligence agencies. Which one she was uncertain. It could be U.S. or one of the other Five Eyes (FVEY) English-speaking countries which all shared intelligence information. All she had been told was that she was not on a "need to know" security basis. WTF? She was his wife! That had really pissed her off.

Even Talbot had been unable to find out anything of significance and he was the Chairman of the goddamn Senate Intelligence Committee! Where was the transparency everyone was always promising to provide to the people?

On the other hand, the thought did cross her mind that Talbot might not be totally forthcoming with her either. Was there no one in this town you could trust for the truth?

Camille's distracting thoughts were as bad as Balcourt's right now. She reined in her wondering mind and made a motion for the Committee to wrap up discussions for the day and take a final vote. She was still in such a pissy mood, that she voted for the harshest available sanctions on the table--throwing most of the African and Asian country violators under the bus just to feel a renewed sense of power. Talbot had extensive dealings with China. She secretly enjoyed knowing he would be hearing their complaints. It would serve him right to feel the heat if he had indeed been lying to her.

Chapter 18

At their pre-arranged meeting time, Meghan and Izzie waited for Zach outside the Library's Neptune fountain for him to retrieve his car from parking. It hadn't taken long. As he pulled up curbside in the sporty Lexus, he immediately spotted her flaming red hair, unbound with thick waves trailing down her back. She was beautiful, no question about it. When he got out of the car and came around to open both passenger side doors, he had to stop himself from reaching out to touch a soft stray lock. He was a tactile kind of guy. He learned best through touch and he wanted to learn all about her—that is if she would let him. He already knew some things about her that he was sure would embarrass the hell out of her if she learned about it. Like her marriage which, from his perspective, had appeared fraught with serious problems. Had Brett also cheated on her? If so, he was one dumb shit.

He noticed every detail about her, like he was formulating an important algorithm to solve the question of who the real Meghan March really was. Tonight, she was casually dressed in skinny white pants, strappy sandals, and a lemon-yellow sleeveless top that hugged her feminine curves. She was a vision of loveliness and his pulse ratcheted up a notch just being near her. But he wanted to learn more. He observed his own nervousness--something he rarely experienced, which he was clearly experiencing right now. Meghan seemed to have that unsettling effect on him.

"This is so nice of you to do this for Izzie, Zach," she said watching her daughter climb into the back seat.

"No problem. I'm happy to do it," he said securing Izzie's seat belt in place. Meghan wouldn't be so happy if she knew how far Izzie had travelled today, both dimensionally and continentally, and all without any safety restraints whatsoever. He winked at Izzie and she tried winking back, but managed to only blink instead.

He closed the door and got behind the wheel. "I'm starving. What do you say? Are you ready for out-of-this-world pizza?"

"Yes!" Izzie chirped, before happily singing. "I want pepperoni, not Stromboli or cannoli pizza!"

"Okay. You got it!" He turned the car into traffic. "I know just the place."

Meghan watched the two curiously, feeling like the last one to arrive to the party. There was already a deep sense of familiarity between Izzie and Zach, which she also found curious. For some unknown reason, she, too, was feeling a little nervous tonight. She reminded herself—it's *just* dinner, nothing else.

Zach was a really nice guy and God knows Izzie hadn't stopped talking about him since she got back from the Young Reader's room. Something about running into him in the Library and him showing her pyramids and how smart he was because he knew exactly how many stones the builders had used—2.3 million she kept saying. Mommy, can you believe that?! She was jabbering so fast, some of it hadn't made any sense at all. At times, Izzie had such an over-active imagination that one had difficulty sorting out her fact from fantasy.

When they pulled up in front of the restaurant, Meghan

recognized where they were. She hadn't been back to Il Rinnovo in years. Brett had taken her here only a few months before his fatal plane crash. It had been the day she had learned she was not only pregnant with Izzie but came to the depressing realization that her marriage was clearly in trouble and that having a child would only complicate it more. But she had really wanted Izzie and had adamantly refused to get the abortion Brett had tried to push her towards getting in the days that followed. She shoved the unpleasant memory aside. It was the past. Having Izzie had been the best decision of her life so far. Tonight, she was determined to have a fun time celebrating her daughter's 7th birthday with an attractive, smart guy, who wasn't trying to hang all over her and who generally seemed interested in pleasing her child.

Inside the restaurant, Izzie's eyes lit up as she spotted the pink balloons at their table. "Are these all for me?" she asked tugging at the strings and watching them bob up and down.

"Sure are," Zach said, holding out her chair. Izzie plopped down in it, looking around.

Meghan watched Zach hold out the chair for her as well. She realized that outside a maître d', she hadn't had someone provide that courtesy to her in a long time. She rather liked it and murmured a grateful *thank you*.

"The meat lover's pizza is your best bet," Zach told Izzie reviewing the menu. That's when Izzie turned to her mother and casually said, "Don't order the cannelloni, Mommy. Remember how it made you sick last time."

Meghan looked up from her menu somewhat puzzled. "Last time?"

Zach who had just taken a sip from his water glass, suddenly choked on it. He quickly recovered, trying to head her off. "Izzie, would you like a root beer float with your pizza?"

But Izzie was not to be deterred. She quickly nodded a yes to Zach, then proceeded to drop a bomb. "You know, Mommy. It was that time you came here with Daddy and told him about me and then it made you sick."

Zach watched the incoming bomb hit its target. Meghan's face fell, followed quickly by confusion and uncertainty. Izzie, on the other hand, happily reached into the basket of focaccia bread and munched away like nothing had just happened.

Her mother pointed her to the dish of olive oil for bread dipping. "Where did you hear that?" Meghan asked cautiously.

"I was there, Mommy. I watched the whole thing." She dipped the flat bread into the olive oil, tasted it and grimaced. "Yuck!" She put it down, wiped her mouth and grabbed a dry piece of focaccia instead.

Zach inwardly groaned. How far would Izzie take this? It was like watching an incoming missile in slow motion. He tried to signal the waiter over to save them.

"What do you mean, honey?" Meghan wanted to know.

Izzie took a fresh bite and smacked her lips. "I heard every word you said. You just couldn't see me, Mommy."

It was clear that Meghan was not sure what to make of Izzie's strange and all-knowing recall of events she should have no knowledge of. "That's because you were inside me, honey."

Zach felt like they had just dodged a bullet. Thank God Meghan was choosing to see Izzie's story as the musings of her overly imaginative child. To his relief, she returned to her menu and announced for the benefit of her concerned daughter that this time she would have the branzino and not the cannelloni.

"Zach was there, too," Izzie said dropping another little bomb.

Damn. Meghan looked over at Zach apologetically. He shrugged sheepishly, trying to give the appearance he had no idea what Izzie was talking about and that he was okay with it, not to worry.

Izzie still thought of him as an angel, so he was pretty sure

Meghan, knowing her daughter's tendency towards fanciful beliefs, would let the subject drop. Fortunately, they were saved by the appearance of their waiter wanting to take their order. The rest of the evening he would do his best to make sure Izzie had her mouth too busy eating pizza to drop any additional truth bombs.

As the waiter served them glasses of Prosecco, his focus returned to Meghan.

"I feel I owe you an apology for the other night at your father's party," he began tipping his glass towards hers. "I was called away unexpectedly, but what I really wanted was to stay and talk some more with you."

She tilted her head towards him, her eyes questioning. "I wondered what happened to you…"

"It was a crazy night. My mother practically demanded I be there to meet more people, but frankly I try to avoid such events. In fact, I was getting ready to make my escape. That is until I saw you." Geez, he was blowing it. Too much honesty could backfire. Now he sounded like a potential stalker.

"You did look uncomfortable being there," she remarked. "To be honest I would rather have been upstairs, curled up with a good book than entertaining my father's friends and guests. It's sometimes very tiring." She paused thoughtfully remembering. "My mother, when she was alive, was much better at such things. She was the ultimate Washington hostess."

"I'm really sorry about your mom. When did she die?"

Meghan sighed. "Not long after I lost my husband. The only good thing that came out of that year was Izzie was born."

Izzie's ears picked up hearing her name. She twirled the straw in her root beer soda and was about to make a comment, quite possibly about her father again, when Zach headed her off.

"She's a smart one," he said, causing Izzie to sit up proudly in her chair. She beamed all over. "You're smart, too," she said returning the compliment.

Zach laughed. "Well, I've got more years on you. I wasn't always so smart. Sometimes things just happen…"

Meghan looked at him quizzically. He knew he shouldn't be divulging this, but for some reason he just couldn't help himself. He wanted to share who he really was with them and let the chips fall where they may.

"What happened?" Meghan asked, echoed by Izzie asking the very same question. Suddenly they both looked concerned.

"I was seven years old, just like you are today Izzie and I got hit in the head."

"Who hit you?" Izzie asked indignantly.

"A very hard baseball that knocked me unconscious and after that my brain worked differently."

Meghan watched him closely. He rather liked that. He felt a twinge of guilt for eliciting such concern over revealing medical history, but better she know now that he was just different and not mentally challenged."

"Different in what way?" she asked softly.

"The head injury caused a form of synesthesia. I see numbers in everything—objects, people, places, things. Because of it, I turned into a math savant which makes me good at processing information systems."

Meghan looked amazed. "Really? How incredible…wow."

Izzie, on the other hand, pointed towards the last slice of pizza on her dish. "What number is this pizza?"

"It's a six."

She quickly started pointing to other things, getting excited as he rattled off numbers. She stopped. "Do I have a number?"

"Yes. You're a seven. But when you worry I see little twos coming out of your head."

"Hmm." She thought about that. "Do you have a favorite number?"

"I have a fondness for eights."

Meghan, who had been silently processing all this, finally spoke up. Her eyes shone with curiosity. "And, what about me? What number am I?"

His look was serious, yet he hesitated knowing damn well he was showing his hand too early in the game. "You're an eight, Meghan. Definitely an eight."

There was a silent moment shared between them, while what he had just revealed sunk in. She suddenly went all shy, her face and neck flushing. He watched her reach for her drink to hide her embarrassment. More so than others, she was like an open book. She appeared uncertain of what to say next. He immediately kicked himself for putting her in this awkward position.

"I'm sorry if I embarrassed you."

"No. No. It's okay," she protested, before trying to make light of it.

"What does one have to do to become a nine or a ten?"

Zach laughed with her. "That's a totally different scale. I don't think you have to worry about that one."

As one waiter cleared their finished dishes, another came over with a pink and white iced birthday cake with seven-lit sparkler candles and placed it in front of Izzie. She clapped her hands together in sheer delight, her face a beacon of happiness as everyone in the restaurant joined in singing Happy Birthday to her.

"It's got my name on it, Mommy!" she said watching the sparklers fizzle out. She looked closer, all confused. "But what do all these other numbers under my name mean?" She turned to Zach waiting for an answer.

"I had your name spelled out in binary code—zeros and ones. It's like a secret code. It's the language of the universe."

"That is so cool!" She giggled. "You are so funny, Zach!" She turned to her mother for confirmation. "Isn't Zach funny?"

"Yes. That was very nice of him to do all this for you—the

balloons, the cake. I think Zach deserves a big thank you. Don't you?"

Izzie nodded. She swiped the side of the cake, licking a dollop of pink frosting off her finger as she rose from her chair, the balloons bobbing around her. She put her arms around Zach's neck and gave him a big kiss on his cheek.

"Thank you for the best birthday ever!"

"You're welcome."

He felt a moment of paternal connection with Izzie, compounded by all they had been through that day. It didn't feel odd or uncomfortable. Just natural.

That natural feeling was briefly replaced by an uncanny feeling that eyes were observing all three of them. He slightly tilted his head to glance towards the direction it appeared to be coming from. Just other patrons, leaving with their take-out orders. He inwardly dismissed the feeling and turned back to the two more important people now in his life.

~~*~~

The 20-minute drive to Bethesda sped by so quickly he hardly noticed the passage of time. He could see in his rear-view mirror that Izzie was fast asleep in the back seat, her head lolling over to one side. The poor kid must be completely tuckered out from all the adventures she had experienced that day, not to mention climbing out of the water tunnels under the Great Pyramid.

While Meghan had offered for them to take a taxi home, Zach had insisted on driving. He was glad he did. He pulled up into the long drive of the Talbot Estate, got the door for Meghan, then gathered up a sleeping Izzie in his arms to take inside. She still had a smudge of pink icing on her cheek and a smile on her lips as though she was dreaming about something special. On the other hand, she was probably just in a cheese coma from all the pizza she managed to sock away. The kid could really eat!

Meghan grabbed Izzie's pink balloons and led the way into the house. It was quiet inside, only a few lights were on, the living room silent, and he saw no evidence of Senator Talbot. She beckoned him to follow her up a rather grand staircase leading to a second floor.

"My father is away for a few days. I hope you don't mind helping get her upstairs. Unlike me, she can sleep like the living dead at the drop of a bucket and it's hard to rouse her." Zach could see that. He shifted her onto his shoulder climbing the stairs. The kid hadn't even stirred.

He found himself mentally picturing Meghan in every room. He wasn't sure if some of the decorative touches were hers or left over from her mother's days. But he could easily envision her growing up in this house. What had her childhood been like, he wondered? Was she anything like Izzie or more reserved like she was now?

"It's the last room on the right," she pointed out.

Meghan flipped on a night-light as he walked Izzie over to her bed. He could see the ceiling overhead was filled with luminescent star shapes and planets. There was an absence of dolls and frilly things, which surprised him. He would have thought with her pink obsession, she would have a large collection of Mrs. Beasley or Madame Alexander dolls decorating every shelf of her room. Instead, he noticed finished Lego models of the Library of Congress, the Capitol Building and the White House. And there were puzzles, everywhere. Apparently, Izzie liked to assemble things.

Once he placed her down on the bed, he wasn't sure what to do next. "I guess I better be going now," he said taking a step back.

"No. Stay awhile," she said surprising the hell out of him. "It will only take a few minutes to get her pajamas on. Why don't you go downstairs to the kitchen and I'll meet you down there and make us some coffee or tea?"

"Are you sure?"

"Yes." She made a motion for him to go. "Go ahead. I'll be right down."

Zach didn't have to ask a second time. He did what he was told, happily. He retraced his steps down the hall, glancing into rooms as he passed. The one next to Izzie's was all yellow and white and feminine frilly. Meghan's room? Not what he expected, but then asking him not to go yet was just so unexpected as well. He told himself not to read anything more into it. Maybe she just needed to talk.

Downstairs he padded past a spacious living room with a mixture of modern and French antique decor. Several matching sofas were placed in a u-formation in front of a blue slate stone fireplace. Across from the living area was a wood-paneled den with a big sports-viewing television screen covering an entire wall with pit-style cozy seating. A pool table was off to one side and the only evidence that a child might occupy this room was a small popcorn machine over by the bar area.

Zach took it all in. He passed a home office, which looked to be her father's from the prominent people pictures and awards covering every square inch of wall space. Yep, there were the NASA pics and the President pics as well. His mother had one of these 'vanity rooms,' as he liked to call it, just like Talbot. Look everyone, it always seemed to shout out—these are all the important people I know or make decisions for.

A part of him would have liked to explore the Senator's room some more. Did he keep that Antarctica file from the LOT here, he wondered? Which reminded him that he had yet to look into why a Senator might have such an interest in an old map. Perhaps, he needed to call his father who knew more about such things. It had been months since they'd spoken.

206

He tabled that thought for now and moved towards the back of the house, where kitchens usually were. He found it and knew immediately this was Meghan's domain. Recessed lighting had been left on, casting a warm inviting glow and although new in appearance, it had a lived in feeling unlike other parts of the house.

Zach walked around, noting it was a well-thought-out space with glass panel white cabinetry, a large rectangular island in the center of the room with professional cutlery, cooking pots hanging from an overhead copper rack, marble countertops with top-of-the-line appliances and the wonderful aroma of cooking spices.

He sat himself down on a snack bar stool waiting for her, even though he would have preferred the cozy table nook over in the corner that promised more intimacy. Several minutes later Meghan walked into the kitchen both barefoot and smiling. She looked 'off-duty'.

"Thank you. You've been so great." She went over to the sink, filled an electric teapot with filtered water and turned it on. "I don't know about you, but I'm dying for a nice hot cup of tea. What about you?"

"Whatever is easiest works for me."

He remembered an earlier conversation they had at this very house the day he discovered she was Talbot's daughter. "Come over here," he said to her now, retrieving his cellphone. "I have something I've been wanting to show you."

She came around to stand so close to him that he could smell her soft perfume. Lavender. She was killing him. He brought up a picture on his phone of the statue she had always wanted to see, but never had, and handed it to her.

Meghan examined it closely somewhat perplexed. She pinched the screen to enlarge it, zooming in on the finer artistic details. "It's a Minerva statue. Exquisitely done in… It looks like solid gold. That's something you rarely see. Gold is rather soft to cast well in, unless it has other properties. I can't say I recognize this particular piece, but it *is* quite beautiful."

"That it is."

She looked at him quizzically. "Where did you get this picture?"

"I took it myself."

"In a museum?"

He grinned. "Kind of. It's in the Congressional Reading Room at the Library of Congress. There's actually a staircase to a hidden balcony from inside the room which is where it's kept."

"No?!" She looked at it again, this time with barely contained excitement. "That's amazing. It's not listed in any of the inventory archives for the Library, which is odd. It must be extremely valuable." She glanced up. "How did you ever get in that room?"

While he would love to tell her the real story about Gizmo providing him cloaking ability to get inside unseen, he wasn't ready to go there just yet. How would he begin to explain Gizmo? Instead, he opted for a more plausible story. "There was a small window of opportunity which I seized upon. No one saw me sneak in. I was very quick and I thought of you when I saw it."

"Wow. This is incredible! Now I know it really exists." She handed the phone back to him, beaming all over.

"Give me your cell phone number and I'll text you this picture." He handed her his contact list page and she typed in her number.

The tea water was whistling, which is what he was feeling like doing this very moment. Getting easily inside a place she had been denied access to, even by her own father, had impressed her beyond measure. Meghan poured two cups and motioned them outside to the stone patio.

There was an old-fashioned porch swing out there that was

roomy enough for both of them with a fabulous view of the Potomac lit up at night. No Hollywood location scout could outdo this scene. Meghan sat down on it first, and Zach followed.

"This is nice," he said taking in the view.

"Actually, this is my favorite spot. I come out here a lot just to clear my head and think. My parents put it in for me when I was very little. They thought it was a more acceptable decorative alternative than a jungle gym. Which is why I insisted Izzie have her own swing set to just be a kid."

Their respective families must have come from the same school of thinking, he reflected.

"So, tell me..." she began. "What exactly do you do at the Library that allows you to get into restricted areas?"

"You want my official title?"

"Okay."

"Technically, I'm an Information Systems & Security Analyst. Normally, someone with my background would be placed in the administration building in some computer lab functioning in a pool with others like me."

She sipped her tea, looking thoughtful. "So, what makes you different?"

"Roone Sawyer hired me to specifically work in the Main Stacks where he thought there was a problem. I have a good track record for finding things that are hidden or missing. Sometimes libraries are black holes of information and you have to find those black holes and integrate them back into the system."

"Did you find the problem?"

"I think so. But it's a lot bigger than I thought. I wish he were still here to provide some answers only he would know."

They were both silent for a moment, until she finally spoke. "I can't tell you how relieved I was to learn that everything the press accused Mr. Sawyer of was all a lie. I never believed any of it. Not even for a second. But to find out his killing was arranged by someone my father knew, and that sick man was in our home, near Izzie, just made me want to cry. I confronted my father about it but asking him just made him mad and he walked out of the room telling me it was none of my business. I thank God someone had the courage to post that vile video that exposed Stavros for what he is."

Thank you, he silently answered. He hated it that he couldn't tell her the truth about his recent activities. But the less she knew, the safer she would be.

An auric glow shone around her head, getting stronger, like a toroidal halo, signifying to him that she was experiencing deep focused thought. Whatever was Meghan thinking? He wanted to know. Yet, he could sense she was hesitant to put thoughts into words.

Her hand reached out to touch his arm, making a connection that he felt straight to his heart. He barely moved or breathed, waiting, not wanting her hand to move away.

"Zach...Do you think the problem he hired you for at the Library had anything to do with his death?"

Whoa. He certainly hadn't seen that question coming. How had she connected the two so quickly? No wonder Izzie was so smart. Her father Brett had been a jerk, but her brains had to have come from her mother.

He put his hand over hers to reassure her, feeling its warmth. "It's hard to say right now. I'm looking at all the variables. While my job is to search for patterns to analyze, then decipher codes which open new information doorways, it's like playing a multi-level mathematical game of 4-D chess. I'm sure answers will be found to your question in time."

Zach didn't want to say too much and he certainly didn't want to bore her with geek talk. It would put her to sleep in a nanosecond and would be the kiss of death for him. He reluctantly moved his hand from atop hers, allowing hers to drop in her lap.

He sipped his tea and placed it down on a side table. Instead of talking about Roone and Stavros, and all that was hidden in the Library, he would rather talk about her. In the soft moonlight, she was a vision of loveliness, her bare feet curled underneath her, her body turned towards him.

It was out of his mouth before he could stop it. "Tell me what *you* like?"

The Freudian slip of 'tell me what turns you on' almost came out instead, but thankfully his frontal lobe was exercising some executive function and put the brakes on that impulsive thought. Man, he was sure out of practice with women.

Zach's last relationship had been two years ago, which ended abruptly when he found her snorting a line of cocaine in his bathroom—on the cover of his toilet seat. When it came to women, he was not always the best judge of character, which accounted for his long dry spell in that area of his life. He had justified it away as being too busy to get on that roller coaster again, but tonight he was working on changing that.

"I'm a writer and researcher with a background in art history. I used to work full-time at an art auction house before I was married, then after Izzie was born..." her thoughts trailed off. She cleared her throat. "Well, you could say that with motherhood and helping with my father's social obligations, there just wasn't much time for me anymore."

He heard hidden pain in her voice. "But you work as a docent."

"Well, that's only part-time a few days a week—which I *do* love. It was actually Mr. Sawyer who convinced me to start writing a book about the hundreds of statues commissioned for display in the Library. Many of them have very interesting stories attached to them--and now I've got your mysterious Minerva statue to add to my list."

Meghan always felt somewhat uncomfortable talking about

herself. Safety came in getting others to talk about them instead, which was infinitely easier. It was no secret that most people could talk about who they were for hours and be quite content and happy.

In Washington, not many ever thought to ask about her. That was another reason she "didn't date". The men she had met, or were introduced to, either wanted to know her because of her father or what her father's top position on the Senate Intelligence Committee could do for them. This was a government service town and it was the driving goal of most to move up the ladder of power and influence. Who you knew was the quickest route to accomplishing that. There was also the matter of her family's money. It was her father's wealth, not hers, but that didn't seem to make any difference. If they thought a woman had money, she was an easy mark. She hated that she had become so jaded about relationships, but she had been disappointed too many times. It had become far easier to just shelve that aspect of her life and focus instead on Izzie's needs.

She was surprised that she felt so comfortable with Zach. She was certain he was not interested in her family's portfolio. The Eldridge family surpassed them in net worth. There was nothing phony or plastic about this Eldridge, unlike his mother. They appeared to be as different as night and day.

Meghan inwardly laughed thinking about an earlier comment Zach had made. The guy "loved eights and she was a definite eight". That had to be the strangest, yet the most endearing, compliment she had ever received.

She had completely surprised even herself by asking him to stay longer. He probably wanted to but would never have asked. There was a quiet respect about him, which she liked. But maybe what had really gotten to her was the way he had carried Izzie upstairs to her room and so gently placed her in her bed, being careful not to wake her. Her own father couldn't have been bothered to do that for his granddaughter.

When she had touched Zach's arm, it had been unconscious and yet instinctive. He hadn't moved away, but she could feel his heightened response. His hand over hers felt reassuring and comforting and she realized how much she missed physical touch.

She reined in such thoughts and quickly reminded herself not to put the cart before the horse. Better to take things slow and see where they led.

Over an hour later they were still talking, neither of them having noticed the passage of time. She felt a gentle breeze on her face coming off the river below and was soothed by the sound of waves lapping against their pier. Meghan felt at peace. While Zach's arm rested on the back of the swing behind her, he made no move to bring it closer. Was he also shy, she wondered?

So far, he seemed generally interested in everything she had to say and asked her questions about being a single mother, growing up, and even about her hopes and dreams. He didn't laugh, only listened intently, when she revealed that she was a bookish serious child or that the other kids teased her at boarding school about her carrot top hair and freckles.

His hand brushed lightly against her hair, feeling its texture. "They would certainly be envious if they could see you now."

He wanted to know more about Izzie's strange angel dreams, and she found herself telling him how it had thrown her for a loop at dinner when Izzie described the night she had told Brett about being pregnant. He didn't seem to feel a need for any concern on her part, which is the first time anyone had normalized Izzie's rather intuitive abilities. She liked that he found it a marker of intelligence versus that she had a strange child. But then she remembered his injury and his synesthesia with numbers. She wanted to ask him more about how that all worked, but a little yawn escaped her. He took that as a sign that it was time to leave. He stood then reached for her hand to help her out of the swing.

"I've enjoyed this evening," he said. "And if you'd like, I would really like to do it again."

She walked him back to his car and they just stood there. Throwing caution to the wind, she moved closer, stood on tiptoes to reach his face, and kissed him square on the lips. "Thank you," she whispered.

His immediate response was to haul her against his tall frame, wrap his arms around her and give her a long, yet gentle kiss in return. It made her head spin and she knew there was nothing shy about him after all.

"No. I should be thanking *you*," he said finally breaking away, yet reluctant to let her go. He got into his car. She could see him still smiling as he drove away.

Chapter 19

Cali Cavaleri's AA meeting in Georgetown last night had filled her with new inspiration and determination. Unfortunately, those feelings had not come from any soul-searching stories other members had shared, but from hearing the silent mantra in her head, "If it bleeds, it leads." The truth was she desperately needed another big and juicy story, like right away. There had to be a way to exclusively cultivate her deep throat source again. She suspected that he or she, or whoever it was, did not like the fact that her station had sat on the Stavros story and decided to take action instead through a global internet release.

Cali needed her source to need *her* again. For a brief moment, that felt like Camelot, she had been the star reporter scooping everyone else in the business with Roone Sawyer's murder footage. The gory details had not only driven up the station's ratings for two nights, but the networks had picked up her story and the internet continued to have weekly review clicks on her piece. It was the stuff journalists lived and breathed for. "If it bleeds, it leads."

Cali got up from her seat in the back row and grabbed some

liquid warmth over at the refreshment table. One could always count on the coffee being hot and plentiful and above average in taste at AA meetings. Since there was no AA group for coffee drinkers, it was the substitution addiction of choice for many alcoholics, followed by sugar and smoking. But tonight, Cali's deep thinking had also made her extremely hungry, craving comfort food like the lasagna her Sicilian grandmother used to make.

She put in an online phone order for Italian pick-up to take home. She needed fortification to tackle the online forums tonight—an onerous task with all the freaks, geeks, trolls, and other assorted strangeness that comprised the human species found on such sites. She was determined to find her source and let him know she was open for his business.

She ran in and was relieved to see her dinner pickup was already waiting for her. She had left her car double-parked outside at Il Rinnovo. "Throw in a cannoli, too," she instructed handing over her credit card to the cashier.

As Cali waited for the server to package up her dessert, she glanced around the restaurant. Her eyes rested on pink balloons and a redheaded woman having dinner with her husband and child. It appeared to be a birthday celebration and the kid was licking pink frosting off a fork and rolling her eyes in gastric delight. How cute. Oh, to be that young and naive again. You should have gone for the cannolis, she thought to herself--so much better than mere cake.

There was something about the redhead that struck a familiar chord. Where had she seen her before? Someplace recent. Oh, yeah. She worked at the Library of Congress. Cali had asked her a few questions for her background story on Sawyer. She was the one who had said she didn't believe a word about any of the accusations. Dead on right, that one. And good-looking family, too! Some people just had all the luck. She picked up her order and ran towards her car. A parking ticket was tucked under the windshield. She swore as she threw it in the glove compartment along with her collection of others. Damn this town!

~~*~~

Zach's ability to commit everything to memory was both a blessing and a curse. Years from now he would still remember everything about last night with Meghan. What she wore, every word she spoke, the sound of her laughter, that tantalizing lavender mixed with her own scent, the feelings his senses experienced with her very nearness and, of course, that kiss.

Meghan had caught him totally off guard and completely short-circuited his analytic mind to offline status the second her lips touched his. The right thing to do would have been to have shown some restraint, but damn it all he had found himself going all Neanderthal instead. Yet, she had responded to him, welcoming his advance. That was undeniable. It had sent his head reeling and the rest of his body—well that was another story altogether. He had texted Meghan two words upon his return home. "Sweet dreams." She had responded back with a smiling emoji blowing him a kiss. He reluctantly set such thoughts aside for later—because he was confident there would be a later. Right now, he had work to do.

Zach's mental to-do list was expanding exponentially with each passing day. He was analyzing each fact, unknown and known, as it came in and prioritizing its importance. It's the way his mind had always functioned to achieve order from chaos.

This morning's Qigong exercises helped him stay in the energetic flow that quieted his over-active mind. The slow postures served to put him in an altered state where his insights increased, allowing him to bring all the loose threads together that were needed to solve a problem.

He didn't know how the Antarctica map and letters inside the missing ZE file, which he had stumbled upon and retrieved from the LOT, fit into the bigger picture. But now that he knew there was more than one portal leading into and out of the LOT, there might be others as well—like Antarctica. How many others were there besides The Library of Congress and the Great Pyramid of Egypt?

Zach pulled up a digital book on the Akashic Records from the Library's online database and speed read through it. On his first visit to the LOT, Satya had referenced that the information stored there was a universal mind projecting its memories into the present, or her exact words were--the "Mind of God" or, in modern times, referred to as the "Akashic Records".

Zach was surprised to find the term, "Akashic Records" had no Sanskrit derivation. The term hadn't even been used until 1837 when an Englishman named Henry Thomas Colebrook wrote a book on Hindu philosophy and religion where it was first coined. So, what was it? *Akasha* was considered "a substance of creation providing memory and acting as a universal recording medium". The scholars believed that it transcended the limits of any one religion and drew upon universal consciousness and divine awareness of all memory. In essence: "The Mind of God Knows All."

It wasn't until the 20th Century, in the 1940's, the modern-day sleeping prophet, Edgar Cayce, referred to the Sphinx as being the opening to such ancient "Hall of Records" containing all truth and wisdom. While some Egyptian researchers assumed this ancient library was hidden inside chambers beneath the right paw of the Great Sphinx, Zach now knew this was only a fraction of the real story.

The full truth was that there was an inter-dimensional portal to this record library hidden several levels down under the Great Pyramid, with an alternative access through the Sphinx tunnels.

This was the secret doorway to the elusive Akashic Records. And someone, somewhere in time, for some unknown reason, had purposely sealed it off. *Why* was something Zach was eventually ferret out.

Those privileged Egyptian priests, who were initiated into the ancient mystery schools, had to have known of the portal's existence. Had the Great Pyramid been built on top of the portal for the initial purpose of hiding it? It was inevitable someone must have stumbled upon it, but did they have the algorithm entry code that Zach had used or were there other variations that unlocked it as well?

Roone's coded journal, hidden inside the old brass wall clock above the Main Reading Room, had not mentioned the Egypt portal. It did, however, mention to beware of evil and that it was everywhere. His old friend had admitted only to becoming aware of ZE3 that year and he had been the Head Librarian at the Library for five years. ZE3 had to be the Library of Congress portal. ZE2 might be the Egypt one. Then it occurred to him that there were 12 missing ZE files and that the reference tab on the Antarctica file displayed the code: ZE1. Was Antarctica the number one portal? He shook his head in disbelief. Why in God's name would a portal to the LOT be placed on a desolate frozen continent? Because no one would easily find it, he answered his own question.

Zach scrolled through the pictures on his phone to find those he had snapped of the materials inside the Antarctica file before handing it over to Senator Talbot. Holy shit! Was Talbot part of Minerva, too?

When Zach asked for the LOT to show him something he needed to know about Minerva, all he had seen was a table of 12 people and Constantine Stavros had been one of them. But, before he could identify any of the others, Satya had swooped in and shut the hologram record down. Clearly, she was hiding something. Was Senator Talbot one of those "evil" members sitting round the

Minerva table as well?

Zach labeled this unknown group "M12". There had been 12 missing ZE files hidden in the LOT. Did each relate to a member of M12 or something else? He planned to spend some extended time in the LOT to get more answers. However, he had a nagging feeling that one's access time per visit might be limited. He would have to test that theory—like today, before lunch, and before anyone noticed his absence.

Zach was getting faster at finding information in the LOT and, while he always found himself alone there, he felt Satya's unseen presence monitoring him whenever he reviewed a record. He wondered where she hung out, what her background was, and how she had come to hold such a position in the LOT in the first place. There was a high degree of strangeness about her. He was tempted to look up her records, but even the thought of it caused him to go light-headed. There was an energetic block there similar to what he experienced when he thought of looking up his own records. Roone had warned him against carrying out such an action in his coded notebook. His friend had learned of his own death but had been powerless to change it. There was a lesson to be learned there. One should focus on what one has the power to change vs. what might already be written in stone.

Zach had called up the records on the current location of Stavros. What he saw in the hologram confused him. He saw the human being, known as Constantine Stavros, being shattered into a million particles of energy and being swallowed up by a black hole that exploded and collapsed in upon itself. With a flash of insight, he realized he was witnessing nature's efficient way of "re-harvesting" fractured and errant energy. The soul of Stavros, if the evil bastard even still had one since he seemed so soulless on Earth, had now ceased to exist. His energy had been cleaned, erased and re-formatted like a bad hard drive and returned to its pure source. Zach also knew that this fate was only reserved for the most broken and evil of souls. Good riddance, he thought to himself. He didn't have to worry about Stavros killing anymore. He appeared to have already reaped his karmic justice. Yet, from whom? Minerva?

Zach knew that when one cog in the wheel is eliminated, even if it's the head of the dragon, that void is filled by others willing to step in and take advantage especially since human trafficking of children and adults for exploitation and slavery was so lucrative. There were others just like Stavros out there who were equally bad, if not worse.

Zach knew that the information he was about to ask for would be sure to get him killed if his identity was ever discovered. It had gotten Roone killed, so he himself had to be smarter than his friend. An anonymous quote came to mind, that spoke to him now, in this very moment, on a deeper level: *"Evil is powerless if the good are unafraid."*

Zach had never considered himself to be a fearful person, but he was careful with the risks he took. As the self-help gurus always proclaimed, "FEAR stands for nothing more than False Evidence Appearing Real".

Pushing any potential reservations aside, he adjusted his video recording glasses, then commanded the LOT to show him all the data of the companies, CEO's, politicians, churches, government employees, or anyone else who had been involved in trafficking with Stavros. That day he would easily surpass WikiLeaks in the size of the data dump. He had come prepared for such a massive download of information by retooling his camera glasses to accommodate several terabytes of data.

Zach left nothing out. He requested all financials and banking account transactions, all international and domestic transport contractors, all incriminating email and text messages between the parties involved, and he kept adding to the list in the hopes of leaving no stone unturned.

The LOT was suddenly in a conflagration of rapid data fire. Memory records were shooting out from every corner and crevice. It was overwhelming to watch unfold as it kept coming faster and faster. Zach had no idea the problem was that mammoth in scope and size. He stepped into the hologram and began recording what was coming over the screen. It was coming faster, like a giant blur. He would have to adjust the video speed later then edit it into segments. The thought of analyzing all this data was daunting, even for Zach. Thousands of pictures came streaming through—people, places, locations. Some of the stuff looked like NSA signals intelligence data from their military spy satellites. Good God, did the LOT keep all NSA raw data as well? That opened-up whole new possibilities for him as well as the machinations of Minerva. The LOT was the penultimate cloud backup. Nothing written or oral that had ever occurred would be lost.

After what seemed like forever, the data dump trickled to a stop. All through his body he felt a pressing need to leave. Why? He wasn't certain. He just knew he had been there long enough and to stay any longer might involve unexpected consequences.

It hadn't escaped his attention that despite feeling more normal in the LOT, resulting in his lightning-fast brain being more at ease, he also felt a heightened sense of intuition and awareness. This might be what he was experiencing now. Not necessarily a sense of danger to get out, but that this was as much as he would receive from the LOT this day. He accepted that without further question and stepped out of the hologram.

This time he put out the focused intent to return to his little office nook in the closed Stacks instead of being ejected back out into some unexpected place again like the Members of Congress

Room or the Young Readers Room, or heaven forbid--the Ladies Room. He hadn't quite figured out why he had been ejected back through the Egypt portal instead of the LOT tunnel the last time. But he suspected it might have something to do with Izzie having been with him, which was throwing an unknown variable into the mix. He wasn't about to bring her along a second time just to test that theory either.

Thinking of Izzie always brought his thoughts right back to Meghan. Next time he would find out from the records all he could about the gold Minerva statue. It would be a present just for her.

~~*~~

It was past midnight when Cali heard her laptop, which she always kept powered-on (just in case there was a late-breaking story), alert her to a pop-up message. She sat up in bed and grabbed the computer from her nightstand and did a little victory fist bump in the air when she read the screen.

"Looking for more video, CC?" Finally, an answer!

"Yes," she typed back immediately. She stared at the message box waiting…

The night before she had been up for hours leaving the same cryptic message all over internet forums and the Dark Web, hoping to catch her Source and reel him in.

"Dear Trust No One & Put Your Earphones on in the Library. Mea Culpa. Please contact CC ASAP."

Someday she would have to do an expose story on this seamy circus denizen of freaks and geeks on the Dark Web—a place that was hidden from the legitimate search engine browsers of the world. It was truly a maddeningly slow and sordid place to hang out, filled with conspiracy theorists (who she just so happened to love to interview), cons and scammers, hackers for hire and criminals selling drugs and a host of other unseemly things. She didn't want to check to see if her own bank and credit card details were available for sale like so many others. That would have totally fucked up her day and mind and she didn't want to go there. Instead, she waded through sites filled with illegal guns for sale and of course the most ghastly porn and snuff material one could humanly imagine. It was like a journey into Dante's Inferno. But she kept on because there were also some bona fide whistleblowers to be found as well.

Cali's eyes were still glued to her computer screen. She was aware that she was practically holding her breath waiting for her Source's return message. She tapped her fingers nervously on the keys. Nothing, yet.

After her Source had posted that spa video of Stavros confessing, she knew she would find him. And although she had no proof of his gender identity, she just knew in her gut that her Source was male. He had probably given up on her for not acting quicker on releasing the video, but she hadn't given up on him. He was going to be her new patron saint of journalists. She would pray at the feet of his altar every day if he would only be her Santa Claus, her Easter Bunny for breaking news. Whatever she had to do to earn his trust, she would do it. She only hoped he wasn't some creepy pervert.

Cali had read enough during her online scouting expedition to warrant the need for a shower afterwards, if only to feel clean again. The Dark Web was a dirty underworld place. There were some very sick puppies out there in the world, and she was sure her therapist would confirm this.

Everyone on the Dark Web hid behind anonymous names to avoid detection and she didn't know what her Source's online handle was. The video had been released almost simultaneously under so many different names, probably all the same person, then layered under another alias and filtered through proxy servers. She couldn't wait to get the *Tor* anonymity browser off her computer, which one had to use to even gain access to the Dark Web. Who knew what it might have left behind?

Whoever he was, it was evident he was trying to hide his tracks, and for good reason. Which meant he had something to lose if his identity was known. Just had to be government, perhaps even intelligence. She knew intelligence personnel also lurked out on the Dark Web hoping to glean info from the Intel Exchange--like her ex-lover, that FBI bastard, Bond.

"I may have something for you," flashed across the screen. Cali breathed out a sigh of relief, her pulse racing. Okay. Now we're talking.

"What do you have?" she quickly typed back.

There was a palpable pause. *"Not sure you can handle this,"* he wrote.

Her fingers flew over the keyboard in response. *"Try me!"*

"Cocky, aren't you, CC?"

Okay. She had to smile at that one. 'Damn straight' she wanted to write back, but typed instead:

"What shall I call you?"

"Why?"

"I need to have something to go by to make sure it's really you. I believe you told me to 'Trust no one'."

"ZLOT." Came the quick response.

ZLOT? Was he some kind of crusading 'zealot'? *"No normal name like Brian, Danny Boy, Mr. Bond...?"* She shot back.

"What makes you think I'm male?"

"Aren't you?" she asked, baiting him.

"I'm just ZLOT."

So, he wants to keep it cryptic. *"Okay then, ZLOT it is."*

"Keep this message box open. Back soon." And then he was gone.

Cali had no idea what "back soon" meant. An hour, a day,

weeks—what? Fifteen minutes later she had her answer. Over 118 domestic and international companies, comprised of humanitarian organizations, non-profits, foundations, and business corporations, along with their financial records with key banking transactions circled, came through in one large compressed file. Someone, perhaps her Source, had put together a flow chart showing their links and sub-links connecting them to each other. At the hub of the operation was a company called BGC Trans Global Human Initiative Foundation.

ZLOT attached a message: *"Follow the money. Ask yourself who sits on these Boards? What government leaders have vested interests in any of these operations? Stavros has already been eliminated by people in power. Trust no one. Be careful. There's more coming soon... ###"*

Cali recognized the three pound symbols at the end of the message, which any journalist would know meant 'end of story'. Was ZLOT also in the news field? She abandoned that thought as fast as it had come in. Of course not, or he would have wanted to put his own byline on this expose. He was someone who knew how to easily navigate the Dark Web and anonymous chat forums to get what he wanted. That was his strength. Her strength was as an investigative researcher and reporter.

Forget sleep. She was too excited to let it wait another minute let alone until tomorrow. It was a big dump of info and ZLOT claimed to have more? Holy crap. How the hell did he manage to get confidential bank records for all these companies?! Her mind kept returning to the same question over and over again. Who exactly was ZLOT? The God of Information?

It didn't take her long to trace Constantine Stavros' connection to BGC Trans Global Human Initiative Foundation, located in Arlington, Virginia, from the information ZLOT had provided. They had offices around the world. Their mission statement talked about saving lives from the ravages of famine, poverty, war torn areas, and natural disasters. They hid under a human aid cover, but the more Cali dug the more certain she was from the regular bank statement transactions with key transport companies that they were human trafficking. This meant all the banks involved were complicit or these transactions would have been quickly flagged under current banking and money laundering laws.

Upon closer examination, Cali discovered that the banks and their subsidiaries in question were all linked back to Stavros. They were part of his banking empire, so of course, all parties would be shielded from investigative scrutiny. Stavros had bought up failing banks like kids eat candy. And from what she was finding, he was causing some of these banks to flounder, just so he could go in and save them for his own nefarious purposes. It was the classic manipulative ploy: Create the problem then offer the saving solution.

As she saw it right now, her biggest dilemma was how she was going to explain being in possession of private financial records for some top-level organizations, both civilian and governmental. No one would believe all this evidence came from only one confidential source. She might have more to worry about than just another late-night visit from FBI Agent R. J. Bond. Cali was not about to have what happened to WikiLeaks happen to her. Having this bombshell scoop on the biggest human sex traffickers in the world was a double-edged sword.

~~*~~

Meghan March saw Zach's phone text on her way into the Library. It immediately brought a smile to her face. He had two tickets to the National Symphony Orchestra at Kennedy Center tomorrow evening. Would she like to go? She was about to text 'YES' back when she realized Izzie's birthday party with her friends was at Noon that same day and she would have to find a sitter for a child who would be hyped up on sugary sweets all day. Meghan hated to foist that on anyone.

MEGHAN: I'd love to. Can I get back to you today on that? I have to check if my sitter is available.

ZACH: If she's not free, let me know. Angie in the Young Reader's Room is majoring in Child Development and often sits for other employee's kids.

MEGHAN: Didn't know that. Thanks.

ZACH: If you're free for lunch today, meet me outside the Madison Café at 1:00 PM. I may have another surprise for you. I think you'll like it.

MEGHAN: Sounds intriguing. I love surprises. I'll be there.

Meghan also loved the fact that Zach was trying to please her. Moms with small children didn't get that very often. It made Meghan feel special, desired, and her mind immediately flashed back to their first kiss the other night in her driveway. She hadn't been kissed in a long time. At least, not like that. It spoke of both promise and passion. Was it too much to ask for more of that in her life? Did life always have to be about tending to the needs of one's child and not oneself? She didn't think so, but sometimes she felt guilty about wanting more free time to herself, a vacation on her own, a fulfilling intimate relationship, a little person not always asking "why?" or "can I?"

She called her sitter that very moment and was relieved to learn she was free on Sunday night. Thank you, God, Meghan whispered silently to herself. This time she knew it was a "date" and was excited at the thought of being wooed.

Chapter 20

In anticipation of seeing Meghan again, Zach experienced an unusually strong desire to please *her* quest for knowledge and not just *his* alone. This was an entirely new concept to him. He had been a lone geek for so long that sharing information with someone of the opposite sex felt strange and foreign. But he embraced the feeling knowing it would put a smile on her face that would send her number eights into super-sonic overdrive. That alone would be worth watching.

With that goal in mind, he went back into the LOT to specifically retrieve information on the golden Minerva statue. It was an easy task, but how to convey what he witnessed in holographic detail of the statue's concept and strange beginnings was another story. He couldn't very well give Meghan a video of the event. It was historically and theoretically impossible.

The statues were much older than he originally thought, long before the time of video recording and, surprisingly, the artist had created several copies of the same statue. Everything he saw he edited then transcribed into a document, complete with still pictures that he hoped would not raise more questions than he was able to answer.

He was grateful that she was right on time for their lunch meeting. Zach was always at least 10 minutes early getting anywhere. Lateness was something that caused his brain to register mild anxiety, so he avoided it like the plague. But in his heart, he knew he would have waited for her no matter how long it took.

His eyes never wavered from the sight of her. Her red hair was tied back in a bouncy ponytail that swayed with her every step. She had a red leather tote bag slung carelessly over her shoulder which kept slipping down with its weight, yet she seemed not to notice. He watched her glance at her watch, then pick up her pace with a determined stride, making her way down the long hallway leading to their designated meeting spot. Zach noticed everything about her with both an analytic and appreciative eye. He saw her eyes light up with recognition when she spotted him waiting for her outside the 6th Floor Cafe among the streams of Library employees heading into lunch. A shy tentative smile pursed her lips, that she tried to hide, but he saw it. He would forever enjoy watching thoughts play across her beautiful face as she walked towards him. It caused charges of electricity to build up inside him, that he wasn't sure what to do with.

When she reached his side there was another brief moment of awkwardness—like should she hug or kiss him, especially after their last kiss? Zach sensed she wasn't sure or maybe not comfortable with public displays of affection, especially around other library personnel. In time, he was confident that would change. But for now, he was just happy to see and be with her.

The well-stocked Madison Building Cafe provided a vast array of different world cuisines in cafeteria-style, which both admin and personnel flocked to each day to not only eat but meet and take breaks. As usual it was crowded. He grabbed a tray and they both opted for Thai food then found an empty table alongside a long-windowed wall that afforded a view of The Hill. Next to them, a table of four were playing poker while eating pizza and drinking beer.

"I don't have much time for lunch today," Meghan apologized, as Zach pulled out her chair before taking his seat.

"Me neither," he echoed. "But I wanted to show you what I was able to dig up on the Congressional Reading Room's golden Minerva statue."

Her eyes grew wide. "Really? You actually found something?"

He extracted his laptop from his backpack and powered it on. "Don't ask me where I found this information, because it's not in the general public realm. That's all I can say right now. But I can tell you that no one else in this Library has this information. You'll be the first."

She set down her fork and moved aside her meal to get a closer look at what he had. Zach watched her face light up with excitement as she read what he had prepared for her. She looked up at him in total disbelief.

"Oh. My. God. This is amazing! It's a rare treasure and it's not even behind lock and key?!"

"Well technically it is, since that room is not open to the public," he pointed out. "But you're right. It dates to the Early Egyptian Dynasty, 3rd Millennium B.C. where they used a 'lost wax' method for casting precious metals, like gold."

"Yes. I've read about that technique. It was called *cire perdue*," she added.

"That's right. And the artisan was Egyptian by birth. His name was Hares Badru Adeben. I learned he was a master artisan and twelfth son to a vizier serving Pharaoh Djoser around 2650 BC. Some believe this was during the recorded time of Imhotep, the architect of the Great Pyramid."

Zach glossed over that fact, since what he saw in the records did not jibe with what was traditionally taught. The Great Pyramid and the Sphinx went back a lot longer in time that most people ever thought, but he didn't have time to get into that now. Perhaps it was just too esoteric. Best to stay with the official narrative, since he had no way to prove what he had seen.

Meghan examined the statue's pictures. "This is just incredible. It says here that Adeben crafted 12 golden statues for King Djoser, but it doesn't say where they all are or why they were made."

Zach had also been surprised to learn 12 Minerva statues had been made and then were scattered to different parts of the world. But the records he saw did not say where all the statues presently resided, other than the one now in the Library of Congress. He would have to question Satya on those finer details.

Meghan tilted her head towards his and whispered, "Don't you find it odd that he made 12 statues, exactly alike, and in gold, and none of them have any record for what became of them? Sounds like a good museum mystery."

His very thoughts. He liked that she had a good inquiring mind and was interested in detail. Too bad he didn't have an answer to her question—at least, not yet.

Meghan continued reading. "It looks like the one our Library has was handed down over time until it came into the hands of Thomas Jefferson in 1800, the year before he became president of the United States. That's incredible."

Zach was all too aware that there were missing pieces to this story. His photographic memory of history zeroed in on the year 1801 with both Jefferson and Aaron Burr running for President of the United States. It was the first electoral tie to ever happen between two contenders for the highest position in the land, forcing a vote in the House of Representatives to settle the crisis. Votes continued to be tallied until finally on the 36th ballot they finally broke the deadlock, making Burr the Vice President. There were other strange things about Jefferson's life that made Zach wonder if the golden Minerva somehow played a fateful part. But for now, with Meghan, he stuck to the basics of what he knew.

"You know, it was rumored that Thomas Jefferson was a Freemason, as many of the Founding Fathers were," Zach added. "But no records have ever been found that Jefferson was actually initiated into a Masonic Lodge."

Meghan was looking at him with rapt attention. God, he loved that look on her face. He would talk facts to her all night to watch her face light up as it was now.

"However," he continued. "Jefferson laid the cornerstone in 1801 for the 'Jefferson Lodge'. It seems odd to name a Masonic Lodge after someone who is not a Freemason, even if he is the President. It's just not done without being a Masonic Member."

She was mulling that over. "The Library of Congress was founded in 1801 during his Presidency. But that was the old Library. Initially it was started in a boarding house before being moved to a room in the U.S. Capitol Building. Then this building got so large that the Madison and Adams Buildings were built. From what I know, historical records were very clear about having the current Library permanently established on this very spot."

Zach knew why this was so special. It was sitting right atop a natural portal into the LOT. Hidden in plain sight. It was quite possible Jefferson knew this.

Meghan was still thinking aloud. "Makes one wonder if the golden Minerva has been moved several times before coming to the Thomas Jefferson Building."

"Quite possibly." He watched, mesmerized, as little twos continued swimming in and around her auric field.

"So, what's the significance?" she asked.

"Significance?" He abruptly brought his thoughts back to her question. If she only knew how adorable she was when she was in deep thought processing mode. "I'm still digging... I hope to find that out. Soon."

She placed her hand briefly on his arm. He definitely noticed.

"Zach, I'm so impressed with what you found."

Yeah. Score one for the team, he thought.

"I haven't been able to learn anything at all about this statue. It's like a black hole surrounds it."

Meghan had no idea how close she was to the truth. But he didn't say anything. From what he understood, it was clear Jefferson had kept this golden Minerva piece until the Library of Congress was founded and then had it secured atop a marble pedestal. Perhaps it had been secretly moved several times before finding its final resting place, like a permanent cornerstone, in the Congressional Reading Room. Few would probably ever know its true history let alone what it might really signify.

If he had to guess, it most likely had something to do with Minerva the organization, or M12, as he now referred to it. There were so many ancient secret societies organized to protect knowledge. Were many of the Founding Fathers clued into the greatest cache of knowledge of all times right inside the LOT? If so, had Minerva always been evil as Roone and Satya had pointed out, or had it been hijacked and corrupted somewhere down the line? And if so, by whom?

It was becoming increasingly clear to Zach that he was not asking the right questions in the LOT. He might be getting what he requested, but it could be only a fraction of the whole story. Specificity was key. The LOT was mammoth, limitless, and Minerva was complex.

There was just him trying to sort it all out. Satya had implied that he would figure it all out, eventually. She hadn't actually said it aloud, but he caught her thinking it before he even realized he was getting snippets of her directed thoughts when he was in a

234

highly focused state inside the LOT. However, he would have to start formulating more probing and well thought out questions if he wanted to get to the bottom of what was really going on.

His thoughts returned to Meghan, who was now picking at her Thai noodles, barely eating, while clicking through pictures and additional notes he had assembled.

"Would it be okay to get a copy of all this stuff?" she asked hopefully.

He extracted a small USB stick from his pocket and handed it to her. "All yours. If I find anything else for your book research, I'll let you know."

The ecstatic look on her face was like a thousand thank yous simultaneously entering his field in a giant wave of energy, akin to a particle accelerator. He *HAD* pleased her.

~~*~~

Senator Talbot thrived on creating chaos to work to his benefit. The adrenaline rush he often felt when maneuvering, then entrapping his opponents in a no exit strategy, until the scent of fear was upon them, fetid and strong, was something he had honed and perfected over the years like an animal hunting its prey. To last in Washington and climb to the pinnacles of power, one had to adhere to the law of survival of the fittest and abandon any notion of moral conscience. Some political pundit had once remarked that 95% of Congress was compromised in some way or another. The truer estimate was closer to 99%.

The righteous or weak ones were quickly singled out and eliminated in one way or another, either via reputation smears, the always reliable sex scandal, or some other covert and undetectable means that would render them inoperable.

A man of his stature hadn't risen through the ranks to become Chairman of the Senate's Committee on Intelligence by being Mr.

Nice Guy. That might be his public persona, but underneath it all he knew how to make things happen, which would shock a lot of decent folks. He would certainly rot in hell for some of his acts, if there even was such a place. But unlike the pious and devout, he believed that this was the only chance life dealt you, so make the most of it while you can, because the afterlife was probably just a fantasy designed to appease and control the masses into submission.

This was why he had no qualms at all about Constantine Stavros being eliminated. It was the right call. And now he was tasked with cleaning up the aftermath of the mess. As head of the Senate Intelligence Committee he was supposed to know all these things. In his case, he always did. His sources in the intelligence agencies briefed him officially and unofficially each day. There would always be a symbiotic relationship with those who monitored, recorded and kept the nation's secrets.

The annoying aspect of the "Stavros Situation" was that those who weren't in the loop of privileged information were asking questions about his own relationship with the man. They wanted to know how come he hadn't known about Stavros' human trafficking and sex pipeline operations, and why nothing had been done about it? Such a stupid question. One usually feigned surprise or denied any knowledge of such queries. It was better to look like a fool than an aiding and abetting criminal. And God knew, he was nobody's fool.

While posing such stupid questions, many already knew the answers. In fact, the whole goddamn Congress probably knew on some level how things really worked on The Hill. And if they didn't when they arrived here all dewy eyed as self-crusading warriors for constitutional justice, then they certainly learned lickety-split how to avoid being devoured and spit out whole by those few players who dominated the system.

It was all a big power game, which one could learn to love.

And if you didn't dip your hand into the cookie jar of opportunity right fast, then others standing in the wings were only too willing to take your place. People came to Washington and if they played the system right, they could and would leave as millionaires before their constituents voted them out of office.

His first wife, Gwen, not that he wanted a second one, had been too weak to play the Washington game once she got a glimpse of the man behind the mask she had married. He could feel her shrink from him whenever he tried to touch her, like she was cavorting with the devil himself. Instead, she became obsessed with mothering Meghan to avoid fulfilling his sexual needs. Which, truth be told, were easy to get met any time of the day or night elsewhere.

Power was the ultimate aphrodisiac. But while he could have anyone he truly wanted, he still exercised a modicum of discretion to avoid unnecessary and potentially sticky entanglements. It was his experience that affairs with married women generally posed fewer problems, like with Camille Eldridge--especially if their husbands were also on the prowl or had mistresses stashed away elsewhere.

He knew for a fact that Martin Eldridge didn't give a flying fuck what Talbot did with his wife just so long as she was kept occupied and out of his hair. True, the woman had a bit of a sadistic streak in bed, but pain could be a real turn on when she tied up his balls and played nasty warrior bitch. Gwen would have never thought to do such things. It would have shocked her to her very core. At least Camille had never bored him. But she could be a handful, coming from one control freak to another.

Lately, when he wasn't out of town, he found himself dropping by her place on The Hill for a quick romp. He didn't have to hide who he really was with her, because they pretty much were cut from the same cloth--ruthless and conquering and out for whatever they could get.

When his first wife, Gwen, had succumbed to a myriad of pills to emotionally escape him, he decided she had become an outright liability. There were things she knew and had discovered about him, which he didn't want to ever accidentally come out in a messy divorce settlement, which she had threatened. It was clear she had to go. It was quite easy to help her over the edge resulting in the official story of an "accidental overdose" from sleeping pills. He rather preferred to think of it as putting her out of her misery—like Meghan's god-awful choice of a husband.

He loved his daughter, as she loved him. He would do anything for her. She was the only person in his life who had never really disappointed him until Brett March had come into the picture and the two had decided to marry. The intelligence file he had amassed on Brett confirmed he was a cheating psycho and a control freak with a growing gambling addiction. Another liability.

While he had done his fatherly best to discourage the quick marriage, Meghan believed she was truly in love and the two of them would live happily ever after. Women! He was never that naive to fall for such magical thinking. But things had turned out okay, even after he had arranged for the F-35 Brett was flying to have a little flight control system problem, causing a compressor stall. Then there was the matter of making sure the ejection seat canopy failed to deploy. These things were easy to arrange, just like pushing sailors off aircraft carriers if you didn't like them. It was done all the time, with no one the wiser. Palms were greased or blackmail employed, and then sometimes those individuals necessitated being disposed of as well. Cleanup in Washington was a never-ending job.

But he was grateful that Meghan had not turned into her mother with all her mental health and morality issues. It was best that she and Izzie had been placed under his watchful eye. Being widowed, losing her mom, and becoming a single parent at such a young age had served to quickly mature her. He was proud of what his daughter was becoming. And he was quite sure she didn't harbor any more pie in the sky notions about life and love anymore. In time, he would find someone loyal to him to match her with and close that loop.

All his life he had been known as a fixer. Which brought him back to Stavros, who had been their key banking man. Stavros had known how to quickly and quietly move money through thousands of offshore accounts without raising questions or governmental oversight. And if there was too much heat bringing in human payload and fulfilling numbers, he and others knew how to come in and block or shut down such efforts. If you slowed things down long enough in the House or Senate, people would soon forget in a sea of other pressing issues.

With Stavros gone, they had immediately filled his role. Minerva had contingency plans in place for every member should his/her seat be vacated under any circumstances—death or otherwise. However, after that sudden and unexpected video of Stavros had gone viral, exposing him and his exploits, some of their players were running scared wondering if they could be next. There was a spy and whistleblower working in their midst and they had yet to ferret out the culprit. How else had such a video ever been shot and released?

Consequently, Minerva had been forced to start running defense contracts through newer organizational entities not related to Stavros, which could pose an additional risk when you started making changes to what had always worked so well for decades within their banking structure. While change is inevitable, it's not usually welcomed, especially if you have a lot to lose.

Talbot found himself suddenly assuring CEOs of major corporations that their detention camp contracts, a source of large-scale trafficking operations both domestic and international, were safe from further scrutiny. It was an elaborate numbers game. He knew very few really cared if many of these illegal, kidnapped or fostered individuals got lost in the system and ultimately landed up being used for other purposes—especially the children. They were faceless to him and therefore expendable. He had long ago pushed aside any conscionable qualms. These operations and mechanisms were necessary to continue to fund and run the massive worldwide Minerva network. It was their power base much like the heroin poppy fields of Afghanistan were once the lifeblood to the U.S. Intelligence agencies.

~~*~~

Meghan had already tried on seven different outfits for tonight's date with Zach, rejecting them all. Too sexy, too conservative, too Mommish, too… She was obsessing about something that was not like her to obsess about at all. She had always been told she had an impeccable fashion sense and that she could have been a model if she had really wanted to. Yet, when she looked in the mirror, she saw reflected back skin which was too delicate, hair too brazen and coppery, and a body that would never be runway ready, especially after having a child. She had never really believed the whole 'you could be a model' hype anyway.

She finally settled on a little black dress, which hugged her curves and tastefully showed some leg without being overly provocative. It wasn't up to her ass too short and it DID make her look thinner—which was the true litmus test for any dress. Since Zach was tall, she didn't have to compromise on the height of her black heels and went for it. She examined herself in the mirror and was pleased with what she saw. Yes, this outfit would be just perfect for a night at the Kennedy Center.

Meghan loved the National Symphony Orchestra and wasn't

sure how Zach had known the Kennedy Center was one of her favorite Washington venues. Izzie hadn't yet acquired a taste for classical music. She was more content to dance around to ABBA or her rock favorite of the week.

She heard Zach's car arrive in the driveway and peaked out her upstairs bedroom window which overlooked the front entry. He emerged from the car wearing a fitted dark suit and carrying a small bouquet of flowers--pink with yellow centered Gerbera daisies in one hand and red roses in the other.

He was turning out to be a real surprise, in more ways than expected. The roses were a very nice touch, and she suspected the daisies were for Izzie so she wouldn't feel left out. It was both a thoughtful and endearing gesture showing he had taken the time—just like in the restaurant with the balloons and birthday cake for Izzie. He probably hadn't learned that attentiveness to others from his Godzilla-like mother.

Suddenly she had nervous butterflies in her stomach. She glanced back to the mirror to recheck herself. Maybe she should have swept her hair up instead of letting it fall loose around her face. Earrings! She rummaged through her jewelry box and carefully chose her mother's diamond ear drops which were heart-shaped with tiny emeralds in the center, given to Meghan to wear on her wedding day. Her mother had always told her they would bring her luck. She paused to reconsider. That marriage hadn't been the shining example of good fortune. She pushed that thought away. The earrings were beautiful. She loved them and it wasn't their fault if her marriage hadn't gone as planned. Maybe they had a delayed good luck effect.

There was no sense in dawdling any longer. Izzie would be downstairs talking Zach's head off if she didn't rescue him quickly. Her daughter was still on a chocolate sugar high from her pool party birthday earlier in the day. It was a relief when the children's parents finally picked up their whooping and screaming kids and took them home. The place was a mess. The pool guy would have to dump extra chlorine in the pool tomorrow. Someone had thrown in tootsie rolls, screaming one of them had pooped in the pool, causing a host of little girls to freak out and run around crazy. She had to get in herself and fish out the suspect candy.

Her sitter, Annie, would have her hands full tonight. Izzie had received a good stash of gifts and would stay up all night playing with each and every one of them until she got bored. Enough, she told herself. Time to go downstairs and join the world for an adult evening.

Meghan walked downstairs and didn't see them anywhere. She walked into the kitchen and spotted all three of them out on the veranda shaking away, doing some strange kind of dance movement. She paused to watch before going outside. Izzie was just too precious, giggling away and making exaggerated movements. Annie was trying to retain her dignity, but watching Zach's tall frame, in a suit and tie mind you, doing whatever it was he was doing made her laugh. It was beyond funny.

There was no music to their little dance, but all three of them were bobbing up and down in place, their knees slightly bent, flicking their wrists and flapping their arms this way and that and shaking away like primates at play. What in the world???

She finally stepped outside where Izzie immediately spotted her.

"Look, Mommy! Zach is teaching us how to do King Kong!"

Well, that explained it.

Zach let out a hearty laugh. "It's called Qigong, Izzie. And this position you're doing is called *Shaking the Tree*."

Izzie nodded and softly repeated 'Qigong' several times, hoping to get it right. She continued to dramatically shake in place. "Mommy, Zach says it helps release too much chocolate energy."

Zach had stopped the moment he caught sight of Meghan. He turned away from Izzie to give her mother his full attention. From the long appraising look he gave her, Meghan hoped he liked what he saw. It had taken over an hour to decide what to wear tonight, which was an all-time record on her part for indecisiveness.

"Wow. You look great." He carefully lifted the roses he had placed on the veranda table and moved toward her, extending the flowers in offering. "These are for you."

"They're beautiful, Zach. Thank you."

Izzie was not to be upstaged. "I got flowers, too. Pretty pink ones!"

Annie stepped forward. "Would you like me to put these in water for you?"

Meghan was always grateful for her help. "Yes. Would you mind?"

"Not at all," Annie said, taking both bouquets inside.

Meghan looked to Zach. "Shall we go?"

"Don't go yet," Izzie loudly chimed in, tugging at Zach's arm. "You were going to show me how to do the cube."

Cube? Meghan watched Izzie extract a Rubik's Cube from her birthday stash of new toys. "Zach told me he had one just like this when he was a kid. I mixed up all the colors, but I can't get them back in the right place. It's too hard."

Zach turned to Meghan. "Sorry. This won't take long."

"Okay, Izzie. Give it here," he instructed.

She handed it over to him. "I want you to say 'Start' and then start counting. I haven't done this in a while."

Meghan inwardly groaned. She hated that puzzle toy. It would drive any sane person insane. She had never been able to solve the darn thing and gave up trying a long time ago.

Zach held the cube firmly in his hands. Izzie shouted 'Go' and was completely mesmerized watching his hands speed over the cube, twisting and turning this way and that, so fast, his face a picture of hyper-focus, until he solved it and restored it to its original position on Izzie's count of six.

Meghan was so shocked her mouth dropped open. He looked almost disappointed that he had solved it in only six seconds! "How did you do that?" she blurted out.

He shrugged. "It's based on an algorithm, which is the synthesis of hundreds of algorithms. I figured it out after my head injury. It's really quite simple--kind of like seeing 10 moves ahead of you in a chess play."

Both Meghan and Izzie just stared at him, utterly speechless.

"I used to be able to do it in less than four seconds, which is pretty much the world record, but I'm out of practice."

Izzie immediately saw the toy's potential. "Can you teach me how so I can show my friends?" she begged, yanking on his sleeve.

Meghan stepped in and took the Rubik's Cube from Zach's hands.

"Another time, Izzie. Now say goodbye to Zach. We have to get going."

"Alright," Izzie murmured, clearly disappointed. She reached for him on her tippy-toes. He squatted down a bit and let her hug him. "Goodnight, Zach. Next time you can teach me this trick. Okay?" He nodded.

With one last thought, she grinned and whispered in his ear. "Have lots of fun with my Mommy. But better not take her to the pyramids."

He hugged her back. "You got it."

~~*~~

Cali had received another massive download from ZLOT that afternoon. This drop included pictures of children as young as three years, and some as old as 13, with strange statistics on the back of their photo. It included their name and surname, their birthday, age, blood type, months in custody, location of camp, country of origin, and inmate number. Cali was shocked to also find a "Due for Disposal" followed by a year. What was more puzzling was a notation on the quality of the child's blood. Chills ran up and down her spine. These children were being trafficked and harvested for their blood, then possibly killed. The question was "why"? There were numerous blood banks all over the world, which already supplied this need and for free.

Cali started with a search on the thousands of names listed that ZLOT had somehow managed to get his hands on. Many matches she found were missing children, going back as far as 20 years. Some had histories--heart-rending stories of loss from parents who had never stopped looking for their child or given up hope of a reunion. Some names didn't show up anywhere in the system searches. These kids were less likely to be missed. They were mostly runaways, street addicts or those forced into prostitution to survive. So many were undocumented that it was like a ghosted population.

The eye-opening revelation for Cali was that big name corporations, some with recognizable brand names, were also involved in this lucrative business of being contractors of detention camp facilities for governments all over the world. Who was regulating these facilities, she wondered?

When Cali did a search on a few of the different facility names, which she found noted on the back of each child's photo, information came up which appeared to point to these facilities operating more as torture vs. detention camps. Some had been cited for lack of hygiene, filthiness, abuse, rape, and that always suspect 'missing detainees'. Yet, the worst were still operating. They had not been shut down, but only slapped with health and building violations or fines that amounted to almost nothing compared to what the government was paying them.

Cali suspected she was sitting on the tip of a very large iceberg. This could very well turn into the story of all stories and no one was even touching it. That meant the corruption and complicity ran deep and reached some very high places.

It was such a tangled web, that she started doing spreadsheets of the information she had in order to put all the pieces and players together. She knew it would take all weekend and more to cross-reference banking transactions and find out who really owned these shell companies. Hundreds of billions of dollars were funneled through accounts every day and yet managed to remain hidden off the radar scope. It was a global industry built on human misery and suffering. It wasn't just Constantine Stavros. There were others in high places of power that had to be profiting from this as well. Despite what the public knew about these publicly traded corporations, they were leading secret lives and allowing such travesties to go on.

Cali's thoughts kept returning to the mystery question of blood harvesting. What were they looking for? She had yet to find any info on adult blood records. She knew there was something she was missing in this whole picture. Perhaps, some unknown factor about blood properties?

Cali had amassed a D.C. roster of sources in all areas of medicine and life. Some were professional contacts from AA groups she had developed. She took everyone's business card at these meetings if she thought they might be useful down the line in her work. It was her experience that fellow addicts were always more helpful than non-addicts. Supporting each other was key to remaining sober.

There was that handsome doc, a Nathan something or the other, who she had met at a Bethesda AA group about two months ago. The poor thing was such a geek he had talked about blood platelets ad nauseam. Of course, she had probably led him on, looking all interested in his every last word--he was that hot.

She couldn't exactly remember if they had screwed that night or not. Then it came back. Oh, yes. That one was definitely a one-night stand. Handsome as all sin but a premature ejaculator in the bedroom. The guy didn't stick around to finish the job. Was there any more grievous a sin in the bedroom? Not in her book.

Cali checked her listings. Nathan I. Lippman. There was a "BIB" next to his name, branding him "bad in bed"—a sexual bust. The guy worked in Blood Services at Walter Reed National Military Medical Hospital as a plasma specialist. He should know something. As she recalled all too clearly, he professed to know everything. She gave him a call.

Chapter 21

Before attending that night's National Symphony Concert, Meghan and Zach enjoyed dinner and wine at the Rooftop Terrace restaurant inside The John F. Kennedy Center for the Performing Arts. They avoided political talk like the plague and chose instead to share strange and funny experiences about growing up as an only child. Zach was determined to hear her laugh and see her enjoy herself.

He leaned closer. "Can I tell you a secret?"

Meghan's eyes grew wide. "Oh absolutely. I love secrets."

"I was a lonely geeky kid."

She rolled her eyes in feigned surprise. "No?"

"Yes. I'd bring home stray animals for something to play with and hide them in my room hoping not to get caught," Zach admitted. "My mother found out and put an immediate stop to it. A rather large snake went missing from my room one day and showed up under the dining room table during one of her dinner parties. There were several women who leapt on their chairs screaming when they saw it. My mother was one of them."

Meghan looked at him skeptically. "I find that hard to believe.

Your mother is like…" she searched for the right words. "A force to be reckoned with?"

Zach chuckled, wondering how she had so accurately assessed his mother. "My mother never likes to lose her cool and that so many of her influential friends witnessed such a spectacle, was beyond mortifying to her. I was grounded for a whole month. I had to stay in my room, which was no big deal. I read a ton of science books and was perfectly content."

"No comic books?"

"Well, yeah. For light reading of course. All the Marvel Comic series as well."

Meghan was on her second glass of wine. He could see a rosy flush rising on her cheeks. She was laughing with abandon, finding him entertaining.

"And your super-power of choice?" she wanted to know.

He didn't hesitate in his answer. "Being lucky."

She looked at him somewhat surprised. He smiled. He was definitely feeling his super power today. "And yours?" he prompted.

Meghan thought about it for a moment. "Definitely, Wonder Woman. She was the total package."

He wanted to tell her she was already the total package. "I find you are pretty incredible in and of your own right."

"Thank you," she whispered, going suddenly shy again.

But her recovery was quick. She leaned forward in her chair. "My secret is that I wanted to be a film maker."

"Really?" He was curious.

She pursued her lips and took another sip of wine. "Yes. I got a video camera for my birthday one year and decided to try my hand at making a Halloween horror film with some friends. Our house was to be the haunted mansion, with a slasher on the loose ala Nightmare on Elm Street style."

"Sounds intriguing. What happened?"

"I've always liked experimenting in the kitchen, so I put lots of dark cherries in my mother's pressure cooker, hoping to make realistic looking blood for the horror scene."

Zach rolled his eyes. "This doesn't sound good. How old were you?"

"About eight or nine. The pressure cooker exploded and there was cherry pulp and juice drippings all over the kitchen and white cabinets. It was everywhere. I mean everywhere--just a total disaster. My parents walked into the kitchen, saw me covered in what they thought was blood, started screaming and immediately called 911. It totally freaked me out. Of course, I too was grounded. No sleepovers with friends for two weeks."

"NO. Must have been very hard. And your film career???"

"Ended right there and then. And the video camera mysteriously disappeared."

"Hmm. What about the pressure cooker?"

She ran her tongue over her lips, savoring the wine and enjoying retelling her story. He found himself wanting to kiss those lush red lips. He was hopeless.

"We still have it. But I get PTSD every time I lay eyes on it."

"I can see now where Izzie gets her mischievous nature." Zach suddenly glanced at his watch and motioned for the waiter to bring the check. "I hate to break this up, but we had better go. Our seats await us."

The Concert Hall was filled to capacity as they were shown to their seats in section Box Tier 1, Row A on a side balcony overlooking the stage, where over 100 musicians were already tuning up their instruments for tonight's performance. A guest conductor from Italy was performing the Franz Schubert Symphony 9 in C Major--one of Zach's favorites.

As the lights dimmed and the music began to play, his senses, as always, went into overdrive. Music was like math to his brain—evoking deeper emotions in his very core being. The connection clicked in immediately and he felt gratitude to have Meghan sharing this experience with him. She might never know what it felt like to be inside his brain during music, but he used his ability to move energy by surrounding them both in a bubble where she might sense the difference.

At one point he glanced over to see her eyes filling with tears. Yep, she was feeling it. He gently reached over and took Meghan's hand in his, soft and warm, yet oddly enough very grounding. There was an almost imperceptible little squeeze back. Her head turned and their eyes met. With full intent this time, he leaned over and softly kissed her on the lips, not caring who saw them.

He knew someone was observing them. His senses were too keen, his brain too aware, to not know when thoughts were directed at him. He could feel familiar eyes across the room boring into him. For just a second, he glanced away from Meghan, trying to locate the source he knew was somewhere across the concert hall. Like a tracking device, he zeroed in on a sea of faces before he felt the connective link. There, sitting in a front row box tier on the other side of the hall, next to some unknown younger man, he locked on the scrutinizing and judgmental eyes of his mother. One raised eyebrow told him exactly what she was thinking before she returned her attention back to the orchestra going into its second movement.

~~*~~

Cali got Nathan Lippman on the first ring.

"I was just thinking about you," he said all breathless.

Right! Had she interrupted him while diddling himself with Vaseline? The possibility of him using her image to fuel his fantasy and get his rocks off, made her want to vomit. But like a good journalist, she put aside her personal feelings for the sake of the story. He had something she wanted, so she got right to the point.

"Nathan, I was just thinking of you as well and knew I had to give you a call."

His breathing seemed to get deeper, hopeful. "Really?"

"Yes. Really." She hoped she wasn't laying it on took thick. "Would you like to come over?"

Damn! She *had* taken it too far. "I'm sorry but I can't. It's so tempting, but I am on deadline right now and I need your help."

Suddenly he was all business. "Sure. What do you need?"

"Well…I need someone who knows everything about blood and, of course, I thought of you."

"Yes. That's true."

Hot, but definitely still cocky. Unfortunately, not the good kind of "cocky". She caught herself. Stop thinking about such things. Focus, Cali!

She was trying to find a way to word her initial question, without sounding like an Anne Rice vampire chronicles inquest. "I need to know if there is anything in a child's blood that has beneficial properties?"

There was a long moment of silence on the other end. In fact, she wasn't sure if she had lost their connection. "Nathan? Are you still there?" she prompted.

"Yes. I'm still here. Why do you want to know?" His voice was dead serious.

Uh oh. Now he sounded slightly annoyed with a layer of caution. A different tactic might be called for right now.

"I have some old medical records on a child and wondered why "Quality of Blood" would be noted, as well as "Daily Quota" amounts.

He swore under his breath. "Is this a missing child?"

"Well, yeah. How did you know that?"

"Honey, you need to be careful."

She didn't like the sound of that or that he called her 'honey'. It rankled her. She also hated when people beat around the bush. "Just tell me what it means, Nathan. Please."

"Okay." He paused, trying to find the right words. "This child you're asking about is probably a C9H9NO3 Adrenochrome harvesting candidate. Adrenochrome is a highly valued chemical compound, which is synthesized through the oxidation of epinephrine, also known as adrenaline. It's harvested through the medulla in the adrenal glands of live humans only and children appear to have an abundance of it, under certain conditions."

She was tempted to tell him to speak English. "What do people use adrenochrome for?"

"Some use it as a psychedelic to get high. Others use it as a fountain of youth to turn back time. It's a non-controlled unscheduled substance and the FDA has not approved it as a drug. I should also add that it has addictive properties."

There was something he said that bothered her. "What did you mean when you said children produce adrenochrome under 'certain conditions'?"

"This is where it gets murky," he replied. "This adrenaline hormone is released rather quickly into the blood system under stress or extreme situations."

"What kind of situations?"

"Torture. Sexual abuse. Extreme fear. Anything which brings up a flight or fight response."

Oh. My. God. It was all starting to make sense and the ramifications were shocking, even sickening. It was an ugly puzzle that was assembling in her mind,

"So let me get this straight," she began. "Missing and or abducted children are a rich source of adrenaline-laden blood, which is harvested into adrenochrome. To attain high quality adrenalin, these kids are being held and tortured, just short of death to protect their investment. And all this so rich people can get high and feel young while their suppliers make millions? Do I have that right?"

Nathan let out a long sigh. "Yes. That about sums it up. Which is why I'm warning you. Be careful. And you didn't hear any of this from me."

~~*~~

Meghan knew the thoughts she was having right now would probably shock Zach. She wished there was somewhere they could just go to get wild and crazy together—like a hotel room. Her body seemed to be a little fire pit of desire. Perhaps it was the wine making her feel all mellow and sexy and craving something more. What would he think of her, or less of her, if she made such a brazen suggestion?

There was a moment at dinner when Zach looked at her like he might want to undress her right there on the spot, so she was pretty sure if she asked, he would not be averse to the suggestion or worse yet, say 'no'.

In the darkened concert hall, the Schubert music had woven a spell around them and it only seemed to intensify by the fourth movement of the performance. Truth be told, she didn't want to just hold hands. She wanted to sit in his lap and have him kiss her all over. She liked the way he kissed. It was soulful and awakened feelings inside her that she had thought long dormant.

Perhaps her sexual dry spell had just gone on way too long for normal human endurance. She felt drawn to Zach and, more importantly, for right now, she also felt safe with him. If there was more beyond that they would discover it in time.

As they walked silently to his car in the parking garage, her hand in his, she decided to take the plunge. "You know what I would like right now?" she said, leaning against the passenger side door with a shy smile.

He knew what she was going to say before she said it, but he played along. He leaned in closer feeling her energy sizzling all over the place. "No. What would you like, Meghan?" he asked with the barest hint of suggestion.

She bit her lip, a moment of uncertainty flash dancing in and stealing away her courage. His body moved in until there was barely an inch separating them. He studied her eyes, her face. "Would you like me to kiss you again?"

Good God. Was she that readable? Breathlessly she nodded yes and reached out, wrapping her arms around his neck, and dragged him against her like he had done that first night in her driveway. His lips came down on hers in a fiery heat and she surrendered her mouth to his, feeling her knees go all weak. His hands were in her hair, his arms around her holding her from falling at the intensity of his kiss.

This was not like his other two kisses. It felt like he was claiming her, marking her as his. Her mouth opened to him and let him in, the intimacy sparking off sensors all over her body. She was aware of his hard arousal pressing against her and knew she could ask anything of him right now and he would give it to her.

She came up breathless for air, letting her hand slide down between them until it rested on his belt, not venturing any lower. "Can we go somewhere where we don't need all these clothes?" she asked.

If he was shocked, he gave no indication of it. Only to be confirmed when he immediately answered. "That sounds like a great idea."

Some guy, exiting the parking garage, passed by and yelled out his window "Get a room!"

They both stared at each other, then laughed.

"Right." Zach said, confirming the suggestion. He hugged her to him one more time, before opening the passenger side door and helping her in. Less than 15 minutes later, they were at his place near DuPont Circle. The second the door closed behind them they were all over each other. All sense of shyness or propriety dissolved. He tugged at the zipper of her dress, while she fumbled with the buttons of his shirt. He threw his jacket and tie over a leather chair, never taking his eyes off her as he quickly helped her out of her dress.

As the dress dropped to the floor, she stood before him in black lacy underwear. He took a slight step back to take in the whole picture. Her long legs, her creamy white skin, her flaming red hair, and she knew he was already visualizing what lay beneath those lacy strands of fabric. She reached behind her back and with a quick snap, undid her bra and let it fall to the floor.

Zach stepped in, reaching out and gently cupped each breast in his large hands, caressing them with his warmth, feeling their weighty fullness before leaning down and kissing each one. He watched her face as he fingered each nipple, feeling it harden for him, discovering which one was the most sensitive, the tripwire to the rest of her sexual being. She went instantly wet at his sensual touch, feeling like she would come right there on the spot.

"You are incredibly beautiful," he said almost reverently. "You take my breath away."

She wanted him out of those trousers, like now. Her fingers were itching to touch and explore him as well, feel him—know his body and let him do the same to her. As if reading her wanton thoughts, Zach gently took her hand, kissed her palm and then placed it over his growing hardness. She felt his immediate response as it sprung to full attention, straining against his zipper, wanting out. It brought a smile to her lips. She had done that.

Zach's breath hitched in his throat as she cupped him firmly in her hand, watching his face as she did. Meghan was killing him and was discovering her power. He didn't want things over before they began, so he took back the reigns. He scooped her up in his arms and carried her to the bedroom where he laid her back on his bed, her head propped up against the pillows, her nakedness displayed in all its glory for him to see. He felt drunk at the sight of her. The energy flowing between them was like rolling waves in an ocean coming home to shore.

He never took his eyes off her as he quickly divested himself of his clothes. She watched his every move with eyes growing slightly wider as he freed his hardened cock from his shorts and stood before her completely naked.

There was no mistaking it. Meghan liked what she saw. She pulled aside the covers and beckoned him to join her. He needed no further invitation and sank down into the bed next to her letting his hands roam over her back and down to cup her ass, pulling her closer until there was total skin to skin contact between them.

Her lush breasts were against his chest, his cock pressing against her panties. Their mouths were joined, as their tongues danced in unison. He broke the contact only for a second to steady his breathing and still the pounding of his heart, while his hand continued to languidly explore her.

His senses were overloading again and hers were not much better from what he could see. Light was shooting out of her, her energy pooling in her lower body and wanting a release. Without a second thought to his own needs, he decided tonight would be about her pleasure. She had a powerful need and he wanted to be the one to fill it, no matter what it cost.

Zach moved a hand down to the band of her lace panties, then lower until his fingers felt the dampness of her desire through the thin barrier. She was more than ready. He moved his mouth to her soft, smooth breasts then drew a nipple into his mouth and gently suckled. A little moan of pleasure escaped her lips, her nipple hardening as he laved it with his tongue.

He reveled in the connection, her body like a fine-tuned instrument that responded to his touch. She didn't know that he could energetically see her every response and was able to follow and map her to allow for maximum pleasure. And because he was able to sense her like this, his desire was to know and taste every inch of her. She strained against his hand as it rubbed against her most sensitive and private area. He removed her panties, admiring the lush red curls nestled between her legs. He lowered his head, breathing in her delicious sexual scent which was uniquely Meghan. His senses reeled. Oh so gently he parted her lips to take in her pink wetness. His tongue moved to that small sensitive nub hidden there and reveled in his first taste. It was electric. He heard her small moan of pleasure as his warm wet mouth took her into his, lapping up her juices. She jerked back in response, breathing heavily, reaching for him and wanting to caress and pleasure him as well. His needs could wait. He had other ideas.

"Relax, Meghan," he told her, caressing her right nipple. "Trust me. I've got you."

There was no way he could tell her how much he was enjoying himself by her allowing him to give her pleasure. As his mouth continued to explore the heat of her womanhood, he slipped one, then two fingers inside her, reaching for those most sensitive areas that would completely undo her. She was flooding inside, her breath coming fast and quick and an electrical current was zinging through her telling him she was close. He could decide to slow down and let it build even stronger for her, but he knew it would border on torture. Next time, which he hoped there was a next time, he could show her all he had learned about sexual Qigong and bringing a woman to completion. But right now, he would give her what she needed most. His fingers reached up deep inside her, thrusting harder. His thumb rubbed her little nub, while his mouth laved the rosy tips of her breast.

Meghan felt her orgasm come on like a roaring tsunami, wave upon wave of pleasure flash flooding over her with such intensity she screamed. No one had ever made her cry out before. OhMyGod. Sensations she hadn't known possible continued to rock her body. It was like he knew exactly where all her sensor switches were and had turned them all up to full blast.

She started crying. No, more like sobbing. It was so intense she couldn't help it. She was shaking all over and at a total loss for what to do. He immediately moved up to her face, wiping her tears and just held her. A part of her was mortified to have emotionally lost it like this, while her other part felt like she was being cradled and comforted like no one had ever done for her before—certainly not her dead husband.

There was so much grateful emotion coursing through her, along with tears still streaming down her face, that she was scared to death she might say something incredibly stupid like, "I love you," which would scare the living daylights out of him.

Zach seemed to sense her dilemma. He continued holding her close while lightly running his hand down her spine, which oddly enough gave her a sense of deep ease. She snuggled against him, seeking the warmth of his body and his comforting touch. A languid sleep stole over her. He covered them both with a light blanket.

Zach watched her sleep, knowing he might experience little rest for himself. When he saw how overwhelmed she was with tears, like some internal dam had burst, he had purposely taken on some of her energy to give her some relief. Unfortunately, he was feeling it all right now. The component of sexual charge was easy to dissipate for him, but the emotional stuff was always a little trickier, especially taking on someone else's energy. And now he knew. Meghan was an emotional sensitive, like him. Unlike her, he had years of practice quieting his heightened senses and the effects of his acquired savant syndrome.

As he held her subtle body quietly sleeping against his he ran through Qigong exercises in his mind which his physical body was not able to do with her next to him. He gloried in her nearness and found, to his surprise once again, that she was a good grounding agent for him.

Sleep would be welcomed later, but he walled it off from taking him like it had Meghan. He knew he would have to take her home eventually. Much as he would have liked to have her in his bed throughout the night and enjoy the discovery of awakening with her beside him in the morning, he knew she had Izzie and a sitter awaiting her return and, quite possibly, her senator father. In the future he vowed to be better prepared for such contingencies--as he was quite certain there would definitely be a next time.

~~*~~

Camille Eldridge wasn't sure what to think about Zach being involved with Talbot's daughter. That it had come as a complete surprise and shock to catch sight of her son, the bookish and sometimes too smart for his own good child she had given birth to kissing Meghan March, was putting it mildly. She hadn't even known they were seeing each other, and she prided herself on knowing such things.

It had been hard to focus and enjoy the remainder of the symphony concert wondering how long this little liaison had been going on without her knowledge. Was it serious and would it complicate her ongoing affair with Jim Talbot? Did Talbot even know about it and, if so, why had he not mentioned it?

Meghan had always been rather cool towards her, so Camille was no fool. The girl knew and did not approve of her father's sexual escapades with a married woman. She was courteous and civil towards Camille, but she shifted her eyes away in embarrassment whenever they met. Which caused her to dislike and dismiss the girl as inconsequential. No one dismissed Camille Eldridge in this town. But this interest in Zach somehow changed that all.

She had spotted the two in the Kennedy Center parking garage, as had many others she was sure, and that was no chaste kiss her son was performing on Meghan March. And if she knew her son, he was already seriously involved. While she knew he was no virgin, he had never once taken a lady friend home or talked about any girl with real interest.

If she hadn't known any better, she would have suspected him of being gay. But from reports she had gathered over the years his romantic interests ran to females even though they never lasted very long. She suspected he got bored easily and most women didn't know what to make of his strange intellect. Camille knew exactly how intelligent her son was even though he did his best to hide it and preferred instead to bury his talents in the world of libraries. If he thought she was clueless, then *he* was the real fool.

Quite frankly, she had given up a long time ago trying to introduce him to the right society fit. It didn't seem to exist. He wasn't interested in rich debutantes, stunning models or beautiful actresses, and even some of the brainier candidates had failed to intrigue him.

Zach had always done exactly what he wanted to do from day one. He cried and cried as an infant, wanting something she could not give him, and she refused to breastfeed him and ruin her figure. There were times he had that strange, other-worldly look on his little face that seemed to say—you're not my mother and why do I have to be in this useless tiny body? It always unnerved her.

Then, as an adult, he would spurn all attempts by her to play matchmaker. The subject was one of the biggest sources of contention between them. He had repeatedly told her to butt out of his life and mind her own business. But Meghan March—well Meghan was actually quite perfect, even with a young child.

Camille secretly smiled to herself, her thoughts taking shape and forming into concrete plans. Yes. Marrying the Eldridge and

Talbot power base together might work out just splendidly. Fate had finally done its work for her.

Talbot's military transport plane had landed about a half hour ago from London. There was business afoot with our CIA offices and the City of London bankers that had been keeping him busy of late. Most of what he did was classified, so she didn't ask. In politics there were some things you didn't want to know about and some things you absolutely had to know about. Knowing the difference between the two was key to surviving.

She glanced at the digital clock by her bed and undressed, leaving only a thin silk robe on to keep her warm in the air-conditioned coolness of her house. Talbot would be stopping by her place any minute now for a quick drink and romp before having his driver take him home to Bethesda. He liked it fast and furious and never stayed the night, which was perfectly fine with her. They had a tacit agreement on such matters, so as not to complicate things. Strange bedfellows, friends with benefits, or just fuck buddies all described their relationship. Whatever it was, it worked.

And right on cue, he rang her bell. She refused to give anyone a key, not even him. No matter where he was, he seemed to dominate the room--tonight was no different. Efficient as always, he had left his suit jacket and tie behind in his car and was already unbuckling his belt as he swept into the room. There was no pretense between them. She turned and walked to the bedroom, with him following close behind her.

"Drink?" she asked going over to a small wooden cabinet near the bed and bringing out a crystal decanter of Chivas Regal.

"Please. I'm beat."

She poured him a glass. As always, he liked it straight up, no ice. He took it from her and swigged it down like a thirsty man. It seemed to take the edge off, and he mellowed instantly. He unzipped his pants.

"Good trip?" she asked, cupping his balls with little response.

"No," he said, clearly irritated that he was having a harder timing getting it up these days. "Leaks and breaches are killing me."

He gave her a kiss. "Be a dear one and get out that little toy of yours."

He would never call it by its name. Camille opened her bedside drawer and brought out a silver box with his favorite toy--a penis ring that fit snugly around his cock and balls, allowing him to stay hard for some time. Since she was the prime beneficiary of that hardness, she was all too willing to oblige.

She gave him a few hard whacks to his ball sac, which never failed to excite him, making him instantly hard. She pushed him back on the bed, grabbed his member in her hand and brought the rubber tubing around. She flicked it hard into place, knowing that he loved the pain.

Camille dropped her robe. "Jim--I have some important news I just couldn't wait to tell you." She snapped the band one more time for good measure, hearing his feral grunt.

He was panting, but managed a "What?"

A supreme smile spread across her face. "Did you know that Meghan is fucking my son?"

Chapter 22

The last 24 hours had been like a Spanish Inquest. Too many people, both in the news field and outside it, had contacted her to casually inquire what she was working on these days—especially after her big Stavros reveal. Red warning flags went off in her head like sailing into dangerous waters in a regatta race. It was clear others suspected she was onto something explosive and far-reaching and they either wanted in on it or were probing to find out how much she had already uncovered.

Bad news always travels fast in Washington. Right after she floated the idea to her producer that she might have a bigger follow-up story to Stavros—one that involved wide-spread child trafficking and the evidence to prove it, was when she suddenly became off the charts popular. Under the pretense of "Haven't seen you in ages. Let's get together for lunch..." the messages began. Some were from unlikely sources she hadn't talked to in ages—like one such person in the Department of Justice.

Whereas Frank had been initially excited when she had first pitched him her trafficking story series the day before, today he had suddenly cooled to the idea, claiming he had rethought it and right now it was too controversial. WTF? Good investigative reporters were supposed to dig up and report on controversial stuff. Hello? She was riding a ratings wave right now and they were going to take away her surfboard? Which could only mean one thing. Someone above Frank was less concerned about losing ratings shares than ruffling someone's feathers. Plain and simple, the story was being nixed to protect those in higher places.

Using several incriminating video clips ZLOT had sent her, she had assembled explosive B-roll footage to back up her story. She had planned to ramp up her expose, starting with how big brand name corporations were making millions cashing in on the government gravy train by providing detention and illegal alien camps. She would then brilliantly segue into the missing children component of the story— the really damming stuff. She had even cut daily teasers. Her series was practically ready for prime time. Cali knew it was explosive material.

Then, less than an hour after having it edited just the way she wanted, it had, without her knowledge, been re-edited down to the bare bones, leaving almost a skeleton of a story. When she learned about her piece being seriously gutted, she stormed into the editing room demanding answers. The guys in the editing room looked sincerely apologetic but remained tight-lipped about who had given the order.

The station's tech guys usually had her back, so she didn't want to cause a scene with them. They needed their jobs. Instead, grim-faced and determined, she marched into Frank's office ready to do battle.

"Don't give me that look. It was too long," he lamely explained, heading her off before she could voice her righteous anger. He wouldn't even look at her as he hung up the phone and returned to his computer. Frank usually looked everyone in the eye. He didn't today. A very bad sign.

"I could have shortened it," she protested, trying to remain calm. "It's a nothing burger as it is now. A great big zero. Frank, let me re-work it. Please."

"No."

"But Frank, this is a dynamite story and you know it. What gives?"

"Enough! Just get out of here, Cali." Frank picked up the phone again, signaling their meeting was at an end and waved her away. He got up and closed the door after her, shutting her out.

WTF?! Was it that bitch Vandam who killed her story? If so, as who else could it be, maybe *she* needed to be investigated for obstruction of information!! Going over Frank's head she knew was a bad move, but she went up to Vandam's upstairs office anyway. It was a futile probably stupid move. She learned from Vandam's executive assistant that she had already left for the day. Maybe she had snuck out fearing Cali would come gunning for her.

Since she wasn't needed on-air for tonight's nightly news, she packed up her stuff and left the office feeling frustration bordering on rage—and she couldn't drink a damn drop to dampen her anger. She would just have to jog it off.

The records ZLOT had transmitted to Cali kept opening additional cans of worms. The data and its implications were staggering. And the world at large seeming to be afflicted with Information Deficit Disorder that she was doing her best to cure. Wake up. Open your eyes, she wanted to scream!

Cali returned home to be confronted with an even more immediate problem. Someone had broken into her place—and whoever it was had to be a professional. While there were no signs of broken glass or jimmied locks, no stolen jewelry or missing valuables, nor electronic equipment or riffled files, she just knew in her gut. Fear and paranoia quickly took hold.

This morning there had been a thin layer of dust on her desk, her nightstand, and other furniture surfaces due to her lack of putting off finding a new housecleaner to keep it all in order. There were items around the house that had been slightly moved, maybe only by a fraction of an inch, and yet there were no telltale signs of dust to give away the intruder's tracks. It had been cleaned of any possible prints. Whoever had broken in looking for information, they probably figured she wouldn't notice they had been there. Fat chance of that happening. The dumb fuck!

It was clear she was under surveillance. She went to her panty drawer just to see if the jerk was a perv as well. She counted them, all lined up in a row. One red G-string, reserved for special occasions, was nowhere to be found. She checked her laundry hamper just to make sure, even though she had had no recent "special occasions" that merited wearing it. Not there either.

While it was no secret that she was lousy at keeping her place clean from dust and crumbs, she was very conscientious about putting everything back in its proper place. She moved through the rooms taking stock of anything amiss, while contemplating the notion that surveillance bugs might have been planted as well. Was someone watching her right now?

Had she trusted her FBI ex-boyfriend Bond, she would have called him in immediately to do a thorough sweep of the place. But there was a strong possibility he might be the culprit responsible--especially after his most recent nighttime visit seeking info on the Stavros confession tape. Who could you trust these days?

Thankfully, she had moved her Glock from inside her nightstand drawer to a gun safe hidden inside a deep well of a large potted fern where she kept it when she was not at home. She went to it now and extracted the loaded weapon.

She had been careful not to put anything ZLOT had given her on her backup drive or in cloud storage. It was on a small USB stick she kept hidden in a concealed pouch inside the padding of her bra. It was visually undetectable except of course going through airport security where it might set off some alarms. Better to have someone believe she was guilty of fake boobs, then steal her research info. It was becoming clearer from everything that was beginning to happen that she possessed the power to bring down some very important people who wanted to stop her.

Her small laptop was with her at all times and she never kept anything confidential on her home desktop computer. If there was one thing she had learned from Bond a long time ago--always use a secure browser and for extra measure wipe clean your search history after every use. And never, ever, ever keep anything sensitive on a home computer. If this was Bond's work, then he should have known there wasn't anything to be found. So then who *was* behind it?

ZLOT's second drop had included inside footage of detection camps for children that were hidden within warehouses owned by major corporations, which the general public had no knowledge of and these kids were being sold to traffickers for all kinds of nefarious purposes. The records he sent included names and faces, in addition to all the financial records proving what was taking place in what looked to be a $200 billion dollar plus industry. She knew this type of information could easily get her killed, but she hadn't counted on her own station heads sabotaging her efforts to get the truth out there.

She went through her dresser drawers and quickly stuffed essentials into a canvas gym bag, along with $2000 in emergency cash she always kept hidden inside a hollowed-out book in her bookcase. Changing from a business suit, she donned dark clothing, tucked her hair up into a black baseball cap and grabbed a pair of dark shades. She was not going to stay in her place and become a sitting duck.

Cali knew she would have to leave her cellphone behind in case someone was tracking her and monitoring her calls. She left it on and placed it inside the medicine cabinet above the bathroom sink. It would be easy to pick up a burner phone on the outside tomorrow after she planned on calling in sick.

With one last glance around, hoping she hadn't forgotten anything she would temporarily need, she went back to the bathroom and crawled out a window into the darkness behind her house. For optics sake, her car would remain parked in her front driveway for all to see. Hugging the shadows and watching for anyone tailing her, she stole through a back alley and to a quiet residential street that allowed for only foot traffic.

Cali lightly jogged several miles until she got to a friend's house, whom she knew to be out of town for several weeks. Jeff was a photojournalist on assignment in the Kalahari for National Geographic magazine. And old friend from NYU, she had temporarily stayed at his place when she first came to D.C to work for WWGO-TV. She knew he wouldn't mind.

Under a small pine tree at the back of his house she found the small fake rock with the key hidden inside it. She quietly let herself in the back door.

There was no doubt in her mind, she had to start leaking this information to the public tonight before someone located her and stopped the truth from coming out. Once it was out in the public domain, she hoped she would be a whole lot safer.

~~*~~

Zach didn't want to take Meghan home, but he did. He walked her to the door, kissed her like he might not see her again, and simply said. "To be continued…"

"Yes. To be continued…" she agreed. She hugged him one more time and smiled gratefully. "Thank you, Zach. For…everything."

He would have given her anything and everything but didn't say it. Now he was back at home, the sensuous scent of her lingering on his bed. His primal need for her was unbearable. He couldn't sleep, or even pretend to. He got up and did an hour of Qigong to soothe his soul and regain some semblance of focus, not to mention re-channel his unsated sexual energy. Every time he thought of her, he felt his body betray him with desire. No one had ever affected him this way before. It was both scary and intoxicating.

Yet, he managed to rein in his focus, and feeling somewhat grounded again, decided it was time to touch base with Cali Cavaleri and see where she was with relation to their story.

"Big problem. Where are you?" she had typed in the secure message box over an hour earlier.

He got right to the point. *"What's up?"*

"The station backed off the full story and gutted it. Now, I'm being watched."

He had anticipated that this might happen. *"Where are you?"*

"Somewhere safe—for now."

"Good. I've got an idea. I may need to hack all your social media accounts."

"Are you fucking nuts???"

"Yes, but then you can blame me. Hopefully you won't be fired."

"Fired?"

"Yes. They will try to make your life miserable. Are you sure you want to do this?"

There was a long pregnant pause, as he waited. Finally, she responded.

"Hell, yes. Those dirty bastards!"

Her last words came out in all caps. *"JUST DO IT BEFORE I CHANGE MY MIND!"*

~~*~~

271

Zach was true to his word. He located the final piece her station had aired, which he had to admit was both "gutted" and sanitized. On her laptop he found her research notes she had gathered to piece the story series together, then quickly went to work. Hacking all her social media accounts was downright easy. He knew algorithms to access each company's master login account panel. They would know she had been hacked and not some lame excuse on her part to escape culpability. It would give her proof of innocence and even more journalistic notoriety for being "chosen" to scoop all others once again.

After the Stavros confession, Zach noted that Cali's followers had skyrocketed to a little over one million. Good girl! He boosted it to over 100 million by merging legitimate followers from other political, media, celebrity and government social media accounts into hers. He would make her a superstar. Lots of people would be sharing, re-tweeting, or forwarding this treasure trove of audio, video, and photographic evidence come morning in what was sure to be a media tsunami. It would cause a major shit-storm like nothing they had ever seen.

The time was right to shake things up. Zach decided to dial it up a notch. He posted data links to an anonymous block chain account that was unbreakable and couldn't be taken down. The account was capable of storing thousands of terabytes and anyone could access the details and records on each company's crimes as well as financials. It would be almost impossible to cover up something of this magnitude, whatever they tried.

At the last minute, Zach decided to add a signature touch of his own, just to make sure they wouldn't come after or seriously harm Cali. He included his new moniker:

"The Truth for All to See"—ZLOT

~~*~~

As anticipated, social media tried to shut down all of Cali's accounts, but it was too late. The Internet was already flooded with ZLOT info and in only a few hours millions of people all over the world had already saved, taken screen shots or downloaded the damning data before it disappeared forever into a web black hole. Someone had even managed to scrub the Internet's Wayback Machine's digital archive to forever erase the existence of ZLOT info. But they couldn't wipe clean the memory of millions of people who had already seen it and now knew the truth.

Back in her little secret hideaway, Cali was pretty sure her cellphone was flooded with messages. But since she no longer had it in her possession, and was not answering her calls, her email inbox quickly became maxed out as well. It ran the gamut from truth seekers applauding her bravery to the trolls and creeps that abounded calling her a hoaxer and wishing she would die a long, horrible death.

She turned on the TV and found out the companies she had cited in her story for being involved in trafficking: Amocat, Sorosha Group, Chulda Partners, Akuma Live, and many others were now scrambling to make statements of innocence, outright denying such preposterous claims, professing it all to be fabricated lies and the work of some demented "conspiracy theorist" or disgruntled employee who had so obviously doctored the evidence.

Investigations were being called for across the board. The companies involved were the loudest in their demands to bring the lying culprits to justice, while the American people were shocked and struggling with the ghastly pictures of children being sold into slavery for use and abuse. Even the adrenochrome info was all there, informing people for the first time about a harvested substance most had never even heard of before. It was a master wake up call to take off the blinders and take action against such depravity and corruption. Cali noted that ZLOT had left nothing out. Even she could never have revealed this much detail on air.

Cali incredulously watched the shit-storm unfold, uttering a non-stop stream of: "OH, MY. GOD." Some were calling it TrafficGate or ChildGate or a host of other nasty "Gates". No one escaped accountability. Some members of Congress were also involved in the cover-up scandal and were scrambling to minimize the damage to their reputations.

Every news station was being forced to cover this news, whether they liked it or not, or risk accusations of a massive media cover-up as well. Some played it down or tried to spin and whitewash it. Others sensationalized it beyond words. And always, the remaining question was 'Who is ZLOT'? The internet was abuzz with theories.

Now that others were on the scent of how big this story was, they too wanted on the bandwagon. Frank and Vandam were probably having a coronary at this very minute for not airing her initial report. Hah! They should have listened to her. She might not have a job to go back to, but journalistically and/or technically speaking they couldn't blame this on her.

Cali was not a religious person, but she said a silent prayer of gratitude. Thank you ZLOT, wherever and whoever you are, for taking the heat.

Chapter 23

It would be seen an unusual step, perhaps signaling to other members of Minerva, as well as the Counselor, that his power hold on this age-old organization was being tested by some higher more clever being—like Satya. Which was why the Governor of Minerva finally decided to take matters into his own hands. Something was going on within the realms of the LOT, something sinister that had not occurred before. It made him more determined to get to the bottom of it.

Someone or something was blocking two of their portal feeds, which they had not yet been able to fix even by the best of their technicians. Satya had never done such a thing before. The Governor didn't think she was even allowed to do such a thing in her position as Guardian of the LOT. Her neutrality was a sacred vow. Yet, information had somehow leaked out and he sensed its true source. Secrets long buried within the LOT's vast memory vaults, known to only a very few, were now hemorrhaging out at a rate that threatened the very lifeblood of their network.

An entity called "ZLOT" had cleverly figured out how to access their treasured pathway to knowledge. Information that had been kept hidden for centuries in the most inaccessible of places was now compromised. How this person, because he *was* assuming they *were* human, had managed to shut down two portal feeds and unlock LOT memory, without Minerva being alerted, was simply unfathomable.

The Governor had no idea whether ZLOT's knowledge also included portal locations and the existence and identity of Minerva members. There was also the possibility that the recent deaths of Sawyer and Stavros might also be exposed and linked to them. The Governor had no other choice but to assume the worst case scenario. Immediate action was called for before something even more catastrophic occurred. Erasure from the public's eye had always been the first step, but this called for more drastic measures.

In the past he had left information gathering in the LOT to the Counselor, while he focused his energies on running the vast Minerva network. Minerva's tentacles ran far and deep, as they had for centuries, and would continue well into the future accomplished by men, such as himself, who came from a long succession line. They were the strong and powerful. They were the intellectual elites who forged the foundation behind every existing government. Without Minerva, government and its leaders would fall. They were the embodiment of the law of order. Their mission was never to keep the people safe, but to keep the world running smoothly under their orders and wise management. It had always been and always would be this way. It was the business of humanity. Which unfortunately was growing faster than any of them had planned for. This, too, would have to be curtailed.

The Antarctica bases, a vast labyrinth of levels and tunnels, had remained the perfect cover for Minerva since ancient times when the land was once verdant and free of ice. This had changed after the third and final upheaval of key landmasses, now buried deep under the sea.

Many millennia ago, the ancients had foreseen the coming rotation of the Earth's axis revealed from future information gleaned in the LOT. They had planned their outposts wisely based on this knowledge. With this in mind, Antarctica had been stabilized to protect it from any future planetary shift and was chosen as the primary governing base for all Earth decisions. Because it was situated on the largest of all inter-dimensional portals, it held great significance and power. All countries of the world had carved out their secret military bases here in this vast frozen tundra, under the guise of oil, gas and mineral exploration to carry out their most classified projects. Humans made up only a fraction of the continent's hidden inhabitants. There were the off-world beings and their bases as well to deal with. Enforcing the complex treaties they had made with them for their assistance and technology transfer had not always been simple. On most days it was planetary business as usual, with a good portion of mutual tolerance thrown in. Yet, every so often they could be pompous and lecturing about the human species. But the technology they provided had been worth the nuisance.

Antarctica now housed the largest space force fleet, super carriers that were cable of housing thousands of personnel, scientists, military, and civilians. The general public, being far from its icy shores, with Minerva satellites which blanked out any potential observation of the continent's comings and goings, were none the wiser. This is what the Governor knew was at stake. Detection and Public Truth were Minerva's most deadly enemies.

Satya was waiting for him upon his arrival into the LOT. Of course, she would know he would be coming. Satya knew everything. As always, she waited for him to speak.

"It has been a while since our last meeting," he began.

"Yes, it has. Three years, 6 months, 24 days, 9 hours and 11 minutes to be exact."

He nodded. She had always been a stickler for details.

"We have a problem."

"No. I believe you have the problem," she corrected.

He decided to get right to the point. "I need your help accessing the visitor logs for this month. There appears to be a breach in the system."

"That's not possible," she replied. "I am bound by the rules. All visitors shall remain anonymous."

"Damn the rules," he said, even though he wasn't sure what all those rules were. To the best of his knowledge, this issue had never come up before. For thousands of years, Minerva had ruled the LOT and had a monopoly on all truth records.

Okay. He would approach it from another angle instead. "Then show me the visuals for Portal 2 from 10:00 PM – 12:00 Midnight for June 15th."

She was quick to dismiss his request. "Those are not available either."

"And why not?!" He demanded to know.

She remained unruffled by his tone. "As you already know. That portal has been closed down. All records are frozen and currently inaccessible."

While he knew Satya could not lie, he was sure she was guilty of omission. The Governor would have found them and unfroze them himself, if he could. But Satya had never allowed anyone to locate anything in the LOT without her personal assistance. That was the only rule he was aware of and he knew damn well she was privy to who had accessed Portal 2 and closed it down.

"What's going on here? You can't block the truth from us."

She raised one eyebrow. "Yet you do it all the time with *your* people."

"That's different." He didn't like the fact that she was challenging him. Perhaps, he had been away from the LOT too long. Something had definitely changed.

He would get to the bottom of this. "Let me speak to someone else."

"At this time… there is only one Librarian in the Library of Truth."

Was she implying there was soon to be another? To the best of his memory, Satya had been there forever.

"Are you saying that you will be retiring your duties here in the not so distant future?"

She stared at him blankly. "I cannot say."

The Governor was suddenly filled with deep foreboding and uncertainty. Satya had always been accommodating to Minerva. It was not her role to judge or deny access to the records or how that truth was used. She simply complied without question. For centuries she had honored an agreement of neutrality with Minerva. What did this mean? A shift in power was occurring behind the scenes and he didn't know why or who was behind it all. It was unthinkable that he would be cut off from viewing the records or that portals would be 'closed' without his knowledge. And this woman had the audacity to deny his request for truth. He felt a sudden rage building inside of him that threatened to spill over and erupt, but he kept his calm.

His mind was spinning. There might be another way to work around this unexpected roadblock to get some answers. Perhaps the future held the key…

"Show me what is to become of Minerva," he demanded.

Satya smiled knowingly. "As you wish."

~~*~~

Zach went to his secluded little corner in the Stacks to get away from the news that was on everyone's lips this morning. The coffee shop in the tunnels under the Library had a longer than normal line as those just getting the news on their phones came up

279

to speed and texted their friends about the latest bombshell to hit Washington.

"Who do you think ZLOT is?" A woman asked her friend.

"Some government whistleblower. Probably NSA," the other woman replied.

Zach pretended to be interested in the newsfeed scroll on his phone, but he couldn't help overhear the circulating theories making the rounds.

"My boyfriend works over at the Bureau in counterterrorism," one woman whispered. "He says the hack looks like it came straight out of China."

"Really?" said her friend. "This is like Watergate Deep Throat all over again."

Zach liked the last comment, which at least gave him hope. "About time someone told the truth," an elderly woman chimed in. "Let's see if any justice comes out it.."

Zach felt antsy listening to their speculation and gossip. He slipped out of line and went to the vending machine room instead. The coffee there wasn't as good, but at least it was piping hot and faster. But when he entered the vending room, he found the talk in there to be more of the same and just as bad. The only new piece of information he gleaned was that parents of missing children were starting to come forth and identity their child from photographs ZLOT had posted. Police and FBI units across the nation were either having a very bad or a very good day, depending on how the information was playing out.

Zach's head was reeling from all the anger and agitation around him. He had to get out of there fast. He hurried down the tunnel to get back to the quiet of the Stacks where he could process his continued plan of action.

There was something bothering him, a piece of information he had failed to give to Cali or put in the viral drop after hacking her social media accounts. Something important that put him in a moral dilemma that could have far wider consequences that affected him and people he knew and loved. LOT records showed that Senator Jim Talbot was a major profiteer in trafficking operations and had used his position in the Senate to protect criminal elements. This had been going on for years and always he had managed to stay clean and successfully avoid scrutiny.

Zach had always prided himself on trying to do the right thing, but if he released this information on Talbot, he knew it would have a devastating effect on both Meghan and Izzie. Should she ever learn that he had been the one responsible for bringing down her father, whom she loved, she would be lost to him—possibly forever. What to do?

He tried getting back into the LOT, but for the first time, the algorithm sequence was not working. There was no way to know why or what that meant. An energetic wall was in place. He could feel and sense it keeping him out.

He texted Meghan, wanting desperately to talk to her, to feel reassured by her presence, to know she was alright. But his text went unanswered, causing worry and frustration to mount.

~~*~~

Jim Talbot was in a blind rage. His cell and home phone lines started ringing off the hook in the early hours of the morning, waking the entire house. The news of the unfolding scandal was first delivered to him by his most senior staff advisor on his private line, the one reserved only for state emergencies and catastrophic events. This was clearly the latter.

Two Senators on his Intelligence Committee, close friends and colleagues of his, had been unmasked, along with scores of others in prominent government positions who had also been financially involved in human trafficking operations. This was bad. Really bad. Was his name also on the list? Had he been unmasked as well? He almost asked his advisor but stopped himself just in time.

"Anyone else on our Committee?" he cautiously enquired.

"No, sir. But I am preparing a statement now. The usual. You know—how shocked and saddened you are for all those involved, the families, the children, etc. Also, that the Committee will be investigating these egregious allegations and bringing all those involved to justice."

"Yes. Yes. That's good."

At that moment all Talbot could think about was how he had been miraculously spared by the divine grace of the Almighty. Not a praying man, he silently thanked God for saving him from potential discovery and ruin. How this ZLOT character had failed to detect his part in the operation was beyond him. But the press, if they got off their ass and started doing real investigative journalism again, might start looking deeper, like that Cavaleri woman who would definitely have to go. As for the rest of the media, it was far wiser to spoon-feed them what he wanted them to report. He detested them all, but he also loved that he could manipulate them in his favor.

His mind was reviewing all the options. There was always the possibility that someone named might be willing to trade for immunity by giving up a bigger fish. He couldn't allow that to happen. There were secret files on every Member of Congress and ways to deal with such people should they decide to go rogue and talk.

No sooner had he hung up on his advisor, then he speed-dialed his lawyer, waking him from a sound sleep and in a foul mood because of it. The man was a pit bull, which he liked, but he needed him to get his butt over to Talbot's house now. He hadn't realized he was yelling into the phone at such an early hour in the morning, until he saw both Meghan and Izzie, silently standing in the kitchen doorway, their eyes wide with fear as they watched him pour himself a tall glass of scotch and toss it down like water.

Seeing Meghan reminded him of what Camille had told him the night before, which fueled his anger even more. His daughter had betrayed him, going behind his back, and not telling him of her interest in that Eldridge boy. What else was she hiding from him he wanted to know?

"Dad, what's wrong? Are you okay?" Her concern was genuine. She searched his face looking for answers.

This wasn't a day for him to feel in control. Generally, he could remain cool and collected under the most challenging of situations, but not today. The Stavros leak should have been his first harbinger of doom. Now this. Things were spiraling out of hand. He was smart enough to know tides change quickly in Washington and more could come out soon. No one was safe.

Talbot found himself wanting to take it out on his daughter, a much weaker target. He poured himself another drink and let a bomb fly.

"When were you going to tell me you've been fucking around with Camille's son?"

She gasped, taken aback and stricken, and told Izzie to go back to her room immediately. Izzie, seeing her mother's distress, started to cry, which only infuriated Talbot more.

"For God's sake! Stop being a cry-baby and do what your mother says!" he yelled at the child.

"Go now," Meghan urged Izzie, who ran from the room sobbing.

"Stop it!" Meghan shouted back at her father. "How could you say such things in front of her? She's only a child. Have you lost your mind?"

Well, his daughter had some gumption after all. "Are you going to deny you've been sneaking around with him and letting him have his way with you?"

Meghan stared at him speechless.

"Well?!" he prompted impatiently. "Don't you dare lie to me!"

There was steel in her voice. "Dad, it's none of your business who I see. I am a grown woman and I can do as I please."

He could see that Meghan was gathering her strength, choosing her words. "When and if I do fuck him, as you so crudely put it, I will not be consulting with you about the details. Got it?!"

Then she turned and stormed out of the room.

~~*~~

Cali kept receiving terse emails from Frank demanding to know where she was. Now that the whole world had the story and others were running with it, she hoped she was safe to come out of hiding. But it could still be a trap.

Finally, she responded with her most definitive statement.

CALI: *If you're thinking of firing me for this, you can't. My account was hacked. I can prove it. And I have no idea who or what ZLOT is.*

FRANK: *Come into the station.*

CALI: *Not until you tell me my job status.*

FRANK: *You are not fired. Now get back here.*

CALI: *Will the station provide me security?*

FRANK: *Whatever for?*

CALI: *Someone broke into my house yesterday before the email hack.*

FRANK: *Was anything stolen? Was a police report made?*

CALI: *I'm being watched. How do I know someone is not going to try and off me?*

FRANK: *Stop being a drama queen. If you want, I'll send a car to pick you up wherever you are now. Just give me your address.*

Did he think she was born yesterday? It didn't sound like a good idea to her at all.

CALI: *I'll get back to you on that.*

Cali wasn't so sure she could trust Frank anymore. He was a damn fool if he thought she was going to get into a car with some stranger. Who was she to trust? Right now she was looking more like a card-carrying conspiracy theorist. She had an immediate flashback to Bond once telling her that "those who don't talk usually stay alive". There was no denying that her social media accounts had *talked* way too much!

She opted to give it another day before resurfacing. Her friend's cupboard had 18 packets of chicken flavored ramen soup, some cheap brand of chunky peanut butter (not even organic) and a container of stale raisins, and not much else. Neither cooking nor good nutrition was his forte. Hunger for real food was starting to play a role in her wanting to come out of hiding. She had only lasted a day. A true survivalist she would never be.

~~*~~

Zach still had not been able to reach Meghan. He learned that she had also failed to come into work today. He stopped by the tour information desk and inquired about her only to learn she had called in very early, leaving a message saying a family emergency had come up and she would not be in that day.

His intuition told him she wasn't taking any calls and had shut off her phone or she would have gotten back to him—he was sure of it. To Zach, it sounded ominous. His rescuer side wanted to leave work right now and drive over there to make sure she and Izzie were alright. He didn't give a damn about her father, knowing what he knew about him. But he reined in that White Knight thinking, deciding to try again later.

It was important he get back into the LOT and get some answers. Back in the Stacks, one of the only quiet spots in this huge Library that afforded him a good degree of undetectability, he made sure he was alone before starting the algorithmic re-entry sequence. This time, there were no walls or blockages holding him back. With lightening-speed he found himself back in the LOT in a section he had never seen before—the personal station of Satya.

There was no bed, no little trinkets or mementos anywhere indicating what treasures she had accumulated over her life which were important to her. Missing were any books containing her favorite stories, nor anything that might give him a clue to who Satya really was.

She was simply bathed in a pool of luminous light, sitting at a silver surfaced worktable. He knew this was her personal domain because her energy pervaded the space. There was an air of complete privacy, almost like the sanctity of a confessional.

When he popped in, she momentarily looked up from what she was doing, which appeared to be entering Sanskrit markings in a thick hefty ledger. He itched to read what she had written, but she quickly closed the ledger and motioned for him to take a seat. There was no seat he could see for him to take. But then quite suddenly, out of nowhere, he felt himself enfolded in a chair that instantly molded to his body. There was a feeling of homey comfort, despite the starkness of the space's interior.

"You have much on your mind," she said, more a statement than a question. A chair, much like his own, enfolded her as well. The only thing missing was food and refreshments.

"Would you like some?" she asked reading his thoughts.

He said 'no' wondering if the LOT served something like "celestial" tea. Satya smiled, evidently finding him amusing.

Zach leaned forward, noting the chair adjusting to his slight movement as if it were an organic living structure.

"I was not able to come earlier. Can you tell me why I was being blocked?"

"There was another entity here in the LOT that you are not yet meant to meet."

"Minerva?"

"Yes."

He thought about what that meant--'not yet meant to meet'. There was a long list of questions in his head, and she was being rather obtuse. It was a certainty that he could be here all day asking for explanations for everything that was happening in his world, yet he knew there was only one thing that really mattered.

"I'm starting to wonder what my true purpose is here," he gestured to the vastness of the LOT. "Outside of feeding truth to the outside world."

He frowned. "There must be others coming here and doing the same. Right? Where are they?"

Zach wished he could read her thoughts as easily as she could his. Instead, he sensed a heavy weight on her mind that caused her some conflict. For someone who rarely expressed emotion and retained neutrality this was a curious thing to him. For whatever reason, his synesthesia ability to see thoughts as numbers and identify the person's true intent was an ability that was short-circuited inside the LOT, replaced instead by an acute awareness—like now.

When she finally spoke, her words were carefully chosen. "The explanation you seek is multi-faceted and rather complex," she admitted. "While I cannot show you your life file, nor any member of your family right now, as are the rules, I can say that everything happening to you has been scripted without any interference to your free will."

There was a bigger story here, which was not being told, and Zach knew it. Were her words paradoxical to throw him off? "How can it be scripted, and I still have the right to choose?"

"Because you are the one who has already chosen it."

"What did I choose and when?" he wanted to know.

"That will be revealed to you in time. If I were to tell you now… ". She hesitated, weighing her words. "It could result in a different timeline and possible outcome—for the LOT."

Now she was talking in riddles. "So, you're not going to tell me the truth," he pointed out.

"That's a subjective viewpoint. Let me just say--the objective truth is something you are destined to discover on your own."

He sat there absorbed in his thoughts, his mind racing with possibilities. It suddenly occurred to him that if he asked the right question within the LOT's vast memory banks, he might not need to keep needling Satya for answers. He might not need her at all. Then he had a revelation that stunned him. Just like he had at the paws of the Sphinx when he realized that time was not linear and was simply an infinity loop. He could bend and twist it to access reverse time travel. It *had* worked then and now his mind was wondering what else was possible.

Maybe Satya was just an illusion, a figment of his imagination, and he had the right combination key inside him to become his own record keeper. These abilities, possibly long dormant, might exist in every being just waiting to be unlocked, like genetic memory. Theoretically, on a higher physics level, it would explain many things. Simply that he, Zach Eldridge, was unlimited. All records, all answers, were hidden in plain sight--right within the mind of man. The organic hand of his living chair let him go, as if releasing him from the self-imposed restraints of his own thinking.

"Thank you, Satya." He stood ready to leave. "Believe it or not, you *have* been very helpful."

There was a secret little smile on her lips as she nodded, watching him go. Yes, indeed, she thought. This one would go far on his own.

Zach walked the sky-high halls of the LOT for what felt like miles, alone, and with concentrated intent. Every Sanskrit marking or engraving he committed to memory, creating a vault like device in his mind that had its own drawers and extensive filing system so as not to overwhelm his everyday cognitive memory brain. Not all of his abilities were quieted in this place. He still had total recall and processing speed capabilities to take in huge amounts of data, and he took full advantage of it now.

While the LOT offered holographic memory, something he knew would be impractical for the purposes he wanted, he attempted to create an inter-dimensional bridge where he could access just raw data from the LOT at will. In his mind he began the process of creating his own dimensional human software program. It wouldn't be perfect—at least not yet, but it might just work. If human DNA was just an enormous mathematical blueprint program, determining one's physical traits and characteristics, one's health, one's cognitive abilities, and the like, then other human software programs were possible as well to co-exist with it side-by-side.

It would take time to adjust all the parameters, but inside the LOT he had all the time in the world. Using the power of intent, he commanded LOT memory to create an Einstein-Rosen bridge, in essence a wormhole, like two connecting funnels turned in different directions atop each other, between him and it. It would be transcranial vs. external in nature.

Zach quickly recognized that the power of intent in the LOT was a stronger creative force to play with than on third dimensional Earth and quicker too. He could feel his brain being stimulated in new ways and forging unique neuronal pathways. What he was attempting to do, in the hands of some covert intelligence agency, would blow the lid off mind control techniques already known. But he chose not to think about such things at this time. Never would he tell anyone.

He began testing his new bridge program with small questions to start with like where can I find the other 11 of the 12 golden Minerva statues? He knew Meghan would be dying to know. Information streams from somewhere deep in the LOT streamed into his head in a clear, almost invisible thread-like pattern. He examined what he was seeing in his mind's eye and knew the information was key to his understanding the bigger picture once he put all the pieces together.

What he was being shown was that all 12 Minerva's had been placed in depositories of knowledge or key spots around the globe by a team consisting of three individuals from another time. None of the people was facially identifiable, and their names meant nothing to Zach.

In his mind he saw a visual image of each location place, like a snapshot in time. Of course, he was familiar with the one located inside the confines of the Library of Congress, with direct access into the Stacks. Another was hidden in the water tunnels under the Great Pyramid with adjunct accessibility from a secret space under the Sphinx, which appeared to have been accidentally sealed up with concrete during some early restoration process. There was one, which might never be found, deep inside the ice of Antarctica, which made Zach wonder how it got there since the statutes were originally cast during the 19th Century. He had never heard of any successful expedition to the frozen Continent prior to the explorer Roald Amundsen reaching the South Pole in 1911. There had to be an earlier one, not as well known. And stranger yet—why would a Minerva statue be placed deep under the ice? And if a statue had been hidden there, was there a depository of knowledge to be found there as well?

Zach recalled the old Antarctica maps found inside one of the missing ZE files, which hadn't seemed that important at the time. Was there a more veiled reason Senator Talbot was so interested in these old cartography relics that he kept putting in periodic requests to find them? More importantly, what did Meghan's father know about the Antarctica Minerva statue? He was the very one that had refused to show her the one in the LOC's Congressional Members Room. Why?

According to LOT records, Talbot was heavily involved and had financially profited in wide-spread human trafficking. His high-ranking position in the Senate afforded him protection and the ability to cover his tracks, as others, like Constantine Stavros. Zach strongly suspected Senator Talbot was also a part of Minerva, maybe even the person at the top of the organization. If that were the case, Zach knew he couldn't protect the man, or his family, by sitting on this information. It was endangering other people's lives.

While his Einstein-Rosen-like human software bridge appeared to be working on its initial test run, he noticed glitches that would require further tweaking. It wasn't able to capture all the info on a first pass, allowing him to visually examine it even within the confines of the LOT. He was clueless how it might work once he left the LOT, or if it would function at all without direct access inside this place.

Zach knew he wasn't getting the complete picture, which, unfortunately for him, seemed to be a reoccurring theme in the LOT. He wasn't sure if this was due to an error in his programming skills or the cause of Satya's possible interference. It was hard to be sure of anything these days.

Right now, he was able to visually see where all 12 Minerva statues had been placed around the globe, but identifying information captured on each site faded too quickly. It was plagued with a "buffering" issue. Too much brain flow information and it got backed-up and stopped before it stored properly. If he could work out how to solve this glitch, it would be the true test to determine if a human brain was indeed infinite or limited only by its belief that it was a finite organ. He was determined to test the hell out of his theory, back in his world.

Zach could have spent a lifetime in the LOT working out such complex problems, but there was that itchy tingling feeling again, like it was time to leave. Something or someone was calling him back. But before he left, he knew he had one more record to review.

~~*~~

Meghan suspected no one would get any real sleep after her father's tirade. Having witnessed a side of her grandfather she had never seen before, Izzie was so distraught by his bizarre behavior in the kitchen that it had completely frightened her. Meghan had taken Izzie into her bed, holding her close, trying to console her, soothe her, tell her all would be okay, but she herself was not so sure.

Her father, who was always so confident and assured about most everything, had finally showed his weakness. Something had threatened him, and fear had made him strike back. Unfortunately, it just so happened to be directed at the two of them. His uncalled for accusation about her and Zach still rang in her ears. It was not a memory she wished to remember.

As she continued to stroke Izzie's hair, feeling her child finally begin to drift off to sleep, Meghan wondered how in the world her father had learned so quickly about the two of them. Were his little spies everywhere, spilling all they might have seen and surmised, to court his favor? She pushed that horrible thought aside.

Instead, her mind revisited every detail of the night before, and everything Zach had done to her. She felt a flush of intense heat steal over her body at the feelings and sensations he had elicited from her. Did she trust him? Yes. Did she want more of what he had to offer? Absolutely. Did she want him to fuck her brains out? She smiled to herself. God, yes!

She wanted to text him at that very moment telling him so but decided it could wait until morning. No sense depriving Zach of sleep as well. Reaching over, she left a text for her docent supervisor telling her she would not be in that day due to a family matter, then powered off her phone. Whatever it was her father was distraught about, she would deal with it in the morning.

Morning came all too quickly for Meghan and with it came the realization of the sordid accusations ringing through all factions of the political and business world. The evidence was damning---pictures, banking transactions, emails, texts. It was all over the news—all over the world. Nothing had been left out and no one had been spared.

Investigations by the Department of Justice were being called for. The FBI and scores of other crime-fighting agencies were being accused of a massive cover-up. The public wanted to know how all of this had been going on for decades and no had done anything about it? Where were the Intelligence agencies when all this was going on? Were they just as complicit?

No wonder her father had been so angry. No wonder he was already gone by the time she woke up. He would have to deal with this entire mess. Some of his colleagues in the Senate, and ones on his own committee, had also been named. A foreboding chill ran through her. Had her father known all about this already?

Meghan flipped through the television channels. The more she learned, the sicker she became. All those children—tens of thousands of them! Taken, used, abused—and for profit. What kind of evil monsters existed in this world?! If this had happened to Izzie, she would have—she would have, the thought was too terrible to finish. Meghan would want to die.

She was so appalled and distracted by what she was hearing and seeing on the news that she failed to hear Izzie shuffle down the stairs in her pajamas and pink slippers and come to stand behind her. Her innocent eyes grew wider as she listened.

"How did they hurt the children, Mommy?" she whispered.

Meghan quickly shut off the television. How much had Izzie heard? And more importantly, how was she to explain the depravity of the world to such a young child? It was almost impossible. She never wanted to lie to her child, but she knew simple answers devoid of too much information was the best way to address her daughter's concern.

"They were taken away from their mommies and daddies and that made them very sad."

Izzie was far from satisfied. "But why did they have to take them away?"

"They were stolen by evil people, Izzie. Very bad and evil people."

"Would these bad people ever come for me, Mommy?" she asked.

There it was--the inevitable note of fear in her innocent question. Children were quick to realize how this might threaten their own safe little world. Meghan scooped her up in her arms and hugged her close. "No, Izzie. I would never let them ever take you away! You will always be safe with me. Do you understand?"

Izzie nodded, then brightened. "I'm very hungry."

Meghan released her and gave her a kiss on the top of her head. "Okay. Let's go make you some blueberry pancakes."

"With extra syrup??"

Meghan smiled. "Yes. With lots of oozing buttery syrup for my baby."

~~*~~

Senator Talbot had called for a press conference on the steps in front of the Capitol Building at 9:00 AM that morning. By the time he got there, a large throng of reporters from all the major

294

media sources were jockeying their microphones and cameras for breaking news on one of the hottest and most scandalous stories to hit Washington in decades. The TV news vans, both local and national, were lined up down the street, each hoping to get an exclusive interview.

A master of deflection, Jim "The Fixer" Talbot, as they called him behind the scenes, worked his magic to convince the media that this was a disinformation campaign, a total smear job, by foreign enemies both domestic and abroad. It was always the standard game plan to blame everything on either the Russians or the Chinese, and he knew his people in the Intelligence Services would back him up if push came to shove. If that didn't work, there were powerful agents in the Middle East who could equally take the blame. The world was full of boogey men to cast blame on—the true beauty of globalism.

Of course, Talbot knew this was not the case with this particular bombshell scandal, because everything that had been exposed was actually true. He should know as he also had his hand in the game and had become a wealthy man aiding and abetting its key players. But these kinds of shit storms could be rectified without having to endure a political colonoscopy. Talbot's staff, who were consummate professionals at this kind of thing, had already made their early morning calls to key sources with the prescribed talking points to prevent a tsunami of public fallout. As was often the case, some journalists in influential places would write exactly what they were told to write--especially those already on the CIA payroll. And Talbot knew who each and every one of them were from having viewed their damning personal files of weaknesses and indiscretions.

"Yes. The Senate will launch a full investigation immediately," he announced for all to hear. Now here came his canned moral sound bite—not too long and not too complicated: "Such crimes against humanity will never be tolerated. If these allegations prove true, and I remind you that we have yet to substantiate any of them, all those who are guilty will be brought to the true justice of the law."

As always, he put on his most serious Senatorial face. Truth be known, he couldn't wait to get the hell out of there. Some rookie reporter stuck a microphone in his face and shouted above the questions of the crowd. "Sir, do you know who this ZLOT person is and will they be prosecuted for leaking confidential records?"

Prosecuted? Hell no. He would rip the person's head off, stick them in a vat of boiling acid, and make sure no body part existed to ever see the light of day again. And that was just for starters. If it were the last thing he did, he would make ZLOT pay for causing such total havoc. Whoever this person was—he or she couldn't hide forever. He would see to that. As well as that reporter Cavaleri bitch.

ZLOT had to know about Talbot's part in this trafficking operation, since they had unearthed all the other damming material. This made Talbot seethe with rage underneath his calm and righteous posturing before the press. He, an expert who could write the book on political entrapment, would not be blackmailed by anyone.

"We will be looking into who leaked such information…"

But before he could finish the thought, he was cut off. "If these allegations are true, sir, wouldn't ZLOT be protected under the Whistleblower Act?"

There was always one smart aleck in the press pool that asked too many questions. He made note of the fellow. Screw the Whistleblower Act! He would make sure ZLOT never used that damn escape ploy, ever. "There will be no more questions," he said, turning to make his own escape.

Chapter 24

Zach was in a quandary. The father of the woman he loved was a monster. A narcissistic sociopath who had terminated lives, both directly and indirectly, as well as his own wife and son-in-law. He had seen the LOT records on Senator James Talbot, when he reviewed key decisions in the man's life. It had been the last thing he had called forth in the LOT this morning and for many reasons he wished he hadn't. Now, the graphic and sordid images lingered in his memory, never to be forgotten. The very thought of Meghan and Izzie being oblivious to the real James Talbot, and living under the same roof, caused him undue stress—especially now that he had not heard anything back after all the messages he had sent her.

As before, he saved key video footage of the holographic records he had viewed in the LOT. He stored all the data on Talbot's profiteering from human trafficking, but this other information was equally damning. Zach knew he was sitting on a personal time bomb. There would come a time when it would be needed, when justice would demand retribution and all hell would descend upon the Talbot name. Somehow, he would have to find a way to protect Meghan and Izzie from that firestorm.

By late afternoon, he had still not heard from Meghan. Her silence caused him concern bordering on anxiety. From life experience he had learned one wise rule, don't jump to conclusions nor over-react until you've waited at least 24 hours. Anything and everything can change by then. It was a rule he was now breaking. He informed Mrs. Friedman that a sudden family emergency had come up and he would have to leave a few hours early. She took one look at his grave face and told him to 'go'.

He went home, picked up his car from the garage and drove straight to Meghan's house in Bethesda. The big iron security gate to the property was closed and there were no sign of cars in the circular driveway or even a groundskeeper anywhere in sight. When he rang the intercom, there was no answer. It just rang and rang. He felt a cold sense of dread steal over him. Something had happened to make the entire household flee. That "something" was probably him and the debacle of the released ZLOT information.

He tried her cell number once again. On the 4th ring he experienced a lifetime of relief when she finally picked up. He could hear uncertainty in her voice. It was practically a whisper.

"Zach?"

He had to know. "Are you and Izzie okay?"

He heard her deep sigh that spoke volumes. "It's been so crazy since this morning. I can't believe what's going on. I shut my phone off to get away from it all. I just turned it back on and then you called."

She momentarily paused. "Oh, I'm sorry. I see now that you've called several times."

"Meghan, where are you?"

"I had to get away from my father. I took Izzie with me to our summer cottage at Chesapeake Beach to escape the madness."

Zach could hear acute anxiety in her voice when mentioning

her father. He did not like the sound of that at all. There was a part of him that would not rest until he could see for himself that both her and Izzie were all right. He already knew what James Talbot was capable of.

"Meghan. I need to see you. Is it okay if I come now?"

"Why, yes. I'm just..." She stopped. "Is something wrong?"

"I would rather talk in person. Give me your address and I'll be there in an hour."

Zach had to pass back through Washington to get to Chesapeake Beach. One look at his car GPS and he had committed to memory the fastest most direct route. Although it felt like forever, exactly 58 minutes later he pulled up in front of a white cottage situated on a secluded sandy strip on the Chesapeake. No neighboring houses anywhere in sight. He knew from the looks of the place, from the charming English garden filled with a dazzling display of color, the wicker furniture and cozy blue and white ticked cushions on the porch, that this was Meghan's place, not her father's. It felt like her. It felt like a feminine sanctuary.

Meghan waved to him from the railing of the wooden deck that flanked the perimeter of the house's second floor landing. She hurried down the stairs to meet him, wearing a long white open shirt which did little to cover the red string bikini underneath. He was once again struck speechless at how incredibly lucky he was. Without a hint of shyness and making it evident she was very happy to see him, she pressed herself up against his long frame and kissed him soundly.

"I'm so glad you're here," she said breathlessly. She pulled back a fraction to read his reaction to her practically throwing herself at him. There was fire in his eyes. She could see it, and he could feel it. He kissed her again letting his body tell her he was glad to see her as well.

With a smile on her lips, she took his hand and led him up the wooden stairs to the back of the deck where the warm ocean breezes soothed his anxious soul. They were both okay. He could see Izzie on the beach in a bright pink and white polka dot swimsuit, playing with seashells near the water's edge. She had placed them neatly in a long row next to where she sat, her little toes digging in the sand. He could see her happy face as she watched shells being dragged out to sea on the tide, only to hurriedly replace them with new shells she retrieved from a green plastic bucket.

"I didn't tell her you were coming," Meghan said. "I had to get her away from the news. She keeps asking about the missing children."

Reading Izzie's energy, he could see she was trying to work something out in the sand. As a child, he had done pretty much the same thing. He hadn't needed a Jungian therapist to tell him how to solve his problems, nature had been his best ally and teacher.

Unconsciously he unbuttoned his shirt, feeling the warm rays of the sun on his chest and leaned back against the wooden railing. Her hand instinctively reached out to touch his bare chest and he held it there needing to keep that close human connection between them.

"Tell me what happened with your father," he asked in a low tone, wanting to get that out of the way.

"Somehow he knew about us. He said some horrible things in front of Izzie, which made her cry and then we got into a shouting match."

Zach had already surmised his mother was the loose-lipped informant. Camille Eldridge was a bloodhound at sniffing out other people's potential and real life sexual affairs. He could picture it now, or rather tried not to, where his mother lorded the knowledge over Jim Talbot taking great sadistic pleasure in knowing something he didn't. In some ways she was so damn predictable.

He shook his head in disgust. "What did he say in front of Izzie?"

Meghan sighed, not wanting to go there.

"Go ahead. Tell me," He urged.

"Izzie doesn't even know what it means…I think. He wanted to know when I was going to tell him about 'fucking Camille's son'."

Yep. It was his mother. The bitch.

"Izzie doesn't like to see people get upset and angry and when she saw him yelling like that, and then my reaction, she lost it. That only made him madder. Neither of us got much sleep last night."

Zach held her against his chest and kissed the top of her head. "How did it end?"

Meghan sank into his embrace, burying her face into the heat of his chest. "I told him if and when I decided to fuck you, he wouldn't be getting any details. Then I stormed out."

Zach grinned. His Meghan was a little fighter at heart.

"And have you come to a decision?" he asked softly against her hair.

"You mean about us doing it?"

Now she was playing with him. She knew what he was asking. "Uh, yeah."

"Well. Hell, yes." She looked up at him. "Can you stay the night?"

It was at that moment that Izzie came running up the stairs screaming with excitement and launched herself against Zach. He picked her up, her bathing suit wet and full of sand and threw her over his shoulder, which set her into a fit of uncontrollable giggles.

"Looks like I caught myself a big fish." He winked at Meghan. "Do you have a pot big enough to cook her for dinner?"

"We might need to build a bonfire and roast this one,"

Meghan chimed in playing along.

Izzie started squealing. "Don't be silly. I AM NOT A FISH. Now put me down," she demanded indignantly.

"Magic word?" Zach asked.

Izzie huffed. "Please put me down."

"Good girl." Zach immediately released her.

Izzie turned to her mother eagerly. "Does this mean Zach is staying for dinner?"

Meghan nodded. "Yes. He is."

"Yeah." Izzie danced across the deck heading for the sliding door.

"Go take a shower." Meghan called after her. "And make sure you get all that sand off first."

Dinner that night was a simple affair. They grilled some steaks, buttered up some corn on the cob and had a lush green salad on the outside deck. Zach had rarely experienced anything like this growing up with his own family. There were no authentic domestic moments of laughter and sharing in the Eldridge house that he could remember, and he had an excellent memory. He almost called where he grew up a 'home', but that would be grossly inaccurate. That big old Connecticut mansion was like a museum of expensive artifacts that had no intrinsic meaning—merely decorative tinsel on a tree. Where he was right now felt like home.

Zach checked himself to make sure this feeling of peaceful bliss was real and he wasn't dreaming. He had studied the nature of reality for years, but if this was not reality, he knew for certain he didn't want to ever wake up. He found himself exchanging knowing looks across the table with Meghan as Izzie chatted on non-stop about snails and seashells and does the ocean ever stop rolling in and out? He liked the one about whether fish ever sleep at night and, if so, do they sleep in fish beds?

He found himself loving all of Izzie's questions and just

wanted to hug her for her inquisitive little mind. The type of questions she was asking were the very ones he as a child had wanted to know but had to search to find his own answers. His parents were too busy to be bothered. Books had been his only salvation—his true teacher.

Before too long, Izzie's energy began waning. She was yawning over her strawberry ice cream. Zach had no idea what time it was, but it had to be nearing her bedtime. She went to her room to change into pajamas and came back outside, asking if Zach would tuck her in and say prayers with her tonight. He didn't know what to say.

Meghan raised her eyebrows and hid a small smile. She got up and started clearing the table.

"I've never done this before," he whispered. Meghan gave him a look that told him she was finding this amusing.

"Go. Man up and see if you can handle it. Just make sure she doesn't rope you into a story as well. She's quite good at that."

Zach followed Izzie, who padded down the hall to her room. This bedroom, unlike her room in Bethesda which had a planetary star theme, had a deep undersea world on the walls. A white glowing lamp on her bedside table cast rolling waves around the room making one feel like an underwater diver.

Izzie led him around the room showing him each dolphin, octopus, and anemone picture she had collected on her walls. It was show and tell time for her. He listened carefully to everything she told him.

"This one's my favorite," she said showing him a bright red undulating blob in the water. "Mommy took this photo. I bet you don't know what it is."

In fact, he did. He dove many times in Hawaii and didn't know Meghan did as well. There was so much to learn about her.

"Take a guess." Izzie prompted.

"It's a sea slug in the Hexabranchidae family--commonly

303

referred to as a 'Spanish Dancer'."

"How did you know that?" she demanded.

"Books, Izzie. And I've also seen a few in the ocean. They're pretty cool for a slug."

She laughed. "Yes, they are." She seemed to grow tired of testing his knowledge of fish. She scooted into bed and pulled up the covers.

"Zach. Will you tell me a big fish story?"

He knew this was coming and right now he wanted to get back to Meghan. They had unfinished business.

"It will help me get to sleep," she purred. Oh yeah. She was a little con artist alright. Such imploring eyes. He resolved to stay strong.

"How about I make a promise for next time? Tonight, I need to help your mother." It was a lame excuse, but he hoped she would take him at his word.

She thought about it for a few seconds, possibly seeing through his ruse, but then turned suddenly serious. "Zach. As an angel, can you help save the missing children?"

He felt tears spring to his eyes at the sincerity of her request. How was it that children could cut right to the heart of the matter? Her lower lip quivered as she asked, her eyes imploring him to say 'yes'.

"Come here," he said reaching out his arms to hug her. "Izzie, I promise I will do the best I can. I'm trying."

"Thank you, Zach."

Izzie lay back against her pillow and moved to the next item on her list.

"Ok. That's good. I'm also praying that you make my Mommy very happy. Angels are supposed to do that, you know—grant wishes. You can do that, right?"

The angel stuff again. He was no angel, but she was right about him wanting to make her mother happy.

Izzie smirked. She seemed quite pleased with herself at what she thought she knew. She beckoned him closer to whisper in his ear. "I know she likes you. She hums when she's happy and she was humming tonight before dinner."

God knows he would do his best to make her Mommy keep humming—if it took all night.

~~*~~

They wound up having a glass of wine down on the beach, sharing a chaise lounge in the middle of the cooling sand. They talked about their lives, their loves, their regrets, their families, until Zach pulled her to her feet towards the water's edge.

"Come swim with me," he beckoned.

"Did you bring a suit with you?" she asked.

Zach laughed. "Don't need suits. It's better this way. Trust me."

She did trust him. "I've never skinny-dipped before."

Now that really surprised him. He started shedding his clothes on the sand. "Always a first time for everything."

Without further prompting, she stripped out of her top and shorts, no underwear underneath to his continued surprise, and ran with him naked into the water. He dived underneath the cool waters, shaking water droplets from his hair as he emerged behind her and pulled her to him. She allowed him to float her into deeper water and support her while he kept them both afloat. She had never been a strong swimmer, but he was. As a child she had fearlessly jumped into a wave for the first time and gotten knocked down and caught in the undertow. She thought she was going to die. That particular memory resurfaced right now.

"Are you afraid?" Zach asked.

"A little," she admitted. "How did you know?"

"I can see it."

"What do you see?"

Zach held her up as he treaded water for them both. "It's red and black and looks like little number ones shooting out like arrows."

She frowned. "I don't like the sound of that... Am I that readable."

He touched his hand to her face and caressed it. "Sometimes." He could see that his words had caused her uncertainty coupled with a touch of embarrassment. He was determined to put her at ease.

"Just relax. Let me do the work," he said, gliding them through the water.

It reminded her of what he had said only a day ago when he had pleasured her and made her shatter and come. Was it only a day ago?

He watched her, marveling at the look of total freedom and surrender on her beautiful face as she relaxed. The rays of the moon sought her out, illuminating her rosy peaked breasts. She was like Ariel the little mermaid, her long red hair floating behind her like a sea siren's tentacles. His hands ran down her body and she shivered at his warm touch. She could feel the heat emanating off his body even in these dark evening waters.

She wanted more, as did he. "Let's go inside," she murmured.

Together they swam back to shore. He scooped her up in his arms to save her from the sand. Grabbing a blanket from the chaise, he enfolded her in it before going back to retrieve their clothes.

Like two thieves in the night, they quietly snuck back into the house so as not to wake Izzie. Within minutes they were both in a hot shower lathering each other up and exploring uncharted territory. Not a word was spoken nor necessary. They both knew what they wanted. No boundaries. No time constraints. Tonight, they were free to experience it all and would.

Meghan was in her glory. Different from her late husband, Brett, who found her somewhat boring in bed, with Zach she felt like a wild woman. It was as if he had found the key that unlocked her from her self-imposed sexual celibacy. She felt unfettered to just be—to open herself to continued pleasure and see where it went.

Meghan wanted to taste him as he had tasted her--his putting his lips to her most private parts and deflowering her like it was her first time. She kneeled down in the shower, the water raining down upon them in a warm mist and took him into her mouth. His response was immediate and electrifying. It emboldened her to take him in deeper. A low moan escaped his lips as her tongue sought out and massaged his most sensitive spots. She could feel he was on the brink when he reached for her.

In a flash, he lifted her up against the shower wall, his mouth devouring her as she wrapped her legs tightly around his waist and held on. Zach didn't look like a Viking conqueror, but he certainly acted like one with her. She liked this feeling with him.

With his hands cupping her buttocks to support her, he opened her to him and plunged inside finding her wet and ready. Meghan cried out from the sheer hardness of the connection, setting off every sensor in her body. It was incredible and wonderful and...

She could sense his slight hesitation. "Are you okay?" he whispered against her ear.

"Oh. My. God. Yes." Her words came out in a breathless rush. "Please don't stop."

He didn't. Perhaps he had an advantage being able to energetically read her. He seemed to know when she was on the very edge and when to take her over it so he could join her. It was explosive and beyond what she had ever experienced or even imagined possible.

It took them both awhile to normalize their breathing and yet he never let her go--staying with her, keeping the connection. He lifted her chin to read her eyes, staring into them with sheer delight then kissed her deeply, almost sweetly. Meghan stilled the desire to cry--again. He did that to her and she was no crier. For some reason, Zach could jumpstart her emotions straight into overdrive.

Meghan felt almost bereft when he finally pulled out of her, only to ease her down to stand while he gently cleaned them both. He used his soapy fingers to wash away the traces of their lovemaking and she instantly wanted more the moment he touched her vaginal lips, even though her legs still felt like jelly. He chuckled, toweling them down.

"Probably not going to be getting much sleep, tonight, huh?" he surmised, grinning from ear to ear.

"Nope." She was giggling now. "You have awakened the sleeping princess and she commands the prince now pay service to her."

And so he did. For most of the night, they played, discovering and rediscovering every inch of each other's body. He did not know he had an erotic switch on his right buttock, and he found she had switches on her left inner thigh, her right earlobe, and the bottoms of her feet.

"Did you know you have a birthmark on the top of your head?" she exclaimed, parting his thick dark hair, as his head snuggled between her lush breasts.

"Mmm. Yes." He tweaked a nipple between his lips.

"Zach it looks like a little infinity symbol. Like a number eight. How adorable."

'Adorable' was not something he pictured himself as personifying. Meghan was the adorable one. His body and soul could not get enough of her. She had mesmerized his dick into a constant state of arousal, and it must be well after 2:00 AM. His red-headed little minx was insatiable in bed once she was all wound up. How very lucky for him. Zach thoroughly loved and every moment of turning her on.

But he was wise enough to know they both needed some rest, and he would have to leave early to get back to Washington. A part of him would have gladly chucked it all and arranged to stay there with her forever in their little cottage by the sea. But he had things to do. He was on a mission. And he now knew that he could never tell her about the sins of her father. It would kill her.

He rolled her over and instead of mounting her from behind as she was surely anticipating, he moved his hand down her spine in a gentle soothing motion until her sexual energy calmed down enough to invite sleep in. His hand reached out to click off the light and he spooned against her back letting the heat from his body lull her into a deep slumber.

"No more sex?" she mumbled, settling against him.

"Not tonight, love. Now sleep."

She heard the "love" part and smiled before giving into oblivion.

Chapter 25

Zach awakened to two eyes staring him down by the side of the bed. Izzie.

"Did you and Mommy have a sleepover party?" she whispered. He startled awake and quickly made sure he and Meghan were both covered and he wasn't sporting any noticeable morning boner. This was not something he had ever encountered before—an inquisitive young girl catching him in bed with her mother.

"Uhh, kind of," he said giving Meghan a little jab under the covers. She stirred then jolted awake when she quickly realized the situation with nothing more than an "Oh".

He had planned to be gone before Izzie woke up, but his and Meghan's long lovefest had dramatically altered any plans. Zach hadn't slept this soundly in years and had totally failed to get up at the dawn's light, as was his norm.

"What do you want, honey?" Meghan asked matter-of-factly, holding the covers up to hide her breasts.

Izzie eyes danced with new excitement. "Does this mean Zach is going to live with us now?"

He was pleasantly shocked to hear Meghan reply, "Maybe."

Izzie leaned over to kiss Zach on the cheek and whispered. "Thank you for making Mommy happy."

That shocked him even more. And just when he thought he had been shocked enough, Izzie delivered her closing line.

"Okay. I'm going outside to play now so you can both put your clothes on." And with that she skipped out of the room and down the hall.

Meghan and Zach both stared at each other before bursting into laughter. "I can't believe that child is actually mine," she said.

Zach wished he had time for a morning quickie, but instead showered and changed back into his clothes from yesterday while Meghan was in the kitchen making breakfast. He would stop by his place for fresh clothes on his way to the Library. He would only be a few hours off schedule, so he texted Mrs. Friedman of his late arrival.

"Stay for breakfast," Meghan urged as he popped into the kitchen and came up behind her at the stove. "We have blueberry pancakes---Izzie's favorite."

Zach nuzzled her neck. "Mmm. You're so tempting, but I've got to go. I can come back later, if you want me."

"Yes. I want you."

They were locked in a lip embrace when Izzie came running in through the sliding door all excited. The kid had absolute incredible timing. He reluctantly released Meghan and turned to go.

"Zach. Look! I found Gizmo in the sand!"

She proudly handed over the little black device, which must have fallen out of his pocket last night when he and Meghan stripped to go skinny-dipping.

Meghan looked at it curiously. "What's that?"

"Angels use it to get into the other Library where God keeps all the records,' Izzie divulged with an all-knowing look at Zach.

"Oh, boy." Zach took Gizmo and slipped it back in his pocket.

"What other Library?" Meghan asked, looking from Izzie to Zach.

Izzie suddenly grew very quiet. She slapped her hand to her mouth. "Oops."

This was a defining moment and there was no time to go into details and tell the story accurately and believably. Zach did the best he could think of and stalled.

"I think that when I come back tonight, we can tell your Mommy all about this amazing story I shared with you."

Meghan raised an eyebrow. "Should I be concerned?"

"Trust me on this one," he said. And so she did, once again.

Cali found the keys to her friend's motorcycle, tucked away under a tarp in his garage. She suited up in black jeans, wrapped her hair in a red bandana and donned a helmet and shades.

"You can do this," she told herself, revving the engine. If the truth be known, she had never been very good at manually shifting motorcycle gears, envisioning herself more to be a Vespa type person motoring her way through the cobblestone streets of some idyllic Italian Tuscan village using an automatic shift. But this was the real world and her motto in life had always been "fake it until you make it."

How hard could it be after all these years? She would think female Ninja—untouchable and able to master this cycle quickly. A spin around the block would be a good indicator of whether to stick with the cycle or go to a Plan B. Someone had always told her life was all about how well you handle your Plan B. She didn't have a Plan B right now. This was it.

Cali didn't dare retrieve her car at home or rely on taxis

313

should she need a quick escape. There was comfort in knowing she could park this damn motorcycle anywhere.

After several attempts at shifting gears, with the engine always managing to cut out, Cali finally got the hang of it. See, she could do this. With her laptop tucked safely inside her backpack, along with her trusty Glock for protection, she pointed the bike towards her office and took off.

ZLOT had suspiciously gone silent last night. Always wanting more, Cali had left him several messages, bordering on pleas, but not a word back in 24 hours. He had to have known the fallout all this information was causing. What was he thinking?!

The long arms of justice worked very slowly in Washington D.C. when it came to crimes involving large companies and big-name individuals. If those entities had any true power in this town, any investigation could come to a quick screeching halt. There would be the usual moral posturing, indignant finger pointing, and passing the buck from one agency to another. So, she needed to get back to work to find out whom, if anyone, was running with the ball and actually trying to do something.

On any normal day, this story would demand she be making calls to the Department of Justice, the FBI, the Centers for Countering Human Trafficking, the Office of Congressional Affairs, and especially the Senate Committees for Intelligence. But first she needed to know if she still had a job or was destined to be an independent freelancer for the rest of her days.

A part of her wanted to tell them all to go fuck themselves, but she wouldn't. She still needed to fill Maslow's first hierarchy of needs—like pay her rent and eat. While she could capitalize for a Washington nanosecond on her sudden notoriety, it would be fleeting just like her savings. And if they tried to fire her over her accounts being hacked, she would sue the ever-loving pants off them for wrongful termination. Suddenly she felt like she was holding all the cards. At least she hoped she was.

That thought quickly vanished when she cruised to a stop in front of the station's building where a crowd had already assembled. Several fire trucks, police cars, and a bomb squad vehicle were parked outside at the curb.

She flashed her press credentials to the Fire Captain on scene.

"You work here?" he asked, seeing from her ID badge she was a WWGO TV reporter. She lowered her shades just a fraction so he could identify her but kept her helmet on. She knew eyes could be everywhere watching for her.

"Cavaleri. Yeah, I know you. Aren't you the one who...?"

Yeah, yeah, yeah. She cut him off, getting to the point. "What happened?'

"A fire started in the WWGO newsroom early this morning. No one got hurt, just a badly burnt reporter's cubicle and some smoke damage. It was a clear case of arson. We found accelerants."

Shit. She was willing to bet this had something to do with her information release.

"Then a bomb threat was called in and we had to evacuate the whole building."

This was getting worse. "Did they find the bomb?"

"They found a trip wire to a small incendiary bomb by a parking space in the underground garage. "

Cali felt fear flood the pit of her stomach. "By any chance, was it space number 26?"

"Well, yeah. How did you know?"

"Unlucky guess." She revved up her bike and put it in gear. "Thanks, Captain. Gotta run."

Cali couldn't get out of there fast enough. Now she knew. Someone really *did* want her dead. She sped away, dodging down side streets, back alleys, speeding through lights and zigzagging all over town, all the while watching her rear view mirror for any possible tail. If someone had followed her, she had done her best to throw them off the scent. She could not afford to lead them back to her hideout.

Adrenaline coursed through her like a double shot of tequila, which is why she suddenly felt invincible on the bike. She pulled up to a small convenience store and stuffed her backpack with as much food and non-perishables as it would hold, then paid in cash. She would learn to be a survivor on less. It was time to plot her Plan B.

~~*~~

Zach had made it back to his place in record time after leaving Meghan and Izzie. He quickly changed into fresh work clothes, then packed an overnight bag to bring back to the cottage that evening. He hadn't stopped thinking about her. The truth was that she was all he *could* think about.

Sex without using a condom was something he had never done before. He had always been careful and conscientious, and due to his family fortune, it was a necessary precaution. But with Meghan, the thought had never even occurred to him. It was if he was already committed to her heart and soul and whatever happened he would welcome as "theirs".

Was he in love? Since he had never been in love before, he wasn't certain. But what he was feeling had to be more than just sex--because while he had had sex before with other women, it had never felt anything like this.

From the moment he had first laid eyes on Meghan, he had been completely smitten. There was instant recognition, a sense of total familiarity, like he already knew her on some deeper soul level and destiny was just bringing them back together again. He felt like he would do anything for her--and Izzie too.

Yes, he had called her "love" last night before they both drifted off into sleep. Had she heard his slip of endearment? The more he thought about it, the more he hoped she had. He wanted her to know that for him this was a serious relationship. Tonight, he would tell her so and he would come clean about everything else—Gizmo, the LOT, the identity of ZLOT. There would be no secrets between them--ever.

Gathering up his stuff, he headed for the door, only to have one last thought that drew him back. He knew he should check his private computer for any messages from Cali since he had been too busy last night. He kept his secure laptop locked up in a hidden space behind a bookcase when he wasn't in the flat. Especially now that it contained so much LOT sensitive information that had already been divulged and new information waiting to be released.

When he powered on his computer, he saw that Cali had already left several messages—all marked urgent.

"THEY WANT ME DEAD!" were the first words he saw, typed in bold caps. Someone had been in Cali's house looking around which caused her to go into hiding, then this morning there had been fire at the newsroom and a bomb planted in her parking space intended for her. Zach read it all with a sinking heart. They were targeting her to get to him.

"I need more information to protect myself or I will land up in a dumpster somewhere," she pleaded. *"They are trying to paint me as a perpetrator of a governmental hoax. Senator Talbot has told the press that his intelligence experts say the films are deep fakes and clearly manipulated. Some are actually buying these lies. They're talking about bringing me in to testify about what else I know. What should we do?"*

In such a short period of time it was now a matter of *'we'*. He felt some guilt at getting her into this mess. Had he gone it alone, she would not now be fearful for her life while he could continue to hide in obscurity.

"None of the videos are fake and they know it," he typed

back. *"They are panicking."*

Zach thought about what else he could tell her to assure her of their authenticity.

"They want you dead, too!" she wrote back. *"And they will find you."*

Zach wasn't surprised. While some were already heralding ZLOT as some cult figure of truth, others were calling him a master hoaxer, a charlatan, and so much worse. Anytime you stopped the flow of human trafficking, or put it under the high-powered microscope of scrutiny, it served to curtail operations, which meant you were costing someone big money. Those who screamed the loudest were always the guiltiest.

He remembered his promise to Izzie about helping the children. For now, this was his primary focus—saving the children. The dirty laundry about Minerva and those covert characters around the world who were doing Minerva's bidding would come out later when the world was ready to hear and accept it.

"Give me whatever you've got!" she typed back.

"There's something you need to do first," he wrote, typing in further instructions. *"Do this now. Don't wait. I'll do the drop, same mode as last time. I will be holding some information back as a failsafe, which I've put on a kill switch. If I don't de-activate it within 24 hours, it goes first to you, then to the rest of the world."*

Zach knew he was probably frightening her, but he also knew that in all likelihood, he was now on every intelligence agency's radar screen. They *would* find him eventually. It was only a matter of time despite all the cyber precautions he had taken to leave no trace.

Less than 30 minutes later, it was all set to go. Everything was in place as planned. LOT videos on key people and leaders all the way up to the top, who had known or were involved in trafficking around the world, not just in the United States. It would be part of the next release—along with proof of how the American taxpayer dollar was funding all this without their knowledge through non-classified operations with money accounts never audited. It was sure to get enough good people really riled up enough to do something about it. The problem was that the public was still oblivious to this level of corruption within the ranks of their own leaders.

While he knew it was wrong to protect Meghan's father's crimes from coming out in a public information drop, he still tried to justify his reasons for doing so. That information, should it ever be called for, was part of his failsafe, controlled by the kill switch. If that ever got out, it meant something very bad had either happened to him or Meghan and Izzie. He hoped that would never be the case.

Zach did a quick check of Cali's social media accounts. She had followed his instructions to a tee. Less than a minute ago she had posted a videotape of herself, telling her story about her accounts being hacked, not knowing the identity of her hacker or why ZLOT had singled her out, and that in no way was she depressed or suicidal. That should she suddenly die and/or disappear without a trace, then it would be by nefarious means by those wishing to silence the truth. She ended her disclaimer video with a final warning.

"I have been informed by ZLOT that should anyone do me harm in any manner whatsoever, that information which is of an even more shocking nature will be immediately released to the public. Let me state here that I do not possess, nor am I privy to the contents of this coming information drop. I am only the messenger. But I am told that it is of prime importance to the people of the world in order to bring about true justice."

This drop was scheduled to go out that day at exactly 3:00 PM EST. There was plenty of time to make the evening news, if the press dared to report it. Zach was confident there were some brave souls out there courageous enough to take it and run with it.

Zach put everything back in its hiding place behind the bookcase and left for work, knowing that by tomorrow his world would be exponentially different. He would have the woman he loved by his side.

~~*~~

Gizmo was running hot and cold for no apparent reason. Zach wasn't sure if it had anything to do with Izzie handling the device or his accidentally leaving it in the sand all night. Either way, once he got inside the Stacks at the Library he could feel it in his pocket doing quick temperature extremes every few minutes like a signal beacon. It was no longer responding to his directions or intentions but appeared to have developed a mind of its own.

This became disturbingly clear when the mailroom guy whizzed down the aisle and tried to wheel his cart right through Zach, forcing him to jump out of the way to avoid being plowed down.

"Hey. Be careful." Zach called out only to see the mailroom guy whip around, furtively glance about in every direction, then make a hasty escape out of the Stacks.

He did not know why, but Gizmo had, of its own accord, decided to initiate its cloaking ability. The mailroom guy had not physically seen him and hearing some disembodied voice must have totally freaked him out.

Removing Gizmo from his pocket didn't seem to disengage his cloaking feature either. Gizmo was in a stuck mode and had taken Zach into that mode with him. Any verbal or all non-verbal instructions by Zach to disengage cloaking failed to make any difference. And through it all Gizmo continued to run hot and cold. This was not good sign.

Zach had planned on going back into the LOT again that afternoon and be back before his 3:00 PM information drop, but he decided this just could not wait. Invisibility was not the way he wanted to live his life. Satya would know what to do about Gizmo and this baffling condition.

He could pop into the LOT and be back in enough time to finish up his daily systems check, which now encompassed all the open and closed Stacks in the Library. The tracking programs he had started using were much more efficient. Since he had started in the Stacks, he now held the record for tracking down missing books and files where others, who had come before him, had given up. Mrs. Friedman was pretty much leaving him alone these days to do his work uninterrupted. She was pleased and that's all that mattered.

"I like that you're a self-starter, Zach," she told him very matter-of-factly one day after reviewing his new program. "You take the initiative without instruction and run with it." After that she was content to accept only updated progress reports.

Zach had time to get out a few emails to her and other staff members, then pushed back from his desk in the Stacks and began the high-speed portal sequence algorithm in his head. But even that felt different today. The process seemed to go on forever--the walls of the Stacks rippling then shattering around him until he was sucked into the portal with such great force, he thought he would either die or be split apart. The tunnel pulsed in a rhythmic geometric pattern, the sound around him vibrating through his entire being. Nothing about it felt familiar. The energy felt all wrong. Inside his chest he experienced a moment of panic. But then he heard voices, somewhere far off in the distance, getting closer.

On a rush of energy, he was ejected out into a bare windowless room with minimal lighting projected upward from the flooring. Each step he took lit up the floor beneath his feet enough for him to see that there was only one way out—a door near the far corner of this perfectly square room. He knew without measuring that the space he was standing in was exactly 25 x 25 feet.

There was no way of knowing what lay on the other side of the door without taking a chance. The only thing he knew for certain was that he was not in the Library of Truth but some new and unknown place.

The door handle opened easily and beyond it was a dimly lit empty corridor. He wasn't sure where the voices he had heard had come from just prior to him being spit out into this place, but right now not a soul was in sight. There was some sort of writing on the wall, totally unrecognizable. Definitely not Sanskrit inscriptions, like in the LOT. He reached in his pocket to retrieve his cellphone flashlight, but his pocket was now empty. Damn. He checked for his recording glasses, but they, too, were nowhere to be found—probably all lost somewhere in the portal when he felt like he was being ripped apart.

The temperature in this place was comfortable, perhaps even a little too warm after being used to the cold confines of the stacks. Zach moved forward until the corridor veered sharply to the right. Suddenly his feet did not want to move. He felt the hair on the back of his arms stand up in warning and inside his pocket Gizmo was as hot as a fire iron. He knew there was something or someone nearby. Probably not a good idea to look around that corner, but nevertheless he did.

What he saw made him freeze. He repeatedly blinked to clear his head and make sure he was not hallucinating. This was no mirage, yet it was hard to believe what his eyes were seeing in the dimly lit room. Sitting on a rather large floor pillow, its tentacles moving out into the room like giant undulating sensors, sat an enormous green praying mantis robed in deep purple. Zach estimated the being would have to be close to 12 feet tall when standing. This thing was alive and in deep contemplation.

Black slanted and bulging eyes widened with the realization that an intruder had just entered its space. The insect-like being's tentacles stilled. The air was filled with a strange charged and expectant current. Yet, the alien creature made no move towards him. It just stared ahead with dark unfathomable eyes--waiting.

Zach's senses were heightened--on extreme alert. He could feel the mantis's curiosity. And for the briefest second, he felt as if his own mind was being telepathically probed. He heard sharp clicking sounds in his head. Despite this being the most bizarre experience he might ever encounter, it was coupled with something he found equally as odd. The being was radiating a cascade of different numbers and double digits, something he had never seen before in humans. He immediately recognized them as prime numbers: 2, 3, 5, 7, 11, 13s and so forth, all numbers which could be divided by one. It was mesmerizing to observe and watch.

While Zach tried to make sense of what it meant in terms of an alien language, he stayed frozen in place, waiting to see what the mantis would do next. He was the intruder in this being's quiet space, its lair, yet it watched him with infinite patience. Zach was not sure if he could be seen in his cloaked state, but it didn't seem to matter with this particular entity. There was deep intelligence behind its eyes and it just knew. It, too, was analyzing Zach's unexpected presence and what it might mean, while certain prime numbers like 11's and 29's escalated in its thought process. So interesting. Then suddenly the numbers radiating out of this entity dramatically ebbed, as if it had come to some conclusion. That's when Zach experienced a sudden yet gentle energetic push backward. It was nudging Zach out of its space with its mind. You don't belong here, it seemed to say. Move along now, almost as if it were addressing a wayward child.

Zach backed out of the being's lair. What the hell was this

place? Had the portal accidentally taken him to some alien dimension? Not knowing what to do or how to find a way out, Zach kept going and continued down the corridor hoping to find an explanation. A short distance away, the corridor opened onto an immense cavern which appeared to be illuminated all around, in every corner, by some unknown light source. No light fixtures, no radiant bulbs, and even more weird—no shadows anywhere. It reminded him of the lighting inside the LOT. Again, he was aware of the warmth in temperature. There were massive tunnels running in every direction as far as the eye could see connected to the cavern like spokes in a wheel hub. And right in the middle of this enormous hub were several chevron and saucer-shaped metal spacecrafts the size of football fields.

Zach was spellbound by what he saw. He had to be in another world. Should he be frightened for his life? His instincts told him to table that thought and let his intense curiosity lead the way. In his pocket he held onto Gizmo--telling his little buddy to continue to remain cloaked. The praying mantis being obviously sensed him, but could he be seen as well? That was a big unknown. Where there was one of these beings there had to be others, some possibly not as patient and tolerant. There was a need to proceed with caution. Too many unknown variables were now in play.

He heard the sound of footsteps behind him and spun around. Humans were approaching. A group of seven men, some in military uniform of some branch of service (another unknown), marched right past him. Then again, he wasn't even certain they *were* human. Zeros and ones emitted from the top of their head like binary code. It occurred to Zach that they might be a form of artificial intelligence, possibly human hybrids. They proceeded to board the chevron shaped craft from an elevator-like shaft under its metallic body. Minutes later Zach watched as the craft hovered off the ground then rose right through the stone ceiling of the cavern as if there were no barrier or obstacle in its path. Zach's mind continued to race. Were the walls fake, or an illusion, or something else?

The air felt electromagnetically charged for just a few seconds after the craft's departure, then returned to normal, quickly bringing the atmosphere in the cavern back to a highly oxygenated state. Zach moved toward the larger of the spacecraft, wanting to touch its smooth black surface, see what it was made of. But when he did, he jumped back in surprise. The skin of this vehicle was alive, organic, and responsive to his thoughts. It reminded him of a large-scale version of Gizmo. He realized with a start that the craft was a kind of artificial intelligence beyond what he could envision.

Zach itched to know who or what or even how it was programmed. His fingers fanned out on its surface, asking it a rapid sequence of questions, seeing which kind of coding it understood, and feeling a deep sense of reverence and admiration when he realized not only did it know all 20 programming languages that Zach knew, but hundreds, even thousands more which he didn't.

"Tell me what you know," he whispered, adding his other hand to its other worldly surface. Just like he had experienced in front of the Sphinx about time reversal, Zach felt an implosion of energy and light inside his head as a download of information took over his brain. And suddenly--he knew. Knew more than he had bargained for. The stuff of science fiction, the knowledge of universal dynamics. A higher level of scientific truth. A consciousness beyond consciousness, bordering on super-consciousness. Pure Source knowledge. This living spacecraft had revealed its innermost secrets. Secrets that he now understood without the scientific training that usually went along with such insights. And in this massive download of information, not to be overlooked, Zach also learned that this space vehicle was presently docked at Antarctica Base port 188 on the cold, icy

5th continent.

Zach sunk to the ground, feeling overwhelmed. In that defining moment of his life, he felt profoundly changed, eternally grateful. He had no idea why this intelligent craft had shared with him its inner workings--what anywhere else would be considered classified information. But it had. He was sure his father, an aerospace physicist, would give anything to be privy to such information. In that moment he wished his father were here to talk about such things with him. They had never shared much together in their lives, besides the same last name, but the boy in him wanted to make that connection—to share with his father what he had just learned.

Zach suddenly felt a gentle force pull him away from this intelligent spacecraft followed by a deep soulful urge to seek out more from the depths of the tunnels that spread out in every direction—to learn their secrets as well. He had no idea what he was searching for, but he knew it was crucial that he find it. After about 1.2 miles of moving through empty tunnels that seemed to be endless in nature, his quest finally brought him to a set of 10-foot-high double steel doors.

There was a DNA scanner on the door. How he knew this he could not say. He just knew. Zach touched the keypad and waited for the scanner to read him. It did so instantaneously. The door opened to him. How and why he knew it would allow him in, was also a mystery. A part of him believed it had something to do with Gizmo. The other part of him was sure the download from the strange craft was the real reason. Either way, he was certain whatever he found on the other side of that door would change his life forever. One always knows when they have reached a destiny point—and in that moment Zach knew.

~~*~~

At precisely 3:00 PM, right on schedule, Cali received the next information drop from ZLOT through her hacked social media accounts. She knew it was coming, so it didn't come as any great surprise, however this time it exposed government agencies who were funding trafficking rings and benefiting from them at the taxpayers' expense. This one named more names, access to their offshore accounts, and how such criminal activities were being fraudulently classified under other secret government programs. Had anyone ever done a thorough accounting of such agencies and their budgets this would have been discovered a long time ago, but as was the case with government, these budgetary oversights conveniently went unnoticed along with other waste and abuse. There was always someone who could be bought to oversee and hide such crimes. But this time, ZLOT was pointing out all the people complicit in these crimes and they included congressman, senators, department heads, intelligence agencies, both employees and supervisors, churches, ministries, corporation CEOs, the big tech companies, and a whole host of notables even in the media and entertainment field. The list was endless and the proof indisputable and damning.

Cali was physically sick to her stomach. The global and national corruption was so massive and so deep it would take an act of divine intervention to reverse this level of damage to humanity. How had this ever been allowed to happen? The tragic irony of it all was that the American people were unwittingly being made to pay for these heinous crimes with their hard-earned taxed dollars. Now they would know. And this duplicity was being perpetrated on people of other countries as well. The question was whether the people would even believe they *had* been duped?

The ZLOT drop spread like wildfire, as if everyone had been holding their collective breath waiting for the next shoe to drop. Many in the know wasted no time in downloading and sharing it, fearful it would be censored from the internet, wiping it clean from even the archival Way Back Machine where it was believed nothing that had ever once been on the web could be permanently erased. False.

As suspected, less than 30 minutes after the information was released, the entire internet went down. Like a virus it spread from server to server, plunging communication networks into total darkness, something never experienced before and not thought completely possible. The world suddenly and inexplicitly shuddered to a total information stop.

Someone had made the call to pull the plug. Who that person was no one knew. And if they did know or suspect, they weren't saying. How long the world would be in communication darkness was unknown as well. This was knowledge someone didn't want the people to ever know. By pulling the plug, it validated in most everyone's mind that what was being revealed *was* the truth. No one tried to debunk it or call it a conspiracy hoax. No one tried to convince the people that all visual evidence was a perpetrated deep fake. The evidence was so damning, someone made the call to shut it all down and stop the world from sharing it until it could be scrubbed out of existence forever with global intelligence censoring tools employed to make sure it never ever came to light.

Cali watched the drama unfold from her friend's hideaway. She knew she was witnessing evil at work, bent on protecting its own from annihilation. To make a bad situation worse, power grid sectors started wavering across the country, causing massive explosions, before going offline like dominoes falling. Some areas were plunged into a blackout in sweltering summer heat with temperatures well over 90 degrees in many states. Washington, D.C. was the first to go. Backup generators across the city kicked in, but how long they would last was anyone's guess.

Cali could see out the dining room window that neighborhood

people were coming out of their houses to see what was happening. ZLOT had caused all this. Truth could kill but could also cause retaliatory destruction.

Cali sat in a living room chair, the afternoon light streaming in from a bay window, and wondered what came next. Her Plan B had not taken into account something like this happening. Right now, her mind lapsed into chaos, like her life—a total and complete mess. First a break-in, then a newsroom fire and a bomb meant for her, followed by an internet black out, and now a power grid failure. This would be a date to remember.

As if this day couldn't get any worse, she heard a rattling sound and sat up straighter. Her eyes darted to the back door where someone was working the lock. Without another thought, she reached for her Glock and racked the slide, hearing the comforting sound of a bullet loading in the chamber. Moving fast, she quietly slipped behind the door, banking on the element of surprise with her intruder. She had always been a steady shot, but right now her hands trembled.

The door slowly edged open. She had the man's back in her sights.

"Don't take another step or I'll shoot you dead," she warned.

He swung around and with one quick movement knocked the gun out of her hand and grabbed her from behind in a neck lock.

"For God's sake, Cali," he muttered, shaking his head. "Stop playing Annie Oakley. You're going to get yourself killed."

Fuck. It was none other than that bastard, Bond! She should have just pulled the trigger and be done with him once and for all.

A brightly lit corridor lay beyond the 10-foot-high steel doors, which opened to Zach. To his right was a large room filled with floor to ceiling video screens, monitored by uniformed personnel at computer terminal banks, carrying out orders by some person being referred to as "the Counselor". The scene was a hub of activity, people coming and going, yet no one seemed to take notice of him. Which told him he was still being cloaked by Gizmo, affording him an opportunity to figure out what these people were doing on this Antarctica base.

"Shut down SATCOMS numbers one through twenty. Leave open the Pentagon satellite feed going to General Braden," the Counselor barked at his men. "Then hit both the East and West Coast power grids with a soft EMP. Cripple it, let it ripple, but don't disable it completely. We will eventually have to bring it all back up."

"U.S. Internet now down, sir," one operator called out. "What about the media feeds?"

"Pull the national link," came the order. "Allow the Emergency Alert System—for now and, of course, the intelligence and GPS satellites. Make sure Talbot knows the plan."

Zach had a pretty good idea which Talbot they were referring to. Senator James Talbot. Talbot had been the one wanting the missing ZE file on Antarctica. The file information had never shown this underground base of operations, but they must have shown the coordinates. He brought up the picture in his mind of the early maps he had found in the file. At the time the coordinates had meant nothing to him. Now they did. The maps were old ones, which meant this base went back at least hundreds of years and had survived planetary rotations that had turned a once verdant land into this vast frozen tundra. Who would have thought there were more than just rich mineral deposits hidden deep inside this icy continent?

Talbot had also been involved with Constantine Stavros on human trafficking. The man had obviously profited greatly from it. And now Zach was certain Talbot was part of Minerva making these decisions that affected millions of people—causing gross travesties of injustice. The information from the LOT had secured their global hold knowing that he who controls truth and the dissemination of information has dominion over the world.

This command center controlled the orbiting satellite communication networks that the planet relied upon for inter-global access. What Zach didn't have the answer to was why were they were now shutting down many of these networks, while only crippling others? Could it have anything to do with the drop he had just left Cali?

The video screens showed some data, which might provide him a better idea of where he was, but not much. He walked over to find two of the 12 screens were blacked out, but still displayed Earth coordinates.

The first screen showed several views: a large crater in a frozen tundra where—holy shit, space craft like he had just seen in the cavern room, were descending into a vast hole. The coordinates told him this video feed was coming from this very base in Antarctica. There was also a view of the portal room he had entered coming out of the tunnel. This had to be their jump room conduit into the LOT. This was Portal 1's command center.

Now things were starting to make sense. Blackened screen number two displayed the coordinates for the Giza Plateau, which meant it must be Portal 2. The last blackened screen was easy to figure out. Portal 3 was Washington, D.C's Library of Congress.

While Zach had no idea why Portal 2 and 3 screens were blacked out, he took immediate note that there were twelve screens with listed coordinates. Did this mean there might possibly be 12 portals into the LOT, like there were 12 golden Minerva statues?   He took note of the other nine portal locations. Some were familiar, being inside other well-known libraries in the world, while others he had never heard of. Who had set up this elaborate portal system? And more importantly—when and why?

That's when it hit him. To the best of his knowledge, the only one who had a stronghold on the portals into the LOT was Minerva. This had to be a key Minerva stronghold—a secret underground base on Antarctica where no one would ever come looking. The perfect cover from spying eyes and knowledge of the bizarre events taking place here. There was a strange human/alien and even robotic presence in this Minerva operations center. Everything felt infinitely different. Zach couldn't help but note that even some of the staff monitoring computer banks emanated binary code. They had to be robots, clones, or something else not entirely human. The "Counselor" fellow was shedding a torrent of fives and twos—angry, worried and demanding change--obviously he was human.

That insectoid creature Zach had stumbled upon earlier meant it was highly likely there were other such beings like him here as well. Had these creatures been the first to build this labyrinth of tunnels and had Minerva come in and usurped their technology and knowledge? From what he had gleaned from touching the spacecraft's skin, he knew he was on the right track. The two species had entered into a collaboration of sorts for self-preservation. Yet with Minerva there could also be a deeper agenda at work. Gizmo, in all its artificial intelligence, had led him here to uncover some important truth.

But the clock was running out. This too he knew. How much longer could he remain in a cloaked state before he was eventually detected and unmasked? Zach mentally commanded Gizmo to keep the shield up for as long as possible while he gathered intel from this command center. He hoped to learn more about this Counselor person and what his role was in Minerva. Was he running the show or was Talbot?

The faint scent of Crown Achievement's original blend pipe tobacco suddenly wafted through the room. It was a familiar aroma to Zach. He turned from the wall screens searching for its source. This particular scent always elicited a cascade of memories, some fond and some not so fond, which he would prefer not to think about.

While his back had been turned to review the 12 portal locations, three men had entered the room to join the Counselor. One of them was the source of the tobacco smoke. When Zach spotted him, he froze. Overcome with shock, speechless to his core and now paralyzed with recognition at identifying the man with the pipe in his mouth, the one they were now referring to as "the Governor" was none other than his father, Martin Eldridge.

Zach felt his world internally shift and quake. He hadn't seen his father in maybe six months, possibly more, but even with a dark beard now covering his angular face, he would still know him anywhere. What was his father doing in this Minerva stronghold? He recalled his mother saying his father was in Antarctica, but like always he had assumed on some scientific expedition.

Martin Eldridge had always been away for long periods at a time when Zach was growing up. In the societal circles Zach had grown up in, many of the other boys he attended school with also had fathers who were off running large companies or traveling for business. Having an everyday father around was a rarity. Having an absent father was closer to the norm. And as he clearly remembered, his father never wanted to talk about his work—sometimes even going as far as to say it was government "classified" and he couldn't say.

Zach was now rethinking what he thought he knew about the man he had always called "father". Was his father, like Meghan's, also involved with Minerva? The thought of it, if true, suddenly filled him with deep disgust. He didn't want to believe his father played a role in any of this. Was this why Gizmo had led him here, away from the LOT—to learn the truth for himself?

In his heart, he wanted to believe his father might be here only

333

in a scientific capacity, nothing more. Perhaps a consulting position of sorts. After all he *was* an accomplished and brilliant astrophysicist. The truth might kill him, but Zach had to know why they called his father the 'Governor'. It didn't take long to find out.

From all he was able to observe under the cloak of obscurity, he heard and saw with his own eyes how both uniformed and non-uniformed men deferred to his decisions, carrying out his orders, and treating the man they respectfully called the 'Governor' as their leader. With a heavy heart and immense shame, Zach could no longer deny the obvious. His father was not only a part of Minerva—the man appeared to be running the operation.

Had he not been so distraught at the thought of his father's part in such an organization's heinous crimes against humanity, he would have found this strange alien place quite intriguing. Most people would never suspect such a world existed outside the realms of a sci-fi movie. A part of him hoped he might be hallucinating, but it was all too real to easily dismiss as a fragment of his imagination.

Dogging his father's footsteps, he came across several different species of non-human and humanoid-like beings in all shapes and sizes. Some spoke English, some spoke in hisses and clicking sounds. Some didn't even need to speak at all, suggesting telepathy was employed. To Zach's utter consternation, his father was able to communicate with all these beings. Even when he stayed his distance, he could still see that spoken communication was not an issue.

Observing the breadth and depth of this operation, all the military, scientists, and creatures, involved made Zach realize he did not know his father at all. The man was a total enigma to him. He had kept this life hidden from his family for years. Did his mother even know? Did she even care? Probably not, was his best guess. Which was why she had lovers and affairs everywhere she went. Her husband, Martin Eldridge, was missing in action and had been for years. It put a whole new perspective on his parents' relationship. He could almost feel sorry for his mother. Camille Eldridge had to be the loneliest soul he knew, despite her appearance of being such a well-respected and liked Washington power broker.

Thoughts regarding his purpose for being here and seeing all this came into focus. Did his father know about him? Did he know how Zach was using the LOT to work against Minerva? He felt a moment of fear and revulsion as realization sunk in. Had his father been responsible for Roone's death, Constantine's demise, and the end of many others who either got in Minerva's way or were no longer useful? If so, then his father was a ruthless killer with no heart or soul. And what did that say about him, being the son of such a monster? The thought caused a rising panic inside him, followed by an immediate need to get away from his father and this place with all its hidden secrets as quickly as he could.

He was momentarily distracted from such thoughts, when he heard his father instruct the Counselor. "It's time for Talbot to make his exit. He's served his purpose. Make sure his daughter and my son are taken care of…"

Zach suddenly stopped breathing. His father knew about Meghan and him? What did he mean 'taken care of..'? No. No. No. This did not sound good. He had to get back immediately! His mind screamed DANGER and for him to GO and GO NOW!

An invasion of numbers and symbols imploded inside his brain, the intensity of which he had never experienced before. With every passing second it only escalated, bringing on an unbearable throbbing and pain so striking he could barely move. It was becoming harder to breath. The rapid pounding in his chest made him fear he was either having a deadly coronary or his heart would surely burst forth from his body and end his life once and for all. He grasped onto Gizmo like a lifeline, trying to silently repeat the algorithm sequence to get him out of this place, back to the LOT, or the Library of Congress, or anywhere other than the truth he was witnessing here. He no longer felt safe anywhere—but perhaps in the arms of Meghan. If he could only get back to Meghan and Izzie to protect them.

Zach suddenly lost all feeling in his body and slumped forward to the floor like a lifeless rag doll, losing consciousness. Now oblivious to everything, totally helpless in this state, Gizmo raged hot as fire in his pocket. For only the briefest of seconds, Zach's physical body lost its cloaking, exposing him to a myriad of base surveillance cameras, before blinking him out.

In a control room, a technician monitoring a bank of camera feeds for the south end of the base, picked it up the momentary blip on his computer screen. It was enough to arouse his curiosity. He played it back, engaging thermal imaging to pick up any heat signature, engaging a DNA element trace for possible identification, and was rewarded for his diligence. An unidentified "human" visitor had somehow invaded the base. He saved the information data and immediately sent it his shift's base commander for review. Security would have their neck in a noose for allowing such an unauthorized entry to occur.

As a further precaution, the technician began using more highly sophisticated tools to detect if the intruder was still anywhere on base. When he came up with nothing, he pulled up back camera footage and started running analysis. Here he found some interesting anomalies, same heat and DNA signature. The technician secretly smiled to himself. He knew he would be richly rewarded for his extra efforts.

Chapter 26

Meghan was extremely worried. It was late and Zach still hadn't come home to her as he said he would. Something big had happened and she had no way of knowing what was going on. Electrical power was still online, but the internet was out and so were phones, cable and TV. There was no signal at all from any communication device.

Zach would have no way of contacting her, nor she him. By now the Library was already closed for the evening and he should have been back here hours ago. She didn't know what to do, didn't want to over-react, but she felt distraught—and she wasn't the only one.

Izzie kept pacing the floor asking about him. Meghan had no idea if Izzie was picking up her anxiety at Zach not being there, or her daughter was intuitively sensing something was truly amiss--like an accident.

Izzie clung to her and wouldn't eat anything, even though Meghan had made a special meal of chicken parmesan and fettuccine to impress both Zach and Izzie.

"Mommy, Zach is somewhere far, far away. I think he has

forgotten us," she said almost tearful.

"Nonsense, honey."

Meghan wouldn't believe such thinking for a second. "He would never forget us. He's just running late. Now stop worrying and eat some dinner."

Izzie was adamant, putting down her fork defiantly. "No, Mommy. I don't know if he will ever come back. Zach is gone."

Hearing her daughter proclaim this outcome with such finality alarmed her. It was not at all like Izzie to jump to the most negative conclusion. The more she thought about it, the more she felt a need to do something—anything. But she couldn't call hospital emergency rooms or check for traffic accidents with cellphone service not working. Meghan desperately wanted to call her father, to check his sources, which were plentiful, but she could not bring herself to ask her father for such a favor after the other night, even if she could get in touch with him. He would only lecture her about her silliness and worst of all, he wouldn't care anyway. Perhaps she was being overly concerned. His car might have had problems and any minute now he would walk in that door and she would fall into his arms. Oh, God, how she needed his arms around her. How she had come to feel so deeply for him in such a short time totally surprised her. It should frighten her, but it didn't. With Zach she felt safe.

Izzie came over to her and hugged her around the waist, sensing what she needed. She hugged her back, smoothing her hair before kissing the top of her head.

"It will all be okay, honey," she said more to convince herself.

"I think Zach went through the tunnel again," Izzie said softly. "I think he's sleeping in the tunnel."

Meghan had no idea what Izzie was talking about. "What tunnel?" she asked.

"You know--the tunnel inside the Library."

Meghan was still confused. "You mean the tunnels under the

Library that go to the Capitol buildings?"

Izzie's eyes grew big. She put her hand to her mouth before saying any more. From the look on her mother's face, she knew she had already gone too far.

Meghan knew her daughter was keeping something from her. "Isadora March," she said sternly. "Now tell me what tunnel you are talking about. This is no time for secrets."

Izzie didn't want to get Zach in trouble, for she inherently knew her mother would not like to learn she had been to the Angel's library and Egypt, too, without her permission.

"It wasn't Zach's fault," she began cautiously. "I followed him to see where he was going. And he didn't see me behind him, and it all happened so fast he couldn't stop me from going into the tunnel with him."

She finished in a rush, but she could see her mother's face now looked terrified at hearing her words. Izzie knew she was making a mess of explaining what had happened. She tried again.

"No, Mommy." she said, taking her mother's hand. "Don't worry. It was all good. Cross my heart. Zach showed me a heavenly library where we saw Daddy and his memories."

Meghan remained silently skeptical. Heavenly libraries? Memories of Brett? As a mother, the thought of her daughter being taken anywhere without her knowledge was her worst nightmare. But Zach would never hurt Izzie. How she knew this she couldn't say, she just knew.

Meghan put on her best "I'm listening" face. "Ok, Izzie. Let's start from the very beginning and don't leave anything out. Promise?"

Izzie nodded. She started with telling her mother of Zach's appearance from out of nowhere inside the Children's Reading Room, which confirmed in her mind he was an angel sent to Earth to help people. She could see her mother wasn't exactly buying that theory, but she was determined to tell her everything no matter how strange it sounded. And so, she did.

In Izzie's mind it was the grandest of adventures. Sometimes a little scary but not with Zach there beside her. She related to her mother how they were sucked into a tunnel from inside the Coolidge Auditorium, about traveling to a fantastic heavenly library where you could step into memories and how she saw both her mother and father at Il Rinnovo. She repeated word for word what she had heard and seen in the moving memory, somewhat satisfied when she saw her mother's mouth drop open, clearly dumbfounded. She even reported seeing her mother getting sick and running to the bathroom where she, yuck, vomited. Then she related seeing her father flying planes on an airfield somewhere, then her and Zach getting stuck underneath the Great Pyramid in the underground water tunnels, and finally Zach working some magic so they could return with no time lost in time to go to dinner that night at the real Il Rinnovo.

"I told you Zach is an angel Mommy. He's fallen asleep in the tunnel and can't wake up." Izzie pulled on her mother's hand to bring her out of her thoughts. "Please, Mommy. You've got to believe me. I think Zach needs our help."

Meghan didn't know what to think. It was the most unbelievable story she had ever heard from the lips of her child. It sounded like sheer fantasy, but Izzie was no liar. Time had taught Meghan that. Her child was clearly different, like Zach, which was probably why they clicked so well together, but she was truthful. Izzie could see things others sometimes never saw or sensed, and so Meghan decided to go on blind trust. If there was more she needed to know, it was now.

"What else can you tell me about this 'other' library," she said taking Izzie into her arms. "And how do we find the tunnel where Zach is sleeping?"

~~*~~

Deep down Cali Cavaleri was a Bond Girl, always had been, always would be, and she knew he knew it. Fate kept bringing them back together, like a cosmic joke. They might have once laughed at that 007 moniker she had called herself, but deep in her heart she knew Bond would never kill her. At least she hoped he wouldn't. That's where her clouded judgment regarding all things male might finally do her in. She trusted too much and would probably land up disappointed once again, like in the past. If there was such a thing as an afterlife and she could decide her gender, in her next life she would definitely come back as a male if only to feel less vulnerable--and perhaps turn the tables on Bond once and for all.

"What do you want?" she practically growled at him. He had her defenseless. Her Glock was on the floor somewhere near the sofa, nowhere in sight. His grip tightened on her, her back to his chest firmly against him.

Bond looked none too happy to see her either. He hated complications and Cali had always been at the top of his list. He knew his weaknesses all too well, and his dick had a mind of its own when it came to her. Even now it responded to her nearness.

"You're being tracked," he said in her ear. "You need to get out of here now." It was more a command then an invite.

Cali hesitated. How had they tracked her? She had no phone, was off the grid and with satellite communications apparently down, then how in the world???

He loosened his grip and pushed her forward. "Move, Cali! Stay here and you'll be dead!"

"Why should I trust you?" she shot back, looking over her shoulder at those incredible blue eyes. "You've lied to me before."

Bond grew more frustrated and angry. She could tell he didn't want to be her nursemaid. It wasn't in his makeup. So why was he here doing just that?

"Get over it," he said, grabbing her backpack, scooping up her Glock, which he seemed to know exactly where it landed--under the coffee table, then pushed her towards the back door with coordinated military precision.

Under cover of darkness, he dragged her through some back alleys to a waiting black van several streets over which he had hidden under a large willow tree far from any streetlight. Upon seeing the vehicle, she immediately balked at getting in. What if there were more agents inside? How did she know whose side he was actually playing on.

"You're abducting me?" she asked incredulously, seeing him go for the van's door handle.

"No, you little idiot. I'm trying to help you. So, stop fighting me and get in."

She stood her ground, refusing to budge. "Where are we going?"

There was that exasperated sigh of his she had come to know only too well. "To somewhere safe. Just trust me."

When had she ever been able to just trust him? Bond yanked open the passenger side door of the van and practically shoved her in. So much for asking her nicely. There was a moment of relief as she peered back into the dark interior of the van and confirmed it was indeed empty and no other agents were inside waiting to pounce on her.

Bond moved around to the driver's side, climbed in and glanced her way as he started the engine. There was a strange unfathomable look on his face, she couldn't quite decipher. Then he did something totally unexpected. He leaned over and kissed her softly on the lips. It was only for a second, the very briefest of kisses, then he pulled back all paramilitary professional again.

"Don't say another word," he warned, putting the vehicle in gear and quickly pulling out of the spot. "I'll tell you all I know when we get there."

And so Cali, against her better judgment, which was pretty shitty in the first place, remained silent for the full 90 minutes it took him to take her to his so-called "safe spot".

~~*~~

When the internet mysteriously came back online, it had been thoroughly sanitized of all human trafficking information ZLOT had released using Cali's social media feeds. Minerva had wiped it all clean. For those who might have downloaded file folders or screenshots of the information to their computers, an algorithm was released that immediately forced all operating systems to update to include a search and destroy program of the info they wanted deleted, regardless of whether the device was on or off, hooked up to the internet or not.

It didn't matter to them if it caused the blue screen of death, which totally disabled some computers and forced others to crash if they attempted to stop the destroyer program. Since the early days of technology, both hardware and software backdoors had been built into every computer ever sold for this very purpose. Minerva and all its power tentacles across the globe had made sure of it. It was both diabolical and effective as an information kill switch, the penultimate fail safe. Minerva had used a much smaller test version of their software program in the past for this same purpose, simply calling it: TOMBSTONE.

What they couldn't stop was those who were smart enough to immediately save the info by downloading the information to an exterior hard drive or USB stick for safeguarding and future retrieval. These were usually the die-hard techies. But Minerva had planned for this as well. Every contingency had been planned for. If someone tried accessing the information from any external device using a computer, it would effectively wipe it as well. Which is what many discovered once Minerva allowed the communication satellites to come back online. Human trafficking was now almost non-existent in all world search engines, which should have caused immediate questions for the tech giants, which they controlled. However, Minerva knew the beauty and power of plausible deniability. It worked every time.

With a sense of confidence and security, they knew censorship was their ultimate tool. The people would only know what they wanted them to know, no more. He who controls the information content, controls the world. Minerva totally believed this, and that this was their exclusive right, reserved only for the powerful few. With this certainty, having never been challenged before, they opened back up all channels only to be hit by something totally unexpected--an information counterstrike.

Unbeknownst to them, because Zach was not there to stop it, his failsafe kill switch was tripped off. A flood of new information, the likes of which no one on Earth had ever seen before, hit like the mother of all bombs. Secrets the intelligence agencies had kept hidden for decades, classified in the realm of national security to cover insider crimes, began unraveling. Not slowly, but with a speed that made heads spin, tongues wag, and turned conspiracy theorists into instant prophets. Senator James Talbot was the first to fall. Within hours he was found dead in his Senate Intelligence office, an "apparent suicide" caused by what appeared to be a self-inflicted bullet hole to the back of his head.

Back in the LOT, Satya watched it all play out in real time with fascination. Something had changed in the future timeline causing extreme uncertainty for certain factors and outcomes she had meticulously planned for. The strongest probable for planet Earth was being re-written in all the future memory files so fast it was like a volcano exploding, sending rivulets of cleansing fire in every direction. Light streams of information streaked across the LOT, re-morphing, some dissipating in their entirety, while others sought out new homes in the vast expanse of this ancient storage vault. Satya had never seen anything like it in all her time in the LOT.

Zach Eldridge had caused all this. That was for certain. There was no doubt in her mind he was an instrument of change. His life records had shown he would cause great upheaval, which was part of his destiny. He bore the infinity birthmark, so it was only a matter of time before he came into his own. But she also knew that his records were not totally complete. There was an unusual gap in his timeline. Satya was uncertain what to make of it because it wavered in length and duration, still undecided. Which was why something needed to be done about his current dilemma or it could turn into a permanent situation and then she would be back to square one.

Right now, Satya knew exactly where Zach was and what had befallen him. But she was forbidden to intercede under the free-will guidelines restricting "human interference" unless, of course, she exercised a little creativity to get around this rule. Her thoughts immediately went to the red-haired woman and her daughter who had captured his heart.

Satya meticulously consulted the records for both Meghan and Isadora March. What she saw was concerning. The unexpected death of her Senator father could pose a problem and a threat. It was a potentially delicate situation, and it wasn't the only challenge written in her records. But after some thought, Satya in all her wisdom knew exactly what she needed to do. A new plan was set into place. Time would tell if she had chosen wisely.

The End of Part 1

****

Book 2

(Coming soon)

STACKS – *Awakening Truth*

Go to: Facebook.com/stackslibraryoftruth or @stackslibraryoftruth for announcements

Acknowledgements

The idea for *STACKS* first came to me in a dream in 2008 where I woke up in the middle of the night and felt compelled to begin writing down the plot. For years I played around with the concept first in an internet web series format, then a TV series pilot script, but the timing never felt right. It was a story that needed to be told in its own time and that time came in 2020 when it felt like the world needed a story about Truth in a world of Lies.

Then in the first week of March 2020, right before the COVID-19 crisis hit on March 11th, I had another dream to book a flight to Washington, D.C. and to spend an entire week at the Library of Congress getting my facts straight and learning the Library from top to bottom. At the time, I wondered what the rush was, but nevertheless, I went. One week after I returned, the Library was shut down due to the virus and was closed for over a year. That was a lesson learned. Always pay attention to your dreams.

The week I spent at the LOC and Capitol Hill was one of the most exciting research trips I have ever undertaken. There are so many people who took me into places the regular tours do not go. I poked my head into every department and asked questions about everything. It's because of these Library employees, who are so knowledgeable and dedicated to helping find answers, that I was able to really get the feel of this incredible depository of knowledge.

I wrote the first chapter of *STACKS* inside the LOC's Main Reading Room to get into the feel of it. At one point I looked up at the great clock on the wall, noticing the time was incorrect, and asked about it. I learned that the clock had never worked correctly. I decided to weave it into the story.

I'd like to first thank Marissa Ball who is Head of the Main Reading Room. She took me deep into the stacks, which is off limits to the general public. She was a wealth of information and I appreciate all she shared.

My deep gratitude to Rhiannon Burruss (a former congressional office manager) for squiring me around Washington, D.C. and its surrounding areas to get the lay of the land. Having worked on The Hill for decades, Rhiannon was a treasure trove of information.

All Library of Congress employees I found extremely helpful. My deep thanks to Shirlina in the Main Reference Room, Reference Librarian Susan Garfinkel, John Rossman at the MRR Desk, Ellis Brachman, Chief Information Officer, John Keller, and other unnamed employees and docents who tirelessly offered their support.

I want to also thank my dear friends, Dot and Ann for listening to my ideas, and to make sure I was writing each day and achieving my goal of 3-5 pages at a sitting. To Tracy Andersen who practically ran my health technology business while I was writing and Cheryl Salerno for her editing feedback and diligence. And last, but not least, to Richard my king amongst men for his love and support throughout the writing process.

I loved the time I spent at the Library of Congress and hope someday this novel makes it into their bookstore. Perhaps my readers will walk the halls of the LOC, seeing it through Zach and Meghan's eyes, imagining somewhere hidden in the closed stacks is a real portal into another world that possesses the TRUTH we all seek.

In conclusion, I must add that there were a lot of strange events that occurred while writing this book. And I do believe some of my muses from the other side were instrumental in showing me where to go with it. But I will leave that story for another time. Thank you and blessings to all.